Sydney-based Karina May is a former magazine journalist turned digital marketer and writer of lively love stories that span the globe. When she's not dreaming up her next meet-cute, you'll likely find her rescuing her paperback from the bath, or out guzzling espresso martinis in the name of research.

Also by Karina May
Duck à l'Orange for Breakfast

never ever forever

Karina May

MACMILLAN
Pan Macmillan Australia

This is a work of fiction. Characters, institutions and organisations mentioned in this novel are either the product of the author's imagination or, if real, used fictitiously without any intent to describe actual conduct.

First published 2023 in Macmillan by Pan Macmillan Australia Pty Ltd
1 Market Street, Sydney, New South Wales, Australia, 2000

A catalogue record for this book is available from the National Library of Australia

Typeset in 12.5/16 pt Sabon by Midland Typesetters, Australia

Printed by IVE
Dinkus by Hein Nouwens/Adobe Stock

The author and the publisher have made every effort to contact copyright holders for material used in this book. Any person or organisation that may have been overlooked should contact the publisher.

The paper in this book is FSC® certified. FSC® promotes environmentally responsible, socially beneficial and economically viable management of the world's forests.

For my first-ever reader, Danica, who believed

You can't go back and change the beginning, but
you can start where you are and change the ending.
Attributed to C.S. Lewis

Chapter One

How to stand out in a country pub 101: wear a suit and order a cocktail. Dr Markus Abrahams has succeeded spectacularly at both. Even in a modern establishment like Lesters, his snug-fit pants and olive-garnished martini have no place in Mudgee. Although I have to admit, begrudgingly, that he looks even better in real life than he does on TV.

I'm rarely fooled by a chiselled jawline but even from across the room it's hard not to notice his razor-sharp cheekbones and alarmingly white smile.

'Table for one, ma'am?' My stare is interrupted by the clipped accent of the attractive hostess.

Shit. I hadn't expected to be seated. Perhaps I'm the one who's underdressed. I glance down at my Chuck Taylors. They're freshly starched and about as subtle as Dr Markus Abrahams' teeth.

Lace-ups are Satan's shoes, Rosie. They're more offensive than ballet flats. I smile as Penny's disapproving voice sounds in my head. It doesn't help my case that my laces are often undone. Rogue shoelaces don't sit well with me either, but they're a by-product of Dad's simple yet incredibly ineffective bunny-ear tying method. My fine-motor skills may have suffered under his tutelage, but almost three decades later, I still find myself humming his sweet rhyme.

Over, under, around and through. Meet Mr Bunny Rabbit, pull and through.

Nostalgia rushes through my body and I momentarily savour the warm, tingly feeling. Like the first sip of hot, salty ramen the morning after a big night out.

The hostess is staring at me expectantly. She reminds me of Meghan Markle. Her dark hair is pulled into a perfect 'messy' bun – the kind I can never quite master. I should have made more effort with my appearance. I just prefer not to pretend to be someone I'm not. This is who I am: frequently Converse-clad, fiercely passionate and notoriously punctual. I've arrived at the bar with five minutes to spare.

'Actually, for two please.'

'Right this way.'

We weave around the tables of smartly dressed couples and sidestep the queues of thirsty miners and farmers snaked around the bar. I'm relieved at the sight of their dirty work-boots. It's certainly a mixed crowd. From behind, the hostess is also less polished. A biro sticks out from the top of her bun and the back of her neck is peeling from sunburn. No doubt she's fresh from fruit picking and temporarily settled in town to replenish her travel funds. Mudgee isn't exactly on the backpacker hit-list.

We come to a stop at a high table in the back corner.

'Can I get you something to drink? I'm Bee, by the way.' Her smile reaches her pretty eyes. They're the colour of bowling greens, slightly darker than mine. Mine also have tiny muted-yellow flecks, like a stray dog has made its way onto the green and killed some patches with its pee.

I settle onto one of the vinyl stools. 'A vodka soda please.' I raise my voice so I can be heard over the din of excited weekend chatter and Ed Sheeran.

'Perfect. And your name?' she shouts back, head bowed over a shiny iPad. 'For when your guest arrives.' She nods to the empty stool as her chipped blue nails key in my order to the beat of 'Shape of You'.

Yikes. Is it that obvious I'm here on a blind date? You'd think I'd be a pro by now – Tinder Olympic team worthy. This is my third date this week.

'It's Rosie.'

'Sorry?'

'It's Rosie,' I repeat.

Bee stares back blankly.

'Rosie,' I'm practically yelling now. 'Rhymes with – um – ah – posie . . .?'

I wince as I say it. It's been years since I heard that old nickname.

It seems to do the trick as Bee nods enthusiastically, like the dashboard bobbleheads my mum used to make me sell to strangers for pocket money, in her twisted version of mother–daughter time.

'Rosie. Okay. Got it, got it.' Some dark strands of hair fall free from Bee's bun and dangle delicately around her face, making her look more like an elegant art piece than a student on a gap year. I'm sure she's never had to swipe for a date in her life.

'One vodka, coming right up!' She sweeps off towards the increasingly packed bar.

I turn my attention to the sticky table, take hand sani-tiser from my bag and squeeze some onto a serviette and start vigorously wiping. Once I'm satisfied, I give my hands a quick slather for good measure, then return the mini bottle to my bag and look around the packed room.

I've spent countless nights at similar Sydney spots with Pen and Ange, checking out suits downing after-work schooners. But tonight, I'm not in Sydney and thankfully there are no investment bankers here, just a roomful of lovely country folk. And one TV celebrity. I glance over to where Dr Markus Abrahams is sitting at the bar. He's finished his martini and started signalling for another. What a schmuck. Even if the evening ends up being a complete waste of time, I'll at least have a good story for Penny.

'How ya' going, Rosie. I'm Lachy.' I jump as a man with thick eyebrows appears in front of me, plants a kiss on my cheek and plonks down on the stool to my left. My online photos are recent – I make a point of keeping them up-to-date – but it still takes some balls to take a seat without a quick check that I am, in fact, *the* Rosie, twenty-eight, he's meant to be meeting. Very confident.

'Nice to meet you, Lachy.'

On first impression he ticks most of my appearance boxes: dark, with broad shoulders and a rough-and-ready look. Not as scruffy as Wes, although he had a short front, back and sides by the time he left for London.

Why are you thinking about Wes, Rosie? Focus on the perfectly good guy sitting right next to you. Well, good guy until proven otherwise.

Lachy's hair is thinning. A turn-off for many, but I think it adds a sweet vulnerability, a marker that he's been through some sort of loss – even if it's only of key hair follicles. He's spiked up the strands at the front in an attempt to create the illusion of a full head of hair. The look is fooling no one, except perhaps himself. His online photos had him smiling widely under a selection of different baseball caps. You can tell a lot about a man by the way he handles his impending baldness. I can't imagine Dr Markus handling it well at all. He's probably taken out an insurance policy on that mane.

'See something you like over there?' Lachy swivels his bar stool, following my gaze.

He doesn't exactly fit the *Markus & Pup* demographic, but then again, Markus's face is plastered everywhere – including several highway billboards on the drive from Sydney. You'd have to be living under an Uluru-sized rock not to know who he is.

Lachy's eyes fix on Markus. 'Ahhh yes, Dr Perfect. Our resident celebrity vet. Used to be like one of us, but turned all fancy when he got that model girlfriend.'

As if on cue, Markus pushes back his stool and stands up. He puts some bills down on the bar and turns to survey the room. His suit pants are tight around his crotch. I wonder how many wriggles it took to squeeze his sizeable package into those pants. Markus plucks a glass of red wine off the counter before he and his pants strut towards us. He reaches our table and places the wine down in front of me.

'Not ours, mate.' Lachy speaks before Markus has a chance to.

'Oh, I don't work here. It's for the lady,' Markus responds in his signature *Markus & Pup* honey-smooth tone. His words are served with a whack of expensive-smelling spiced cologne.

'What? For my date?' Lachy scoffs. I want to tell him not to feel threatened by Markus's celebrity status – or his full head of hair.

'That's right.' Markus's eyes flick over me, taking in my striped V-neck, jeans and high-tops. 'It's about time Mudgee got a place with some city style. Don't you think?'

Lachy grunts in response.

I can't help but quietly agree – Lesters hasn't been open long, but it's a welcome addition to the town, reviving a beautiful historic building. I'd never stepped foot in the old pharmacy, but I knew it to be one of Mudgee's first business establishments, built well before the town developed into a burgeoning wine-producing and mining region. It eventually lost out to a discount chemist and closed its doors a few years ago – until the space was finally purchased six months back, along with a nearby vineyard, by a bright-eyed twenty-something couple who, like many of us, had swapped their busy Sydney life for a tree change. I'm yet to meet Cameron and Joanna Lester, but I'm hopeful we'll become friends.

'Have a sip. I promise you'll like it. Full-bodied, with rich, lingering flavours.'

'No, thank you.' I glance over at Lachy, who has fallen silent.

'Aww come on. What's your name anyway, gorgeous?'

'Rosie.'

'I'm Dr Markus Abrahams.'

'I know who you are.'

'Oh, you do, do you? I thought you might . . . I saw you watching me.' A smug smile tugs at his full, clean-shaven lips as he cocks his head to one side. His dark Lego hair doesn't move.

Bee reappears at the table and sets down my drink and some water. I try to catch her eye. Maybe she can use that lovely British accent to lure Markus away. But she doesn't look up as she pushes an embossed coaster towards me.

'A vodka soda for you too?' she asks Lachy. 'Or would you prefer a wine?'

'Vodka sounds good,' he replies. Nice and no-fuss. I don't want to get ahead of myself, but he is looking more promising than usual. Plus, later I won't have to deal with wine-stained lips. Now I'm *really* getting ahead of myself. I don't have an allergy in a classical 'burning, itching, wheezing or swelling' sense of the word, but the taste, and sometimes even the thought of wine, still makes my stomach roil.

'You're doing a stellar job, Bee-utiful,' Markus coos in his honeyed TV voice.

'Thanks, Markus,' she responds plainly, still not bothering to look up. Thank God I'm not the only female on this planet immune to the charms of Dr Markus Abrahams. 'Can I get you another drink?'

'Sorry to disappoint, but I can't stay long –'

Bee is off again before Markus can finish his sentence. I like this girl.

The dark red wine looms in front of me, and my tastebuds betray me as they salivate over the heady aromas emanating from the glass. It looks and smells like a shiraz or, perhaps it's a syrah? Wes's eye for colour was so good that he could discern a variety or blend just by examining its pigment, chased by a quick whiff for confirmation. He could even tell in a glance if a wine was corked, sending it back without ever taking a sip. I'm not sure if he thought the weird flex would impress me; instead, it scared me how quickly he appeared to be morphing into his dad.

I drown thoughts of Wes by polishing off my drink in a succession of large gulps. Not terribly ladylike, but there's a point to be made.

'I hate wine,' I say once I've swallowed. 'And I know better than to accept a drink from a stranger, Markus.' This is far from my first rodeo. 'Especially when said stranger is not even drinking the product he's peddling.'

His eyebrows flick upwards in amusement.

'Touché, babe. But I've had more glasses of this drop than you've had breakfasts. I live at Horizons, the huge mansion next to the Lesters Estate, so my cellar is packed with cases of this delicious shiraz. Trust me when I say, it's viscous and ripe. And it tastes like sex.' There's a devilish gleam in his bright blue eyes.

'It sounds awful,' I manage, while an annoying zing skates down my spine.

Ugh. He's so practised at this whole act that it's almost working. Almost. I wonder if he makes a sport out of hitting on every new girl in town? I know I'm not completely hideous, but I'm no glamour either – especially in my lace-ups and jeans. If the gossip magazines have it right, then he's supposedly ditched his bachelor ways and is engaged to Polish model Eryka 'Glamazon' Polanski. A *model*. So, what the hell is he playing at?

I scooch my chair away.

'C'mon mate. Would you mind leaving us to it?' Lachy interrupts, running a hand through the front of his barely there hair. He's been very patient. Perhaps he really is one of those elusive good guys.

Although I'm new to the Tinder scene in Mudgee, I'm positive I've already exhausted all of my eligible matches. And I use the term 'eligible' loosely . . . Penny almost had me convinced that I could actually find love here with her glorified tales of cashed-up miners and winemakers. Not that I'm one for riches, but they are supposed to breed them more honest in the country. So far the dating pool has been as dismal as Sydney's – worse, even. Instead of terribly angled pics of blokes holding fish, they're posing proudly with dead pigs.

As a teacher at Mudgee Primary, Lachy has a good, solid profile. Shaping the minds of youth is a promising start, although much further digging is obviously required.

'Okay, I get it, man. Hands off your property, right?' Markus says, while simultaneously placing a hand on the small of my back. My nerve endings leap to attention as his cold hand presses through the thin fabric of my top.

'It's been a pleasure meeting you, Rosie.' He winks again.

I sit up straighter and arch my back until a cavity opens up between my body and his hand.

'Oh no, the pleasure was all mine, Markus,' I say, coldly.

He turns to Lachy and lowers his voice. 'I'd be careful with this one. Bit of a firecracker, isn't she?'

I can still hear you, arsehole.

Dr Markus Abrahams gives me a final flash of his pearly whites before turning and folding into the crowd.

Did that actually happen? Pen is going to lose her mind when I tell her.

I trace the rim of my empty glass with my index finger and look up at Lachy. 'Well, that was a memorable start,' I say, laughing nervously. 'Where were we?'

'Very memorable. Scandalous, even. It's not every day a dreamy celebrity TV vet buys you a drink, is it now?' he says.

'Definitely not,' I respond uneasily, eyeing the full glass of wine still sitting between us.

Lachy's sarcasm and notable absence of emojis appealed online but in real life it's a little confronting. Is he annoyed with me? Jealous even? Surely not. There's not much I could have done about Markus. I think I made my disinterest abundantly clear.

'I've got a hell of a thirst, Rosie. Not sure where my drink has gotten to. If you're not drinking it, I might smash this wine then go chase down that bar girl and order a steak while I'm at it. I'm guessing you want a salad or something?'

Oh.

'I'll take a look at the menu first,' I say, voice stretched thin.

'Trust me. I ate here last week. You really can't go past the caesar salad.' He misinterprets my stormy expression, raising his palms in the air. 'Okay, sprung. I was here on a date, but don't worry – she was batshit crazy.'

My stomach drops. Why, oh why, did I think things were going to be any different here? At least we've wasted no time in getting to the reveal quickly.

The big fat *never ever.*

Chapter Two

The town is quiet. I don't spot a soul as I stroll down the middle of the crumbly road. It feels reckless not to have to stick to the pavement. One of the first things that struck me about the roads was their width – then it was the absence of gutters.

I'm still not sure if I feel safer wandering the streets at night solo here than in Sydney. There's not as many street-lights, but then the stars are a hell of a lot brighter . . .

During the day, and especially on the weekends, Mudgee is heaving with visitors. They breeze into town for tastings of wine and that 'good country life'. They're here just long enough to admire the magnificent copper-clad spire at St Mary's, declare they've found 'the spot' for decent coffee, peruse K hub for stock long sold out in city Kmarts, and choose their 'very reasonable' fixer upper from the windows of the local real estate before returning to their high-rise apartments on adaptive cruise control. Weekdays are an entirely different story. You can practically hear the town's baristas breathe a collective sigh of relief as they no longer have litres of oat milk crowding their fridge.

I've worked out that weekday mornings are more lively than the nights, and I can get a decent coffee before heading to the station thanks to the brigade of MAMILs – middle-aged men in lycra – that descend on Mudgee at approximately 5 am on their way through to Gulong on the Central West Cycle trail. On an evening like tonight, most folk – Lesters' patrons aside – are already snug in bed, ready to rise at dawn to tend to their livestock or work in the mines.

A taxi pulls up next to me, windows wound all the way down.

'Do you need a lift to your motel, miss?' an older male voice calls.

I must look like one of those painful oat-milk-guzzling out-of-towners – and to be fair, six weeks ago I was.

'I'm right. Thank you.' I smile at the driver and keep walking, picking up my pace slightly. The man's eyes are kind and not narrow like Ivan Milat's but you can never be too careful.

He keeps driving slowly beside me. 'You do know we're a taxi town, not an Uber town, love. You won't have much luck using that newfangled app at this time.'

I look down and realise I'm gripping my phone. A habit – in case I need the torch or to make an emergency call.

'I'm actually from here,' I say, my voice with an edge of pride. 'I live just around the corner up there.'

I'm not going to reveal my exact co-ordinates.

'Ah, a local. My mistake, I'll leave you to it then. You have a good night and get home safe now.'

The cabbie tips his hat and drives off.

Ten minutes later, once I'm home, I fumble for my keys at the door – I really need to notify someone about that light.

My apartment is not the dream country home I'd had in mind when I'd been one of those city slickers window shopping local real estate – no bubbling brook at the end of a cobbled stone driveway, garden filled with plump strawberries or fire pit under the stars. Not even a milk-can letterbox. But I'm walking distance to the radio station and it's the best I can manage for now. Once I find my feet I'll head out of town and find the perfect home somewhere up in the hills, or perhaps out near the Lesters Estate. We'd had a girl's weekend in Mudgee for Ange's hen's seven years ago. It was one of those cup-filling holidays where the pinot flowed freely, we ate camembert for breakfast and ogled Christian Grey's abs in our pyjamas. Back when I could still tolerate wine and Ange was still speaking to me. Gosh, I could do with some of Ange's signature pitch-perfect advice right now. I'm sure she'll come around soon – once the shock wears off.

In six months or so, when she and Penny finally visit, I'll have my own country chateau, perhaps fringed with grape-bearing vines. I can still appreciate vineyards for their aesthetics, if not their associated fermented fruit beverage.

Or maybe I'll even own a small eco-home on an acreage with solar panels and plenty of space for alfresco dining. I'll get one of those long, rustic timber tables perfect for Insta-grammable mezze platters overflowing with cured meats and fresh figs. Assuming my radio career takes off, that is.

But for now, this shabby apartment in a converted three-storey terrace just off the main street will have to do. With white paint peeling off the wrought-iron balustrades, broken shutters, a faded striped awning and the lawns crying out for a good mow, the building would be right at home in any number of Sydney's inner-city suburbs. There is some comfort in that.

So far Cedric has been my only visitor. Cedric Cool, Mudgee's king of drive-time radio, is the reason I moved here. He'd appeared at my side as I'd walked off stage at The Marketing Leaders' Summit. 'How ChatGPT is Disrupting Digital Marketing' was the keynote I was supposed to be delivering, but things didn't go to plan. Instead, I found myself comparing AI marketing to modern dating – an impossibility; a farce. Destined to go dreadfully wrong once you discover that it's not the shiny new thing it's made itself out to be. I went on a long, windy tangent drawing very shaky parallels to my failed dates of recent times. Ben, who whipped out his iPhone mid-date and started swiping in front of me; Mick, who was pulled over while driving me home from dinner and issued a DUI on the spot; and Patrick, who was a complete no-show . . . I came alive as I told sad story after sad story. If I wasn't laughing, I'd sure as shit be crying with the miserable reality of it all. Except for the deranged fact that somehow, I still held out hope.

The keynote was unfortunately timed. The previous night I had suffered through a date with 'one-word Juan'. If he happened to respond with more than a 'yeah' or 'nah', he simply parroted back what I'd said, like he'd never had a unique thought of his own. Quite frankly, it was exhausting.

But it was the conference swag that properly triggered my menty-b. I'd been handed a bobblehead of 'Milly the Millennial Moose', the event's absurd mascot, just before I stepped on stage. The oversized head and bouncing antlers had jolted me back to 2002, and a seven-year-old Rosie taking pictures of dashboard knick-knacks for an eBay seller's page while my mother submitted fake bids on our items. It was an unwelcome memory at a most inopportune time.

Probation for two months. That's what Slice's management team deemed appropriate for my outburst. Demeaning.

That's how it felt. All because of one off day. Yes, that off day happened to be in front of a thousand or so industry peers, but still.

I'd loved my job as marketing manager at Slice, one of Sydney's top creative agencies. It was interesting, fast-paced and for a while there, it took the sting out of my flailing love life. Over the years, I had given it my absolute all. But in the months leading up to the conference, around the same time Dad and Naomi got engaged, I found myself caring less and less about it. Emails went unanswered for more than twenty-four hours, weekend work was replaced with Netflix binges and I was home each night in time to iron my socks in front of *The Project*. No client – no matter how 'emerging' or 'disruptive' the brand – excited me. The rush was gone. I guess it was the realisation that my Mac, even my sleek fifteen-inch Pro, made a terrible big spoon.

Luckily Dad wasn't there to witness my embarrassing on-stage meltdown, but Cedric Cool was. I'd turned my back on the gaping mouths in the audience, walked offstage and ran straight into him. I know now that our 'collision' had been perfectly planned. Ceddie informed me later that he was there scouting talent with 'in-built marketing smarts', someone he could train up on-air but who understood the importance of engaging authentically to build a loyal listener-ship. For reasons I'm still not entirely sure I understand, he wanted me, and offered me a job on the spot hosting a new morning radio show in Mudgee. One week later, when I was asked to step down as lead of a Spotify campaign I'd been working on for months and given an account for a small, family-run winery instead, I called Cedric and accepted.

I push open the front door slowly, carefully removing my keys so as not to startle Squash – my house-warming present from Cedric and Simon. You'd typically ask someone before gifting them a cat to house and feed. Thank goodness I'm not allergic. But my move coincided with their British Short-hair, Madge, having kittens, and I guess they figured it would be good company for me. At the very least, it would stop me monopolising Cedric's weekends with constant requests for coffee and drink dates. Perhaps it would have been more effective to have given me a dog to walk – Squash is quite self-sufficient. On his second night with me, I completely forgot he was there and decided to rearrange my furniture – almost squashing him between the couch and wall in the process. At least the incident resulted in his name. Six weeks on and I still haven't made any friends outside of Squash, Cedric and Simon. I suppose I should start prioritising friend dates over date-dates. It's guaranteed to be a better use of my time.

My apartment is exactly how I left it. The ceramic tile floors have a so-clean-you-could-eat-off-it sparkle, the walls are a light-reflecting white and the glass coffee table gleams of fresh Mr Sheen. There's not so much as one dog-ear marking the magazines sitting squarely in the centre of the table. They're also all in date. My new living room has as much personality as an IKEA showroom.

I head to the kitchen, open the pantry, select a tin of Delightful Tuna Gourmet and spoon it into a gold-rimmed bowl. Squash is suddenly at my side.

'Where have you been hiding, bud? Sorry I'm late. Another waste of time.'

Squash lifts his tail and looks expectantly at me.

I laugh. 'You can answer me later.'

I set the bowl on the floor at my feet, and he attacks it immediately, as if it's about to sprout legs and scurry off. It's time to make my move. I hurry to my bedroom at the back of the apartment before Squash realises that I've disap-peared. We're still getting used to each other.

The floor around the bed is littered with discarded outfits. Very un-Rosie-like. There are jeans in various shades of denim flung across the back of my armchair and striped shirts hanging off the doorknob. It's as though my wardrobe has literally spewed out every single item I own. And yes, most of the items happen to be identical. Like a cartoon character, I have a trademark outfit, which varies only slightly with the occasion and seasons. My disinterest in fashion horrifies Penny, but – as I take great joy in reminding her – there are plenty of geniuses, both past and present, known for wearing the same clothes each day. 'Steve Jobs shouldn't be your fashion icon, Rosie,' is Penny's broken-record reply.

I bend down and scoop up the stray ankle socks off the floor. In my anxious flurry to prepare for the weekend away, my usual standards have slipped. Dad and I always had a place for everything. A tumultuous, single-parent household we were not. Everything was lists and Excel spreadsheets. Dad ran our household like his small accountancy firm – with military precision, but plenty of heart. We may have had to downsize to a tiny weatherboard house once Mum left, but she took with her most of the chaos – and her stupid get-rich schemes. Naomi is Mum's polar opposite. As generous and warm as Dad – with as much smart business sense – but bucketloads more style. Theirs had been a fairly ordinary workplace meeting. I knew he'd struck up an instant friendship with the 'new hire' but was delighted as it slowly progressed into something more. And now with the engagement . . . well, I couldn't be happier for him. It almost makes me believe it could happen for me again, too.

I sigh as I continue to refold and hang my litter of 'uniform' clothes. Mudgee is it for me. One last serious go. I've uprooted my whole life not just for a career change, but on the promise of romantic potential. My wish list isn't unrealistic – a kind, loyal man who sticks to his word, is confident in who he is, and who doesn't try to sleep with me on the first date. No outlandish requests. I'm flexible on dietary habits, hobbies, professions and appearance. Yes, I have my preferences – but no real deal-breakers. I'm searching for good 'bones'. In the same way as when purchasing a home, you expect the basics: a roof, four walls and sound plumbing. Not a leaky-arse shack.

At least tonight was eventful. It's not every day you come face to face with an egomaniac celebrity in a country town. Otherwise, I may as well have been back in Sydney, wasting another night on yet another good-guy-on-paper/ fuck-boy-in-real-life.

Perhaps there really is no one decent left to meet. Not even a nice country boy. It appears the 'kind farmer who wants a wife' is as real as a bunyip. A mythical creature lurking nowhere.

Tonight, I can't swing by Pen's apartment to drown my sorrows with a G&T nightcap. She'd typically nod along patiently, be outraged in the right moments and, although she may insult my outfits, she'd never call me too picky. I briefly consider phoning but we'd spoken earlier, and she was off to an art gallery opening in Surry Hills. The party would be in full swing by now and Penny would be at least five champagnes deep, with some unsuspecting hipster completely enamoured with her theatrics. She does life *balls in*, something I beyond admire. There's no point calling Ange. Besides, I'll be seeing them both tomorrow at the reunion.

The reunion.

My stomach starts churning at the mere thought.

I'd considered not going. I haven't been in Mudgee long but it's St Bernard's Class of 2013 10 Year Reunion. Ten years since graduating from high school. Many of those years spent recovering from side-splitting heartbreak.

I finish returning the last of my clothes to the wardrobe and settle onto the bed. There are still a few items on my pink slipper chair. The purgatory pile: clothes that have been worn but aren't dirty enough to wash.

I'll deal with that later. First up, I need to work out my plan of attack for facing Wes Preston.

The dreadful shrill of my alarm clock wakes me. Six am. *Arrgggh*. It's an hour later than it blares during the week, but I've barely slept a wink.

I've been pre-empting the alarm going off all night, checking my watch constantly. I finally settled into a deep sleep for what feels like only moments before the alarm sounded. I'd been dreaming. One of those lucid dreams where you feel like you're the puppetmaster and in full control of the action. But you're not.

Wes was there. I had walked into the St Bernard's hall and seen him smiling widely near the stage. Our eyes met, and he tilted his head towards the ceiling. I looked up to see a replica of Michelangelo's Sistine Chapel painting. Except Wes was Adam and his girlfriend was God. Her lush, blonde hair replaced God's mane. Their arms were outstretched, hands almost touching, and then – *beep-beep-beep*.

I hit snooze. I want to escape the remnants of my nightmare hanging thick in the air, but leaving the safety of my bed also means that the day will officially begin. A day that I've simultaneously dreaded and anticipated for years. Although there are no guarantees he is even going to show up.

C'mon, body . . . move. I could easily stay cocooned in my satin down doona, close my eyes and use my ventriloquist powers to get the answers I need from my imaginary Wes.

Those are coward's thoughts, Rosie. Enough! I'd never forgive myself for passing up the opportunity to finally see him after all these years. Plus, I can hardly bear picturing Dad's disappointed face when he discovers that I'm not coming. Or Penny's. There's a good chance she's driven straight to the airport from her night out and is already stationed at Mascot Krispy Kreme car park, diluting her champagne-blood with half a dozen original glaze and some bad coffee. *Coffeeeeeeeee.* The thought of caffeine makes me sit up.

I take a deep breath, stretch my arms to the ceiling, let out a big yawn and swing my legs over the side of the bed. I plant my feet on the floor and stand up, forcing a smile. *You've got this, Rosie.*

Squash is lying flat on his back at the base of the bed, licking one of his paws, but pauses when he spies me. He jumps up on all fours, pads towards me and starts rubbing up against my legs. *Purrrrrrrrrrrrrrrrrr.* This cat lady thing isn't too bad at all.

'Are you going to be good for Uncy Cool, Squashy?' I crouch down and scratch the top of his head. More purring, then a flick of his feathery tail over my cheek. I give him one last gentle stroke then text Cedric.

All food is labelled in the fridge. Just top up his water and change the kitty litter. Thanks a million. I owe you

Cedric replies. **He can always come around here to hang out with mama Madge?**

I hesitate, my mind going to the detailed meal instructions I've taped to the fridge, then my gaze falls on Squash as he makes his way over to his favourite slice of sunshine near the TV cabinet and curls up like a cinnamon scroll.

I think he's pretty comfy here ☺

No problems, doll. Can't wait to see you on Tuesday. Bring GOSS

Are you sure you're right to do Monday's show without me?

I hate the thought of letting Cedric down, especially when I've really only just started, but this long weekend had been in the calendar when I'd signed on.

Pffft. Who do you think was in control of that mic before I found you on the marketing scrap heap?

I grin. **Thank youuuuuuuu**

You're most welcome. Btw how was your date?

Huge fail, I reply.

Next comes a series of emojis. Fire flame, devil, girl with crossed arms.

I laugh and write back. **You never mentioned Dr Markus Abrahams was a local. What a tosser!**

I wait a few moments but there's no text back. It is Saturday morning . . . it could be some time before he makes it out of bed with Simon. I check my phone again: 7.30 am. Now I really need to get going. The reunion isn't until this evening, but I want to see Dad. Some Dutch courage is also in order. I can't go full mid-noughties Lindsay Lohan though. I need to keep it together in front of Wes.

Penny's convinced me to help her out at some fashion event on Sunday too. It's supposed to be a star-studded affair, with a handful of the nation's favourite radio broadcasters on the guest list. Rubbing shoulders with my new industry peers could be a good career move. Networking aside, I'm happy to spend bonus time with my bestie.

I make it to the airport in plenty of time and as soon as my Pelican Air flight lifts up off the ground, it seems like we're touching back down again.

A sloppy kiss is planted on the side of my face as I stroll out of the terminal in Sydney. *Mwah!* 'Surprise, darling!'

I'm face to face with a beaming Penny. She looks stunning in a tight, neon coral dress, which perfectly complements her brown skin. An almost thigh-high split in the skirt shows off her short yet slender legs.

'Your personal chariot has arrived,' she trills, reaching down to grab my carry-on suitcase.

'You look fab, Pen!'

'Thanks. I was going for fuckable. Last night's outfit.' She winks.

Love it. So typically Pen. I instantly feel lighter.

She looks me up and down, clearly disapproving of my basic combo. 'And what sort of revenge outfit do you call this? This better be your plane clothes.'

I'm feeling proud that I've thrown a black blazer over my striped tee and my hair is not its usual mess. I styled it so it no longer puffs around my head like a frizzy halo, but falls silkily over my shoulders. I've even managed a sort of soft, side-sweeping fringe thingy. My Converse have stayed for now, but I have heels in my bag. I don't think I've done too badly at all. The embellished jacquard cocktail dress I wore to Dad and Naomi's engagement party almost got a look in, but that was before I rationalised that there's no better armour than feeling like oneself. I also don't want to give Wes the satisfaction of thinking I've dressed up for him.

'A practical one?' I reply. 'Anyway, how was your night? Better than mine, I hope! You'll never believe who I ran into . . .' I quickly fill Penny in on my chance encounter with Markus.

'Whaaaaaaaaaaaaat? Dr Markus Abrahams bought you a drink?' she screams like a banshee. Thankfully there's such a commotion of squeaking luggage trolleys and transfer logistics around us that no one looks our way. 'You lucky thing! He's a total stud muffin. Tell me more. I demand it!' She drops my bag and squeezes me excitedly. I'm describing how slimy and gross he was when she switches into a hushed tone.

'Actually, I think he's coming to the Scuttlebutt event on Sunday. You didn't hear it from me. You can have first dibs; he's more your type than mine anyway!'

'Eww. He's definitely *not* my type at all,' I say with a laugh. 'And he has a fiancée. Eryka Polanski. That absolutely breathtaking Polish model?'

Penny's eyes are shining, any residual hangover completely evaporated at the prospect of playing cupid. 'Fiancée, schmiancée. This is perfect! A new focus for the weekend.' She pauses, stealing a cautious look at me.

Even though Penny was there to witness every step of our relationship, she'll still never know exactly what Wes meant to me – what I thought we meant to each other. Penny might not one hundred per cent get it, but I appreciate her 'tough love for the sake of guarding my heart' approach. She's always taken that responsibility very seriously.

'Thanks so much for coming to collect me, Pen.'

I'm well aware that she could have continued her night into the early hours of this morning. She waves her hand, dismissing my words as unnecessary platitudes.

'I can sleep when I'm dead. And now there's plenty of time to get the full lowdown on your fancy new country life in Mudgee. The dates, the radio station, Dr Markus – I want to hear it all!'

She starts jogging towards the exit, pulling my bag behind her. A crazed vision in coral.

'Come on. We have seven minutes to get to the car before I can't afford to eat for the next week.'

It's good to be back.

Chapter Three

'You are an absolute snack, babe!' Pen squeals. 'Except I do like this one too,' she says, eyeing up a lime cut-out dress that's definitely more her vibe than mine.

'It's a bit – ahem – loud, isn't it?' Dad chimes in. It's scary that a man whose wardrobe consists primarily of Led Zeppelin T-shirts is the voice of reason.

We're in Naomi's boutique in Double Bay. Penny insisted on accompanying me the moment she found out I was meeting Dad here. Hangover or no hangover, not much can get between Pen and couture – not to mention the promise of a makeover montage.

Naomi's done a fabulous job with Blossoms. In less than twelve months she's built a name for herself on the prized Bay shopping strip and a strong following of local yummy mummies. She credits Dad with encouraging her to make the leap from actuary. He credits her with keeping him young. These days he's in his Zeppelin tees more often than business suits. His new 'fun accountant' act is equal parts amusing and heart-warming.

The interior of Blossoms is more like a museum than a shop. I count a total of twelve items, including the lime number. Each piece is separated by at least a one-metre buffer, as if the clothing needs its own space to breathe. The featured exhibit, a red dress splayed on a glass block in the centre of the room and illuminated by a spotlight, has somehow made its way onto my body. Naomi pinches the extra fabric at my waist and pulls it tight. I breathe in sharply.

'Ooh, yes! Much better. It's always hard to see your gorgeous figure under all of those T-shirts.'

Even when Naomi worked at Royce Tax & Accounting, she sported immaculate designer outfits, complete with matching shoes and jewellery. The beige carpet was her catwalk, the cubicles an unglamorous backdrop. Yet she's never shamed me for my more 'casual' style. Perhaps she assumed my tomboy look was all part of growing up without a mother.

'I keep telling her she needs to show off that hot bod,' exclaims Penny, who is still enamoured with the green dress.

'Righto girls, leave her be.' Dad comes over to my side. He takes my hand and twirls me. 'You do look gorgeous, honey.' He gives me a gruff peck on the cheek.

'It's a Sebastian Worthington. His latest design,' Naomi says, slipping into sales mode. There's a sparkle in her perfectly made-up eyes. 'Now, how about a glass of champagne, girls?'

'That would be lovely,' Penny says smoothly, well-versed in accepting free drinks.

Champagne I can do. Preston Imports, Wes's family's company, deals strictly in wine.

'A bottle of Dom Perignon coming right up!'

Dom Perignon? How much is the dress going to cost? I have a flashback to being offered sushi at a new hair salon on this same strip a few years ago and walking out with a four-hundred dollar cut. Although anyone who is able to tame my unruly hair deserves a small fortune.

'Naomi, that's really not necessary,' I say, one eye still on the three-panelled floor-length mirror.

I can't deny that I look good. The dress hugs my curves in all the right places. A fitted bodice meets a skirt with a cinched waist that skims over my midsection and finishes below the knees. The light from outside shines through the raw silk fabric so that every last stitch and thread is visible. I may not be a fashionista, but I have to admit the transformation is kind of miraculous.

Penny catches me admiring my reflection and wolf whistles. 'Just admit it. You're a total knockout, Rosie. Wes Preston better watch out!'

I can't help but laugh at her enthusiasm, and for a brief moment the butterflies that have settled in my stomach since waking go from inducing nausea to an excited swarm. Maybe a hot, completely out-of-character dress is what's needed. I don't want Wes back, not even close. But it'd be nice to hear him say he fucked up, and that he regrets it.

'I'm sure it's way out of my budget,' I say to Pen. 'I'm only trying it on for fun. It's totally inappropriate for the weather.' I swivel to see how it hugs my bum – not bad at all.

'Budget? What budget?' Dad exclaims as he fills glasses with the bubbly Naomi's fetched from the storeroom. 'If this is to stick it to that Wes, then I say go for it! I'm sure Naomi can nudge the price down.' He takes a big gulp of his champagne and wriggles his face as the bubbles tickle his nose. Fun Dad is the best. I never even saw him so much as sip a beer before Naomi.

'Half price for you, my dear,' Naomi offers warmly.

I reach behind my neck for the price tag. I can't believe I'm even considering such lavishness – or that Dad is talking about Wes. I guess the whole thing was a bit of an ordeal. He'd given me sound advice at the time, encouraging me to take a leaf out of his own book and throw myself into work to distract myself. As he'd said, 'It did the trick for me.' I wonder if he'd dish out that same advice now. Sure, it eventually led him to Naomi, but he'd clocked up close to two decades of hard work before that. There was definitely no champagne fizzy nose.

Penny hands me a pair of strappy silver sandals. I perch on the cushioned bench seat in the corner while I buckle them up, then stand and toddle back to Dad. He passes the champagne around and then raises his half-drunk glass.

'To Rosie. We miss you. We love you. We're so very proud of you.' His voice cracks with emotion.

'Dad, it hasn't even been two months,' I say. Inside, I'm chuffed.

'We've been listening online,' Naomi says. 'That Cedric's a real character, isn't he? Even if he did steal you away from us!'

'He's the best.' My phone has been beeping non-stop with Squash selfies since touching down in Sydney. I couldn't help but zoom in to check his water bowl was full. 'But I should be congratulating *you* guys. I cannot wait for the wedding of the century. Now, if you'd only set a date!'

'We've been toasted enough. This is about you, sweetie, and your brave decision to try something new.' Naomi's voice is full of admiration.

I blush. What with the work probation and my washed-up dating life, it didn't feel like I had much of a choice. I hadn't reached a fork in the road, but a dead end.

'Well let's cheers to the *almost* first birthday of Blossoms, then,' I say. 'I don't know how you do it, Naomi, building a fashion empire and all the while putting up with Dad!'

'Hear, hear!' Dad grabs hold of Naomi's arm and squeezes it before pulling her towards him for a kiss. If it were anyone else, I'd be vomming in my mouth at the blatant PDA, but I don't think I'll ever tire of seeing Dad so deliriously happy.

I'm paranoid about spilling champagne all over the delicate red silk so I return to the change room to de-robe. Before I have a chance to make up my mind about the purchase, Penny has the dress nestled firmly in a garment bag. 'If you don't wear it, I will. Think of the return on investment on that thing,' she hisses at me.

As we're preparing to head off, Dad starts orbiting me awkwardly. He's going to have to get better at these goodbyes. I'm planning on visiting every month, so that's at least twelve goodbyes per year.

He clears his throat. 'Ah-ummmmm . . . so, are you going to know anyone at the reunion?'

'Of course, Dad, it's my school reunion – full of people I know.' I hold back my eye roll. I love him to bits, but he's often oh-so Dad-like.

'You're right.' He still sounds odd. Is this small talk his way of checking in about Wes?

He glances over his shoulder to where Penny and Naomi are chatting away about some young, up-and-coming designer. He lowers his voice. 'Look, I've been meaning to ask, love, and I do hate bringing it up . . .' he trails off.

'Yes?' Surely, he hasn't left some special-occasion present for Naomi to the eleventh hour? Although I'd rather deal with a last-minute surprise gift than discuss Wes. It's already a terrifying thought that I'll likely be seeing him in a few short hours.

'Have you heard anything from your mother recently?'

His question comes as a surprise, landing with a giant thud in my chest. It's been so long since we've spoken about her.

'No?' I reply, voice climbing an octave.

That wasn't unusual. We only ever exchanged a few words here and there online anyway – never in person. Our last face-to-face contact was on that fateful day twenty years ago when she'd kissed me on the top of my head and said she was off on another urgent business trip to Japan. After two weeks of not hearing from her, Dad filed a missing person's report. He was beside himself. And then the email came.

From: marie@carsfromjapan.com
To: john@roycetaxandaccounting.com
Subject line: Update
Hi John and Rosalie,

I did try calling. It seems there is a great opportunity to expand my business in Hiroshima, so I have decided to relocate here. Being at the heart of the manufacturing action means that I get first pick of defective cars before they go to auction, which gives me a clear advantage over my competitors (no more wasted $ on lemons!!!). I've also met a contact who is helping me import into the US too (their automotive industry is worth over $100 billion – imagine a piece of that market!!!!) I'm sure you both understand what this could mean for me.

I know that the biggest regret I'll have isn't failing, but never trying to make something of myself.

As much as I've tried, I don't think that I'm cut out to be a mother, or a wife. I bit off more than I could chew there. The best thing I can do for the both of you is recognise that and move on.

Rosalie, I leave you with the gift of entrepreneurship. Although you'll no longer have my car trinkets to sell, I have no doubt that you share my natural affinity for

*business. I can only hope that one day you'll have the
courage to follow in my footsteps.*
For now, we must go our separate ways.
I'm sorry.
Mum/Marie

They're not words an eight-year-old was ever going to
comprehend. Dad still let me read it – probably because he
was in shock. A few weeks followed where he couldn't get
out of bed and I stayed at Wes's house, but we soon 'got on
with it'. Just the two of us. Schedules and rosters were drawn
up and happy(ish) routines formed.

Dad never said whether he tried to convince her to come
home. I suspect he did. She'd been so absent in my life anyway
that I don't think I was terribly fussed. The best thing she
ever did was deliver the news straight up like that instead
of making promises about coming home that she knew she
wouldn't keep. It allowed us to move on. It would have been
even nicer if she hadn't drained Dad's bank account before
jetting off, but you can't win them all.

She'd better not be making some grand reappearance in
time to fuck things up for Dad.

'Why? Have you heard from her?' There's no hiding the
edge in my voice.

Please don't say yes.

'No, no not specifically. Well, she just left a strange link in
the comments of one of the photos from the engagement party.'

'You didn't click on it did you?'

'Well, I –'

'Dad!'

'It was a website to buy tea . . .'

'It sounds like spam, Dad. Just delete it. And pray that
she didn't give your computer some virus.'

Typical Mum. We're both 'friends' with her and occasionally check her Facebook profile just to keep track of her whereabouts – although her page hasn't been updated in months.

'Okay, not to worry love. I just thought it was worth mentioning. You can't prevent a father's urge to protect his only daughter. I've acquired a very particular set of skills, you know . . .' He winks, instantly lightening the mood.

I groan. 'What? Number-crunching? You're a dag, Dad.' I think he's the only accountant alive who insists on quoting *Taken* on a daily basis.

'I know, I know. I'm an old-fashioned dinosaur – turned ninja by night.' He karate chops the air and moves to kick up a leg. I raise an arm to block him. He looks dangerously close to throwing out his back again.

'Message received loud and clear,' I say with a laugh. 'Now, cut the theatrics. Naomi won't be impressed if you knock over a mannequin.'

He resumes his regular stance and steady voice. 'Enjoy the reunion, won't you, love. And let me know once you're back in Mudgee safely.'

'I will. And thanks for always having my back, Liam Neeson. You're the bestest.'

Chapter Four

We arrive at the reunion half an hour late (Penny's fault, not mine), which means we have to slip in the back and creep quietly to our allocated table. I'm in the Sebastian Worthington. I can barely breathe, but Penny's assured me that it's 'giving'.

'Time to slay, girl!' she whispers as we make our way across the room. It's dimly lit, making it hard to see the faces of those who are already seated. My anxiety is at an all-time high. I can't believe that I'm actually here. That Wes is likely here too.

Ange is already sitting at our table. She purses her lips as I slide in next to her. She's wearing a black jumpsuit with a red statement lip. She looks amazing. Her face softens as she sees Penny, who has swapped her coral ensemble for an equally show-stopping baby blue number. Teamed with a Chanel clutch and shell-pink manicured nails, the dress makes her look every inch the PR professional. It's little wonder clients – and men in general – flock to her.

A middle-aged woman dressed in a tight leather skirt is addressing the room. Mrs Slattery? She's certainly transformed from the unassuming librarian type who took my Year 8 English class.

'Well, how the years have flown!' She punctuates the sentence with a violent thrust of her chest. 'The last time I looked out over this sea of faces everyone was a lot younger. But no doubt you are all now a lot wiser!' Her silk blouse stretches across her rock-hard boobs and with every word a gaping hole is opening between her two top buttons.

'Tonight is all about reconnecting and sharing what we've learnt over the past decade.'

The microphone squeals and index fingers instinctively go into ears to block out the awful high-pitched noise. We could be right back in an assembly at St Bernard's listening to Principal Carmel reprimand the Year 11s for smoking behind the church. We're not in the gymnasium tonight – the ex-students' committee has sprung for a function room at the hotel down the road.

I pluck up the courage to scan the room. There are lots of familiar – albeit changed – faces at the nearby tables. The painful insecurities that plagued our teenage years have gone, and in their place are an excellent assortment of beards and tasteful fashion that testosterone levels and budgets of yesteryear had forbidden. But no Wes. I swallow the bile that's surfaced in my mouth and mask it with a sip of sparkling. I can't spend the entire night in this state.

The technical hiccup has derailed Mrs Slattery's address. The room has erupted into chatter, and she's struggling to regain control.

'Shhhhhh, guys, guys . . . I only need a few more seconds of your time.' I could be sitting in English class reading *To Kill a Mockingbird* while watching Mrs Slattery attempt to silence the back row.

There's a kerfuffle down the front. Next comes loud snickering, then someone is pushed to their feet.

'Mrs Slattery. Or, is it *Miss* Slattery now? You seem to be having some difficulties. I was wondering if I could offer some tech support.'

It's Trent Dell. Wes's best friend. Wes is probably right alongside him, egging him on. I crane my neck for a better view but there's too many backs of heads between me and the front of the stage.

Mrs Slattery ignores Trent's heckling and continues. 'Thank you to the ex-students' committee for all of their hard work putting this event together, as well as our generous hosts for the night, The Regency.' She pauses only briefly for applause. It's obvious she wants to finish her lines and get the hell off that stage. I don't blame her.

'For those interested, we'll be ending the evening down at the school campus for a tour of the new buildings and an unveiling of the renovated Year 12 common room, kindly painted by one of our former students.'

There's more whistling and yahoo-ing. Realising that the crowd is beyond taming, Mrs Slattery wraps up her address. 'Now without further ado, welcome Class of '13!'

Before the poor teacher has even stepped back from the mic, Penny is approached by a grey-haired man in a black turtleneck. Is that Jimmy McGuire? Gosh, he's aged. We all have. Shaky hands tug at his snug polo neck as he stands in front of Penny, mouth opening and closing like a guppy fish.

You've got this, Jimmy, I will silently. *Pen always had a thing for you.*

'Hi.'

The voice doesn't come from Jimmy, but from behind me, immediately sending a rush of goosebumps down my arms and legs.

Shit. No, no, no. You let yourself get distracted, Rosie. You are not mentally prepared for this.

Yes, you are, another voice challenges. *This is what your weeks of breathwork have been for.*

I'm still mid pep-talk as I stand, slowly push back my chair, and turn to face him.

Wes's wide-set jaw is relaxed into an easy, genuine smile, which is framed by a heavily stubbled beard. Unlike the last time I saw him, he could actually do with a shave and a haircut, but he's definitely retained the boyish good looks that helped me bloody well fall for him in the first place.

The frills of my red dress flounce around like a flamenco dancer, betraying my nerves.

Breathe. Just breathe.

This is not the time for a panic attack. I thought I could do this, but I can't. Toilet break time.

'Evening, Wes,' I say. 'Would you excuse me? I need to pop to the ladies.' I'm careful not to meet his gaze. It would take the moving of some serious Everest-size mountains to be drawn back in, but I still don't want to risk it. That puppy-dog face used to turn me straight to putty.

'Really? I was hoping we could talk . . .'

'Sorry,' I offer in a way that says I'm anything but.

I want to tell him exactly where to go, but I don't think I can manage it without bursting into tears.

'Can we chat later then, Posie?'

Argh, that name.

How dare he behave so casually, like nothing has changed? I want to yell down this fancy reception room. Instead, I focus on the big-girl pants I purposely pulled on this morning and give him a smile as controlled as my under-wear. I didn't squeeze myself into this fabulous dress only to come apart at the seams in front of him.

'Please don't call me that,' I say quietly. 'Maybe we can speak later. No guarantees, though.'

'Sure.' His tone is forlorn.

I try to ignore the way his voice pulls at my heart by staring down at my glass. It's empty. I could use another refill right now – or half a dozen tequila shots.

'I'm going to get another drink,' I say.

'Let me get it.' He extends a hand for my cup. 'Wine?'

My eyes finally flick up at him. 'No. Not wine,' I say flatly, my gaze unwavering.

He stares back at me, unblinking, and my gut squirms as I see guilt swimming at the edges of his rust-coloured eyes.

Warning bells jangle. *Abort mission, Rosie. Now.*

I try to brush past him, but he catches my arm. His touch elicits another round of goosebumps, this time down my spine.

'Please. Don't go. I have some things I'd like to say.' His hurried words are warm on my ear. I can almost taste them. Taste *him*.

No. This is not the way it's supposed to go down. I won't allow it.

'Are you wanting to recommend a fine drop to complement the Cheezels? A Preston-approved riesling, perhaps? Rarely disappoints, I hear. The tropical and mineral notes pair perfectly with cheddar additives and palm oil.'

'What? No.' His brow furrows.

'Look, I've really got to go, Wes,' I say, yanking my arm from his grip. 'Shouldn't you go catch up with Trent?'

'I haven't seen the bloke in years, Rosie.'

I thought they'd been joined at the hip in the UK. Smug in their suits. I wonder what happened?

Stop. Caring. Rosie.

'Last I heard you were pretty buddy-buddy.'

'Last you heard was six years ago, Rosie,' Wes says flatly.

Yes, I suppose that's true. Six whole years. In some ways it feels like a lifetime ago, in others it feels like only yester-day. I'd stupidly thought we were soulmates, with a love that didn't have an expiry date. When it finally computed that it was over, I blocked him everywhere. It was easier for me to move on pretending that he had met someone new. That he went to his fancy wine sales job, came home every evening to kiss a girlfriend who wasn't me, and went on weekend road trips in his expensive, upgraded car.

It's now or never, Rosie.

'How could you just leave me like that?' I blurt. I want to sound icy, but I'm trembling like there's an earthquake underfoot. I feel dizzy and unbalanced. It's a question that's cycled over and over in my head for years, so furious and frequent that it's burnt a permanent place in my skull.

Wes's eyes widen and a hand goes underneath his chin and starts vigorously twisting the thick plantings of dark whiskers. He's always fidgeted when he's nervous. There's a smudge of inky violet on his knuckles. My breath catches. He's still painting? He swallows deeply and his inky hand slides down below his protruding Adam's apple.

'Trust me. I've thought about it plenty over the years,' he mumbles.

I wonder if he can hear the irony of his own words. *Trust me.* I'd tried that. It hadn't worked out so well for me.

'So, how?' I ask again.

'It was a huge mistake. Leaving without –'

Blood thunders to my head. I need to sit down. I was right. I'm not ready for this yet. Perhaps I won't ever be.

'Mistake. Yes, I know a fair bit about those too. Unfor-tunately, you were mine. But it taught me *never ever* to date a guy whose career becomes their entire identity again. I suppose I should be thanking you, shouldn't I?' I spit.

'Rosie, please . . .'

'Wes, I can't.'

I'm shaking as I walk away. I want to crawl under the refreshments table, curl up in a ball, put my fingers in my ears and stay that way until the end of the night. Coming here was a mistake – yet another one.

I spend the next few hours doing my best to stay on the fringes of the room and avoid any further run-ins with Wes. At one point I see him deep in conversation with Ange. She may as well have picked up one of the plastic party knives and plunged it into my back.

Wicked grins and encouraging bum slaps from Penny each time she flits past help me stay upright. We sit and watch a bunch of slides of old school pics. If I hadn't recognised the faces and locations, I would never have guessed that we were the people in these photos. When a photo of me, Pen and Ange in our ugly brown sports uniforms flashes up, I'm shocked at how young we look. Our knobbly knees poke out from our too-short skorts and our arms are flung carelessly over each other's shoulders. My wild hair is caught in a scrunchie, Ange's mouth is full of metal, and Penny's face is caked in contraband foundation a few shades too light. A warmth invades me. I think I can remember an indignant Penny getting detention that day.

I have to turn my head when a picture of me and Wes splashes across the screen. It's one I've seen before: Wes is carrying two backpacks, one strapped to his front and the other to his back. We must only be twelve or thirteen as his small frame is overwhelmed by the bulky bags – he looks like a pregnant tortoise. I'd been tasked with holding the snacks. One packet of chicken chips and a can of Coke to split for recess.

The night is wrapping up when I see Wes re-entering the room. He's part of a large group led by Mrs Slattery – presumably the returning school tour. Wes breaks away from the pack and makes a beeline for me.

My heart hammers violently. I'm alone at a high table. Penny has swanned off to fetch us one last drink. I glance around wildly for a flash of baby blue. She's halfway across the room already. Too late to call her back over. The table is littered with Dorito crumbs, empty plates and half-drunk glasses of wine. I nudge aside the garlic-bread crusts, put my elbows on the tabletop and rest my chin in my cupped hands. If I feign a relaxed demeanour, perhaps the rest will follow. I sneak a peek over my shoulder. He's right there.

'Hey, Rosie.'

'Hey.' An evening of general cheer and lots of champagne has taken some of the fight out of me.

'I don't want to ruin your night. I really don't. But this might be my last chance to speak to you.' His voice drips with desperation.

I nod. An acknowledgement that he's spoken, rather than any sort of commitment that I'll hear him out.

His hand is back at his neck, twisting furiously. 'I should never have left. If I could take it back, I would. In a heartbeat.'

Okay, that's a start.

'I know that you deserve to know why. And I'd like to explain it to you as best as I can. Not here though. Can we maybe meet up to talk properly?'

'I live in Mudgee now.'

'I've heard. That's amazing. I can come to you?'

I don't say anything, just pick at the Dorito crumbs. The room around us is alive with chatter and laughter, but I can only focus on the heavy silence that has fallen between us.

I should say no, but it's hard to give up the chance of getting an actual explanation. It's a sobering feeling being with someone you used to know so well, knowing that things will never ever be like they were.

Eventually, Wes breaks the silence. 'I'm sorry, Rosie.' He reaches his violet-smudged hand across the table.

'Hey! Hands where I can see them, Preston.' Penny returns with our drinks – and turtleneck Jimmy on her arm.

'Well, if it isn't my favourite garden gnome.' It's always been like this between them.

'Great job on the common room, man.' Jimmy clasps Wes's hand and gives it a firm shake. 'Can you imagine if it looked like that back in the day? So pimpin'.'

Wes's face flushes. 'Thanks mate, it's really no big deal.'

Wes painted the common room?

'Whatever Preston,' Penny scoffs. 'What's next in your new-found philanthropic quest? Volunteer work at a soup kitchen?'

Of course Penny is not sold on his good-guy act either.

'I think it's time I got going,' Wes sighs, clearly dispirited. 'Please just think about it, Rosie.'

I busy myself smoothing down my dress, erasing invisible crinkles in the fine silk, and don't allow his eyes to find mine before he walks away.

'Don't let the door hit you on the way out, Preston!' Penny cries.

We're pretty tipsy by the time our ride arrives, so Ange ends up piling in with us instead of ordering her own Uber. She's going home to the babysitter while Penny has made me pinky promise that we'll go out.

'Well. We did it!' I exclaim.

'Not only did we survive, I'd say it was a successful night. You survived Wes and I pashed Jimmy in the bathrooms – for old time's sake,' Penny boasts. Her dress is hitched up at her thighs, revealing a hint of lacy black underwear.

'Um, ah-mazing!' I am genuinely delighted for her. 'How about you, Ange? How are you holding up?' I turn to look at her in the back seat. The flush in her cheeks matches her worn lipstick and she has mascara smudged on her right upper lid and under her left eye. She's wasted.

I turn to Penny for assistance, but she's grown bored of our conversation and is engrossed in some serious Insta-filter selection on her phone.

'I spoke to Wes,' Ange slurs.

My stomach lurches.

'Now's probably not the best time to talk about it,' I say. I'm already wrecked, and we haven't spoken properly all night. I really can't get into it with her now. 'I'm still in Sydney tomorrow; maybe we can do brunch?'

'Brunch?' Ange squawks. 'And what do you suggest I do with the boys? Shall I call Dave?'

Yet another wrong move.

I know that tonight would have been difficult for her, too. Like Wes and I, Dave and Ange had been childhood sweethearts – the difference being they'd successfully navigated their relationship through to marriage and children. Every girl at school was in love with Dave. He was two years our senior and your typical hunky footy star. He even played reserves for the Roosters for a bit. But he fell for Ange like a ton of bricks. Even right now, her blotchy red skin and glazed panda eyes can't hide her enviable porcelain complexion and general gorgeousness. They married while we were still at university. Pen and I were bridesmaids in God-awful apricot chiffon.

I never really gelled with Dave. But he made Ange deliriously happy, and that's what counted – until the week before I left for Mudgee, when I was in the unfortunate position of witnessing him kiss someone who wasn't Ange. I told her straightaway and now, nearly two months later, they're separated, set to divorce as soon as they can. She's been pretending to cope ever since, and shut me and Penny out. Me more so, since I'm the one who 'blew up' her marriage.

With any luck she'll soon realise that I was only trying to look out for her. Penny will back me up on that. Better now than being blindsided later, once the boys are older. Unfortunately for me, Ange doesn't see it that way yet. Still, I'm hopeful we'll patch things up soon enough.

It's hard not being able to talk to her. Ange would have known how much I was dreading seeing Wes tonight. Yet not so much as a, 'Hey, how are you feeling?' had come my way.

Nothing. Hopefully I'm out of the 'Ange freezer' soon.

'Rosieeeeeee, babeeeeeeee. What are you waiting for? You'll mess up my five stars.' Penny is standing on the pavement yelling through the closed window.

Shit, I hadn't even noticed we'd arrived at King Street.

'Ange is still in here!' I yell back at her.

'Agggggh,' comes a moan from the backseat.

I poke my head around my seat to find that Ange's head is dropped between her legs like she's about to be sick.

'Oh God, are you okay? Do you want me to stay with you for the ride home?'

But as I reach for her, her head snaps up.

'No, thank you. Your shouting is giving me a headache.'

I'm the one giving her a headache? I keep my mouth shut about the copious amounts of cheap chardonnay she's consumed and instead ask her to text me when she's home safely. I thank the driver and jump out of the car into Penny's outstretched arms.

'I hope you are ready to bring your A-game,' she howls as she lurches towards me, stumbling over a non-existent hazard on the sidewalk.

'You bet I am.' I laugh as I picture the chaotic night that lies ahead. I'm ready to twerk the bad vibes of the Class of 2013 away.

Chapter Five

Given we danced until the early hours of Sunday morning, my red dress has fared relatively well. I'm so hungover that I break my strict 'wear once, wash once' rule and, one deodorant treatment later, it's ready to go again. It passes the sniff test, rid of any lingering odours – and dark high-school memories.

We have spent the best part of the day laying on the lounge in Penny's Bondi beach pad. All of our slovenliness, UberEATS and intermittent debriefing of the night before has done its magic, so by the time 6 pm creeps around I'm looking forward to going out again. My head has finally stopped thumping and Wes is old news. Well, older news – filed away to dissect with Squash from the comfort of my couch.

'This is a big event, Rosie. Lots of networking opportunities,' Penny lectures on the way over. 'You'll be out of Mudgee and heading up a breakfast slot in Sydney in no time.' I go along with her enthusiasm, although I'm not sure that's even what I want. The whole point of moving to Mudgee was to escape it all.

We step onto the red carpet outside Sydney Town Hall, and I prepare myself for an onslaught of flashing cameras. Instead, we're greeted by a pair of gruff security guards sporting high-tech earpieces and pulling last-minute barricades into place.

'Passes, ladies?'

'Here.' Pen presses an official-looking lanyard into my hand and hisses. 'Tonight you're my assistant.'

We flash our credentials and the security guards wave us through. Penny strides ahead, eager to check on the last-minute prep, and starts fussing over the bottles of Scuttlebutt in the VIP section. She'd failed to inform me until the very last moment that Scuttlebutt was, in fact, a wine brand.

The paparazzi have assumed their positions and the crowd behind the roped-off area is starting to build. All eyes are eagerly anticipating the arrival of the who's who of showbiz. The crowd erupts into hysterical screams as a willowy blonde in a daringly short emerald sequinned skirt steps onto the red carpet.

'Eryka, Eryka! Over here, over here!'

Eryka Polanski. The ultimate glamazon, current 'It' girl and Dr Markus Abrahams' fiancée. She glides up the carpet, pausing to pout and pose for the photographers, making the peace sign like she's in a Tokyo schoolyard and not at the hottest fashion event of the season. Yet, she totally rocks it. She's sweet schoolgirl and sex on legs, rolled into one. Rumour has it that she's nice, too. Like, disgustingly so.

Even in my stupid heels I'm not tall enough to see if Markus is behind her. I still can't believe how forward he was the other night. Did he actually think he was charming? I can only imagine that overinflated ego on the set of *Markus & Pup*.

He probably clicks his fingers, Beyoncé style, and expects everyone to fall at his feet. I wonder how Eryka puts up with his antics.

I grip my event pass and push my way towards the pack of photographers to secure a better vantage point. Cedric has provided me with a comprehensive list of who I should be sucking up to.

Someone catches my elbow. Penny. 'Am I going to have to watch you all night? You don't have to panic. I'll make it happen with Markus.'

'Yuck! No thanks – you can have him. I was getting a head start on Cedric's hit-list.'

'There will be plenty of time for that later, girl. You need to play it cool – this is an industry event. Besides, I need your help backstage.'

For all of her play, Penny is a ferocious worker. I spend the next few hours stocking and restocking the Scuttlebutt VIP bar and miss the fashion show completely – not that I mind. I'm impressed that Penny has swung things to seem like she's doing me a favour when, really, I'm a whole lot of free labour. By the time I'm released from my bar duties, the afterparty is in full swing. Selected guests have been invited to hang out in the Scuttlebutt lounge, and I have full access. A waitress with a tray of delicious-smelling meat pies heads in my direction, but I'm too slow off the mark and she sails right past and sits the tray down on an empty table in the middle of the room.

I stare longingly at the plate. I'm famished. *The fried foods are strictly for husbands only.* Penny has briefed me. Hilarious considering her well-known penchant for anything fried or glazed. The much hipper fringe dwellers seem happy enough pretending they're filling up on hummus. Not wanting to risk Pen's rep, I look around for the dips and carrot-sticks.

'Oh, sod it, let's do it. I want one too.' The glamazon has

materialised beside me, grinning wickedly. She sounds a bit like Anna Kournikova, and she looks a lot like her too. Her perfect blow wave has been scraped back into a ponytail and she's wearing thick-frame glasses.

'I know, right,' she says, as my eyes fix on her ripped jeans. 'When the clock strikes midnight, my ballgown turns right back into rags. I prefer it this way.'

This chick is cool. What on earth is she doing with Markus?

'Eryka Polanksi.' She smiles and extends an arm.

'Rosie Royce.' I clasp her hand and give it a hearty shake. Her skin is delicate and soft.

'Lovely to meet you. And what brings you to this absolute wank fest, Rosie?'

I swallow a snort and am in the midst of formulating a witty reply when Markus sidles up next to Eryka and hands her a glass of sparkling. Gah. He *is* here. Once again, he's completely TV ready: clean-shaven, with jet-black hair that's slicked down into his signature *Markus & Pup* do, and a crisp white shirt that clings to his sculpted body. Markus Abrahams' body is his one saving grace. Not that I would ever allow my eyes to linger long enough for him to know that. I'd rather die than give him that satisfaction.

'Hi, Markus.' I may as well get this over with.

'Gorgeous! Fancy seeing you here! How are you?' Markus's voice booms, amplifying across the room like he's performing in front of an audience. I half expect him to take a bow.

'I'm well, thank you,' I respond cautiously.

'Champagne?' He thrusts his glass into my hand before I can respond.

Why does this man insist on giving me his beverages? Surely he won't make a pass at me while Eryka is standing right here. That would be beyond stupid.

'Thank you.' I take a hesitant sip.

The alcohol rushes straight to my head. My bravery is buoyed by the sweet bubbles.

'We have to stop running into each other like this, Markus.'

'I couldn't disagree more, gorgeous. What a treat!'

Eryka's smooth-as-a-baby's-bum brow is slightly furrowed as she looks from Markus's face to mine and then back again.

'Your fiancé bought me a drink in Mudgee,' I say softly.

I'm sure I'm not the first female to approach Eryka with suggestions of Markus's dodgy behaviour, but it still can't be nice to hear.

'On Friday night,' I finish off, to timestamp his antics as recent.

And drop mic, mofo.

But Markus doesn't seem at all rattled. Instead, he slips an arm around Eryka's non-existent waist, and whispers something in her ear.

Eryka's near-perfect features brighten with what can only be described as sweet relief.

'Oh, you're Rosie!'

'Yes . . .'

Has Markus mentioned me? What could he possibly have said?

'Well, introduce me properly, Markus!' Eryka exclaims and playfully punches his solid arm.

Markus pulls a mock pained face before giving me an approving once-over. 'We didn't get very far with introductions the other night, did we Rosie? How did things go with your gentleman friend?'

'He wasn't for me,' I blurt.

I don't know why I answer honestly. It's none of his business and also largely his fault.

'Oh, *reallllllly* . . .' His mouth turns over the words care-fully like he's inspecting the underside of a pancake, ensuring it's cooked through before committing to the flip. Next comes his trademark Colgate smile. 'I'm sorry to hear that, beautiful.' He looks the very opposite of sorry.

'It's fine.'

'I'm sure Rosie doesn't want to talk about that,' Eryka jumps in. 'So, what is it that you do, Rosie?'

'I've just started hosting a morning radio show,' I can't help but boast.

Finally, a leg up in this conversation.

Markus's head snaps up. 'In Mudgee, or here?'

'Mudgee.'

Markus and Eryka exchange a glance, no doubt surprised that I work in media. Even the Sebastian Worthington isn't fooling anyone. After my stint behind the bar, I know I'm looking worse for wear. I've pushed my reunion hairstyle with a spray of dry shampoo, but my next-day hair is rapidly resuming its frizz.

Eryka smiles warmly at me. 'Sounds like a great gig, Rosie. Although I must say, that adorable face of yours shouldn't be hidden away in a radio studio. Markus said that you were very pretty – and he was right.'

Okay . . .

I'm not accustomed to compliments – especially from a supermodel. I've either stepped into a warped twilight zone, or I'm being groomed for a ménage à trois and a room key is about to be slipped into my cleavage.

'Um . . . Thank you?'

I'm relieved when Markus starts coughing loudly. He plucks Eryka's champagne flute out of her hands and downs the contents.

'Are you okay, babe?' Eryka whacks him on the back.

'Just a little parched . . .' He glances pointedly at his glass in my hands.

I didn't ask for his champagne. In fact, I didn't want it.

'How about I go grab us some more drinks? Refill, Rosie?' Eryka asks.

'Sure,' I say, even though I want nothing more than to exit this conversation and find someone else on Cedric's list to talk to.

'Can you see if they'll make me a martini, babe? Shaken not stirred, please.'

'I'll ask.' She rolls her eyes at me but it's clearly affectionate.

'Thanks babe. I'll hold down the fort here.' He winks.

'Behave yourself, Markus,' Eryka warns. She flashes me an apologetic smile before sashaying off in the direction of the Scuttlebutt bar. My eyes follow her pert ponytail as it swings from side to side. As soon as Eryka is out of sight, Markus turns back to me and drops into his honeyed TV voice.

'So, tell me, gorgeous. Are you looking for Mr Right, or Mr Right Now?' He folds his arms and flexes his muscles against his chest.

Urgh.

Get. Me. Out. Of. Here.

Chapter Six

The Sebastian Worthington is safely in the closet of its rightful owner, one Penny Santos, and I'm back in Mudgee, in my uniform of comfy jeans and Converse. I'm relieved to return to my new, quieter, *anonymous* existence here – where there's no past chasing me down, or best friends to fight with.

It feels good knowing that I have Penny's support, even when I'm in Mudgee. I've been home for two days, and last night she sent me a photo from the Scuttlebutt event. I'm looking away from the camera, one of the frilly red dress straps has slipped down off my shoulder and my hand tickles my collarbone. Even I must admit that I look wistful and pretty – even though in reality I was on high alert for another Markus run-in. I'd only just managed to hold my tongue on Sunday night. Eryka had returned with more drinks just as Markus had begun to shower me with compliments.

Beautiful, that dress is divine on you.

Tell me, how is it that a stunning woman like yourself is single?

I'd sculled my champagne and hightailed it back to Penny. A narrow escape.

Penny insisted the pic was too good to waste, and that I send screenshot proof once I'd updated my Tinder profile to include it. Once I had her tick of approval, I'd swiped half-heartedly for a bit, delaying my pre-show bedtime. I ended up having a chat with a local photographer. I'd tried to overlook the fact that his Brazil travel photos had Rio 2016 flags flapping in the background. I may never have been overseas – which I'm highly aware is unusual in itself – but surely they don't keep Olympic memorabilia up forever? If his photos were seven years old, that did not bode well.

After making plans to meet the possible-catfish photographer at Lesters next Saturday – mainly because I appreciated his ability to actually lock in a date – I'd closed the app and gone to bed, suddenly struck with the thought that I might come across Markus on there.

I'm pondering the possibility again as I get ready for my post-show errands. Markus wouldn't be stupid enough to use his photos, would he? But he might be one of the many faceless profiles lurking for their next prey. Disgusting. But who knows – he and Eryka could have an open relationship.

I shake my head to rid it of yucky Markus thoughts, grab my grocery list – meticulously ordered by aisle number – and walk out the door. (One of the upsides to a limited social life is plenty of time to plot the most efficient supermarket route.)

I walk in the direction of Woolies. It's mac 'n' cheese again for dinner tonight, and for Squash, a tin of the finest Delightful Tuna Gourmet. Despite the rain, there's a delicious crunch underfoot as I kick my feet through the fresh fall of golden autumn leaves. It's not like this in Sydney, with noisy street cleaners mandated by cautious council workers quickly erasing any slip hazards and potential lawsuits.

It was apparently raining heavily here all weekend, which meant aggressive turbulence during Monday night's landing and getting completely soaked as I ran from the tarmac into the terminal. But you don't complain about rain in the country; I've learnt that quick enough. Despite the downpour, I was informed by both Cedric and yesterday's astute Tuesday callers that it hasn't been anywhere near enough to break the drought. Sadly, it's still the fourth-driest May since the Bureau of Meteorology started taking records.

The weak autumn sun warms my back and bounces off the beautiful old buildings casting low shadows beyond the kerb line. There's the flamingo pink post office, town hall and civic theatre. One of the perks of early morning starts is the stretches of afternoon to enjoy. I squeeze my eyes shut for a moment, picturing the original businesses that operated along here in the 1900s, buzzing with locals. There was the general store and bootmaker on one side, and the butcher on the other, all now turned boutiques, op shops and chain stores. On the corner was the grand tearoom, ready to receive mothers and daughters in their Sunday best. It's almost laughable to think mothers did such enjoyable things with their daughters. My mum was always too busy 'working' – no time for tea and tiny cucumber sandwiches – only to coach me on the expected ROI (return on investment) on a Japanese solar-powered, head-shaking dashboard Kokeshi Doll. She didn't even come to collect me on the first day of kindergarten, when I split my head open chasing Kate Adams around the schoolyard. Three stitches later at hospital and it was Dad who was there to console me. But it wasn't until Wes stopped by later that afternoon with melted Mr Whippy, transported via skateboard from a steamy Galdwell Park, that I finally cracked a smile.

There's no point dwelling on the past, I remind myself as I enter the supermarket. I grab a basket, pull a disinfectant wipe from the packet in my handbag, and sanitise the basket's handles before beginning my tracked route through the fruit and veg section.

Another perk of moving somewhere new is fewer nostalgia-triggering landmarks, yet the moment I reach for a bunch of extra-large Cavendish bananas I'm hit with another wave of memories. I pick up the bananas and put them in my basket, but in my head I'm back in October 2015 – one of the final days of Wes and Rosie's BIG Adventure.

Wes enters our motel room first, doing his usual hygiene sweep before calling out to me that it's safe to proceed. I shuffle through the doorway behind him like I'm on death row.

It's not in the least bit sanitary. The visible cobwebs caught in the corners of the windows means there's invisible filth that lurks in the carpet threads and, worse still, the bedding.

'Eww, look at that stain.' I point out the brown smudge like it can't already be seen from outer space.

'You know that we're just going to be adding to that filth.' Wes grins mischievously, before reaching forward and pulling me over to the bed.

I don't put up a fight as I flop down on top of him. He's literally the only person in the world who can get me this close to suspected faecal matter.

I plant a kiss on his full lips. Better to inhale his car-chip breath than the respiratory virus lingering in the stale motel room air. He kisses me back, sliding his tongue inside my mouth. As our kisses become deeper and more urgent, I begin to slip off his body.

Instead of catching me and adjusting me back on top of his hips, he turns on his side, causing me to topple onto the bed.

I shuffle back on top of him like the bedspread is lava.

'*I can see what you're doing, Posie.*'

'*Urgh,*' *I groan into his mouth.* '*It's just so gross.*'

'*Would you prefer the floor?*'

If looks could kill.

'*How about the shower?*' *he tries again.*

'*Fine.*' *I relent.* '*I'll grab our thongs.*'

It's not like it's hard to convince me. I want him just as much as he wants me. Just look at those muscular legs. He's wearing his absurdly small footy shorts again, the pair he usually wears when he's painting.

I move to roll off him, but his arms go around me, and his fingers sink into my sides.

'*Wesssssssssss!*' *I screech, squirming uncontrollably as he tickles me until I fall, arms flailing, right on top of the brown stain.*

After our shower, the room is suitably steamed and we're sitting flushed-faced across from each other on steel dining chairs, our feet grazing underneath the table.

'*So, what's the plan?*' *I ask, giving him an extra kick.*

A smile plays on his lips. '*The plan, Rosie, is that there is no plan. That's the purpose of a road trip.*'

'*But hypothetically speaking. Like, if you had to make one . . .*'

'*I don't know, maybe watch some terrible cable TV, then a walk into town to –*'

I clear my throat, then stare pointedly at the remote like it's a detonating bomb. Everyone knows TV remotes are as bad as bar peanuts. More semen than channel-surfing going on there.

He sighs, but his nostrils flare, a tell-tale sign that he's amused.

'*Okay, we'll skip the TV. Let's walk into town and find a local spot for some dinner and people watching, then get an early night and head up to the Big Banana first thing for sunrise?'*

A grin dances across my face. 'Sounds like a plan.'

'You and your bloody plans . . .'

I stick my tongue out at him. 'You love them.'

He leans over, tucks the strand of hair I've been twisting behind my ear and kisses the tip of my nose.

'Incorrect. But I do love you. Despite your incessant planning.'

A few hours later we fall back into bed, bellies full of creamy pesto pasta from the Coffs Harbour RSL. We'd planned on playing Keno, but we'd gotten too caught up watching an elderly couple eating dinner together. There's nothing we love more than observing grey-haired couples and wondering how long they've been good to each other for. Wes sketched on the back of a coaster while I commentated.

'Ohhh he's cutting up her chicken for her! Will you cut up my chicken for me?'

'Without a doubt, Posie-pants.'

It takes me a full hour to get to sleep that night, even with the disease-ridden bedspread removed and bundled into a corner of the room. I wish we'd decided to drive south to north, not the other way around, so we were at the beginning of our BIG Adventure and not the end. I hadn't even wanted to come. But as was the case with most things, Wes had managed to convince me. In this moment I'm happier than I ever thought possible, even with bed bugs nipping my ankles.

I'm in the frozen food section, the final stop of my grocery route, before I even realise it. My cheek feels wet. I reach up to wipe away the single tear that's slid silently down my face.

It's slim pickings in TV dinner land here – not like in Sydney where professionals live on a diet of frozen dinners and UberEATS. I throw a couple of mac 'n' cheese boxes into my basket and head for the checkout. It seems I've completed the rest of my list on autopilot.

The friendly cashier with a name badge that says 'Shelly' scans and bags up my items slowly, instead of pelting them at me like we're engaged in a competitive game of paintball. Yet another big plus for country living. *I hope my face isn't blotchy*, I think as she cradles the bananas, before sliding them carefully into the bag on top of the mac 'n' cheese stack. Like she's aware of their time-travelling powers.

I thank Shelly with a shy smile. I'm feeling extra tender after my BIG Adventure down memory lane. The sooner I can forget about Wes and get back to my new life here, the better.

Although my Tinder dates have been epic disappointments, so far all the 'side' characters in this town have proven to be every bit as enchanting as rural romances depict. I'm yet to witness any 'small-town blow-in' hierarchy nonsense, but maybe that's because I've been subconsciously keeping the locals at arm's length so I can romanticise life here. Or maybe I'm the one being kept at arm's length?

A flash of yellow catches my eye and I turn to see a taxi pulling up beside me.

The driver winds their window down and I instantly recognise the wide-brimmed hat. It's the driver from the other night. His hat is adorned with a stripy rainbow band and studded with an assortment of pins. A golden gumboot glints in the sun and my heart skips a beat. The Golden Gumboot in Tully, in Far North Queensland, was a part of our BIG Adventure too.

My mind goes to the motel with the murky pool in the shape of the boot. Wes had pushed me in fully clothed – Converse and all. I'd emerged from the swamp like some creature from the deep with a serious case of the giggles. So serious that Wes had insisted on giving me 'CPR' on the pool's edge until I pulled him in too.

'Hi girlie. Can I give you a lift home?' the cabbie asks, eyeing my grocery-laden arms.

'I'm okay, thank you,' I say. 'It's not far.'

Yes, the bags are heavy, but I'm in no rush. Prior to this week, I'd been spending most afternoons poring over show notes for the next day, but Ceddie has put a stop to that, refusing to let me know what's planned until I arrive at the station the morning of the show. He says the magic happens when I'm 'woefully underprepared'. I'm still not sure about that – it's nowhere close to my natural state. I'd also like to platform *some* local stories, and that will require some planning.

For all of its headaches, I suppose dating has helped me handle curveballs like a pro. I hate that I am crediting any of those losers for my adept ability to think fast on my feet, but I guess it's true. The moment I identify the 'never ever' I throw out a quick one-liner excuse and skedaddle.

The cab continues idling beside me. The driver rests a roughened elbow out the window.

'Yes, I know, dear. You're in one of those old terraces off Court Street.'

Oh! He recognises me. I feel like I've earned some type of small-town Scouts badge.

'Let me take you. On the house.'

'Okay,' I agree. 'That's very kind. Thank you.'

I move to the rear of the car, opening one of doors and placing my groceries on the back seat. I hesitate for a moment, wondering if I should slide in next to my bags, before making a firm decision to close the door and sit up next to the driver. Time to get my head out of the past and into the present.

'I'm Jack.' He introduces himself as I fasten my seatbelt.

'Nice to meet you, Jack. I'm Rosie. Thanks again for the lift.'

'You're very welcome,' he says, one hand on the steering wheel, the other on the gear stick and eyes on the road. I can't remember the last time I was in an old-fashioned taxi. Sydney is all slick leather seat Ubers with complimentary waters. 'Have you been in Mudgee long?' Jack asks.

'Almost two months. I'm working at the radio station.'

'You really are a local then.' His eyes shift sideways and his mouth curves into a toothy smile.

'Not quite.' I laugh. 'Hopefully one day. How long have you lived here?'

'About forty or so years,' Jack says, glancing at me. 'I'm from Thubbo initially – you know it as Dubbo. I moved to Mudgee for work and fell in love with the place.'

'Oh, that's nice,' I mumble, suddenly at a loss for words. I've gotten too used to city Ubers and selecting the 'quiet preferred' option.

'Have you always driven cabs?'

Okay. Basic, but at least something.

'Only since retiring, love. I'm a paramedic by trade, but after decades of heart-racing trips on the road it was impossible to put my feet up completely without getting restless. Besides, I knew the town needed drivers. I take all these short trips the other cabbies don't think are worth their while.'

As we round the corner into my street, my left bum cheek vibrates. I ignore it.

Jack's hand drums the steering wheel. 'But the people need to get places, the places don't come to the people, now, do they?'

I laugh as we come to a stop outside of my terrace flat, and Jack tips his hat at me.

'Thank you so much for the lift.'

'You're welcome. I've gotta rush and take one of my regulars to Bingo, otherwise I'd whizz you around town for a quick 'locals only' tour.'

'That's very kind of you, thanks Jack. Another time?'

'Certainly. There's more to this area than just great wineries, you know. There's a lot of history too.'

As I climb out of the car, and collect my groceries from the back, Jack reaches over and presses a business card into my palm.

'Call me anytime you get stuck,' he says, voice gruff but warm. 'Or if you ever fancy me joining you on air to tell you a bit about Mudgee's Indigenous history. I know a thing or two.'

'Thanks, Jack. That's a lovely offer.'

I'd love to learn more about this place I now call home, and I'm sure our listeners would too.

'Now if this were an audition – which it ain't 'cause I'd have to charge you for that – I'd tell you that the name Mudgee comes from the Wiradjuri word *Moothi*, which means 'nest in the hills'.'

'Ooh, that's beautiful,' I say. Mudgee does feel a bit like a nest to me actually, somewhere I've sought refuge.

'Lots more facts where that came from – you get your people to call my people.'

I laugh again. 'Sure. We'll be in touch. Thanks again for the ride,' I say as I shut the door. I wave at the taxi's rear as it bumps down the road, before glancing down at the card in my hand to read the small print underneath the mobile number.

Jack Ballard
Call for lifts, a good yarn, or emergency first-aid*
*only if desperate and you've tried the ambos first

I carefully slide the business card into my back pocket like it's a winning lotto ticket and retrieve my mobile. The heavy shopping bags lassoed over my arms knock into my thighs as I bring the phone into view.

My Tinder notifications are muted, otherwise I'd assume it was the photographer already cancelling our date. I was half-thinking about doing the same anyway. I've given it a good crack here, but it might be time to call it quits and focus on the show, and put some real effort into making friends. I look down at the screen and see I have a text from an unknown number.

My heart skips a beat as my brain instantly goes to Mum. I wasn't bluffing when I told Dad that I haven't heard from her in ages, but I wasn't honest about how unsettled that made me. I like having eyes on her to minimise any element of surprise. The last time she went MIA on Facebook she popped up in my LinkedIn messages a few months later with a 'Business Opportunity' that was 'guaranteed to make me millions'. It was like a bullet to my side. I'd long since given up hope of any meaningful interactions, and learnt to endure the infrequent *'Hope you're doing well and smashing your business goals'* Facebook comments, but I drew the line at outright scams. I acknowledged the message with a 'thumbs up' emoji, then promptly updated my LinkedIn privacy settings to receive mail from first-degree connections only, before heading to my next meeting, ten minutes ahead of schedule.

I can't wait until I'm inside to find out who the message is from, so I perch on the edge of the nature strip and hold my breath as I swipe.

Hi Rosie, I hope it's okay that I'm messaging. Ange gave me your number. It was great seeing you the other night. Would you be open to meeting me for a drink? I can come to you. I'd like to talk properly

Oh, this is Wes

In an instant, my bones feel like they've turned to jelly. It's a good thing I'm already sitting down. I stare at the message for a moment, hands wobbly and weak, before my screaming brain kicks in.

Goddammit, Ange.

I banned myself from stalking Wes years ago. After those initial few weeks of checking his whereabouts hourly, while simultaneously ignoring all of his messages, I decided that it was making me feel worse. Mostly because it didn't change anything. He was still in London and I – well, I wasn't. I felt like the little matchgirl looking through a glass pane at the brilliant, colourful life that wasn't mine. It was different from keeping tabs on my mum; I was never a part of her world anyway.

The girls set me up with a stalker jar. I had to drop twenty bucks in every time I checked his page. A week later, Penny and Ange were sporting designer handbags care of the 'Wes Preston stalker fund'. I stopped completely right after that, and blocked him for good measure. I suppose that's when my 'precise life' stepped up a notch. Like father, like daughter. Suddenly I found great delight in colour coding my bookshelves and scheduling my weekends. Penny and Ange even joked that they'd have to send me calendar invites months in advance for a chance to see me. Textbook, really. One habit replacing another.

I wait until I've unpacked the shopping, fed Squash, heated up my cheesy mac and re-fluffed the couch cushions before I text back. Wes has had six years to get in touch with me. Seeing him at the reunion hasn't changed anything. I'm still no closer to understanding how he could have hurt me so much when I'd trusted him more than anyone. If you squinted and looked past Wes's rust-coloured eyes, you'd see the words 'selfish prick' strung together around his head in an unfortunate halo. He's a 'proper fuckstick' as Pen would say. And why that fuckstick thinks that there's any part of me that wants to hear from him now is completely beyond me.

Hi Wes, I don't want to be rude, but I'd like you to leave me alone. Rosie.

I'm happy with the mature way in which I've responded. I place my phone on the coffee table and resume my pillow plumping.

My phone beeps again. This time it's just one word.

Okay

Chapter Seven

It's the next morning and the car park outside the radio station is decidedly sparse. To be fair, there's only four spots anyway, and it's 6 am. Back in Sydney this ungodly hour would be classified as the middle of the night – in my previous agency life, anyway. It wasn't uncommon for my team to roll into the office at 11 am.

Getting up early isn't my forte, but being on time is. I'd never admit it, but I'm still finding the pre-dawn starts a struggle – although Squash's early morning pawing and scratching at the door helps. At least a make-up–free look is perfectly acceptable for radio. I can roll straight out of bed, splash water on my face, pull on a fresh set of clothes and I'm good to go. Cedric says it won't be long before I start rocking up in my flannelette PJs and bed socks – especially when the weather really starts to turn. But there's a fine line between efficiency and slovenliness. Time saving: yes. Unhygienic: never.

But I'm slowly adjusting to the hours, although I wasn't able to sleep much last night and have been gifted dark crescent moons under both eyes. Bloody Wes. His messages had sparked another Michelangelo nightmare with his imaginary girlfriend and her sheet of golden hair resuming the starring role.

I'm standing at the edge of the car park when a loud black ute turns into the driveway then gracefully reverses into the space directly in front of the entrance. Who could that be? Cedric rides a mulberry Vespa that he insists on lifting into the tiled foyer each day, and the only other early morning regular is Stacey, the Gen-Z sound guy with a cool name and ever 'cooler' beaten-up sedan.

The roar quietens as the engine is switched off. A head emerges, then broad shoulders in a white linen shirt, followed by dark denim jeans. I gasp as I recognise him. Markus! What is he doing here? He appears to look right at me across the darkened car park as he shuts his door but then turns and strides up the stairs towards the entrance and disappears inside the building.

There's no sign of Markus or Cedric as I walk to my desk, weaving between the piles of magazines, boxes of CDs, a bulky printer and rogue Dyson. A mountain of products balances precariously over my keyboard. I start sorting the jumble of tinned dog food, two-minute noodles and hair removal creams, ordering them in neat piles on the floor by the side of the desk. I should be chuffed that I'm receiving free stuff – Penny's always boasting about swag – but I'm annoyed at the mess. The walls are no better, paint peeling and covered in an explosion of framed certificates and posters of popstars. It's challenging to do the show prep Cedric actually allows in this chaos.

'Score anything decent? I'm the proud new owner of a pair of Toe Tunes. Apparently, musical slippers are the next big wardrobe staple.' Cedric has materialised at my desk, dressed in a paisley shirt and matching purple spectacles. Markus is next to him. Smiling. Not his usual Colgate smile, but a small smile. If I didn't know any better, I'd call it shy.

'Just your everyday glow-in-the-dark squeegee.' I point to the spongey-looking fluoro item on the ground. Best to appear nonchalant until I know exactly what I'm dealing with here.

Cedric smiles widely, his face luminous. 'Rosie, allow me to present to you the godly Dr Markus Abrahams.' For all of his years of experience, Cedric is quick to turn into a teenager on heat at the first whiff of a hot guy.

'That's quite the introduction. Thanks Cedric,' Markus says, his face flushed.

Oh, puh-lease! If we'd never met, perhaps I could have remained as deluded as the rest of the *Markus & Pup* viewers and believed that he was as sweet as his on-air persona. But I now know that Dr Markus Abrahams is no 'nice guy' – he's just another cookie-cutter TV star who thinks he has rights to whatever and whomever he wants because of his handsome face and celebrity status.

'Nice to see you, Rosie.' Markus leans in to kiss me on the cheek. I'm quick on my feet and jump back, sticking out a hand instead. I wait for the whiff of criminally expensive-smelling cologne, but thankfully, it doesn't arrive. Still, this new 'bashful country boy' act isn't fooling me for a second. Not when I know he's a big, flash city knob.

I give his hand a firm shake. 'Hi, Markus.'

I'm curt, but polite, although my stare perhaps says otherwise. I hold eye contact, chin high, colossal under-eye circles and all.

'Hi . . .' Streaks of confusion settle in his piercing blue eyes, giving them a depth not visible on screen.

Gah, they are very striking . . . I force a blink to sever any spell he's busy casting and fold my arms across my chest.

'I hope you've been well . . .?' Markus continues. He sounds unsure, like he's considering where to move his next chess piece.

I stand up taller, defensive stance activated.

You're not going to get anything out of me, buddy. I'm happy for you to do all the talking – you normally have plenty to say.

'You seem like you're not a huge fan of mine, Rosie?'

Now there's the understatement of the century. But I know how to behave for Cedric's sake. I've dealt with worse.

'Not at all, Markus. We barely know each other,' I coo.

'Right . . .' Markus is still hesitant. 'I'm really sorry if I've offended you at some point or another, Rosie. I haven't been – ah – quite myself of late.'

He smiles with the same false warmth I've just used on him. I'm surprised he has a job on prime time with these terrible acting skills. Cedric had better not be making me interview this over-inflated Ken doll.

Markus continues. 'I'd really love if we could start afresh, Rosie. Especially as we're going to be spending so much time together.'

Wait. What? *Why* are we going to be spending so much time together?

My eyes narrow as I glare at Cedric, but he averts his gaze to my pile of freebies, plucks the squeegee from the top and starts fiddling with its handle.

'Cedric?'

He looks up, eyes guilty. 'Okay, let me explain. Gold 86.7 FM has been missing out on a fair chunk of listeners for a while now – regardless of how much Daryl Braithwaite we play. Rosie, you have the social set covered, but we're still in need of a voice for the horsey people of this town.' He lets out a nervous laugh, the same uncontrollable tinkle that escaped on the phone yesterday while trying to convince his fiancé, Simon, that he didn't eat a bacon and egg roll for breakfast. (He did.)

The outside frostiness instantly materialises inside, and I hug my crossed arms tighter to my chest. What was the point of recruiting me in Sydney – wooing me to come here – only to send in backup a couple of months later? Or was this his plan the whole time?

'Enter Dr Markus Abrahams,' Cedric continues, gesturing towards Markus with an exaggerated flourish. 'When I heard that you'd be basing yourself in Mudgee more with the clinic, Markus, I thought, why not give it a try? And here we all are! I was delighted that you said yes. Isn't it fabulous?'

He throws an arm around each of our shoulders and smiles like Squash after he's demolished his tin of Delightful Tuna Gourmet.

'Thanks, Cedric. I'm really looking forward to working with you both and trying out this radio thing,' Markus mumbles while staring down at his scuffed RM Williams. The fancy leather loafers must be off getting shined.

'So, we'll be co-hosting together? Every show?' I ask, my voice becoming pitchier with each question.

'We can discuss the finer details after today's show. You're due on air any second, Rosie. I want Markus to witness your natural brilliance firsthand.'

Oh no, Cedric, you don't get to smooth everything over with a quick burst of flattery. 'We still have a few minutes,' I respond coolly.

Cedric sighs. What did he expect? He saw me on that stage at Millennial Marketing. I'm no wallflower. In fact, I'm sure the passionate, opinionated me is the 'natural brilliance' that he's referring to. I'm not one to let things go easily.

'Very well, Rosie. You'll still be hosting the show and we'll have Markus as a regular guest taking calls and answering any animal-related questions. He still has his TV commitments, so we'll try to work around that where we can.'

'I'm not sure how I'll go, but I'll give it my best shot,' Markus chimes in.

I'll give it my best shot. So blisteringly arrogant. He's got to know that he has years of media experience on me.

I'm sure he can't wait to show me up.

It's not a nuclear disaster, but it's not my finest. Following the show's usual loose formula, I kick things off by opening the newspaper and selecting a story for discussion. Today's hot topic is food wastage and the local IGA's pledge to take overripe bananas and turn them into banana bread – a noble, largely uncontroversial cause – aside from the NSW Food Authority's eye-roll–inducing comments that its officers will be monitoring the new venture.

Next is a chat with Jack, which is definitely the highlight of the show. I knew from our call late last night that he would be perfect on air.

'*Ten minutes, you say? I might need an hour,*' he'd said. '*Do you need me to explain how to correctly bandage a snake bite too?*'

I'd laughed, only for Jack to reply: '*Not a laughing matter, girlie. We have some of the deadliest snakes in the world here. Eastern browns, inland taipans, you name it!*'

'*Let's maybe stick with Indigenous history for now,*' I said as my skin crawled.

'*Right you are, young pup.*'

This morning, Jack is patient and informative as he gives me, and our listeners, an overview of the First Nations people who traditionally inhabit the area, tribes from the Wiradjuri Nation. When caller, Abby, phones in to ask more specifics about how far Wiradjuri country stretches, Jack describes how it is bordered by three rivers, Macquarie (*Wambuul*), Lachlan (*Kalari*) and Murrumbidgee (*Murrumbidjeri*), then directs us to an online resource with a helpful colour-coded map.

Then comes the 'entertainment' interview, the only segment Cedric allows me to vaguely prepare for. I speak with Candice Shell, the star of the new Australian teen drama *Sugar High*. She's lovely and chatty and surprisingly humble for a thirteen-year-old child actress prodigy, although perhaps a demographic mismatch with the more mature Mudgee listeners.

As soon as Stacey hits the final button and the 'On Air' sign dulls, I'm out of my chair and bursting into Cedric's office. He's in the downward dog position.

'Where is Markus?' I demand.

Cedric stays put in his pose for another thirty seconds, looking at me from between his legs, eyes bulged, face flushed. I tap my foot impatiently. He eventually stands and then crouches back down again to roll up his mat.

'Simon says I'm getting fat,' he says, sticking out his bottom lip.

I glance purposefully at his desk, which is littered with a week's worth of fast-food wrappers and coffee cups. The yoga mat is as out of place as a nun at Sexpo.

'Simon doesn't understand the toll these hours take on the body,' he moans.

'You could try doing yoga for longer than a minute.' I'm not feeling at all charitable.

'Okay, Rosie, I suppose I deserve that.' He stands, throwing his right arm up in a surrender. 'Please just hear me out.'

'You have one minute.' I'm aware of my insolence. Cedric is my boss, but I can't help feeling like he's my friend first and foremost. Besides, he approached me for this gig.

He launches straight in, not the self-assured Cedric from two hours ago, but talking a mile a minute. 'Firstly, you are amazing, Rosie. I know that you think I'm blowing smoke when I say that, but it's the truth. What you do on air can't be learnt. You have the za-za-zing. That X factor that can't be taught or trained.'

'Okay . . .' I say hesitantly.

'It really is a case of having the full demographics covered. It's my first time producing, and I don't want this to be a great show – I want it to be the best. Cedric Cool only knows perfection. I had the Markus idea planned for a while, but I didn't say anything because I wanted it to be a surprise. I thought you'd jump at the chance to work with such a hunk of spunk. But then you ran into him, and it didn't go so well . . . so, I panicked. I didn't know how to tell you. Please say you don't hate me.'

I watch as a bead of sweat rolls down his face. It's definitely not from his performative yoga, so he's clearly distressed. There's no question – Cedric Cool's heart had unequivocally been in the right place, which is where it is the majority of the time. It's that same heart of gold that brought him back to Mudgee five years ago – once he was already a household name in radio. He could have taken a job anywhere, but he chose to go back to the town he grew up in. That meant something.

I should put him out of his misery.

'You're a turkey.'

'A forgivable turkey?' He takes a step towards me.

'Yes, Cedric. A loveable, forgivable turkey.'

He breathes deeply. 'So, you're not going to quit the show?'

'No. Not today.' I couldn't possibly do that when he'd taken such a risk on me. Cedric propels forward and pulls me into a hug, squeezing tightly. The same you're-cracking-a-rib-embrace he gave me after my first show.

'Praise the Lord! I couldn't bear the thought of losing you. A few polishes here and there and you're going to be radio's brightest star.' He's still gripping me and rocking from side to side.

'Don't get carried away,' I say, laughing. 'Let's wait and see how much two-dimensional TV vet I can possibly stand first. Where is he, by the way?'

'He had a few things to do at the practice before tonight. I said we could reconvene then.'

'Tonight?'

Cedric is quiet for a second before murmuring something almost inaudible. 'Umm, I didn't mention that the station is throwing a belated show-launch-welcome-Markus party at Lesters?'

I swallow and mentally cycle through all the things I love about him before responding calmly.

'No, Cedric. You definitely failed to mention that.'

Chapter Eight

'So, Rosie, how did you get into radio?' Markus asks.

I'm in Jack's cab headed to Lesters. Cedric has struck once again and kindly arranged a complimentary ride to the event – I only accepted the offer because I've forced myself into yet another pair of heels and don't fancy navigating the block and a half from my apartment looking like a wobbly baby deer. And once I found out that Jack would be the one collecting me, I'd been excited about doing a quick post-mortem of our earlier on-air chat. I already had some ideas about turning his guest appearance into a regular weekly segment – I even had a working title: 'Jack of All Yarns'.

But instead of brainstorming with Jack, I am in the backseat, making small talk with a tuxedo-wearing Markus. We're two minutes into our journey. Luckily there's only one minute to go.

'Fate, I guess,' I say, purposely cagey.

'In what way?'

Dammit. Why the sudden interest in something other than my looks? I'm trying my best to tolerate him for Cedric's sake, but I'm not interested in being friends. I hate that we're in a confined space and there's no quick escape. My hand is already on the door.

'I studied media but ended up in marketing. I met Cedric earlier this year and he offered me this job. The timing was right, so I thought, why the hell not?'

'That was my thinking too! Why the hell not? A job where I can actually help folk out – while using my brain,' Markus responds enthusiastically.

Is that not what you've done for five seasons of Markus & Pup *on a national television network?*

'Unfortunately, *Markus & Pup* is a lot of hot air and not a whole lot of action,' he continues, as if reading my mind. Sounds like his dream scenario. If hot air was a business, surely Dr Markus Abrahams would be a mogul.

'What do you mean?' I ask coldly. If there was ever permission to be a bitch, it's now. His big creep energy has lost him the right to any niceties – except when in the company of Cedric.

'I don't exactly get to be very hands-on. It's all scripted.'

I thought he'd love that. Someone else doing the actual work so that he can lap up the limelight?

'And that's different from radio, how?' I keep tight-lipped about Cedric's reluctance to let me plan much of anything.

'I guess it seems more authentic. I'll have to do more thinking on my feet with the live calls – which is scary, but I'm excited to make a difference.'

Sure, I'm super convinced that this gig at a country radio station in Mudgee is going to challenge a national TV star. There's got to be something more to this 'career' move. I'm just not sure what.

'We're here, kids,' Jack announces, rescuing me from a snarky response that I may regret.

I go to open the door, but Markus reaches over and wraps his large hand around my wrist. 'Do you mind waiting a sec, Rosie?'

My face warms at his touch and for a fleeting moment I wonder if I'd be attracted to him if he wasn't such an arsehole. He may be good-looking but . . . yuck. I flick my wrist to free it from his grip.

'Sorry Rosie. I – ah – I need a moment to prepare myself.'

How silly of me . . . we've skipped the mandatory self-loving. I wait for Markus to pull out his phone to perfect his Blue Steel look and start slicking back his hair and re-adjusting his bow tie. Despite the smart suit, he is looking less polished tonight. He's still stupidly handsome, but his top button is undone and there's not the usual truckload of wax in his Lego hair. It's a pity Eryka isn't on hand for last-minute fluffing. I wonder if she's planned a graceful late entry?

But instead of stretching over the front seat to check his reflection in the rear-view mirror, Markus doesn't move. What on earth is he up to? I want to get out of this car.

'It's been a while since I've done an appearance,' he offers with a stiff smile. 'I get last-minute jitters.'

'You were plenty comfortable at the fashion show.' I can't help but shoot back. My patience is already frayed. I don't know how I'm going to tolerate this sham-of-an-act all night.

'Oh yes,' Markus is clearly taken aback that I've called him out on his horse shit. 'I suppose I mean an event without Eryka. We've actually – um – ah . . . We've broken up.'

Wow. That explains why Eryka was behaving so oddly the other night. She was trying to beat him at his own game.

'I'm fine. I just need to brace myself. For any media,' Markus continues.

Of course. It's still all about the photo op. He's probably the one who broke the story for the added attention.

'I'm sure you'll survive,' I say sharply as I force open the door. I'm relieved for Eryka that she dodged that bullet. 'Thanks for the ride, Jack,' I say as I climb out of the car. Markus follows behind me.

Out on the street, people in formal evening wear have spilled off the pavement and are milling around the edge of the road. I've been so focused on Markus that I haven't paid much attention to the way I'm feeling: I'm a ball of nerves. I've spoken at plenty of marketing conferences, but this scale of attention – even regional – is new. Cedric didn't let on that this was such a big deal. Although, he hasn't let on much of anything lately. I fiddle with my clutch, mentally thanking my past self for dressing up. With no access to the Sebastian Worthington, I've opted for the jacquard dress from Dad and Naomi's engagement party.

'Where's Eryka? Is it true?'

A man with a dictaphone pushes past me to get closer to Markus, almost sending me flying.

'Did she leave you? Has she really jetted off to Paris with a millionaire? Any comment, Markus?'

I recognise the man as a local journo from the *Mudgee Gazette*. Since arriving in town, I've combed that newspaper daily for new show material.

Fury begins to burn in my lower abdomen.

I refuse to let Markus's incessant need for attention overshadow the reason we're all here. Tonight is about the radio show. If the press is going to talk about anything, it's that.

'I have a comment,' I say loudly.

The dictaphone is thrust in my direction. Markus spins to face me, his eyes wide with fear.

'Markus and I are here tonight to officially launch our breakfast radio show – not fuel some soap opera,' I announce with a confidence that almost fools me. 'If you want to hear Markus's take on these rumours, you'll have to tune into Gold 86.7 FM from 7 am weekdays.'

I grab hold of Markus's clammy hand and drag him to the entry. I thought he lived for this sort of attention? Granted, it isn't the nicest line of questioning. But isn't any publicity good publicity? Besides, he brought this on himself. Eryka wouldn't have flown the coop if he was a decent human being.

By the time we're inside and at the bar, some colour has returned to Markus's face and he's looking at me with a strange expression.

'Thank you, Rosie,' he says quietly.

'The show needs to be the priority,' I say.

I wasn't rescuing you to spare your feelings, Dr Perfect. I don't give a damn about you. Even in my head the words sound a little harsh. But the truth can be that way.

Glasses of sparkling are lined up on the bar, ready for the taking, and platters of oysters and sashimi have been placed at the high tables around the room. It's all so fancy. It's surreal that we're back at Lesters. Together. I'd hoped to never lay eyes on Markus again after that night. It's funny how the world works. Constantly crossing paths with the wrong people, yet those whose love and attention you seek can be lost to you.

'Shall we get this party started?' a voice calls from below the bar. I recognise the posh accent before spotting the top of a brunette bird's nest, complete with sticky-outy biro. Bee's bronzed face pops up over the teak bar. 'Well, if it isn't the guests of honour!'

Bee would have served her fair share of drinks in Lesters' first few weeks of trading, so I'm delighted that she not only remembers me but knows about the radio show. There are no posters promoting the show in town – Cedric said he hadn't gotten around to printing them yet. I hadn't minded, since I wasn't in it for the small-town fame, but it occurs to me now that he was probably waiting on my photogenic new co-star.

Bee sets some freshly polished glasses down on the bar and stands up. 'Go on. Grab a champs, Rosie.'

'Thanks, Bee.' I make a point of using her name as I select one of the pre-poured glasses.

'Markus, can I get you something special to drink? A martini perhaps?' Her smile tightens. We exchange a look and I resist the urge to roll my eyes. We're both on the clock. Instead, I give a discreet nod and return her knowing smile. Nothing bonds two people like a common enemy.

'No, this is perfect. Thank you so much.' Markus plucks the champagne closest to him and takes a sip. Not the demanding diva move I was expecting. This Eryka break-up must be hitting him hard.

'Sushi?' Bee gestures to the plates laden with a selection of mouth-watering multi-coloured rolls. 'I'm going to sneak one.' She plucks a tuna roll from the platter and submerges it into the dish of wasabi. She wriggles the roll around until it is coated in a layer of thick green paste and then takes a big bite. Her eyes grow wider and brighter, but there are no tears or cries for water. I can't even handle that much Vegemite.

'Do *not* try this at home. I grew up on this stuff so I'm immune to the burnnnnnn.' She pops the last of the roll into her mouth. 'I-s ow-why they-he call meh Bee.' She swallows and grins. 'It's short for Wasabi.'

'Don't encourage her!' A woman I recognise from the paper as Joanna Lester calls from across the bar. Her bright pink floral skirt billows out around her as she swivels and starts heading in our direction. It's hitched up high on her waist and sits right under her breasts. Tucked into her skirt is a sheer mustard polka-dot blouse with puff sleeves. A red headscarf is knotted on top of her head, a short blunt fringe just visible. She's mastered the vintage cool style that's hard to wear well and looks every inch the owner of a hip new bar.

'Welcome. I'm Joanna Lester,' she says as she approaches. 'I own this place with my partner, Cam. He's here some-where, too.' She glances over her shoulder. 'Probably off doing something completely unnecessary, like stripping a wall. We're still finishing off bits and pieces, but I told him that it was tools down tonight!' She's brimming with an energy that's as colourful as her clothing.

'Lovely to meet you, Joanna. I'm Rosie. You might already know Dr Markus Abrahams?' I hate that we have to present as a united front.

'Rosie! Cedric has told me so much about you. And good to see you again, Markus.' Joanna is still smiling warmly. If she feels the same way about Markus as Bee and I do, then she's better at hiding it.

'Well, it's clearly the best bar in town,' Markus responds smoothly. Right, here comes the Markus we know – with compliments thick and fast. But instead of following up with any over-the-top remarks, he drains the rest of his champagne, selects another glass and takes a huge gulp.

Joanna wipes some non-existent crumbs from the counter and restraightens the front row of glasses. I suspected from her perfectly blunt bangs that we were going to get on just fine. 'This looks fab, Bee,' she says. 'Thanks for getting everything sorted.'

'You're most welcome.' Bee dips into a joke curtsey. 'Now, can I get you guys anything else?'

'Actually, have you seen Cedric around?' I ask. 'About yea high,' I say gesturing to my forehead. 'Glasses. Possibly wearing purple and resembling a good-looking eggplant?'

Everyone laughs.

'He must be here somewhere.' Joanna scans the well-dressed room. 'Why don't we go find him and I can give you a quick tour of the bar?'

'Sounds great. Markus?' I assume he'll also want to locate Cedric.

Markus shakes his head. 'Unfortunately I'm not feeling the best. I don't think I can handle the crowd.' He settles onto one of the bar stools and undoes another shirt button. There's a hint of heavily forested chest. I'm surprised. I thought he'd be all about the manscaping.

'I might stick here with Bee,' he adds. His legs are spread wide over the stool. Poor Bee. He's a few centimetres away from a full manspread.

'That's no good, Markus,' Joanna sympathises. 'How about a glass of water? Bee, lovely, can you sort Markus out?'

'One water, coming right up,' Bee responds extra brightly.

She catches my eye as she scoops some ice into a glass and pretends to spit in it. I clamp a hand over my mouth, but a small giggle escapes through my fingers. I glance over at Joanna, but she's busy scraping together another pile of imaginary crumbs. Markus continues to guzzle his champagne. He's about as sick as a kid with Mondayitis; he just wants to stay put to flirt with Bee.

Joanna gives the bar a final wipe then turns to me. 'Right. Let's go eggplant hunting!'

Her impressively white patent-leather brogues lead the way through the space. The crowds of people from the street have made their way inside and are standing in clusters around tables laden with wine and dainty finger food. The men sport a variety of K hub straight-legged jeans and press-stud shirts teamed with boots, while the women are elegant in high-street fashion a few seasons behind what's being worn in the city. As I glance around the room, I can't help but wonder how many of these strangers will eventually become friends.

Joanna points out the gorgeous finishes as we make our way across the room, including many details I failed to notice the other night, like a beautiful timber jukebox that Cam rescued from a deceased estate and carefully restored. It's the sort of fun retro detail I can picture at Dad and Naomi's wedding – if they ever get around to planning the damn thing!

We stop in front of a closed door. 'Still a work zone,' Joanna informs me. Her eyes sparkle as she describes her grand plans to create the mother of all function rooms, a space that's equally suited to first birthday parties, weddings and rowdy bucks' nights. The door swings open and a man I assume is Cam pokes his head around the doorway. He's dressed more conservatively than Joanna in a pair of jeans and plain black T-shirt. White powder has settled on his shoulders and in his dark hair.

'Cam! Get out of there. Everyone is here!' Joanna exclaims.

Cam smiles bashfully and tucks a hammer behind his back. 'Just finishing up some prep for the painting . . .'

'Of course you are.' She tries to sound stern but fails. 'I'd like you to meet Rosie Royce.'

'Hullo, Rosie. Sorry, no rest for the small business owner. I promise I'll be out on the DF with you all soon.'

'All good,' I say with a laugh. 'The party's just getting started.' I imagine the jukebox is full of juicy golden oldies. Dad would have a field day.

'Didn't you hire a guy to finish this all off, Cam?'

As Joanna rouses, Cam's eyes cloud over in a dreamlike haze. He's got it bad. 'Isn't my wife gorgeous?'

Joanna pretends not to hear him. 'I swear Cam would curl up in his ute tray and sleep with his tools if I let him,' she says to me.

'It's true. It's a close call between spooning Jo or my adjustable crescent wrench.' His eyes twinkle.

This is the kind of love that looks easy.

We leave Cam to his handiwork and complete our lap of the room. There's no sign of Cedric. Where is he? There's no way he'd flake on an event he's hosting. Joanna excuses herself and I fire off a text to him as I approach the bar.

I'm not prepared for the scene that greets me. Markus is no longer spread over his stool but is slumped against the bar, his elbows resting on the surface like he's depending on the thick teak to prop him up. His sleeve is in the wasabi dish.

'Cannawe get goin'?' he slurs in my ear. 'I do-nna think-a my med . . . medi . . . medication mix welllll.'

Seriously? We've been gone for twenty minutes tops. And what medication? I look around to see if anyone is watching us, but Joanna is herding people over to where a microphone is set up in the corner of the room. Oh, God.

'You'll need to keep your shit together for a few more minutes, Markus,' I hiss. 'I think we're about to give a speech.'

Joanna addresses the room. 'Lesters is delighted to welcome you all to the official launch of Gold 86.7 FM's new morning radio show with Rosie Royce and Dr Markus Abrahams. I'd now like to invite them up to say a few words.'

There's a round of applause. I check my phone. No text back from Cedric. We're on our own.

'Wha . . . whadda ya doin'?' Markus slurs at me as I hook

an arm into his. It's either this or dragging him by the scruff of his neck. I ignore his confused protests as I walk us over to where Joanna is standing. Ideally, I would have liked time to prepare, but the show must go on . . . I step up to the mic.

'Thanks, Joanna. Hi, everyone,' I start. 'I'm Rosie Royce, city marketing girl turned country radio host. You may have already spotted me wandering around town like a lost Labrador . . .'

I've learnt that when you lead with authenticity the rest follows.

'You might be wondering what brought me to Mudgee. To be honest, my life was at a bit of a standstill, so I decided that it was time for a change.'

It's like riding a bike.

'It was still a big decision to leave my life in Sydney, but it already feels like the right one. Your very own Cedric Cool – who I'm sure will be joining us very shortly – has rolled out the red carpet for me. I've felt so welcomed by everyone I've crossed paths with so far.' My eyes settle on Bee who is wedged between a lady in a shocking pink frock and a man in a tartan vest. She winks.

I can hear Markus breathing heavily beside me – a good indicator that he's at least still upright.

'You've got yourselves an amazing town here and I can't wait to get to know it, and all of you, so much better – both as listeners and guests of the show. And let's not forget our exciting announcement!'

I pause for dramatic effect.

'As you may have heard, from tomorrow Dr Markus Abrahams will be joining me live on air. I can hardly wait!'

I mentally remind myself that my blatant dishonestly is necessary for the sake of the show. I don't move from in front of the mic and thankfully Markus doesn't try to elbow me out of the way. He simply raises a cupped hand and flails it around in the air, acknowledging the crowd like a royal. They clap enthusiastically in response. Thank God he has the sense not to try to speak.

'We want to ensure our voices are in tip-top shape for our first show together, so if you don't mind, we're going to sneak out and leave you to enjoy this fabulous party while we get our beauty sleep. Please, eat, drink, be merry – just not too merry. We're expecting you to tune into Gold 86.7 FM tomorrow at 7 am! Until then!'

Not a mind-blowing TED talk, but hopefully it's done the job and I've managed to keep Markus's professional integrity intact.

I guide Markus towards the door to the soundtrack of applause. He grips my arm to steady himself. I hope Joanna has worked out what's going on and doesn't think I'm rude. We push past a pair of women attempting to take a selfie and eventually step out onto the darkened street.

'I'm calling you a taxi, Markus.'

He hangs his head. 'Imma sor . . . sorry, Rosieee.'

'Let's talk about it tomorrow.'

We wait in silence for Jack to arrive. I kick off my heels and stand barefoot on the asphalt. He was tall before, but Markus now towers over me. His broad shoulders are in line with the top of my head, and his chest is at eye level. He reminds me of a pile of Jenga blocks threatening to topple over at the wrong puff of air.

'Have some water when you get home,' I instruct into his broad chest as Jack's cab finally pulls up. I don't care about Markus's wellbeing, only that he makes it on air. We've promised our listeners Dr Markus bloody Abrahams, so they'll get Dr Markus bloody Abrahams. I always make good on my promises.

'Areya comin, Rosieee?' Markus calls from the open car window once he's clambered in the back seat.

'I think she's happy right where she is, son,' Jack answers for me, and I flash him a grateful smile.

I know that I should get back to the party, but I'm suddenly exhausted. Plus, I need to go home and figure out how I'm going to tackle my first official work day with my newly single, horribly hungover TV vet co-star.

Chapter Nine

I wake to insistent pounding.

It takes me a moment to remember that I ended the night on a peppermint tea and not tequila, and realise it's not my head that's thumping, but someone banging ferociously on the front door.

'Rosie, can you open up?' a male voice booms. There's a brief pause and then more banging. 'Rosie . . . are you home?'

'Yes, coming!' I swing my legs over the bed and stuff my feet into my Uggs.

Good grief. I've heard tales of Cedric's benders. He must have finally got to Lesters and made up for lost time. He and Markus certainly make quite the pair. I wrap a hoodie over my pyjama top and open the door.

'Honestly, Cedric, what are you –' I stop as I see the dishevelled figure in front of me.

Wes Preston is leaning up against the door frame. He's wearing a thick navy coat and has pulled a beanie over his scruffy hair. He looks like a drug dealer – except his beanie has a pompom.

'Wes?' He's the last person I'm expecting to see. I'm glad I had the sense to conceal my floppy bedtime boobs.

'What are you doing here?' I reach a hand up to smooth down my *Something About Mary*–style hair. 'I don't understand . . .' My sleepy haze is making it hard to think straight. Or, perhaps I am still asleep, and my Wes dreams have become a whole lot more vivid.

'Thought I'd drop by to say hi.' He says it like he's just popped around to borrow a cup of sugar.

He definitely looks and sounds real, and I'm not sure my imagination would have bothered with the pompom detail. 'Is now a bad time?' His pitchy tone betrays his confident door stance, like it's only dawning on him now how absurd this scene is.

'Ah, 2 am is not typically the time for house calls.' My loud voice bounces up the hallway. The confusion is gone, and fury has arrived in force. My neighbour coughs pointedly – a reminder of the building's old, paper-thin walls, and that it's the middle of the night.

'You better come in.' I grab Wes's khaki sleeve and yank him through the doorway, shutting the door firmly behind us.

Wes seems surprised by my sudden hospitality.

'We were making a scene.' I don't want him thinking that we're about to curl up on the couch and catch up on old times. 'Let's make this quick. I –'

I stop as he pulls a painted rainbow canvas from behind his back.

'I brought you something,' Wes says quietly.

He steps forward and thrusts the canvas into my hands.

In an instant, I'm transported back to visions of a younger, paint-smeared Wes bent over his easel. I can almost taste the turpentine.

'This is an original. I painted it years ago. Just never got the chance to give it to you.' He shrugs, but I can see his hands shaking.

I know what it is before I even look at it. I always hated flowers, especially sorry flowers. Who wants a ten-dollar bunch of servo lilies dropping pollen and staining the carpet as a permanent reminder their significant other has fucked up? But Wes had found a loophole and introduced the 'peace posie' painting. The painted flowers ranged in size and density, depending on the seriousness of his offence. This artwork has red, purple, pink, green and yellow blooms crammed in so tightly that there's no space for any background colour. It's the lushest design I've seen, although I have nothing to compare it to – the old gallery of posies, which once hung proudly on my bedroom wall, is now in the Vinnies' discount bin.

Wes tugs at his beanie like he's trying to busy his hands and stop them from reaching for me. 'I'm sorry, Rosie . . . I thought you'd like it.'

I place the painting on the floor, leaning it up against the wall and stay staring at the carpet for a moment as I attempt to compose myself. Tears prick my eyes and threaten to spill down my cheeks, but I manage to swallow them away.

'What do you want from me, Wes?' I eventually ask.

'I need you to know that I'm sorry.'

I grit my teeth. He may have fooled the St Bernard's community with the freshly painted common room, but it would take more than an old painting to convince me that he deserves my forgiveness. This is not the story of a man who suffers more than anything because of a mistake he's made, then makes a token gesture to win back the girl. He knows I'm not that kind of girl. Yet here he is, arriving unannounced in the middle of the night, expecting to be absolved for his sins. Did he drive from Sydney expecting a movie moment?

Squash brushes past my ankles and I scoop him up and bury my face in his ginger hair. I don't have the energy for the ghosts of unwanted memories.

'I'm back painting a bit again,' Wes says quietly.

He's looking at me expectantly, like he's waiting for me to pat his head and feed him a treat. I can't deny there's a part of me that's happy to hear that.

I also can't help wondering what Ron – Wes's Dad – thinks. I'll never forget an excited fourteen-year-old Wes giving Ron a Father's Day portrait for his desk at work, and the crushing disappointment when he'd found the painting in the bin the following week. Ron's approval was so important to Wes that he eventually transferred from Fine Arts into a business degree and started interning at Preston Imports – 'Australia's finest wines sent direct to the UK'.

I guess I understood why Wes switched careers. I just didn't expect him to trade in other areas of his life, too. Soon, pencil skirts became his thing, not pencils. His childhood sweetheart girlfriend from home didn't match his shiny new life in the UK. To him, I was a corked chardonnay, musty and damp, like a woollen jumper worn to death each winter yet never washed.

I set Squash back on the floor, alongside the painting. He meows loudly and then darts up the hall.

'I don't know how I fit into any of this, Wes,' I say. 'And why you're here now. At 2 am?'

'I know, I know. It's a lot.' Wes fiddles with his pompom. 'It's just the reunion is the first time in years you'd actually speak to me. I know it wasn't the greatest conversation, but I finally had the tiniest amount of hope that our door was still ajar.'

I've spent years convincing myself that he no longer thinks of me, let alone cares. Especially since he stopped trying to contact me. Yes, I may have blocked him. But if he really wanted to get in touch, he could have.

'By the way, it's not 2 am, Rosie. It's 9 pm.'

'Don't be silly.' I glance fruitlessly at my wrist before remembering that my watch is laying neatly on my bedside table.

'See for yourself.' Wes extends his arm so I can read his old-school Casio.

21:06. An amused smile creeps across his face, his mouth framed by dark facial hair. His beard has grown wilder since the reunion.

I instinctively stick out my tongue. 'Okay, fine. You're right. So, I may be twenty-eight going on eighty-eight.'

'I look forward to the blue rinse and matching twin sets.'

His words remind me that banter was never our problem. In fact, we excelled at it. But it's easy to have fun and laugh with anyone. We were always so much more than that. The strength of our relationship had been more than being each other's favourite; it was knowing that we could count on each other. That's the part he messed with.

Wes runs a hand through his beard. 'I know, I know. Teasing doesn't help my cause.' He grins.

How is it that he still knows what I'm thinking? Is that what close to a decade together gifts you, some serious ESP? We didn't make things boyfriend/girlfriend official until we were thirteen – well after Mum had left. But by that time, it was already hard to distinguish where I ended and Wes began.

I don't want to think about what once was.

'How long have you had that thing?' I point at his beard. The tip of my finger brushes a few of the straggly hairs.

'A few years. It's in need of a tidy up. Didn't really fit in with tonight's crowd – especially that TV vet in his fancy tux.'

I can feel my heartbeat pick up pace.

'You were at the Lesters event?'

'Yeah. Well, kind of.' He pauses to clear his throat. 'I had some – ah – business to sort with Cam and time got away a bit.'

My chest compresses with the weight of a sandbag. He needn't say any more. Some of Preston Imports' bestselling winemakers are from the Mudgee region. I bet he was here doing his sales thing, getting the new Lesters Estate on his books.

I clench my lips and Wes shifts his weight from side to side, like he's preparing for the moment I snap and demand he walk back out through the door. His eyes dart around my sterile-looking living room. At some stage in our conversation Squash has stalked back into the room and is now curled up in a neat ball on the sofa.

'Nice place,' he deflects. 'I could always add a splash of colour in here for you if you like.'

'It's a rental.'

He looks taken aback by my frosty tone. 'Honestly, I didn't realise there was even an event tonight, Rosie, let alone that you were one of the guests of honour! I freaked out when you walked in with that TV guy and made myself scarce.'

'And then you followed me to my apartment?'

'It wasn't like that! I wanted to make sure you got home okay. I saw you walking on your own, and I know how you can be with directions. I went straight back to my motel once I saw that you were home safely. I'd planned on reaching out via text tomorrow, but after a few minutes of sitting in my room alone, I realised that I couldn't lose the opportunity to speak with you. I need you to know how sorry I am, Rosie. Like, *really* know it.'

The words hurry from his mouth in a flurry of emotion and lodge themselves somewhere beneath my breastbone. They don't quite hit the heart, but they've found some sort of in. It's nothing that I'm sure wasn't said in those initial emails, texts and voicemails that went unanswered. The difference is that I suddenly feel more ready to hear them now. Maybe it's the unhinged way he's just shown up on my doorstep with a peace posie, or perhaps it's simply that enough time has passed . . .

We study each other in silence. I'm conscious that his rust eyes are finding new lines and creases that have deepened since he was last this close to me.

Eventually, I speak. 'Well, since you've already dragged me out of bed in what *is* the middle of the night for anyone who works in breakfast radio, I should at least put the kettle on. Tea?'

Wes grins at me. 'That depends.'

Huh? I'm literally extending an olive branch right now.

'On how clean your kettle is,' he continues. 'You don't boil your dirty underwear in it, do you?'

Ohhh, I'm following now. Cute. I had put a blanket ban on using motel kettles after I'd read that it was a travel hack holidaymakers used to wash their undies.

I grin back at him. 'No, Wes. I don't.' I wink, feeling a sudden boost of confidence. 'I only use it for my bras.'

'Ah, that explains it then,' he remarks, sparkly eyes now fixated on my unsupported chest.

My cheeks burn. Damn. I'd forgotten how good he was at this.

Chapter Ten

Wes stopped by for a cuppa last night. Oh, and Dr Markus Abrahams is my new co-host

I fire off the text to Penny as I walk into the radio station.

WHAT THE ACTUAL FUCK ROSIE

She starts calling me over and over.

It was cruel of me to text when I won't have time to respond properly for a few hours, but I had to let her know what was going on.

I'd woken this morning unsure if I had dreamt my encounter with Wes, but then padded out to the living room to see Squash snuggled up beside the peace posie.

Wes had left behind more than the painting – he'd delivered a mix of emotions and plenty of unresolved feelings, too. I'd found myself agreeing to meet him on Saturday. I was tired and he'd caught me off guard. There's always time to change my mind.

But today is the big on-air date with Markus and I need to be on my game, which means no more Wes thoughts. I take a deep breath as I round the corner to my desk, steeling myself for the morning ahead. I'm sure that even a nasty hangover won't stop Markus from copious amounts of big-noting. I just hope that Cedric is on hand to help manage his ego. That's if he bothers showing up.

Cedric breezes in five minutes after I've arrived at the station. He's wearing black, oversized shades like Anna Wintour perusing a high-fashion catwalk.

'You're in deep shit, girlfriend,' I call. I do a quick scan of the room to make sure there's no Markus. 'Are you sure we're friends? Because it really seems like you're actively trying to achieve frenemy status.'

'I'm sorry, Rosie.' His voice is thick and hoarse and he's sniffing like he's trying not to cry, or he's just finished sobbing.

Aside from a brief moment of concern, I'd assumed that Cedric had suffered some type of wardrobe malfunction but had eventually made it to Lesters. It was even possible that he'd be mad at me for leaving the event early – although I'd texted him again to explain the Markus fiasco. It hadn't occurred to me there could be something seriously wrong.

'Ceddie! What's the matter?' I've seen him cry uncontrollably listening to Taylor's rerecorded version of 'Red'. But this emotion is different.

Cedric lifts his sunglasses. His eyes are puffy and bloodshot. I hurry over to him and place a hand on his shoulder. Tears well up in his eyes and start streaming down his face.

'It's Siiiiiiiiiiiiimon. He told me that if I keep putting on weight he doesn't know if he'll find me attractive anymoooooooore.' He's heaving and struggling to breathe.

I find a crumpled tissue in my pocket and hand it to him. I'm aware that Cedric often exaggerates. It's likely that Simon – probably not very tactfully – suggested Ceddie sharpen up for the wedding, and he's twisted Si's words and run screaming for the hills.

'I'm sure Simon didn't mean it. I bet it was one of those "in the heat of the moment" things.' I hate seeing Cedric this upset.

'It waasssn't, he saiid the weddinnng mighhhht be offfff.'

I rub his shoulders in a futile attempt to calm him. His sobs deepen so I pull him close for a hug. Eventually, his breathing returns to a steady peace. When I release him, Markus is standing silently in the corner.

Cedric doesn't notice him. He'd be absolutely mortified knowing that his new celebrity talent has witnessed him in such a state. Markus catches my eye. 'Coffee?' he mouths.

I nod and he tiptoes off towards the kitchen.

'Sorry, Rosie. I promise that as soon as Markus arrives, I'll control the waterworks,' Cedric pledges with another loud sniff.

'Don't be silly. That's what friends are for. And we *are* friends.' Given his current emotional state it's important to emphasise that I'm no longer harbouring any hostility.

'I think you should go home and patch things up with Simon. You're not going to be of any use to us like this.'

'But you need me. It's the first day with Markus and I told you I'd handle it.' Cedric is so sweet in his sincerity. It's one of his many qualities that sparked our instant love affair.

'Handle, schmandle.' I wave his words away. 'How about I just deal. Markus is a seasoned entertainer. I'm sure we'll be fine.' *Entertainer, all right.* I decide not to remind Cedric of Markus's night of excess.

'Espresso? Latte? I've frothed milk just in case.' Markus reappears with a tray of coffees. I'm surprised that he knows his way around a Nespresso machine. He sets down the tray on my desk and selects a cup filled with dark liquid. 'Boy, do I need this . . .' He steals a quick look at me.

Yes, Markus, your secret is safe with me. I only texted Cedric the basics and it seems that, amid his own dramas, it's been forgotten. Despite what Markus may think, I have no intention of discussing last night's shenanigans. My night had taken its own Wes-shaped turn. But I know better than to bring my personal life to my workplace. Markus had better check his Eryka issues at the studio door. I just need him to remain professional and get on with it. Cedric isn't exactly in the right frame of mind to deal with a radio disaster, and I'm still finding my on-air legs.

'What five-star service, Markus!' Cedric says with so much faux cheer I can practically see his back strain as he high-kicks. 'We could get used to this, right, Rosie?'

'Sure,' I say. I turn to Markus. 'I was just saying to Ceddie that he really should go home. He has a dreadful stomach-ache. I think he needs some rest.'

'Yes, sorry, Markus. That's why I didn't make it last night. But I'm fine now.' Cedric takes a long sip of his milky latte to demonstrate his ironclad stomach.

'Really, mate?' Markus jumps in. 'You're not looking the best. I agree with Rosie; go home and let us take it from here.'

So much more perceptive than I would have imagined. I wonder if it has anything to do with his own break-up. When things aren't happy at home, it's much easier to sniff out the relationship woes of others.

It seems Markus's words are all the permission Cedric needs. He bids us farewell and is out the door before I've even taken a sip of coffee.

'Break a leg, guys,' he says and blows me a kiss.

'Ditto, Ceddie,' I whisper as he brushes past.

We do a quick run-through to sort timings, such as where Markus will take the lead and where I'll be driving. I have most of the show covered except our joint introduction – and the animal advice. We hadn't exactly been a *Beethoven* kind of household. Raising me on his own was enough for Dad without having the added responsibility of feeding a labradoodle. Squash is new territory. We've been cohabiting well, but like a new pair of jeans purchased in a hurry at the Boxing Day sales, the jury is still out on the fit.

'Thirty seconds!' Stacey announces.

My stomach churns. I think it's good to get nervous. It helps boost the show's energy.

'Ready, Markus?' I exclaim. My wild swirl of emotions has temporarily numbed my disdain for him.

I glance over at my co-host to see the colour draining from his face. He looks like he's about to hurl. He pulls a bottle from his pocket, unscrews the cap and empties two white pills into his hand. He must be suffering from one of Pen's famed 'false dawn' hangovers – fine one minute and horrid the next. Once Markus has swallowed the tablets, his head drops between his legs and he begins breathing deeply.

'Markussssssssss,' I hiss. Does he realise that it's go time?

The on-air sign starts flashing.

I launch in, not missing a beat. 'Playing the best mix of pop, rock and smooth jazz, you're listening to Breakfast on Gold 86.7 FM with Rosie Royce, and my brand-new co-host, Dr Markus Abrahams. Welcome, Markus!'

I silently will Markus to right himself and lean into the mic. He doesn't look up.

I continue. 'We're all about home-grown content and sharing stories with heart. We want to chat about the issues that matter to you, big and small. Because they matter to us, too.'

Still no movement from Markus's side of the table. I keep my voice steady and focus on maintaining the liveliness. 'From today, we'll be opening up the lines so Markus can answer all of your animal questions. As the star of Channel 19's hit show *Markus & Pup*, Markus is as experienced as they come about all things animals.' My forced fanfare is like nails on a chalkboard. 'He's also recently opened up a vet practice at the beautiful Horizons Mudgee.' *Ugh*. Why am I promo-ing his business while he's comatose in his chair?

'He can help you out with your horses, alpacas, sheep, cows, turkeys, dogs, cats, miniature donkeys and even – ah – sloths . . .' I swing my legs wildly to try to make contact with Markus's shin. I'm clearly struggling.

'Tell us more about what brought you here, Markus. Our listeners have heard all about my tree change . . .' Maybe a direct address will elicit a response.

Silence.

This is more than a bad hangover. This is sabotage.

It's only been a couple of seconds of dead air, but it feels like twenty. Markus still won't look up and even the quietest whisper will be audible to listeners so I can't even hiss again – let alone drop the F-bomb.

I'd do anything to hear that stupid honeyed voice right now.

Markus coughs. 'Well, um . . .' he croaks.

Halle-bloody-lujah! I nod encouragingly.

'Yes . . .?' I continue to prompt.

'Let's see . . . well, ahh, the Mudgee region is spectacular.'

Not brilliant, but spoken words, nonetheless.

I have to nudge Markus a few more times before he begins to loosen up and our chitchat flows okay. Once the calls start, green-faced Markus is all but gone. He's terrible at sticking to the five-minute time limit per caller, but his enthusiasm is obvious. When horse breeder Natalie phones in about her beloved thoroughbred, Fred, not shedding his coat last summer, Markus suggests getting him tested for Cushing's disease. He delivers the prognosis perfectly. Not over-explaining or causing huge alarm, but still giving detail where necessary.

There's the occasional stutter, but the energy is bang-on.

Next, Jack calls in again. I'd waited half an hour after he drove off with Markus slumped in the backseat before sending a thank you text and introducing my 'Jack of All Yarns' segment idea. He replied straightaway with a suggested time slot of 8.30 am Fridays. Today he tells us about some of the area's sacred sites. Markus is curious yet respectful as we discuss the cultural significance of the local gullies, ridges and watering holes that were used for shelter and food. When Jack rings off, not only do I feel like I've learnt a heap, but I'm hopeful we've provided a productive discussion for listeners.

By the time the end-of-show jingle sounds, I'm fairly certain we've managed an entertaining couple of hours. As much as I hate to admit it, I'm impressed with Markus. I've even almost forgotten about our rocky start.

We receive a congratulatory group text from Cedric.

Amazeballs show! You guys killed it. Now go celebrate. Lunch on the station, I insist. Credit card is in top drawer of my desk

My phone beeps again with another message. Just to me this time.

P.S. Simon and I have checked in for a romantic night at Evanslea! Back on track x

I've never understood the 'fight hard, love harder' school of romance, but I'm happy he's feeling better. Although, lunch with Markus? Cedric must be high on frankincense oils from a couple's massage if he thinks that more time with Markus is any sort of reward.

Markus is standing by the studio door tapping quietly away on his phone. I hope he doesn't think we're actually going to lunch. We may have pulled off a decent show, but that doesn't make us bosom buddies.

'Markus?'

His head snaps up. 'Oh, so we *can* talk now. I wasn't sure if we were still on air, and I didn't want to mess up again.'

At least he's acknowledging he screwed up and isn't hiding behind his hangover.

'I was awful. I'm so sorry, Rosie – I choked. I don't know what happened.'

Wow. I wasn't expecting an apology.

'Don't be silly, Markus. It was your first show; you'll get better. You were really firing by the end there.' I can't believe that I'm comforting him. 'It can't be much different from TV, can it?'

'I thought it would be easier. Since I get to hide this mug.' Markus gestures to his perfect face. 'But I was wrong. There are no second takes. You're a star, Rosie. Seriously. The way you can keep everything on track like that, but you're also so entertaining . . .'

I lap up his compliments – I'm only human. I guess I could split nachos with this guy after all.

'Did you see Cedric's offer? Want to grab lunch?' I'm proud of this mature Rosie, even if she's partial to flattery . . . 'Meet over at Lesters in an hour or so?' I should at least have a quick shower and swap my sneakers for some boots.

'I'd love that, I really would. But I have to get back to the practice.'

His response is like a kick in the guts. 'Sure. Another time, then.'

I should feel relieved. I've done the 'right' thing and now I'm free to go home, eat nachos and swipe in peace.

'But I'd like the chance to thank you for being a complete lifesaver last night – and now today,' Markus says. 'Can I interest you in dinner tonight at mine instead? Nothing fancy, just some takeaway or something.'

At Horizons?

'Say 5 pm? For sunset,' he continues.

'Umm . . . sure. Okay.'

Skipping out on the opportunity to visit Horizons Mudgee is not worth Penny's wrath. Plus, I'm intrigued to see inside the famed mansion for myself. I'm sure that I can suffer through one dinner with Markus for a serving of juicy content.

Chapter Eleven

I feel like I've stepped onto the set of *The Bachelor*.

Horizons Mudgee is a grand, sandstone beast of a home perched at the top of a long, cobblestone driveway. Rather than driving right up to the impressive entry, my taxi has dropped me near the front gate so I can admire the home in all its glory. With the sun starting to dip down behind Mount Frome and the home aglow in early evening light, it's easy to see what all the fuss is about.

Penny had taken her role of briefing me for the night very seriously, sending me a YouTube link to the *Grand Designs* episode featuring the property. In the clip, the architect and former owner, Alfred Zurich, describes how he designed the seven-bedroom home to hero the landscape with 360-degree country views up and down the Cudgegong River. I've promised Penny that I'll try to take a selfie on the famed 'grassy balcony', which is said to drop out over the rolling hills, vineyards and river valley.

Lush plants fringe the walkway as I make my way towards

the entry, enveloping me in soothing green. There's no noise from the nearby road, only the soft trickle of running water and the occasional bird squawk. It's the type of setting I'd pictured for my own country home. I'd even take a shoebox out here.

I'm half expecting to see a suited-up Markus standing at the end of the walkway with a long-stemmed rose in hand. But the entry is deserted.

Loud music drifts out from the open louvre windows. I hope Markus has remembered our dinner plans and isn't inside 'getting over' Eryka with a poor, unsuspecting fan.

Before I can press the doorbell, the solid glass door swings open.

'I thought I heard something.' Markus greets me as though he hasn't been eyeballing the security camera. 'Did you enjoy the walk up?'

'I did. Thank you. Your home is amazing,' I can't help gushing. I've arrived empty handed and already feel foolish. At least Markus is casually dressed in a white shirt, navy trousers and his scuffed RM Williams. It didn't seem right to rock up to an almost-castle in my Levi's, so I'm wearing an understated black jersey dress. Teamed with black knee-high boots, Penny deemed my outfit 'passable'. She'd also insisted that I bring a bottle of something, but I'd ignored her.

'Thanks. I do love it here. Come on in.' Markus ushers me inside and shuts the door behind us.

Bleached timber floors run as far as the eye can see. We walk up a long hallway, past the open door of what appears to be a formal dining room and enter the second door on the left. We step into an enormous open-plan living area. There's an ultra-modern stainless-steel kitchen with a marble island and a large stone fireplace. The room is about ten times the size of my apartment. At the far end is a stretch of bi-fold doors, which presumably open out onto the grassy balcony. I resist the urge to reach for my phone and document the lot.

'Can I grab you a drink, Rosie? What would you like?'

'Whatever you're having is fine.' I hope he doesn't offer me wine.

'Sparkling?'

'Perfect.'

'Great, make yourself at home. I'll go grab our drinks and some takeaway menus.'

I plonk down on the oversized sofa, directly in front of the crackling fire. The butter-soft suede practically swallows me whole. The fire gives the room a cosy glow, and with assistance from a stilt walnut floor lamp in the corner, casts a soft light over the living room. The interiors are more breathtaking IRL than on my computer screen. I can't believe that I'm actually here, seated in Dr Markus Abrahams' living room. I hope tonight passes without too much drama – and quickly. I don't want to end up regretting my decision to come.

A few minutes tick by before I notice the walls. Covering the polished concrete are frames of all shapes and sizes. Markus is everywhere. In some photos he's showcasing his bright white smile, in others it's his blue eyes, which are made brighter by the gilded gold frames. His ego truly knows no bounds.

I haul myself up out of the downy couch and stand for a closer look. I can't see any of Eryka. All evidence of the former couple has probably been carefully stashed away at the top of a cupboard, or stowed face-down in drawers somewhere.

The flickering of a tea light candle on the fireplace mantle catches my eye, drawing my attention to a carved wood frame that's different from the rest. In it is a picture of

Markus crouched down next to an elephant that's stretched out on the ground. Markus is in a baseball cap and squinting into the sun. It looks like a regular tourist snap.

The fire burns hot on my legs and I take a step back.

'That's Eddie,' a proud voice says behind me.

I turn to see Markus holding a glass of champagne and a beer. Tucked under his arm are some paper menus.

He hands me the champagne. 'That photo is one of my favourites. From my first visit to Kindred Spirit.'

'Kindred Spirit?'

'It's an elephant conservation centre I help out in India. I'm hoping to film an episode there soon.'

I wasn't aware that between the sausage dogs with bad backs and pugs with bung eyes, *Markus & Pup* covered serious international animal welfare stories. The show seemed firmly rooted in the Australian suburbs. I'd caught an episode a few months back when I was still in Sydney – on one of those rare evenings where I'd made myself switch off my computer early and head home. Channel 19 had been hyping up a story on a masturbating budgie for weeks and in lieu of any decent Tinder chat, I'd succumbed. I'd been slightly amused when Markus had explained in his honeyed-vet voice that Jonathan the budgie was suffering from Randy Budgie Syndrome, a very normal condition, apparently.

'It'll be a completely new angle for the show. But an important one,' Markus continues. 'Unfortunately, Indian elephants are severely endangered, because of poaching. The population has halved in the last fifty years alone.' His voice roughens with emotion. He actually sounds genuine.

'That's awful.'

'It really is. I've been there a few times, but never filmed anything. I can't help but think about the amazing exposure the show could bring. The tourism industry is just as bad.

We saved Eddie from a training camp near Kerala. He was being beaten every day with iron rods, wooden planks and metal spikes. I'll never forget the sight of Eddie in shackles, standing in the burning sun with open wounds.'

He speaks with the same passion from today's show, but with added sadness. We're not on air and there's no cameras or crowds of fans around, so there doesn't seem to be any reason to fake it.

'Sorry, Rosie, I could go on about this for hours. It's something incredibly dear to my heart, but it's not exactly great dinner conversation.'

I disagree. Surprisingly, I haven't had to restrain myself from rolling my eyes even once.

'Speaking of dinner – should we get ourselves sorted?' Markus sets the pile of menus down on the coffee table, slips off his boots and drops down onto the floorboards. He leans over and plucks a cushion from the end of the couch and tucks it underneath him. He's traded his tight pants for a more relaxed fit, so his legs cross easily.

'I could murder a Thai curry. What takes your fancy?' he asks.

I grab my own cushion and settle next to him. I was expecting Markus to try to wine and dine me with his smooth act, à la the Scuttlebutt fashion show, but this is surprisingly casual.

I grab the top menu and scan the list of dishes. 'How about a green curry and maybe a pad Thai?'

'Yum, sounds good – do you mind if we get tofu?'

'You're vegetarian?'

'Pescatarian. I realise it's completely cliché, but I can't bring myself to eat furry animals.'

'Completely understand. Tofu is fine with me.'

'Prawn crackers?'

'Sounds good.'

As Markus phones in our order, I sip my champagne. In front of us, the fire roars and I bask in the heat thrown out by the curling flames. I find myself stretching out my legs and leaning over to unzip my own boots. This evening is shaping up to be better than expected. It's not every day you get to eat your Thai fireside.

Markus's hand covers the end of the phone.

'Fifty minutes. Is that okay?' he asks me.

'Sure.'

He resumes ordering. 'Yup, no problems. And we better add a large steamed rice, too. Thanks mate.'

'Don't forget to use the company card,' I whisper.

This is all so normal. Not at all what I would have expected from Dr Markus Abrahams and his big Horizons house.

Markus hangs up, a triumphant expression strung across his face.

'I got them to throw in the prawn crackers for free. But if the wait is too long, we can try the other Thai joint or order pizza?'

'I'm good to wait.'

'Perfect.' Markus takes a swig of his beer. 'Their curry is sensational.'

'Did you put it on Ceddie's tab?' I ask. I hadn't heard him read out the details on the company card.

'Nah. It's my shout. I'd like to treat you, Rosie.'

Oh. 'I would have ordered the lobster then . . .'

Markus laughs.

'I had you pegged as more of a truffle rather than Thai kind of guy by the way,' I say, to curb the strange, flirtatious energy that zings between us.

'Not a chance. I have pretty simple tastes. In food and in life. As long as I'm fed, watered and have somewhere to lay my head at night, I'm a happy man.'

Simple tastes. It certainly doesn't look that way.

'So, why Horizons then?'

'What?'

'This fancy mansion doesn't exactly lend itself to the simple life.'

I look pointedly at the 98-inch TV above the fireplace mantle. It's basically the size of a football field.

Markus's face flushes, the heat of the fire adding to the rose in his chiselled cheeks.

'True. You got me there. It was definitely a compromise. It's the location that sold me. It's so quiet and still out here.'

If this place is the compromise, then I hope that Eryka has moved on to an even bigger estate.

'Speaking of location, shall we go admire the awesome view, Rosie?'

'Sure.'

We stand and pad out in our socks through the bi-fold doors and onto an expansive deck. Stretches of green reach out to the fairy-floss horizon. The grassy balcony. The day is rapidly darkening against the pink sky. We stand in silence and watch the last sliver of sun dip below the horizon and the surrounding hills melt into a silhouette. Next door, the Lesters Estate is cloaked in complete darkness while the bright lights of Mudgee sparkle in the distance.

'It's beautiful,' I murmur involuntarily.

'Isn't it?' Markus exhales loudly. 'The view gets me every time. It's so calming. The architect was a renowned ladies' man – still is. Apparently, he wanted to create an outlook so mesmerising that any girl who stepped out onto the grassy balcony would be so overcome with its beauty they'd sleep with him immediately.'

I shudder. That little piece of information certainly wasn't on *Grand Designs*. Revealing it to me is like a magician explaining how he just pulled a rabbit out of his hat. I wait for Markus to follow with a 'smooth' line, but thankfully he doesn't.

I've finished my champagne and Markus drains the rest of his beer, then disappears into the kitchen and returns with a bottle of red and two long-stemmed glasses. It's the Lesters Estate shiraz. The same wine he'd tried to 'gift' me the night we'd met.

Markus uncorks the bottle and starts pouring.

'None for me,' I say just before the liquid slips into the second glass.

'Oh, I thought you weren't driving?'

'I'm not, but I'm not the biggest wine fan.' I keep quiet about the fact I've already told him this.

'More champagne then?'

'Lovely. Thanks.'

We take a seat at one end of the ginormous concrete outdoor table. Markus tops up my glass and soon the conversation is flowing as easily as the alcohol. After we've finished discussing Kindred Spirit, my move from Sydney and Cedric's penchant for purple, Markus's tone changes.

'Thanks for coming tonight, Rosie. I wasn't sure you liked me very much.'

I bite my tongue. We still need to work together and so far – shockingly – this has been a suitably pleasant experience.

'I think it's just going to take us some time to get used to one another,' I say.

'I know that I behaved like a right fool the other night. I thought drinking would help calm my nerves, but it back-fired big time.'

'Can happen to the best of us,' I say generously. I can't help but wonder if he's referring to all of his obnoxious behaviour.

'I'm sorry about all of it. It's no excuse, but this is so new to me – being without Eryka, I mean.'

I'm not sure if it's all the champagne, but I'm starting to think that Markus could actually be okay. Our conversation is interrupted by the sharp dinging of an oven timer.

'I popped in some wedges to snack on while we wait,' Markus says. 'I hope you're hungry.'

I'm starving. Hunger pains have been clawing at my stomach since I arrived, deepening with each glass of bubbly.

'Yum.' I manage to swallow the excess excitement.

Markus balances his empty glass atop the balcony railing and turns in the direction of the kitchen.

'How do you feel about some more sparkling? I might duck down to the cellar and grab another bottle of that shiraz,' he asks over his shoulder.

Of course there's a wine cellar here.

'Sure.' There's no harm in one more glass.

'And sour cream or sweet chilli for the wedges?'

'Both?'

'Good choice.' He gives me a thumbs-up and continues back through the bi-fold doors.

I wait until he's disappeared inside before I remove my phone from my purse and pull a quick face for the camera. One for Penny. There's no filter needed. My eyes are alight and the sky behind me is dusted with thousands of tiny stars. You definitely can't see this many in the city.

I've just tucked away my phone when the doorbell chimes.

That was quick. I wonder if we'll still get our free prawn crackers?

I listen for Markus's footsteps, but there's no movement inside.

The door chimes again.

'Markus? I think the food is here?' I call. He must still be in the cellar.

When the bell rings for a third time, I set my glass down and hurry towards the entrance.

'Coming!' I yell.

I swing open the door to see a man in a helmet shouldering an enormous bunch of flowers.

'Rosie Royce?'

'Yes?'

'These are for you.'

The man thrusts the bouquet into my arms, then turns and darts back to his waiting scooter.

'Sorry? What are these for?' I call out after him, but he's already sped off down the driveway.

An angry realisation starts to build as I look down at the pink blooms. How could Wes have possibly thought this was a good idea? Given the circumstances, turning up on my doorstep was only just excusable, but following me here? That was going way too far. I shudder. I'll be cancelling tomorrow's coffee.

I rip off the tiny envelope pinned to the brown wrapping.

This is no way to impress me. He knows how much I hate flowers.

I open the card.

Meet you in the dining room. M x

M? The flowers are from Markus?

I shut the door and edge up the hall, cradling the bouquet. I re-read the card as I walk, looking for clues. The words are written in fancy calligraphy script.

As I enter the dining room, I'm immediately hit with the scent of coconut and vanilla, muddled with eucalyptus and pine. The Top 40 music that had been humming in the background all evening has been replaced with classical music that pipes softly from the speakers overhead. The dining table is carefully arranged with silver cutlery, crystal wine glasses, sparkling crockery and half a dozen ornate silver candelabras ablaze with white tapering candles. In the middle of it all is the pièce de résistance – an oversized platter piled high with freshly shucked oysters.

Shit. Shit. Shit.

There's no doubt about it – this table is set for romance. What is Markus playing at? I thought he was done with these ridiculous grand gestures? Just when we were starting to finally get on . . .

I almost knock over one of the candelabras with my flowers as I take a hesitant seat. I'll stay long enough to eat, then make my apologies and get the hell out of here.

The music reaches a crescendo and is finishing on a beautiful, drawn-out note when Markus enters the room. He has a striped tea towel draped over one shoulder and is carrying an aluminium tray filled with wedges.

'There you are, Rosie! I wondered where you'd gotten to . . .'

He stops as his eyes focus on the table, his eyebrows becoming high and arched as he admires his own handiwork.

'That was Elgar's Salut d'Amour. *Wasn't it gorgeous?'* The radio announcer says in a slow, schmaltzy voice.

'Next up we have Puccini's 'O mio babbino caro', *with a special dedication from Markus. Rosie, this one goes out to you.'*

What the hell? I push back my chair and spring up from the table. 'Do you have a bathroom I can use?'

Markus looks distressed, like he's realised he's gone too far.

'Sure – ah – yes, no worries. Up the stairs, turn left and then fourth door on your right.'

'Thank you.'

I find the bathroom and close the door behind me. I lean against the cold timber, take a deep breath and focus on the giant claw-foot tub in front of me. A love-song dedication? This guy is all over the shop. I need to leave immediately.

I've left my phone downstairs, otherwise I'd call Penny – although she'd probably tell me to get my arse back downstairs and throw myself into Markus's muscly arms. No effing way.

I turn on the basin taps and cup my hands to collect the water. I splash some coldness onto my face and then reach for the hand towel and pat my skin dry, careful not to leave an imprint of my face behind. I'm not successful. Smears of foundation cover the fluffy whiteness in my hands, and when I look into the mirrored cabinet, there's patches of red where my make-up used to be. For once I couldn't care less about ruining starchy whites, but I don't want Markus thinking that he's gotten to me. I open the bathroom cabinet. Surely Eryka has left behind some beauty supplies. A discarded powder brush hiding excess product in its bristles is all I need to tidy myself up so that I can go downstairs, collect my things and leave.

The cabinet shelves hold a wide variety of lotions, hair products, mouthwash – and medications. I instinctively reach for one of the little white pill bottles on the top shelf and read the label. *Markus Abrahams. 10mg. Valium.*

Valium. How has this not occurred to me before now? Along with his hundreds of other flaws, Dr Markus Abrahams is your regular pill-popping celebrity. He's probably high right now. This explains so much. I'm sure if I went digging further, I'd find a nice collection of prescription – and, likely, illegal – drugs that he washes down regularly with an ice-cold martini. I need to fix my face and leave.

Among the bathroom paraphernalia is an impressive assortment of make-up – full MAC foundation bottles, concealer and mascara wands. Strange, considering Eryka no longer lives here.

I apply a quick touch-up, flush the toilet for effect and then step out into the long hallway. Crap. Was it left, or right? Identical white timber doors run up both sides of the hall. They're all firmly shut, except for the very last door on the left. I find myself moving towards it. It's only ajar a centimetre, but there's light pouring through the crack.

I tentatively push it all the way open.

At a first glance it appears to be a standard master bedroom, just with far more grandeur. A pair of chrome lamps sit on marble round tables on either side of a king-sized bed, which has a studded charcoal linen bedhead and striped duvet. An ivory faux fur cushion is propped up against the mountain of crisp white pillows.

On the far-right wall there's more frames like the ones downstairs. But these ones feature Eryka. Markus and Eryka at the beach, walking red carpets and flanked by equally good-looking people. There's his Julia Roberts doppelganger mum, who I've seen in plenty of pap shots, as well as his definitely-not-a-dad-bod dad.

I take a step into the room, careful not to bump any furniture or leave any DNA.

Why would Markus have gone to the trouble of de-glamazoning downstairs when the bedroom is one hundred per cent pure Eryka Polanski concentrate?

'What are you doing in here, beautiful?'

I jump as a honeyed voice sounds behind me. I spin to see Markus standing in the doorway. He's pulled a dark grey cashmere knit over his shirt.

'Sorry, I got lost on the way back from the bathroom.'

I realise that doesn't explain how I've ended up in his bedroom.

Markus runs a hand across his designer stubble.

'Are you up here hiding? Didn't you like my little set-up downstairs? Or my dedication?'

He's acting like we're not standing in the middle of a shrine to his ex-girlfriend. How high is he? I don't want to look too closely at his eyes in case he gets the wrong idea.

'I did, thank you, Markus. But I'm not feeling the best so I might get going.' He's not in his right mind and I still want to keep the peace.

'Can I tempt you with a nightcap? How about a nip of whiskey?'

'Maybe next time.'

We go downstairs and I retrieve my bag and boots while Markus waits for me at the door. The music has been switched off and the dining room is deserted. I leave the flowers on the table.

Markus is still trying to convince me to stay with offers of more champagne and chocolate-dipped strawberries as I step out the door.

'Are you sure, beautiful? We could get all cosy on the couch.'

Ewww. No. Hell would have to freeze over first.

If there's any outdoor lighting Markus doesn't bother to switch it on, so I take the long stretch of driveway slowly, careful not to trip on the uneven stones. Once I reach the road, I pull out my phone and call Jack.

'You're all the way out there?' he asks, after I've given him my pick-up address.

'Yesssss,' I half-wail.

'Not to worry, love. I'm a good thirty minutes away but I'll be there.'

I hug my arms to my chest to keep myself warm and edge closer to the shrubs that frame the driveway. A blustery wind whips at my shins and I press myself further into the bush.

I'm still camouflaged in the shrubs when the Thai delivery guy speeds past.

Chapter Twelve

'I don't want to go, Pen.'

'Cancel then.' Penny huffs on the other end of the phone. She's in the middle of setting up for a new Scuttlebutt event at Luna Park and is always more matter-of-fact when elbow-deep in work.

'I don't think I can. I mean, it's too late. He's probably already there.'

Here I was thinking that I'd agreed to a coffee, but Wes had upped the ante by asking me to meet him at mini golf. I half thought about flat-out refusing but then wondered if an activity-oriented meeting might take some of the pressure off. Provided I wore a bra this time.

But the night at Horizons hasn't helped. Markus has me armed and ready.

'Since when do you care about blowing guys off?'

I hadn't even told her about tonight's date with the Tinder photographer and how I was already thinking that it might be too much what with meeting up with Wes this afternoon and all . . .

'. . . Judy! I told you that we needed twenty bottles of the red. Why can I only count ten?' Penny takes a break from berating me to snap at her assistant. 'One sec, Rosie.' There's a kerfuffle of sound while the phone is set down and then some more muffled yells.

I'm glad she's my friend and not my boss.

The phone rustles again. 'Okay. I'm back.'

'What did you mean by that, Pen?'

'Ah, Judy. So well intentioned, but a complete disaster. I should have fired her years ago – before I got attached.'

'No. About me.'

'Oh, right. You know what I'm talking about, Rosie. Since when do you hand out second chances? You normally don't even give a first one. Your Tinder matches need only send the wrong emoji and they're blacklisted. I'm not saying it's bad. It's just your deal, woman. And I totally respect it. El respeto, darling!'

'Have you been tasting the Scuttlebutt wines again?'

'Ha! I wish. I could use a bottle right now. All I'm saying is that you can be a harsh critic, Rosie.'

'That's so not true. Hello! I went to Horizons last night, didn't I?'

I shudder as I replay the cringe-worthy end in my head. What a complete disaster. Luckily, Jack and his yellow cab had arrived eventually to whisk me home safely.

'Give it time, young pup,' he'd attempted consoling me. *'You'll find your way.'*

He wasn't to know the use of the word 'pup' triggered yet another emotional response in me. My chest had heaved silently in the passenger seat.

'Come off it, babe. You ran out of there so fast. You didn't even stay for dinner!'

I'd called Penny to fill her in on last night's craziness and help settle my nerves before my catch up with Wes. Instead, she's doing an excellent job of working me up.

'I still got you your pic of the grassy balcony, didn't I? And I had no choice. Markus was being – well – horribly Markus, again.'

I shift the phone to my other hand so I can lock my front door. The odd thing was he'd been relatively normal until the flowers turned up.

'You know that Preston isn't my favourite, but Ange thinks he deserves a chance. You never really did hear him out about why he left . . .'

'*Ange* thinks I should give him a chance?'

I can't believe what I'm hearing.

'Sorry. I may have let it slip that he popped by, and you were seeing him again.'

'Mhmmpf,' I grunt. I still can't believe Ange gave out my phone number willy-nilly.

'Wes came to Mudgee to see you. That's some serious *Sleepless in Seattle* shit, Rosie.'

'He came for Preston Imports,' I correct her.

'Judy! No! That's where the centrepieces are going! We've been through this!'

I take my cue to wish Penny good luck for the event and hang up before shit gets really real for Judy.

'You've got this, babe,' are Penny's parting words.

Wes spots me across the car park as soon as I step out of the car and strides towards me. He's a solid figure with broad shoulders that look even broader in the low afternoon light. I'd fear for my life if I ran into him in a dark alley, he's that kind of built. Although his neon orange checked shirt, the same shade as a hi-vis safety vest, makes him seem less menacing.

'You look nice,' he greets me.

'I'm wearing Converse.' We were always well-matched when it came to our fashion sense. Or – as according to Penny – lack thereof.

'Well, they're looking spotlessly clean. Are you polishing once or twice per week these days?' His nostrils flare. And he's apparently amusing himself these days.

'Just the once.' I swallow a laugh. *Dammit.* 'On Sundays.'

We head over to the entrance to Putt Putt Planet. Wes is walking dangerously close to me. I hang back a little.

'You know, I'm lucky I found this place. Your directions were terrible. Ten minutes out of town? More like half an hour.'

I'd tallied ten vineyards and about the same number of roadkill on the way – though at least it was in the opposite direction of Horizons.

We reach the counter and Wes pulls out his wallet to pay.

'Uh-uh no you don't. I'm happy to split it.' I plunge my hand into my bag.

'Let me shout.' He hands a fifty-dollar note to the moody teenager behind the counter.

'I don't want to feel like there's some sort of expectation now . . . like we're suddenly friends or something.'

'Of course not.' A bemused smile spreads across his face. The same smile he used to give me on an hourly basis. The only difference is that his dimples are now covered in stubble.

The teenager hands over our putters and scorecards, then we dip our hands into a bucket of colourful golf balls. Wes chooses a white ball and I select a bright orange one to match his checks.

We follow the curve of the path until it spits us out at a bright red lobster, which sits alongside a timber '*Catch of the day*' sign with its mouth wide open, ready to feast on a buffet of golf balls. Its black beady eyes, the size of bowling balls, appear to follow me. Hold on. It might even be a prawn . . . I see a sign that this is the sixteenth hole.

'How did we miss the first hole?' I ask.

Wes grins. 'We could just start here and go against the crowd?'

'We can't do that!' I protest. Too quickly.

A familiar irritating, knowing expression crosses his face. *Oh*. 'You're stress-testing my rule stickling, aren't you?'

'I am.'

'I just threw it all in and moved to the country, remember?'

'Yes. You did do that.' He pauses for a moment. 'Kinda.'

'Kinda?'

'Well, you earned yourself what sounds like a fantastic opportunity, so it wasn't a complete step into the unknown. And at the risk of sounding condescending . . . I'm proud of you, Rosie.' Wes holds my gaze for so long that I feel a heat rise in my cheeks. I avert my eyes to regulate my body temperature.

'Thank you,' I mutter to the patchy ground.

We find ourselves back on the dirt track and head in the direction of the entrance until we eventually turn off onto a narrower path. We walk in single file – Wes trailing behind me – until a minute or so later, when we almost collide with a pair of giant green webbed feet. I look up to see a frog squatting over the seventh hole.

'At least we're making progress.' A grinning Wes sidles up next to me.

'It's like bloody Godzilla out here. Wait, are they warts?' I move closer to inspect one of the lumps on the underside of the frog's darkly mottled belly. I run a hand over the bump – half expecting it to be slimy – but it's the roughened texture of fibreglass.

'Yeah, I think it's a big cane toad.'

I snap around to look at Wes, searching his face for any sign that his flippant-sounding remark is anything but. It's too late. The memory has already taken hold.

I'm in his HiLux, travelling down the Bruce Highway, windows wound all the way down and hair whipping in the breeze. We slow down as we pass through Sarina and follow the belt of green trees until we reach the cane toad in the centre of town – in the centre of the road, to be precise. Smack-bang in the middle of a roundabout. It's drizzling and we watch tourists struggle with their umbrellas. Wes dubs our ready-made entertainment 'umbrella politics'. Who is the 'chosen one' from each group, the one worthy enough to hold the group umbrella? In a nuclear family of four, it's the husband who leans awkwardly like a freshly lopped tree shielding nothing but his own elbow. At a deafening crack of thunder, the heavens open properly, and the families and couples scamper underneath the awnings of the adjacent muffler shop and real-estate agency.

Wes turns to me, a twinkle in his eye and his mop of dark hair already slick against his skull, then scampers underneath the toad. I follow him, begrudgingly at first, like I am a cadet involuntarily consigned to the military, then less so as the hilarity of the situation gradually takes hold. We huddle under the cane toad equal parts delighted and horrified at its existence, relieved we aren't cowering with the families outside the muffler shop.

'What a pest. Remind me again why we're celebrating cane toads?' I say.

'I couldn't tell you,' Wes responds, swiping a droplet of water from my chin. 'It is very close quarters under here.'

'Not that close,' I shoot back, eyeing the bulge in his pants. 'There are families over there.'

'Oh pffttt. They're busy shopping for mufflers.'

I allow him to muffle my laughs with a sloppy rain kiss. I taste salt and metal.

'Why couldn't they have done a nice shoot of sugar cane,' I say when I eventually pull away, head dizzy.

'Not much shelter offered from a shoot.'

'You're right. My soaked Converse appreciate the toad's girth. Now, there's a sentence I didn't think I'd ever say!'

We cling to each other as we shake with laughter. We stay crouched in this position for at least half an hour, until the rain finally clears and we crawl out from underneath the toad.

I swing around to face Wes. 'Hey, remember when –'

But he's already up ahead at the next hole. Luckily. The nostalgia nearly had me.

I pick up my pace and duck and weave across the course, sidestepping the myriad obstacles, including a smattering of abandoned balls and putters, to catch up with him as he's hurrying towards a large pineapple.

A pack of yahoo-ing, sticky-faced boys come charging around the side of the jumbo fruit at full speed. I instinctively lift my putter to shield my face.

'Woah! Watch out, rug rats,' Wes says, laughing and grabbing the putter off me.

'I'm the one who should watch out. They've got protective headwear!' I exclaim, motioning to their colourful party hats.

Wes grins and hands me back my putter. 'Now remember, they're children. Not motel bed bugs,' he cautions.

Before I let his casual reference to our BIG Adventure faze me, I change the subject.

'Where is the bloody start?' I feel like we've been traipsing around this course for the better part of an hour. I'm almost tempted just to get started at the next hole.

'I can see it. Just up ahead.'

I look in the distance to where Wes is pointing and see a large, yellow object sitting on the green.

First there was a big prawn, next a big cane toad, then a big pineapple – and now a Big Banana.

He's studying my face as it finally dawns on me. My throat aches and my eyes start to sting. I'd forgotten this feeling. A feeling so intensely visceral that it has a temperature. Everything is suddenly fever-hot – my head, my putting arm; my heart.

'It's why I wanted to bring you here, Rosie,' Wes murmurs, voice thick with emotion.

Wes takes his coffee the same way he used to: as hot chocolate. We're sitting at the Putt Putt Planet cafe, located in the clouds above the Big Things course. Well, maybe not in the clouds, but a level up from the green. I'm still recovering from the shock that he invited me *here*.

Once my body temperature returned to what felt like a normal range and we finally teed off, Wes made a healthy scorecard of holes-in-ones as I racked up countless numbers of failed swings, all while trying to ignore the jibes of the infant peanut gallery. At the final Big Prawn hole, I'd tried a different approach to settle my nerves – eyes wide shut. I'd swung, then moments later heard Wes's cheers and slowly peeled my eyes open to find my ball nestled comfortably in its hole.

Now, the excitement of my mini golf success has dulled, and silence has settled between us as we drink our post–putt-putt 'coffees'.

There already doesn't seem to be as much pain here as there was the other night. With him turning up unannounced with the posie-painting, and now with the 'Big Things' surprise, it's obvious that he does care. But I know I won't be able to even think about forgiving him until I understand *why*. I need answers.

The day he called me and told me he wasn't coming home from London was something beyond my wildest nightmares. In those first few days, I'd jolt myself awake screaming his name and then reach for him, only to find a cold, lumpy pillow. In the weeks that followed, I'd peel open my eyes tentatively, scared of the emotions waiting to greet me. If I found an ethereal emptiness – as I so frequently did – I knew I'd be crying all day. It was like *50 First Dates* – sans sunshine and pineapples. No more Big Pineapple. I'd make so much progress during the day, but it would all get erased once I went to sleep. I'd wake up and have to re-remember everything.

If he'd given me a heads up before he left, there still wouldn't have been a miraculous fast-forward through the heartbreak, but I could have escaped some of the sting of a blindside. If I'd had even the smallest of inklings, I could have used the time to mentally prep myself – to adjust to the idea of us not being together. It would have been hard, but at least I could have started to imagine a future without Wes. As it so happens, I woke up that morning completely oblivious to the fact that the course of my life was about to be drastically altered.

'How did you know this was even here?' I ask eventually, once I've used my teaspoon to skim all the foam off the top of my cappuccino.

'Google told me.'

Some of the double-whipped cream from his hot chocolate catches in the thick hair on his upper lip. Young Rosie, of Rosie and Wes vintage, would have leant in and kissed off the sweetness, groaning loudly at his grubby ways while secretly loving every second of it.

'What did you even google?' He has me curious now.

'I was searching for the closest big thing to here. It's the Big Merino in Goulburn, by the way. I just didn't think there was any chance I could get you all the way there, when I could barely get you to open your door the other night.'

I take another sip of coffee, processing what he's just said. I offered him tea!

'Which is very fair,' he adds quickly. 'I was just happy that you agreed to meet me at all.'

Sometimes I wish that I'd had a proper relationship since Wes, so that I knew what a 'normal' connection was and that even after all this time it didn't feel like there was this invisible string still attaching us. There had been other guys. Countless failed Tinder dates and some 'situationships' spanning three or four months at a time. But none had stuck. I don't doubt that what Wes and I had was special, but that doesn't automatically mean that we belong back in each other's lives now.

'I just don't understand, Wes,' I say eventually.

His face crumples. 'What? Was this the wrong thing to do?' His fingers play nervously with his beard, wiping away the last of the cream. 'I was worried it might be too much. I had this whole thing planned with the table, too. I was going to bring my hygiene kit and wipe it down with Glen 20, the way I used to, but I –'

'Not about this,' I interrupt, gesturing out the window to where Big Prawn's stringy antennae and beady eyes are watching over us. 'About *this*.'

My hands flip back and forth in the space between us. In addition to our coffee cups, there's a pair of salt and pepper shakers, a bowl of sugar and eons upon eons of loaded history and unanswered questions.

'Did you think we'd play a round of putt-putt and things would magically be fine?'

'No, no. Not at all.' Wes hangs his head. 'I suppose I thought we made some progress the other night. And I'm now realising that we maybe didn't.'

'I'm here now, aren't I?' I exclaim. 'No more big gestures, Wes. Literally or otherwise. Just give it to me straight. I need you to explain it to me.'

He exhales loudly. 'Okay, so here goes. But first – and please don't take this the wrong way, Rosie – I want to acknowledge that this is the first time you've ever let me try to explain what happened.'

'Well, I –' I start to protest but Wes reaches across the table, nudging the salt and pepper shakers out of the way and placing a hand on top of mine.

'It's okay, Rosie. I understand. To be honest, I'm not sure that I could have explained it at the time anyway – I didn't even understand it myself.'

'Okay . . .' I say shakily, drawing my hand back to my lap. I know there's some truth in what he's saying. After that phone call came, I shut down completely. I never wanted to hear another thing from him.

I look at him expectantly and he takes a steadying breath.

'As I'm sure you remember, I went to London with Dad to check out operations there. The whole thing was a set-up – I just didn't realise it at the time. I should have twigged when Dad insisted that I apply for a working visa in case I liked the place – so it was easy to return. London was a place that never went dark. I could literally feel the electricity buzzing off the buildings, the people, the parks. I felt alive there in a way I hadn't for a while,' he pauses, his eyes searching my face – perhaps for a sign that his words aren't hurting me.

I can't give him one. His actions broke me, but it almost pains me more to hear him say that a city excited him more than I did.

'I know now that it was mostly the prospect of getting as far away from Dad as possible that excited me. I realise that sounds ironic when I was effectively still working for him, but being on the other side of the world meant that I could keep him at arm's length.'

We'd both had toxic parents. However, while Wes's mum had watched on idly from his father's side, my dad had done his darnedest to remind me of my worth. It was better once Mum was out of the picture – almost a relief not to have the constant no-shows and disappointments. But unfortunately, Wes had continued to suffer, and the casualty had been my heart.

'I thought I could convince you to come with me. Or that we could try long distance.'

'You knew exactly how I felt about going overseas!' I exclaim.

He knew it. Out of everyone in my life, he knew it all. How I was terrified of leaving the safety net I'd created with Dad.

I shudder as my mind returns to that night before Mum's Japan trip. The evening had been like any other. She'd worked in the study while Dad was on the bolognaise. Instead of sorting through Mum's latest second-hand car finds like she'd asked me to, and cataloguing them ready for sale on eBay, I'd locked myself in my bedroom to practise tricks from the Super Magic showbag I'd 'frivolously' (Mum's assessment) purchased from the Easter Show. I distinctly recall practising the vanishing coin trick over and over, and just as I'd mastered it, Dad had asked if I wanted parmesan and I'd dropped the twenty-cent piece down into my spaghetti sauce.

You'd think that if she was planning on leaving for good the next day, Mum would have at least sat at the table to eat. But Dad had served her in the study and the whoopie cushion I'd placed on her dining chair had remained inflated.

Wes turns to stare out the window. 'You know, the thing about family is that I don't think you ever stop seeking their approval,' he says in the direction of the Big Prawn. 'I somehow convinced myself that I was doing it for us. Instead of dealing with winemakers, I was selling to some big UK supermarket chains. That meant big commissions. I thought if I put in a year or two there, Dad would stop hounding me about "contributing to the family business", and then I could get us set up properly, then get back to painting and, well, you would be free to do whatever it was that made you happy.'

'I never asked you to do that,' I say quietly.

'I know that.'

'And you never came back.'

'No.' His voice cracks. 'When you refused to respond to any of my messages, I threw myself into my work. I started setting up a life there. I had a nice apartment, nice friends, a nice dog . . . I thought it's what I wanted. Dad ended up hiring Trent, too, and a year or so in, I managed to convince him to let us open a boutique bottle shop in Islington stocking Australian wine – The Drunken Duck.'

'And how did that go?' I can't help but snark. Going into business with Trent Dell tops the list of toxic to-dos.

Wes shrugs, sheepish. 'Look, it went well at first. I had lots of fun painting the place. On each of the walls I painted a tiny duck floating on a sea of red wine – shades of burgundy, mauve and ruby. But once I was done, the shelves stocked, and the doors opened, I was left with that same emptyish feeling I'd basically had since I'd made the decision to stay. Heavens knows why I stuck around for five years after that. Maybe because I assumed you would have moved on. My dad should have handed the Drunken Duck to Trent long before he did.' Wes is muttering more to himself now.

Gosh, no wonder Wes is no longer a member of the Trent Dell fan club. It almost sounds as though *he* has assumed the role of 'golden son'.

But before I can say anything about what shitheads both Trent and Ron are, Wes swings back to face me, gaze burning intensely. 'You see. I didn't just lose you Rosie. I lost myself.'

His emotional outburst takes me by surprise and tears spring to my eyes. I bite down on my lip and focus on stopping them from spilling down my cheeks. I'm not sure if the tears are for him, or for myself. If Wes notices, he does a good job of pretending not to.

'I was a damn fool. I went ahead and did the very thing to you that you feared the most. Now I hope to have a chance to be there for you again – if you'll let me.'

It's my turn to focus on the prawn's beady bowling ball eyes. Do prawns cry, I wonder? 'I'm just not sure that I can see the person you want me to, Wes. I still see the person who hurt me. I don't know if that can ever be fixed.' My voice quivers.

'I understand. I do. I'm not asking for you to indulge the idea of you and me again. Just for us to be friends.'

'But why?' I turn back to face him.

'That's easy.'

'Because I'm not sure that nostalgia is enough,' I continue.

'Rosie. Please give me the chance to answer your question.'

'Well, I don't know that "because we had fun on that road trip that one time" is a good enough reason.'

'I keep breakfast cereals for nostalgic purposes, Rosie. Not people.'

I simultaneously love and hate that I'm ninety-nine per cent sure he's referring to his beloved Coco Pops.

'But why now, Wes? After all of this time?'

'Some things have –' He clears his throat. 'They've – ah – recently changed for me. Made me stop and really take stock of what's important. I didn't want to steamroll back into your life and interfere with whatever you had going on. My plan was to see how things went at the reunion first . . .'

'And you thought the reunion went well?' I ask more sharply than I intend.

Short of pouring my drink all over him, I thought I'd made it abundantly clear that I wasn't interested in anything he had to say. Even though I evidently was.

'Well, no. But I decided that I didn't care – I want to be back in your life, Rosie. It's easy to pretend that we were nothing when we're not together. It's impossible when you're in the same room as me. And it's absolute torture when we're centimetres apart.'

My stomach flip-flops, not just at his words, but the hungry expression in his eyes. His assertiveness is worlds apart from the complacent Wes who just up and left. I thought he hadn't cared enough to fight for our relationship, but it turned out he was fighting a different kind of battle – one with himself.

'So, what do you say, Rosie? Can we finally be friends?'

I bristle at his tone. It's all well and good to now understand that I was a casualty of something bigger than the both of us, but it's also presumptuous of Wes to think that automatically changes things between us.

'I–I–I have a boyfriend!' I blurt. I regret the lie the moment it slips from my mouth. It's not like me at all, especially when

Wes is being so unguarded. But I'm here now . . . 'I'd just need to clear any sort of friendship . . . given our history and all. You understand?'

Wes's shoulders visibly slump. 'Of course,' he says hurriedly.

'With Hans,' I elaborate.

Fuck. Why didn't I choose a name that sounds less like my made-up boyfriend has stepped straight out of the pages of a Mills & Boon?

'Hans, hey?' There's a glint in his eye. *Dammit, he knows.*

'What I mean to say, Wes, is that it's not that simple. We can't just pick up where we left off.'

There's no point continuing with my lie when – annoyingly – he can see straight through it.

'So, once you've cleared it with Hans what do you say to a trial friendship?' he asks, voice full of hope.

'I say maybe.'

That's all I'm prepared to offer right now – a lot of maybes, I-thinks and I'm-not-sures. At least there's some safety in knowing that Wes is only going to be in town temporarily. No time to creep up close and cross that platonic line.

Our table vibrates and Wes glances at his phone. I look at my watch. It's almost 5 pm. Where did the time go? I'm meeting the photographer in an hour.

'I might have to run,' Wes says. 'I told Cam and Jo that I'd be finished in a few days and I'm way behind schedule already.'

'Behind schedule?' I ask.

His lip curves into a shy smile. 'I'm doing some painting work for them.'

Oh. A very light, fizzing sensation bubbles in my stomach. I'd assumed he was in town with Preston Imports and chatting to the Lesters about the Lesters Estate.

'Nice. What kind of work?'

He clears his throat a little. 'Just some bits and bobs.'

My fizzy tummy erupts into flutters at his sheepish tone. Even if it is windows and doors, at least there's a paintbrush back in his hands where it belongs.

'Well, for what it's worth. I'm glad you're painting again,' I say.

His eyes flash. 'Thanks, Rosie. I'm actually working on some pieces for an art show next month too.'

My heart blooms. 'That's fantastic.' I pause. 'So did your dad gave you some time off or . . .?'

Wes swallows. 'I don't work for him anymore.'

My chest pinches and I will myself not to flood him with a barrage of questions. Does that mean no more Preston Imports? No more selling his soul?

But I remain quiet as we push back our chairs and stand up. We pay for our drinks and walk down the stairs, detouring via all of the big little things that loom as large as our past.

'You know I had a bonfire with all of my suits,' Wes says as we reach the car park. 'The cheap polyester lit up like New Year's Eve fireworks.'

I grin. 'I bet your dad loved that. I hated that he could never see how talented you were. I hope that's changed.'

Wes drops his gaze like he's embarrassed. After a beat of awkward silence he says, 'I was going to ask if you wanted to come to a Paint & Pinot event I'm hosting at Lesters tonight?'

'Sorry, I can't.' I shrug. 'I have a date.'

'Ah, that's a shame.'

A warmth unfurls in my chest as I hear the disappointed edge to his voice. But as I open the door to my car Wes doesn't try to hug me or even give me a peck on the cheek. I slide into the driver's seat.

'Oh, and I almost forgot . . .' he says, kneeling down next to the car like he's a footman in *Cinderella*, about to remove one of my Converse and slide a glass slipper onto my foot.

What is he up to?

A small plastic bottle materialises in his hands. 'Sanitiser?' he offers.

I laugh. 'Yes please.'

I stick out one of my palms and he squeezes out a generous dollop of fluoro green gel. I hold my breath waiting for him to make his usual 'posy-sized' comment but he's too busy groaning as he stands.

'The back is definitely not what it used to be,' he moans. 'Unfortunately, I think my toad-crouching days are over.' But he's grinning as he shuts my car door.

I look down at the neat sanitiser-posy nestled in my palm and rub my hands together with vigour. It takes all my willpower not to watch as he hobbles away.

Chapter Thirteen

Pencils have been sharpened, paints and pinots have been poured and aprons have been donned. Alas, the teacher is late. I didn't even wait to hear back from the photographer when I cancelled. I just sent a message letting him know that I was no longer able to meet him. Then I unmatched him. Even without my strong suspicions that he'll be at least a decade older than his pictures, there's no way I can go on a date at Lesters knowing that Wes is hosting an art class in the other room. So here I am instead. At said art class.

Joanna is taking drink orders and filling bowls with peanuts and pretzels. Lesters' first 'Paint & Pinot' night looks destined to be a hit, at least once Wes actually shows up. Locals support local businesses – especially new local businesses. Plus, hopefully I'll make a few new friends. I'm just crossing everything that Markus stays clear of Lesters tonight, however great his thirst for martinis, or more of that shiraz. I need time to work out how to handle him come

Monday morning. I don't know how much longer I can put up with his BS – even for Ceddie.

There are people dotted all around the room. I spot Bee loading up a table with art supplies. I smile as I approach her.

'Is it okay to sit here?'

Bee pulls out the seat for me. 'Please do. I'm glad you came. I wasn't sure how popular this thing would be. To be honest, I'm a bit miffed Jo didn't ask me to host the class – I consider myself a bit of an amateur artist.'

Unlike the last couple of times I've seen her, Bee's hair is not up, but wild and curly and tumbles just below her shoulders. I run my fingers through my own hair and pull at my bobby pins to loosen a few strands. It was freshly washed and straightened this morning after my night in Markus's hedges, but it feels gross again after our putt-putt session. I didn't want to get changed and give Wes the wrong impression. The fact that I'm even here shows that I am slowly coming around to the idea of a possible friendship. *Possibly* and *slowly*.

'Can I get you anything to drink, Rosie?' Joanna appears beside us with her iPad.

'Hmm, maybe just a lemonade? Thanks Jo.'

'Are you sure I can't fetch you a glass of the Logan Weemala 2021 pinot? It's drinking well right now.'

'I better stick with the soft stuff tonight,' I say. I'm uncertain if it's only wine on offer and I don't want to cause a fuss.

'I'll go grab it for you,' Bee says, before scurrying off.

'Oooh, I won't twist your arm this time,' Jo says. 'But come next year, when our first vintage of pinot is ready, it will be a different story entirely. It's a shame "Paint & Shiraz" doesn't have the same ring to it.'

'So Lesters Estate is coming along?' I ask.

'Now that Cam has his copy of *Beginners Guide to Growing Grapes* we're all a-go!' She laughs. 'No, I'm only joking. Luckily the vineyard was already well-established when we bought it and we've got experts running the entire operation, continuing with the shiraz production and helping us out with some new varieties. Frees us city folk up for fun social events like this.'

'This is a fantastic idea,' I say, gesturing to the full room of thirsty artists.

'You like? I'll try anything to keep those damn pokies at bay. I'm considering changing it up each week. Maybe a board games night, and then knitting, or yoga? I might even ask that talented co-star of yours if he can put on some sort of demonstration. I'm not sure how a petting zoo would go in here, but then I suppose he could draw a crowd with even a poetry reading. Ohhh, maybe a shirtless poetry reading? Shirtless Sonnets & Shiraz, now there's an idea!'

I wince.

Joanna drops into hushed tones. 'By the way, how did things end up after the other night?'

Oh God, don't tell me Markus has been boasting about me going over to Horizons.

'I figured he was a little under the weather when you ducked out early,' Joanna continues.

Relief washes over me. She's talking about the launch event. 'I'm so sorry about that, Jo. Yes, Markus wasn't feeling well. I think he may have even taken a little something . . .' I hope she can read between my not-so-subtle lines.

'Say no more. Don't be silly, hon. You had quite the situation on your hands. Plenty of time to catch up tonight. There's nothing quite like bonding over a little nakey life painting,' she says, laughing.

'It's life painting tonight?' I squeak.

My face burns at the thought of Wes's bare butt. I bet I could still pick it in a line-up. He was always a bit of an exhibitionist. He loved nothing more than prancing around our motel room, completely starkers, curtains not drawn and the car park – with cars and their drivers (aka neighbouring guests) – mere metres away.

'I have no idea.' Joanna laughs again. 'I'm prepared for everything. I even have flour for papier-mâché glue some-where. Wes wasn't exactly clear.'

As if responding to his name, Wes emerges from the back of the bar. He has a sizable black basketball bag slung over one shoulder, a collection of white canvases tucked under his arm, and he's swapped his jeans for his 'lucky' football shorts.

It's a look I've seen a thousand times before, as an eleven-year-old Wes furiously painted artworks to sell at our weekend street stall. We'd set up outside his house on Pittwater Road each Saturday. It had the best vantage point for foot traffic to the beach. He'd colour the local scenery of Freshwater and Manly: the yellowy beaches, frothy waves, sprouting sand dunes and sandstone-block breakwalls. But my favourites were always his paintings of surfers as they spotted, caught and missed their dream waves. He'd capture their expressions perfectly, using his binoculars for more detail and imagining where he had to.

'Sorry I'm late,' he addresses the room. Everyone is staring at his muscular legs – including me. I look down at my hands in case his shorts are about to end up on the floor.

There are some wolf whistles and I hear Joanna groan loudly. 'Clearly all of those paint fumes have gone to your head!'

Curiosity gets the best of me, and I peer up to see Cam standing proudly on the small, raised platform. His hands are on his hips and he's wearing nothing but a pair of budgie smugglers.

The room erupts into laughter.

'Never fear, guys. I would never subject you to that,' Wes reassures the amused room. Cam has already retrieved his jeans and is madly stuffing his legs back into them.

'Now that we've broken the ice, let me show you your real assignment.' Wes unzips his basketball bag and begins assembling a wooden easel. His large hands spin the tiny screws at lightning pace, as though he's set it up many times before. Once everything's in place, he carefully pulls out an A3-sized canvas and sets it down on the easel. The canvas is back-to-front. He turns it around to face us.

It's Wes. Complete with a lazy, lopsided grin.

'If you can't tell already, this is a painting of me. I'm Wes. An artist.' The sentence is a whoosh of words like he's been holding his breath under water and just resurfaced.

'Hi, Wes,' responds a half-dressed Cam, like a diligent member of Art Class Anonymous. I can see how they've become fast friends.

'It feels so weird saying that,' Wes continues. 'Until recently I was still working a sales job, thinking that was it for me. But as I've discovered, it's never too late to chase after what you want.'

His eyes flick over to me and my heart leaps into my throat.

He's talking about his art, Rosie.

'Today we're going to work on self-portraits. By the end of this session, I want you to come away with a painting of you. I have handheld mirrors up here if you need help remembering what you look like. I want this exercise to be about more than the colour of your hair. What do you see? Who do your friends and family see? Who would you like them to see? Who do *you* want to see?'

I don't remember Wes being this existential.

'You can pair up if you need an objective point of view. Use whichever medium you prefer – oils, watercolours, crayons, glitter . . . In true Lesters style, the fabulous Jo has over-catered, so help yourself to whatever materials you like. I'll be walking around and assisting where needed. But please remember, there's no wrong approach.'

Bee arrives back at my table with a highball glass of lemonade in hand. 'Oooh, now who is that gorgeous lad?' she says, turning to the front of the room as she sets the glass down.

'Wes,' I say. 'He's doing some painting here at the moment, I think.'

'That's right. I recognise him now. I just had no idea he had *those* pins on him!'

I laugh nervously. 'I'm a terrible artist,' I say, in an attempt to change the subject. 'So I'm not sure where to start.'

'Bee! Do we have any more ice somewhere?' Jo calls from across the room.

'I say stick figures for the win!' Bee offers enthusiastically, before hurrying off towards the bar.

I turn my attention to my canvas. Once I've sketched a wonky outline of my face, I get to work on my hair. I select a dark brown pencil from the tin in front of me and press down on the canvas. For whatever reason, I decide to draw long, squiggly lines instead of neat, uniform strokes.

I'm deep in concentration when Wes approaches my table, a glass of red wine in hand.

'I thought you had a date,' he says.

'He cancelled,' I lie.

He doesn't seem to react, just studies my drawing. 'Do you ever wear your hair like that anymore?'

'Sometimes.' I shrug. I expect him to respond with how

he prefers my hair *au naturale*, but he doesn't break from teacher mode.

'Well, it's coming along very nicely.'

'Thanks.'

There's no real awkwardness. Our putt-putt 'date' seems to have – unbelievably – catapulted us out of enemy-ex territory.

He takes a sip of his wine.

'No pinot for you?' he asks once he's swallowed.

'I don't drink wine anymore,' I say, reaching for my lemonade.

'Oh, that's a surprise.'

I quirk an eyebrow at him. 'Is it though?'

Wes clears his throat. 'Well, keep up the great work. I look forward to seeing the finished product.'

He's off again, circulating around the class. I finish shading in my face and get to work on my body, paying particular attention to the black and white stripes of my T-shirt.

Occasionally I see Bee out of the corner of my eye, shuffling past with trays of drinks. The last time she passed, her cheeks were swollen, like she'd stuffed an entire sushi roll into her mouth. When she'd doubled back to the bar, I'd watched as she'd munched fiercely before squeezing a dollop of wasabi directly on her tongue like it was a limoncello chaser. I adore how unapologetically herself she seems.

The class is almost over when Wes returns to inspect my work. Considering I don't have an artistic bone in my body, I'm relatively pleased with the face staring back at me. It's a tad misshapen, but I think there's some likeness.

'Not bad,' Wes critiques. 'Except the eyes. They're not quite right.' He leans in to study me closely. His wine breath is warm on my face. 'They haven't changed a bit,' he murmurs. More warmth. I can smell sweetness from his earlier hot chocolate muddled with the fruitiness of the pinot. Notes of spicy black cherries with hints of raspberries. He selects a yellow pencil.

'Oh, I forgot the wee bits.' I laugh.

'I'd call them gorgeous warm autumn flecks.'

He was always the same way about my hair. *Not a frizzy wildebeest, Rosie. Lovely curls.*

Wes bites down on his lip as he concentrates. My insides twist as I watch his steady hand move the pencil in short, sharp strokes, like Penny meticulously drawing on her winged eyeliner.

'There,' he says, setting the pencil back down and stepping back to admire his handiwork. 'Posie's perfect pee eyes.'

Red-hot warmth shoots through my veins. I'm not ready for this.

'Not that name, okay?' I keep my words nice and steady.

'Oh, okay.' Wes's voice is flooded with instant regret. He looks down into his wine and changes the subject. 'You don't drink the stuff because of me.' It's a statement rather than a question.

I answer anyway. 'Correct.'

He groans and I feel my resolve weaken, like superglue on a hot day. 'Oh God. I turned into a bit of a wine wanker, didn't I?'

'Just a bit.'

'I wasn't *that* bad, was I?'

I clear my throat. 'Do you still send wine back without even taking a sip?'

'You can usually tell it's shit by the colour!'

I roll my eyes in response.

'Okay, fair. Point made.' Wes throws his hands up in mock surrender, but doesn't avert his gaze, 'So moving to wine country? Slightly masochistic, no?'

I don't let his intense eye contact unnerve me. 'I like to confront my demons head on,' I say.

'Good on you. So, there may be hope for you and pinot yet?' His rust eyes flare. I can't tell if there's any subtext behind his words.

'Perhaps,' I quip. The vaguer, the better. I've let my guard down enough for tonight.

'Well, let's cheers to that.' He raises his glass and I bring my watery lemonade up to meet him.

Chapter Fourteen

I'm annoyed when I arrive at the station early Monday morning to find Markus already at his desk, and even more annoyed when he greets me normally and tries to hand me Cedric's 'Swiftea' mug.

'Morning, Rosie. Coffee?'

'No, thanks,' I say flatly. 'And that's Cedric's cup.'

I had considered not coming in at all. But not only would my strict work ethic not allow it, I knew I'd have to face Markus eventually anyway. May as well rip that bandaid off.

There is no way he has any genuine interest in me. I can only think that I'm somehow caught up in an elaborate plan to make Eyrka jealous. The charm, free drinks, flowers and over-the-top love song dedication; it was all beyond ridiculous. Things must have already been on the rocks when he approached me that first night at Lesters, and again at the Scuttlebutt event. I just don't think making moves on someone half as hot as your ex-girlfriend is going to help win her back.

Markus is taken aback by my abrupt response. 'How was the rest of your weekend?' he asks before taking a sip of his coffee. I hope he spills it all down his top. He's in a casual blue sweater. Unfortunately, it doesn't look like cashmere. Coffee is impossible to get out of cashmere.

'It was fine.'

It was more than fine actually. I'd enjoyed my putt-putt date with Wes more than I cared to admit to myself, and the art class had been a surprise, welcome continuation of the walk down memory lane.

'Okay, well – ah that's great, Rosie,' Markus stammers after another sip of coffee. 'Look, um, if I made you feel a certain way, like uncomfortable or anything at dinner I–I–I'm really sorry.'

Is he going to address the fact we never even ate dinner? I wonder if he's packed three-day old pad Thai for lunch – he would have had plenty of leftovers after I fled.

'Honestly, Markus. It's fine.'

It's a shame we've had to go back to a stalemate. I thought I'd seen glimpses of someone half-decent, but sadly that hadn't ended up being the case at all.

'Yoo-hoo!'

The smiling face of Kathy from Mudgee Dance Academy peers through the glass office door.

'Come on in, Kathy!' I turn my back on Markus and open the door.

'Hi, Rosie.' Kathy and I have met a couple of times at Lesters. 'Can you introduce me to the doctor?' she whispers straightaway. She smells as though she's bathed in a kiddie pool of Chanel No. 5.

I conceal an eye roll. 'Markus, this is Kathy Jacobs. Former professional ballerina and owner of Mudgee Dance Academy. She's come in to tell us about how it all started.

Kathy, this is my co-host Dr Markus Abrahams. I'm sure you're familiar with his hit show, *Markus & Pup*.'

I hate that I've big-noted him further.

'Pleasure to meet you, Kathy.' Markus moves forward to greet her and she curtseys in response. The breeze from her pleated skirt sends a waft of heavy perfume towards me. I try not to cough.

'I can't believe I'm meeting you,' she gushes.

How is it that, aside from Bee, everyone is so taken with Markus and can't seem to see past his superb bone structure?

I don't want to bear witness to the absurd fanfaring so I look around for something to do. My desk is already pristine (I rehomed the expanding piles of free products into alphabetised containers, and set up a fail-proof system for incoming stock), so I 'busy' myself with restacking the papers, aware that it's already arranged like a flagship Swedish stationery store. My selection of coloured pencils and markers rivals Saturday night's Paint & Pinot selection. Cedric had been so intent on making me feel welcome that he'd let me go crazy with the Officeworks catalogue.

I keep one ear on Markus and Kathy's conversation. It's mostly gushing from Kathy and then a long story about her new chihuahua Noodle's first trip to the dog park. Markus is barely able to get a word in. Eventually, Stacey gives us our five-minute warning. Kathy links her arm in Markus's, and they fall into step towards the studio. Rather, they *glide* towards the studio. The combination of height and their athletic bodies makes it seem like they're about to take the stage for a matinee of *Swan Lake*.

We take a seat on either side of our wide timber desk and Kathy relaxes into the replica Eames chair that's reserved for in-studio guests. Cedric has done his best to create the illusion of designer style on the station's beer budget.

Stacey scurries in and readjusts the mic and hands Kathy a set of headphones. She slides them up over her neat bun and then stretches out her long legs, crossing her dainty ankles.

Markus is staring. I can't tell if he's checking Kathy out or is fixated on the wall behind us. I hope he's not about to do his freak-out routine again. This time I definitely won't be coming to his rescue.

The wave of churning begins in my own stomach. I clear my throat and prepare myself to kick off the show with jovial chatter about the weekend. The art class is perfect fodder. After I'm finished with a thinly veiled promo for Lesters, I turn my attention to Kathy.

Through an upbeat, light-hearted chat, we learn that Kathy is originally from Yass but moved to Melbourne to attend the National Ballet School on a scholarship. While living there she fell in love with, then married, winemaker Greg. Greg eventually decided to swap his Yarra Valley vineyard for one in Mudgee, and Kathy set up Mudgee Dance Academy. Sadly, Kathy and Greg's marriage broke down a few years later, by which time Kathy had already grown fond of the town so stayed put to continue running her dance school. The Academy has now grown to one thousand students and is well known in the surrounding areas for being the best in the biz. When Kathy goes on to offer a free year of tuition live on air, Stacey can barely keep up with the calls.

Markus has resumed his mute mode throughout the segment. When it's finally his turn to take some calls, he starts off with a stutter.

'M–M–Morning everyone. Before we get into some live calls, I wanted to do a quick shout-out to my co-host, Rosie. For being so patient with me while I learn the radio ropes.'

Markus peers over his microphone at me. There must be some sort of optical illusion going on with the reflection of his blue sweater, as his eyes appear sincere.

He's not going to fool me again.

'Surely one on-air dedication is enough for the week, Markus?' I say coolly. 'Now, shall we get on with some calls?'

Cedric barges into the studio shortly after Kathy leaves.

He's in floral activewear and carrying his bright purple yoga mat. If I was at all worried that he wouldn't be a fan of my on-air hostility, I shouldn't have been.

'There's still work to be done, Markus, but you're improving, and, um, hello! I'm love, love, loooving whatever is going on between the two of you. You could cut that sexual tension with a knife!' Cedric exclaims, raising an eyebrow and looking positively delighted with himself. 'Listeners go absolutely gaga over co-host hook-ups.'

Even though I know that's the exact opposite of what's happening here, I still feel heat in my cheeks. I only went to that bloody dinner because he insisted that we celebrate, and look at the mess it's created.

'I'm glad you approve.' I smile thinly.

I'll have a stern word to Cedric later. Although, I'm not sure anything will dampen his fantastic mood. The wedding is back on, he's rested from a glorious weekend away and he's onto a radio ratings bonanza. I know that he's already picturing the new plaque on his desk – *Cedric Cool: Regional Radio King*.

'On that note, we're taking this radio gold on a little excursion tomorrow. Mr Scarecrow has invited us to broadcast live from his farm. I thought that being out in the field doing what you love might help mop up the last of those nerves, Markus.'

'Thanks, Cedric.' Markus smiles widely, clearly enthused by the idea.

'Picture this: Rosie Royce, Mudgee's newest radio sensation, plus a handsome vet and a pen full of piglets!' Cedric claps his hands and lets out a squeal.

Ugh. Even more time with Markus is not what I signed up for.

Chapter Fifteen

The sun still hasn't nudged over the horizon by the time I arrive at Mr Scarecrow's. But the sky is beginning to turn and is streaked in the first greys of dawn. There's just enough light to guide me down the long, red dust driveway. This is a bit more than a city backyard veggie patch. Even from inside my car, I can feel the vastness that surrounds me – acres and acres of farmland. It's a humbling feeling to be reminded that you are but a tiny speck on this planet – and therefore, all of your problems must be the tiniest of specks too. I breathe in deeply as I get out of my car and am hit with the heavy smell of fresh manure. It's so strong and full-bodied that I can taste it. I try not to gag, chasing the wretched flavour with a sip of coffee.

Cedric had issued strict instructions to be at Mr Scarecrow's at 6 am sharp. He mentioned very loudly and repeatedly how much earlier he and Stacey have to be there to set up. *Rosie, it'll be pitch black. But these are the sacrifices I've made and continue to make for brilliant radio.*

There was lots of flailing, dramatic arms to the forehead, so I reminded him that it was all his idea.

The farm is out past Horizons, so I enjoyed the drive, passing vineyard after vineyard and finding quaint roadside stalls selling fresh figs, oranges and honey. I'd stopped at one with a chalkboard out front that read, 'Coffees, breads, pies' and purchased fresh apple pies (they smelt so delicious, I just couldn't resist!) and coffees for everyone – even Markus.

The car's dashboard informs me that it's 8°C outside, and that it's 6.20 am. *Shit!* I pride myself on being punctual, but I got carried away browsing the lovely country fare.

I hurry along the dirt path, trying to make up for lost time, while also trying not to slip on the frost underfoot. It feels closer to 0°C. I shudder to think how icy it will get here next month, once winter arrives.

I hug the coffees to keep warm, a chorus of birds singing sounds overhead – nature's alarm clock. Pity mine sounded an hour ago. The chirping becomes louder and livelier as I get closer to the trees at the edge of the paddock. I stop as I reach a fence. It looks electric. Where to from here? There are no signposts to direct me.

As my eyes adjust to the low light, I spot Markus. He's in gumboots on the other side of the fence, standing ankle deep in mud and bending down over an overturned cow. Even in the half-darkness and clad in a denim shirt, it's impossible not to notice the width of his shoulders. He runs a hand from the cow's head right down along its back, stopping as the animal lets out a deep moo. The movement is not unlike the way I've learnt to elicit a soft, throaty purr from Squash.

I sneeze.

Bloody hay fever.

Markus looks up startled. 'Rosie, hi! I didn't realise you were there!'

He lifts his free hand to greet me. I note that his arm is the size of the cow's hind leg, without the soft skin folds.

'Hey, Markus. Where's Cedric?' I call out.

'Up in the barn, I think,' Markus says.

'Shouldn't you be up there, too?'

'Yup, I was headed there, but poor Braveheart needed a quick hand. Fell victim to some evil cow tipping last night.'

Braveheart doesn't look too fussed. She clamps a tuft of grass between her teeth, tears it from the ground and chews slowly.

'Boozed-up morons,' Markus mutters.

'Is that really a thing though?' I can't stop myself from asking. 'I thought cow tipping was an urban legend, or only happened on, like, *Beavis and Butt-Head*.'

Markus laughs, a real, eye-crinkly laugh. 'Unfortunately, yes. Although, it would have taken the force of three well-built teenagers to topple Braveheart over. Do you want to come say hello?'

Braveheart is eyeballing me like she knows I polished off a medium-rare T-bone last night.

'I'm not really dressed for it . . .' There's no way I'm muddying my Converse.

'Next time then.' Markus smiles and goes back to stroking Braveheart.

I thought he'd try harder to convince me. Where have all of his grand gestures gone? I was half expecting him to pull me into the field and declare that he's named the Milky Way or some constellation after me. Not that there are any stars in sight; daylight has arrived with a vengeance and the early morning sun has cast a golden haze over the paddock.

I guess there's no witnesses here to report back to Eryka and make her jealous. No bar full of people, or thousands (okay, hundreds) of radio listeners . . . just a cow.

'You should wrap it up soon though. Cedric will skin you alive if you're late.'

Braveheart gives a distressed, high-pitched moo.

'Rosie! Slaughterhouse language . . .'

'Whoops. Sorry.'

'All good. We know that I don't always say the right thing . . .'

I assume he's talking about his intermittent on-air awkwardness. 'You are getting better, Markus.'

'You think?' He sounds genuinely happy and not like he's digging around for extra compliments.

'Yup, I do.' I only say it because it's true.

'I wasn't sure that I had it in me. I prefer to be out here.' He closes his eyes and inhales, taking a deep gulp of manure air.

'Well, we won't have a show if we don't get ourselves to that barn quick smart. Cedric will shoo–' I censor myself in the nick of time. Braveheart still lets out a sharp, warning moo.

'You're right. Let's go.'

Markus gives Braveheart a final stroke then squelches towards me, exiting the paddock through the nearby gate and joining me on the other side of the fence.

He glances back at Braveheart. 'Later, girl.'

We start in the direction of the barn.

'Is one of those for me?' Markus asks.

I'd forgotten that I'm holding the carton of coffees.

'Yup,' I say casually, handing him one of the cups.

Maybe it is a sort of peace offering – it's exhausting having to hate him.

The walk is uphill. I match Markus's long strides and I'm out of breath by the time we reach the barn's sliding timber door. He puts an arm to the door and pushes it open in one swift move like it's made of feathers and not solid wood.

Baaaaaa, oinnnnk, hoooonk hoooonk hoooonk.

There's a medley of farmyard noise, followed by the unpleasant odour of what I can only assume is more fresh manure combined with damp feathers and fur. Inside is a brigade of farmyard animals. There's a pen of goats, sheep, a couple of pigs and a gaggle of geese.

Cedric is perched on a haystack in the middle of the chaos. This would be the ideal occasion for activewear, but he's wearing leather pants.

'Welcome to the jungle!' he announces grandly, like he's atop a Mardi Gras float. Perhaps he hasn't noticed that we're late. 'Where the hell have you two been?'

Oops.

I remember the pies and plunge a hand into my pocket to retrieve the paper bag.

'Apple pie?'

Cedric waves it away, motioning to his hips. But of course, the wedding diet.

'My fault, Cedric,' Markus chimes in. 'I needed Rosie's help with something.'

'No, you didn't!' I exclaim.

'Methinks the lady doth protest too much.' Cedric smiles smugly. 'Anyway, enough dilly-dallying, lovebirds, we have a show to do.'

He's having far too much fun with this. I'll have that word with him as soon as we're done recording.

The goats bleat loudly. I haven't been in showbiz long, but I've heard what people say about working with animals (and children): don't!

I follow Cedric over to the plastic trestle table set up in the corner of the barn. A cluster of white plastic chairs and a bunch of tangled cords complete our 'studio' set-up.

'G'day folks.' I hadn't noticed the older man crouching down at the side of the animal pen. He stands and extends a blistered hand. His narrow face is weathered, scored with deep lines that make his face appear full of character, but also older than his sixty or so years. He's tall and thin, and there's tufts of scraggly hair sprouting from underneath his straw hat. In fact, he looks very much like a scarecrow.

'Fred Abbott, howdoyoudo?' His handshake is firm, yet welcoming. 'You can call me Mr Scarecrow, folk usually do.'

'Rosie Royce. Thanks for having us here, Mr Scarecrow.' I try to match the eagerness of his grip. 'I do hope we're not keeping you from the cow milking and all the – ah – tending of things you must need to do.'

I think I hear a snort from Markus on the other side of the barn.

'Not at all, little duck. I'm excited to have you media folk visit. Although Janet here looks like she's not too far off now.' Mr Scarecrow gestures to the sheep at his knees. 'She's showing early signs of labour.'

I look for a bulging belly, but apart from perhaps a thicker than expected fleece, Janet seems like a fairly ordinary sheep.

Markus crosses the barn to us. 'Do you mind if I give her a quick once-over? I'm a vet.'

'Go ahead, boy. Then I'll go get her out of your way. We could be in for a big day – and night.' Mr Scarecrow gives Janet a tender stroke to the head.

Five minutes later and Markus has donned a pair of latex gloves, wrapped a hand around Janet's swollen udder and bent his head under her hind legs. 'Looks like she's been suffering in silence for a while now, Fred. I can already see the amniotic sac.'

I'm watching on, awkwardly shifting my weight from one foot to another, nibbling on a pie.

'We're due on air.' Cedric calls from back atop his bale of hay. 'Like, now!'

I've been so engrossed in the Discovery Channel situation unfolding in front of me that it's completely escaped me why we're in Mr Scarecrow's barn in the first place.

Mr Scarecrow's eyes widen. 'You're not going to leave Janet, are you? I don't think the vet can get up here in time,' he rasps.

Markus's expression tells me the vet *definitely* won't make it here on time.

I swing into action. 'Ceddiiiiie, how far do those cords extend? Stacey, can you bring the mics over here?'

Cedric wanted in the field and he's going to get in the field. He looks confused for a moment, surveys the scene of Markus with his arm up Janet and a worried Mr Scarecrow, and gives me two thumbs-up.

We're on!

My breath catches in my chest as I position myself next to Markus and Janet. Stacey presses a mic into my hand, and I assume we're live on air.

'Ladies and gents, do we have a treat for you this morning! We're down at Mr Scarecrow's farm and our very own Dr Markus Abrahams will be delivering a brand-new lamb live on air. How about that!'

I signal Stacey over.

'Now, I wish you could witness this miracle with us. I'm going to try to talk you all through it every step of the way, but I think that we can do one better . . .'

I pull my phone from my pocket, quickly key in my pin code and hand it to Stacey.

'We'll be broadcasting everything live on Facebook, so head on over to the Gold 86.7 FM page to watch the action live. And give it a like while you're there.'

Stacey is holding the other mic up to Markus's mouth while he hovers over Janet. Markus's arm has now completely disappeared inside the sheep.

He still manages a few words. 'Hello, everyone. If I'm a little quiet, it's because I'm trying to ensure this lamb is birthed safely. It feels like it may be breach, so careful does it.' There's a glistening of sweat on his forehead, but he seems calm and composed. No stuttering in sight.

Ninety minutes later and I've interviewed Mr Scarecrow twice, taken a few calls, and had some piglet cameos. They're no Babe, so they don't offer much in the way of conversation, but we all get a few laughs.

The show is about to wrap up when Janet's bleating becomes deafening. She stretches out her body, then folds back to reveal a muck-covered lamb.

Well, I'll be damned. There's the little guy.

Janet begins licking the stickiness off her baby's head and limbs. Markus's shirt is completely drenched with sweat and slime. He's looking down with besotted eyes at the pair in front of him.

Mr Scarecrow rushes forward to embrace him. 'Thank you, son!'

Markus's all-denim get-up was already a bold look, but his *wet* all-denim look is an even bolder one.

I motion to Stacey to come closer for a better view of the lamb, but just as soon as he assumes the new position Mr Scarecrow whisks it away in a bundle of blankets. My eyes stay on Markus as he unbuttons his shirt. He attacks each button painfully slowly, before finally the shirt is off. He turns it inside out and starts using it to towel down his sticky torso. The magazines might edit out some of his wild chest hair, but they definitely don't photoshop in those abs. He's like a cardboard cut-out.

A loud 'pop' of a cork sounds from somewhere over near the haystack interrupting my ogling. Where did Cedric get champagne from? I glance at the haystack throne, expecting him to summon me over for a glass, but instead he's making frantic motions at me.

Shit. I've been thrown completely off track by the . . . ah . . . excitement and forgotten that we're still live on air.

'Well, wasn't that something!' I eventually manage to say into the mic. 'Now, let's all say a big hello to little Janet Junior.'

A shirtless Markus looks up at me with a grin so wide that it's impossible not to beam back. I try to keep my eyes on his face.

Chapter Sixteen

As I walk in the front door after our eventful morning at Mr Scarecrow's, I see the rainbow puddle first, then I notice the ripped posie painting. I've mopped, dusted and re-plumped the couch cushions at least a dozen times since Wes's visit, yet the painting has remained in the same spot I set it down.

'Squash . . .?'

It's strange he isn't at the door with a greeting meow.

'Squashy . . .?'

I follow the trail of colourful paper shreds. It wraps around the living room doorway and out into the hall.

There's another puddle.

Definitely cat puke.

'Squash!' I'm yelling now.

A faint meow sounds from the bedroom. I race up the hallway and find Squash laying on his belly in the middle of my bed. He lifts his head weakly to look at me, and then drops it straight back down like it's the weight of a bowling ball. I waste no time in scooping him up and bundling him into the car.

'Hold on tight. We'll get you help.' I place a hand on his over-warm body resting on my lap and turn on the ignition.

I make it in record time. There's no stopping at the gate this time; I drive straight up to the front entrance. We're out of the car and I'm pressing the doorbell frantically over and over before I properly register where I am and what's about to happen.

The door of Horizons Mudgee swings open.

'Oh, hi, gorgeous.' Markus has showered off the lamb muck and swapped his denim for chinos and a grey cashmere pullover. 'What a pleasant surprise. And to what do we owe the pleasure?'

'It's Squash,' I manage, throat tight.

The smugness evaporates and his forehead scrunches as he glances down at the listless bundle in my arms.

'Ah, shit,' he exclaims, but instead of sweeping Squash from me and cradling him in his arms, as he'd done with Janet Junior just hours earlier, he rakes a hand through his hair.

'Can you help us, Markus?'

Panicked eyes dart from my face back to Squash, but he doesn't say anything. Why is he acting like we're about to go live on the radio?

Oh God. Maybe this is much worse than I thought.

'He seems to be breathing, but it sounds all horrible and haggard,' I continue urgently. 'What do I do, Markus?'

'Well – ah – Rosie, I, ummm, ah . . .'

I don't have a backup plan. Dr Markus Abrahams is it.

'What do I do, Markus?' I yell. I'm no longer in control.

I'm not sure what I was expecting, but not this. After his quick thinking at Mr Scarecrow's, I guess I assumed he'd instantly know what to do.

'Why don't I meet you down at the practice? Go around the back and follow the path until you come to the fountain, then take a right. I'll join you in a minute.' Markus directs me formally with a stiff smile like a maître d' seating me for a fancy dinner reservation.

At this point, I'm just relieved he's doing something.

'Where exactly do I –'

Markus closes the door in my face.

I stand there momentarily frozen, like I'm back at Mr Scarecrow's and ankle deep in mud. I hug Squash close. His hair smells like my freshly laundered socks. I want nothing more than to feel his hot fishy breath on my face. Right now, I'd trade every pair of starchy white Converse in my closet just to watch the little bugger shit next to his litter box. It's too late to take him somewhere else. I don't even know where that somewhere else would be. I'm going to have to trust that Markus has this handled.

I hurry down the side of the house where he's pointed. Sure enough, there's a fountain bubbling away. It's as grand as the rest of the home – multi-tiered with water streaming from bronze mascarons. The steady splish-splash is a welcome reprieve from the frenzied buzzing in my head. I haven't been this worried since a few years back – before Naomi – when Dad's phone had a dead battery for twenty-four hours straight. I'd ended up having to go around there, only to find him buried in tax returns and none the wiser. He'd been given a stern talking to and an extra phone charger.

Squash still isn't moving. I pull him closer and stride down the path towards a building tucked away at the back of the expansive gardens. It's made of the same sandstone as Horizons, but that's where the similarities end. This structure is single-storey – not three – and is no bigger than our old two-room weatherboard house (which Dad refuses to move from). Instead of a grand entryway, there's a sweet post-box–red door and sash windows trimmed with little painted window boxes holding cascading vines. It looks like one of the cute cottages on the vision board I glued together while trying – albeit unsuccessfully – to convince myself that the law of attraction was a real thing. This quaint building is more like Hansel and Gretel's candy cottage than a veterinary practice.

As I near the front door, Markus appears from around the back of the building. His face is flushed, and his dark hair is tussled like he's just awoken from a deep sleep on the dirt floor of Mr Scarecrow's barn.

'Rosie! Give him here.' He plucks Squash from my arms and nudges the red door open with his hip.

Finally! This is the Markus I need. I'll happily put up with his ego for an eternity of radio shows if it means Squash will be okay.

Markus disappears inside and I follow behind him. Despite the storybook outside, I'm still expecting a linoleum floor, bright UV lights and rows of steel beds. Instead, there's a narrow entry lined with scuffed boots that opens up onto a larger room containing a double bed and a pair of overstuffed couches stacked with cardboard boxes. There are pictures everywhere of a smiling Markus standing alongside elephants.

Markus lays Squash down on the end of the bed and begins examining him, starting at his face and working his way to the tip of his tail.

'He ate a painting. Acrylic, I think. He's already vomited. That's good, right?' I sound like such a lousy, irresponsible, cat mum.

'Anything else I need to know?' Markus doesn't take his eyes off Squash.

'Only that I'm a horrible person.'

'Rosie, no! Accidents happen,' he placates me, but his eyes are still trained on Squash's little furry body.

Please say he'll be okay.

After he's done pushing on Squash's belly, Markus frowns. 'Hmmm, doesn't appear to be any obstruction. I'm going to get some fluids into him.'

He moves quickly to the back of the room, fetches some supplies from a cupboard and then hurries back over to Squash's bedside, laying out a pair of disposable gloves, a bag of IV fluid, a stainless-steel bowl, medical tape, gauze, a bandage, alcohol wipes and a needle alongside him.

My eyes widen.

'Don't worry, Rosie. It's not as scary as it looks. I promise,' Markus reassures me again. He speaks softly to Squash. 'Relax, Squash. You're going to be okay.'

Is that a promise?

Markus works quickly, talking me through each step as he prepares the drip. Once he's done, he fills the stainless-steel bowl with water and submerges the fluid bag. 'I'm warming it up so it's more pleasant for him,' he tells me.

A few minutes of silence pass before Markus rescues the bag from its bath, shakes it free of water and hands it to me.

'I need you to hold this please, Rosie. Make sure that you keep it elevated above Squash's head.'

I nod and stick my arm out straight. I prop my other arm underneath like a support beam to steady the shake.

Markus sits on the edge of the bed and pulls Squash into his lap. 'You might not want to watch this part, Rosie.'

Despite his warning, I don't turn away as Markus grabs the stretch of skin between Squash's shoulder blades and pulls it out to form a tent, then swiftly inserts a needle, parallel to his back.

Squash stirs, his eyes opening into tiny slits.

'Squashy! I'm right here.'

As soon as they've opened, they're closed again. But he's visibly breathing now. With each heave I can feel tension leave my body. For a few minutes – perhaps longer – I'm completely fixated on the rhythmic movement of Squash's tiny form, until Markus speaks and I realise I've been staring directly at his crotch.

'You can relax now, Rosie. He should be fine.'

He pats the spot next to him on the bed. The bed frame squeaks as I lower myself down carefully. I'm still holding the IV fluid, my arm stuck out stiffly like a marching solider. I can't risk messing things up and causing some kind of relapse.

'You don't need to stay that way,' Markus says. 'You should be able to nurse it – so long as it stays above him.'

'Oh, okay.' Embarrassed, I relax my arm and give it a good rub.

'I can fetch the proper IV pole and hook it up in a second. I just wanted to give him a good head start.'

'How long does he need to be on the drip?'

'A few hours should be fine, but I'll keep him here over-night to monitor him.'

Egomaniac or not, there could have been a truly terrible outcome without Markus's help. I shudder. I don't want to think about what could have been.

'Thank you so much, Markus.'

'It's my job, Rosie,' he says matter-of-factly, stretching his legs out on the creamy woollen carpet. Not the most practical of colours for a veterinary practice. Not that it looks at all like one.

'Do you often sleep here?'

'Depends on my patients, but yes, quite a bit. I have every-thing that I need here, really. Only missing the Horizons view.'

And a few hundred bedrooms, I think. I wonder if he's been hiding out here to escape painful memories of Eryka.

'Poor Zurich would have a heart attack if he saw what I've done with this place. This building was originally his office, so he designed the space for a much cleaner, architect's aesthetic. I've kept the clinic rooms at the front as is, but I wanted to make it feel nice and homely back here. I knew I'd be here a lot.'

Ah, this makes more sense. We've come through the back. I'm sure the proper entrance has a fancy reception area with high-end, gold-plated finishes designed specifically to impress. But why didn't he take us through there, instead of stopping in his bedroom? Now it's just the two of us – apart from a snoozing Squash – alone on his bed. He better not have some big seduction act up his sleeve. I've had a huge shock, and I'm not in the mood to fend off any advances. I shuffle towards the end of the bed, conscious that I can't go too far without ripping out Squash's IV line.

'It's certainly very cosy.'

'It's not always this cluttered in here.' Markus gestures to the boxes on the couches. 'I'm collecting bits for Kindred Spirit.'

'Oh?' It sounds like he genuinely cares about that place, beyond the photo op.

'Yes, just some basic stuff. Cotton tips for cleaning wounds, antiseptic cream for infections – that sort of thing.'

'That's really lovely of you, Markus.'

'It's not much, but I won't be able to take too much over with me. That's if I'm ever able to get the trip off the ground.'

He glances down at Squash who now appears to be in a deep sleep. 'Ah, good boy – he's completely passed out now. How long have you had him?'

'Not long – since I moved here. Cedric gave him to me.

I think he wanted me to be one of those cliché single cat ladies.'

I regret the words the moment they spill from my mouth. I've given Markus the perfect opportunity to make a gross pass at me.

Instead, he eyes me carefully and simply says, 'Nice.'

Phew.

'Rosie?'

Gah. I knew he wouldn't be able to resist. If I edge away any further, poor Squash's IV line is going to come right out.

'Yes?' I busy myself with swapping the fluid bag into the other hand – that will add a few extra centimetres to my 'leash'.

'I really want to clear the air once and for all. I know I thanked you on our show the other morning but given how you responded, I'm not sure you thought I meant it. I also wanted to apologise for how I behaved at dinner.'

We'd gotten through the morning at Mr Scarecrow's without him bringing anything up. I was hoping all of the nonsense had ceased.

'I'd just feel much better if we got it all out in the open . . .' he continues hurriedly.

I'm grappling with reconciling the egotistical Markus who thinks he can charm the pants off anyone, and the one who's just saved Squashy's life.

'Look Markus, I know that you're going through a hard time right now, what with your break-up and everything . . . but you need to know that I won't be used as some pawn to make Eryka jealous. If that's what you're even doing?'

He looks taken aback, as if he didn't expect me to call him out like that.

'Ah – Eryka . . . yes . . .' he stammers. 'I shouldn't have brought you into all of that. I'm sorry, Rosie. Let's just say

I've sorted everything now. It won't happen again. I can guarantee it.'

So, he's admitting to it? This is progress.

'And I shouldn't have been such a bitch back, but I wasn't sure what else to do. Especially since we have to work together.'

'That's fair.' As Markus speaks, Squash stirs in his lap. 'Hey there bud, welcome back,' he coos. 'Ready for a cuddle?' he asks me.

'Yes, please.'

Markus gently scoops up Squash and resettles him in my lap. Squash's claws dig into my thighs as he snuggles into my stomach.

'There you go, buddy. All comfy with Mum now.' Markus hands me the fleecy blanket from the end of the bed. For the second time that day I'm unable to stop myself from returning his smile.

And just like that, an unspoken truce settles between us.

Chapter Seventeen

'Have you seen the videos of you on TikTok, Markus? There's a hashtag and everything – #Markushadalittle-lamb. Isn't it perfect?' Cedric whirls into the studio in a flurry of excitement. He turns to me. 'You're the brains behind it all, Rosie. If it wasn't for your fast thinking, we would never have had that footage. There's more than 50,000 videos on the hashtag. The kids are having so much fun duetting it.'

It's nice to get some credit, but it's even sweeter to hear that a whole week after our Mr Scarecrow's excursion we're still receiving attention. The show has already been picked up by some of the surrounding regional stations. Next stop, state-wide syndication. Dad and Naomi had phoned excitedly to tell me they'd heard the show on their road trip down to Kiama. They'd gone for a weekend down south to check out Berry Book Barn, a beautiful bookshop with cathedral ceilings and exposed timber beams – and the perfect wedding venue. It's the type of place I'd always pictured for my own wedding.

'I couldn't agree more – it's all because of you, Rosie.'
I feel Markus's eyes on me.

Squash has made a full recovery, and there hasn't been so much as a wink from Markus in my direction – just a welcome Nespresso quietly delivered to my desk each morning he's in the studio. It seems like we've finally made some headway.

I also spoke to Cedric about ditching the whole Markus and Rosie romance narrative. He was happy to oblige given the public interest in Markus's eligibility.

'Seriously, Rosie, we've got listeners tuning in to see where shirtless Markus is going to pop up next!'

Our audience is growing daily, and Cedric has given me the important task of scouting a location for our next on-air field trip. I'm in my element, with multiple spreadsheets on the go detailing costs and logistics. I'm in search of the ultimate backdrop. I may have left behind my marketing career, but I could never leave behind its teachings. Markus's abs aside, the birth of Janet Junior pulled at the heartstrings because it was so real. Authentic content moves people in a way that makes it more shareable. The difficulty is in planning that authenticity. I've been struggling to come up with a scenario that doesn't feel manufactured. If I know one thing, it's that our listeners don't want to be fooled.

I've been staying well past the show wrap time, doing research and working with Stacey to try to dream up the perfect location. It's left no time for dating, which actually hasn't fazed me in the slightest. At least my time is being put to good use.

'So, where are we off to, Rosie?' Cedric asks.

'I'm still compiling a shortlist. Obviously somewhere with animals, which really narrows things down. But I was thinking maybe the duck pond in Lawson Park? It would be great if we could have Markus discovering a brood of ducklings learning to paddle, but we'd want it all to be completely natural and not staged or anything. Now, I've researched hatching season and we'll have to wait a few months. There's normally a flurry of hatchings at the beginning of spring.'

'Not bad, Rosie. Although, I'm not sure that we can wait that long . . .' Cedric doesn't sound as impressed as I'd hoped. 'How are you with ducklings, Markus?'

'Well – ah – okay . . . I mean, they're cute and all . . .'

'But you're not terribly keen on the idea?' an impatient Cedric prompts.

'It's only – well – I sort of maybe had a slightly different idea . . .' he trails off while shooting me a look that says, 'I'm about to show you the F– up and I'm going to pretend to be sorry about it'.

I thought I'd finally seen the back of this showmanship, yet here we are again like it's bloody Groundhog Day. 'Please do tell, Markus,' I say coldly.

'A while back I put in a request to the *Markus & Pup* production team to film a special at Kindred Spirit, the elephant conservation centre I work with in India, and the approval has just come through!'

'Oh, that's wonderful news, Markus!' I exclaim, forgetting that we've resumed enemy mode.

'The thing is, they want me to go next week. So, I was hoping we could broadcast from there. I know that it's a huge ask.'

Here I was thinking that ducklings might be pushing it and now India could be on the cards?

'I'd love to say yes Markus, you know I would. But even though the show is making amazing strides, we unfortunately don't have the budget for international travel.' And just like that Cedric bursts any excitement that's started to bubble.

'Channel 19 is happy to cover the costs. They know about the radio show and to be honest, I'm sure the latest hype is what helped it get over the line.' Markus flashes me a grateful smile. 'I think they're maybe hoping for a dual broadcast.'

'Reallllly . . .' Now that Cedric knows it won't cost the station a cent and we will to some effect be joining forces with a national TV network, he is practically salivating at the idea. 'What I wouldn't do for a good bout of Delhi belly to shave off a few kilos . . .'

With Cedric in tow this could be a whole lot of fun. I can already picture him at the Taj Mahal, rolling out his purple mat and saluting the sun.

'. . . but Simon would kill me if I disappeared overseas during all the last-minute wedding prep. We still haven't decided on the appetisers.'

Disappointment hits. The wedding is only six weeks away. The invitation didn't reveal much, only that it's in a top-secret Mudgee location and, to quote Cedric, 'It's going to be the wedding of the century!'

I'm sure Stacey will be able to patch in Markus from overseas. As obnoxious as he so often is, he shouldn't have to miss out on the opportunity to help his beloved elephants.

But Cedric hasn't finished delivering his verdict: 'I'm sure you guys will be able to handle things without me. So, provided you're able to arrange the delivery of a baby elephant live on air, and you're both back for my wedding, then, trip approved!' He's positively gleeful. And so is Markus.

Wait a second. No one has checked to see if I'm okay with this. What if I'm not keen on the idea of travelling to a foreign country with a man who I've really only just met, and who up until very recently has been completely unbearable? And I can't be expected to just put my life on hold.

I have Squash to care for, and I've never even been overseas before . . .

My thoughts are interrupted by Stacey bursting through our door, holding my phone.

'Rosie. The hospital has been trying to reach you. It's your dad.'

For a man who's just suffered a minor blockage in one of his coronary arteries, Dad is looking mighty chipper. He's sitting up in his hospital bed spooning fruit salad into his mouth at rapid speed, the television set blaring overhead.

'Rosie, love! What are you doing here?'

We're at Royal North Shore Hospital, just north of the city. Naomi insisted Dad be transferred to the specialised coronary care unit here. Thank goodness for Naomi.

'Gee, I don't know. When my father has a heart attack, I tend to drop everything and rush to his bedside.' I lean over the bed railing and give him a kiss on the cheek. He smells like rockmelon.

'Is that what Naomi told you? She's overreacting. It was a little flutter.'

It's always been Dad's style to downplay. He's done it my whole life. He managed to make Mum leaving feel so completely normal that – at the time – I barely questioned it. It wasn't until I was older that I wanted to know more. That's when words like 'narcissist' were thrown around. Google – and long discussions with the girls and Wes – helped me fill in the gaps. It made sense. Her erratic behaviour, the hubristic pride for her 'million dollar' car business – all of it. Still, it wasn't something that we ever really discussed openly. There's no manual for communicating such things to young daughters. Dad did his best. Perhaps not labouring over the 'why', but showing me that it didn't matter, was how I was able to keep moving forward.

'You gave us quite a scare, Dad.' I fluff his pillows, re-tuck his hospital corners and pull up the thin cotton-weave blanket. It's freezing in here. The metallic tang from the icy stainless-steel rails and smells of disinfectant creep up my nose. 'Right, what's the plan? Have you started your rehab yet?'

I notice a sheet of shiny paper sitting on the plastic chair in the corner of the room and walk over to retrieve it. It's a print-out of a cardiograph, labelled 'John Royce'. How careless of the doctors to leave it laying around! The heart rate line dances all over the page with erratic spikes and troughs and absolutely no rhythmic pattern to speak of. I've watched enough *ER* to know that's not how it should look.

'When is the doctor back in to see you?' I look up to catch Dad about to tuck into a tub of decadent-looking chocolate mousse. 'Dad! That can't be good for you. Where did you get that?'

Dad smiles wickedly like a rebellious kid sprung smoking behind the back sheds. 'I have my ways.'

He continues peeling back the gold foil lid and readies his teaspoon.

I rush over to his bedside, banging my knee on the metal corner. The pain barely registers as I reach down and snatch the mousse away. 'How can you think this is a joke? This is serious!' Blood is thumping loudly in my ears. 'Seriously, Dad, what about this is so funny to you?'

'Rosie. Love. Please calm down.'

'You don't just have a common cold; you've had a heart attack!' I'm aware that I've switched into a high-pitched shriek.

'Rosie –'

'Do you really think that I can afford to lose you?'

'Rosie!'

'Because I can't. You're being completely irresponsible. To me and to Naomi and . . .'

'ROSIE, STOP THIS RIGHT NOW!' Dad throws down his teaspoon with force. There's a loud clatter of metal on the plastic table.

'Okay,' I whisper. I gently place the mousse back on the table and flip the teaspoon over, straightening it so that it's parallel to the TV remote.

Dad's eyes are on me, but he doesn't say anything.

'Do you want to see if the news is on?' I offer. Some current affairs should help take the attention away from my small moment of hysteria – even a weather update. Dad has been known to spend hours in front of the weather channel, watching highs develop over the eastern seaboard and cold fronts roll in, all to a soothing jazz soundtrack.

Dad picks up the remote before I can and silences the television. He then shuffles over to one side of the bed. I slip off my shoes, lift myself over the railing – careful not to bump the machinery – and lie down beside him.

'I'm sorry for giving you a scare, love.' He pauses and swallows. 'Sometimes I feel like I've really let you down.'

How could he think that any of this is his fault? Yes, he could eat better, but how could I blame him for wanting to finally enjoy the finer things in life with Naomi?

I lay my head on his shoulder. 'What do you mean, Dad?'

'I couldn't give you what you needed. As a father, I mean.'

Is he insane? I wanted for nothing. Except, possibly, a labradoodle.

'I made a mistake. I really thought not talking much about your mother was for the best, but in hindsight it really wasn't.'

What has his heart attack got to do with Mum?

'I'm not sure I'm following, Dad . . .'

He sighs. 'It wasn't right of me to sweep things away and encourage you just to get on with things, Rosie.'

I still don't know what he's getting at. Perhaps it's a side effect of the painkillers and next will come the hallucinations of tiny spiders crawling over his skin.

'Why don't you shut your eyes and get some more rest, Dad? It's been a massive day.'

'Rosie. Please listen,' he says in a tone similar to the one he used the other week at Blossoms when 'warning' me about Mum. 'I wish more than anything for you to live your life not afraid of things going a little off course.'

I've never heard Dad talk like this. This quasi life lecture is obviously care of his recent brush with death, I get it. But I'm doing fine. I have lovely friends, an adorable cat and I'm now busy building a brand-new career in radio. I'm not exactly shying away from life.

I don't want to feel irritated, but I do.

'You don't need to worry about me. I'm loving life in Mudgee. Meeting new people, making new friends. And did I mention that we've made it over the border? The show has been picked up in Albury-Wodonga!'

My high voice drifts up towards the panelled ceiling.

'Any gentleman friends?'

'Da-ad!' We definitely never talk like this.

'I know, I know, I've overstepped. I'm sorry, love. It's just that life really is what happens when you're busy making other plans, Rosie. I want you to remember that.'

When did my father turn into a walking motivational Insta-quote? I'll take Liam Neeson's theatrics any day.

'I'm okay, Dad,' I say firmly, pursing my lips to prevent an outburst. *He's not well.* I remind myself.

'We only get one life, Rosie – and it can be a short one. I've been lucky enough to get my second chance with Naomi. I want the same for you.'

Enough! I get it. I'm the one lying next to my dad's fragile body in a hospital bed, my head resting on his awfully bony shoulder.

'I love you, Rosie.'

'I love you too, Dad.'

We lay in silence. I count fifty tinny beeps of Dad's heart machine before I eventually heave myself up into a seated position and reach for his teaspoon.

'Let's eat mousse.'

Chapter Eighteen

I open my laptop to ninety-nine unread emails. How is it that after such a short time in Mudgee, I've managed to recreate my hectic Sydney life? It's evident that the rest of the world doesn't stop just because I've had to.

At least it distracts me from worrying about Dad while I wait for Penny to get home from work.

Penny has arranged the furniture so there's ocean views from most spots in her beautiful Art Deco apartment. I'm seated at the dining table and have a spectacular outlook of waves crashing against the rocky cliffs and washing into Icebergs' iconic ocean pool. It's hard to stay focused on the computer screen in front of me.

I start clearing out my inbox, moving emails straight to trash or marking them for follow-up. I skip over the emails from Cedric requesting my passport details and other information for my visa. There's no way I can even think about going to India now that Dad is sick. Surely Cedric will understand. He's already graciously co-hosting the show – and caring for Squash – in my absence.

There are a few replies from some potential radio guests I've reached out to, including an email from George Primo, the owner of Primo's Donuts. George and his wife, Celia, are the type of business owners who have their customers' orders ready to go the moment they turn into the car park. I'll have to take Penny there to try their traditional buttermilk rings. They put Krispy Kreme to shame.

I move the mouse to the next message, my cursor hovering over the subject line '*Hey*' and the puzzling sender email: callmevangogh@hotmail.com. I'm about to move the email to spam when it occurs to me that it could be another potential radio guest, so I double-click.

The email takes a while to load, and I instantly regret opening it as I start visualising the Trojan virus angrily eating up all of my new segment ideas. I'm frantically hitting backspace when the email finally flashes up on screen. There are a few lines of text.

Hey Rosie,

I thought I'd try emailing in case you've blocked my number again ;)

Sorry that I didn't manage to see you before I left town. I'm currently painting a pub in Goulburn. Of course I plan on stopping by the Big Merino, and thankfully there's some rain due, so I'll report back on any umbrella politics ;)

Joanna mentioned that your dad hasn't been well. I hope he's on the mend now. I know he means everything to you. Please don't hesitate to reach out if you need anything. Anything at all.

Your friend,
Wes.

I immediately feel guilty. Wes texted days ago, but between the Squash scare and all the attention of the show, and now Dad, I'd forgotten to respond.

I type a quick email in reply.

Thanks Wes. He's doing much better now. His favourite Led Zeppelin shirts have somehow made their way over the hospital gowns! Let's definitely stay in touch.

I hesitate for a moment before adding a sign-off.

Posie

I press send before I can overthink things. I continue working away at my inbox for another hour or so. I'm still receiving new emails faster than I'm clearing them out. As soon as I have the count down to a nice round fifty, it jumps back up to fifty-one. A reply from Wes.

Oh, to be a fly on the wall. I'm sure you're creaming your pants over all that hospital bleach. Now don't be a stranger x

'Can Dave really take the boys to Hawaii without your permission?' I ask.

We're at We Rice Above, our favourite Filipino restaurant. It was Penny's idea to do dinner and given Ange agreed to meet, I was more than happy to oblige.

Lots of new spots have opened up on the Grosvenor 'Eat Street' in the last few months – a trendy tapas place, a boutique bar with a menu dedicated to pizza and pét-nats, and a traditional French bistro – yet we can never go past this place. We've been eating here for close to two decades now. It was Pen's mum who first brought us here for our inaugural 'grown-up' dinner at age twelve. We returned the following year sans parentals and have been coming regularly ever since. The blue and red walls, painted to match the Filipino flag, have seen us through it all – when we're joyful, grief-stricken and when we're stark raving mad. We Rice Above is to the three of us what Cosmopolitans are to Carrie and co. We get the same thing every time – three full-sugar Cokes with two servings of Adobo chicken and rice, followed by leche flan. Penny still does all of our ordering.

'That's the point, Rosie,' Ange says icily. 'I don't know.'

I'm not sure why she's even bothered showing up. I thought news of Dad's heart attack may have thawed some of her hostility towards me, but clearly not.

Come on We Rice Above, work your magic, I will. I can't remember one instance in the past where we'd walked in on shaky footing and hadn't walked out on sturdier ground.

Catching Dave in the 'act' had been an unfortunate, unwelcome coincidence. I'd been giving a talk to a media class at Sydney University and headed out afterwards with a few students to continue the conversation. There are dozens of pubs and bars in the area; we could have picked any one, but we'd decided on the Little Drummer for their signature bad apple whiskey, made with fresh apple juice. I hadn't even known who Clare was until the week before, when I'd finally made it to one of Ange's book club nights. Clare was a school mum. She'd been lovely and friendly and had brought over a plate of freshly baked chocolate chip muffins. Guilt muffins.

Because there she was at the Little Drummer, with Dave. Their heads bent over their apple whiskeys. I didn't even get a chance to pretend that they were planning some sort of surprise for Ange – even though she'd just had her birthday – before they started making out like teenagers. It was awful. I didn't confront Dave, I just went straight to Ange's house and recounted exactly what I'd seen. I didn't think twice about it. She needed to know, to save even more heartbreak later. Apparently, she still doesn't see it the same way.

'Sorry, Ange.' I feign nonchalance as I push some of the chicken around on my plate. A few bites ago it was flavourful and tender, but it now tastes too salty and dry. I take a sip of Coke. 'I just don't think Dave's being fair on you and that makes me angry. Right, Penny?'

'Oh, totally. He's a knob.'

'I don't want to talk about it anymore. What's happening with Wes, Rosie?' Ange changes the subject abruptly. Of course she wants to talk about Wes. She's the one who gave him my number in the first place.

I shrug. 'We caught up in Mudgee and decided to let bygones be bygones. He's in Goulburn now, painting another pub.'

I've made the executive decision that any further Wes chat is strictly off limits. Penny obviously knows about our putt putt meet-up, which I can only assume means that Ange now knows too. But I haven't mentioned the art class.

'Anyway, he's no Dr Markus Abrahams . . .' Penny teases. 'What's the latest there?'

I ignore her suggestive tone, even though I'm happier with this line of questioning. 'Nothing much. He wants me to go to India with him next week to record the show from there.'

'What? How was this not the first thing you mentioned? India?!' Penny exclaims.

'Well, I'm not going,' I announce. 'I can't now because of Dad. Even if I wanted to – which I'm not sure I do by the way, since the hot celebrity you speak of is an egomaniac hung up on his ex, with a possible pill problem, who's been a giant pain in my arse.'

I keep quiet about my recent change of heart towards Markus.

Ange raises an eyebrow. 'Always excuses,' she mutters.

'Sorry?'

'I think you heard me,' Ange responds.

'I wouldn't exactly call Wes or Markus eligible bachelors . . .' I hit back.

'Whatever you say, Rosie.'

'You're going to discover how hard it is dating out there soon enough, Ange. And it's no different in Mudgee. I have a 10km radius set and still nothing decent. I can't push my Tinder settings much further. It's too far to drive what with my early morning starts and all . . .'

'Or maybe you just don't want to meet anyone,' Ange says. 'Let's get the bill. I need to get home to the boys.'

There's a sharp pain in my stomach like a bullet has been shot straight through my abdomen.

Pen attempts to comfort me as Ange goes up to the counter. 'Don't listen to her, Rosie. She's still just upset about Dave.'

'I know. It's just not getting any easier though, is it?' My shoulders drop.

'You know, if it wasn't you telling her, she would have found out some other way. Dave has been cheating on her for years. You did her a favour.'

It's sweet that she feels my injustice so vehemently.

'Come on, let's go pay and enjoy the rest of our night. We can make margs and get lost down a TikTok hole. I'm currently on "snail trail girlies tok". How bloody rude. It's like the app accompanies me to my fortnightly waxing appointments or something. Actually, come to think of it, it does . . . well, still, anyway. I need to put in some hours to fix up my algorithm ASAP.'

Thank God for Penny.

Chapter Nineteen

I'm skipping and dancing my way through the long blades *of grass, taking in the various shades of green. Markus calls out to me from the other side of the field.*

'Rosie, my love, can you come and help with the elephants?'

'Yes, Markus. I'll be right over.'

Life in India is fulfilling. Markus is happy tending to the elephants, and I have found joy in the simple things, like milking our dairy cows and churning the fresh milk into cream, cheese, butter and yoghurt.

I grab a bundle of twigs and make my way over to where Markus is with his herd. There are ten elephants under his care that he has rescued from the ivory trade.

Our dear elephants are huddled together in a tight circle, forming an impenetrable barrier around Markus – a wall of muscle and tusks. They're faced inwards, and as I approach, they lift their trunks in unison and shuffle back to reveal him.

He steps towards me with open arms, a soaring, manly, godlike creature. I leap into his strong arms and kiss him

*passionately. Sheer bliss courses through me. A feeling
I never want to be without. Mmmm . . .*

Suddenly I'm jolted awake. Penny's side of the bed is empty.

I stretch and let out a loud groan. I feel like I need to have a cold shower to wash away the Markus ickiness.

I check the alarm clock on the side table: 8 am. I haven't slept in this late for weeks.

'Are you okay, babe?' Penny calls from the bathroom.

'All good,' I shout back. I wonder if I was moaning in my sleep. I should be embarrassed, but it's Penny, so I'm not.

'I'm going to check my email, then I'll be off to visit Dad before I head back to Mudgee and out of your hair.'

I've now been in Sydney for a full week and Naomi and the doctors have assured me that Dad is on the mend. I have a radio show to get back to, and I have to let Cedric know that I won't be going to India.

'No rush! I love having you here.' Penny pokes a shower-capped head around the door. The cap is pink with white polka dots and a lace trim and it makes her look like a little forest mushroom.

What would I do without her? We may not always see eye to eye, but she's been the ultimate bestie of late. Supporting me endlessly with my career change and move to Mudgee. Right there by my side and literally giving up half her bed for me. Even if she did keep me up until 2 am with the bright glow of TikTok.

'Thanks, Pen. Love ya!'

She pushes open the bedroom door and steps into the room. She's wrapped in a very Pen, very bright pink, terry towelling bath sheet.

'I know we don't get all mush-mush often. But I seriously mean that.'

'The feeling's mutual. I regularly ovulate over you too, babe.' She blows me a kiss and turns and shuffles back down the hallway like a sushi roll on legs. I can't help but laugh. Never a dull moment with Pen around, that's for damn sure.

I open my laptop to the blinking red battery light. I reach for my handbag and turn its contents upside down on the bed. My keys, wallet, a tube of hand cream, and two different kinds of whitening toothpaste tumble out, but no laptop cord. Damn. I must have left it in Dad's hospital room.

My eyes settle on Penny's shiny Mac set up in the corner of the room.

'Pennnn . . .' I call towards the open bathroom door. 'Can I borrow your computer real quick? Mine's dead and I don't have my charger.'

'What's mine is yours, doll,' she sings back.

I boot up her computer and a new mail alert pops up as soon as the screen lights up.

Sender: Dave Pritchard
Subject: Re: We need to talk

Why is Dave emailing Penny? That's super weird. Is Penny doing some sort of favour for Ange and liaising with Dave over the Hawaii trip? She hasn't mentioned anything . . .

I keep reading.

Hi Penny,
I really think that's a bad idea. You may want to clear your conscience, but my soon-to-be-ex-wife is already creating nightmares for my new girlfriend and I'd really prefer you didn't poke the Ange bear.
Think of the boys.
Dave.

I scroll down to the message below, my finger frantic on the mouse.

> *Hi Dave,*
> *I know it's been a while. I've been thinking about what happened between us.*
> *I'm really struggling with it. I think I need to tell Ange.*
> *Please let me know if you want to meet to discuss. It might be best coming from me, but I wanted you to know.*
> *Penny.*

OMG.

'Did you get it working?' Penny is behind me in her towel. So casual.

I jump up off the chair. The colour drains from her face as she looks at the computer screen and then back at me.

'What is this, Penny?' I ask carefully.

'An email to Dave.'

'I can see that. But why?'

'Oh, Rosie. It's not what you think!'

Thank fuck. I knew she must have an explanation for this.

'I mean it's not exactly what you think. It's definitely not as bad as it looks.'

Oh God, she's not flat-out denying anything.

'So, something did happen between you and Dave?' My voice wavers. I'm terrified of her response.

Please, please, please choose your words carefully, Pen. Our friendship relies on it.

'I guess it depends on how you define something . . .'

That simple sentence packs the most destructive of forces. Like a carelessly placed domino sending elaborate lines of ivory beauties crashing down.

'Rosie, what I mean is –'

My hand shoots out to silence her. It feels like everything is short-circuiting and my head is about to explode. 'Now is not the time for technicalities, Penny,' I spit. 'Did you or did you not have an affair with Dave?'

'It was eight years ago, Rosie! Way before they had kids. And it was only the one night. Remember when I was partying a lot? We'd done a few lines and . . .'

The pain has moved from my head to my heart. I think I can feel it cracking; jagged pieces slowly breaking off and ricocheting into my bloodstream. Like the *Titanic* as it hit the iceberg. Not *my* Penny.

'How could you do this to Ange?' I yell.

'I know, I know.' Her head drops into her hands. 'I'm so awful,' she moans.

She lifts her head, face haunted. She's still in her towel and that silly shower cap. Her eyes are wet.

For a second, I allow myself to imagine I'm able to erase the emails I've just seen from my mind. After all, if I'm to believe Penny, it was such a long time ago. But then just as quickly it occurs to me that she's not only kept this secret from me, she's also allowed me to cop months of shit from Ange. All the while knowing that if she'd spoken up earlier – years and years ago – things might have been different for Ange, and for us all.

'I've wanted to tell you so many times, Rosie, trust me. But the longer I left it, the more I wasn't sure what to say . . .' She trails off.

'You know what? I don't even want to hear it, Penny.'

My hands are shaking as I move to my bag and start stuffing in my belongings. Penny doesn't stop me as I zip it up and swing it onto my shoulder. She just stands there watching – like she knows that things are beyond saving.

I march towards the door.

She waits until my hand is on the handle before she cries out. 'Don't go, Rosie. Can't we at least sit down and talk this all through?'

I swing around to face her.

'There's really no point, Penny. We Rice Above can't fix this one. I don't know who you are, but you're no friend of mine.'

A strangled sound comes from her throat.

'Rosie! Please!'

'Don't bother trying to call me. I won't answer,' I cry as I storm out.

Once in the safety of my car, I let out a deep breath. I sit and wait for my body to stop shaking before I check my phone.

As expected, there's already a bloody message. No amount of love heart emojis is going to fix this mess. This isn't about a strapless bra borrowed without permission and returned unwashed. It's about a husband. *Ange's* husband. Penny had me convinced that she was one of the good ones. One of the best ones, in fact. But this is a soul-aching reminder that you never really know someone. You can sleep alongside them, bond over countless broken hearts, leche flans and episodes of *Sex and the City* and it could still all be completely meaningless. Twenty years of friendship down the drain.

My hands start shaking again as I swipe at my phone to read her message.

Don't you dare cut me off, Rosie. I'm here when you're ready to talk x

I scoff as I delete the message and find myself scrolling to Ange's contact and pressing 'call'.

'Rosie, hi.' She answers on the first ring.

I have no intention of actually telling her, do I? Even in my strung-out state I can't see what good that would do right now. I just want to hear her voice. Not just to reassure me that she's okay, but to soothe me in the way she used to be so good at.

'Hey Ange, I just thought I'd give you a quick call to check in.'

'I saw you last night.' Her tone is brisk at best.

'Is this a bad time?'

'A bad time? It's almost 9 am. The boys are still busy throwing their breakfast on the floor, I haven't showered, and I have a meeting in, oh would you look at that, twenty-four fucking minutes.'

'Ah shit, sorry. Is there anything I can do to help?'

'Maybe not call me right at the most inconvenient part of the day,' she huffs.

Right, okay then. I almost want to spit out the reason for this impromptu call in this first place. Almost.

'Sure. I'll let you go then. Bye Ange.'

'Bye.'

I throw my phone across to the passenger side and it bounces off the glove box and falls somewhere underneath the seat. While I'm busy losing friendships in her honour, she's busy being an arsehole to me. Is *continuing* to be an arsehole to me. I wouldn't let that fly with anyone else, so why her? I'm officially done now.

I turn my keys in the ignition and lower the handbrake. I need to get as far away from this BS as possible.

Suddenly Mudgee doesn't seem far enough.

Chapter Twenty

My first impression of India is that it's magnificent. And extremely loud. We exit the airport just as the sun begins its lazy fall from heaven. Thank goodness we have a driver organised as both the heat and the jostle of hopeful cabbies are unrelenting while we wait for our car to be brought around to the entrance.

'Madam. Where are you going?'

'Ride? You need one, lady?'

'Here! We have taxi for you!'

It's like Markus doesn't exist as sets of dark eyes bore into me. I'm so tired that the loud, persistent voices sound like the whisperings of magical tongues. The curiosity radiates off them, bathing me in the glow of their marvel. I feel like a collector's item or a movie star.

I rejoice in the peace and quiet once we're safely inside the car. I vaguely register Markus loading my suitcase in the boot and opening my door for me. I can't believe that just a few short days ago I was swerving dead kangaroos on the road back to Mudgee and I'm now halfway around the world sliding into the red leather backseat of an Indian taxicab.

Cedric was delighted when I called him, seconds after hanging up from Ange, and said that I was 'a go' for India. Even if I'd wanted to back out in the days following my rash decision, I know he wouldn't have let me. He practically ripped Squash from my arms and pushed me onto that plane. Not only did he want me to 'have an adventure I deserved', I think he was secretly relieved that I'd be there to handle any surprise stage fright from Markus. Markus had been cool, calm and collected – much more akin to his smooth *Markus & Pup* self – since he went viral on TikTok, but Cedric was right to still proceed with caution. With the show on the rise, the last thing we needed was the re-emergence of a mute Markus to cause a ratings demise.

Somewhere over Hong Kong, with our fellow business class passengers (yes, business class!) out for the count on varying mixes of Scotch and Valium, Markus had taken off his headphones and quietly asked how Dad was doing. I was impressed he wasn't also indulging in the free-flowing business class drinks, or his pills. We chatted on and off for the next six hours. I didn't even finish plotting my Mumbai temple tour; I was attempting to map it out in a similar fashion and efficiency to my grocery shop, but the maze of laneways was proving more of a challenge than the meticulously organised supermarket aisles. So I'd closed my planner and slipped it into the seat pocket, choosing to talk to Markus instead. Just like that night at Horizons, it surprised me how much we had to chat about. Ceddie, the show, his elephants . . .

The sun is still a blazing fire, glimmering off the tin roofs as we grind to a complete stop in front of a cow lounging in the middle of the road. Horns blare and I wind down my window to get some fresh air. Kids run past our car, giggling and with tousled hair; a toothless man sits on a roof, brushing his gums with a twig and spitting down onto the street below; pop music blares from the concrete block homes that fringe the street; a woman swathed in orange crouches by the side of the road stirring a pan of vibrant yellow dal over a smoky coal fire. The smell of fragrant spices makes my tummy grumble. The whole scene is an assault to my senses – a welcome one. Is this what was out here waiting for me this entire time? A kaleidoscope of colours, sounds and aromas, so unlike the mac 'n' cheese world I had moulded around me.

A tiny, grimy hand stretches through the car window. I look down to see a small boy smiling shyly and rubbing his bloated belly. Markus, and then the driver, gesture for me to wind my window back up. Before following their instruction, I rustle around in my backpack for a packet of plane biscuits and press them into the tiny palm. I watch as he skips away back to his shoeless friends.

We're staying at a hotel in the middle of Mumbai. The building appears modern, with an all-glass façade and a neon blue 'HOTEL' sign affixed to the roof. On closer inspection, though, I see that the glass panelling doesn't reach the sides, leaving cracked and worn exposed brickwork. It's not dilapidated, like some of the buildings we passed on our car ride while winding our way around complacent cows roaming freely in the streets, but the buff-coloured Kurla stone has aged well beyond its colonial days. I wonder why they've chosen to cover up a building so rich with history, rather than restore it.

We check in and are given keys to our hotel rooms. Our two *separate* rooms.

My room is more like a suite, with a bedroom off a large living area. Who gets a lounge suite in their hotel room?

The bathroom is gorgeous, too. Not only does the marble gleam in way that says 'industrially cleaned', there's a TV built inside the mirror that you can watch while in the bath. *Thank you*, Markus & Pup.

I switch on the TV to some Bollywood dancing and shimmy over to the minibar. It's sitting under a spotlight and looking particularly seductive. I'm scared that if I even open the mini-fridge door I'll get slapped with a hefty fee, but I put on my complimentary fluffy robe and slippers and peek inside. A whole 7-Eleven aisle has been crammed into a 50cm x 50cm space. I pop a mini bottle of champagne to celebrate – celebrate what, I'm not sure. That after twenty-eight years on earth I have *finally* left the country? I allow my mind to wander to Wes. I just know that he'd be proud – this is a far cry from the two-star Bananarama Motel in Coffs!

I pair my bubbles with a jumbo KitKat, then swiftly move onto a can of Pringles. As I'm scoffing the last of the Sour Cream & Onion crumbs, an unsettled feeling washes over me, as though I've reached into my bag for my phone only to realise that I've left it at home. This munchie situation would have been Penny's idea of heaven. My stomach turns when I remember how we left things. Luckily the feeling doesn't last long. *She brought this on herself*, I remind myself.

Jittery from all the junk food and ashamed of my inauthentic, confectionary dinner, I make an executive decision to order room service.

My chicken tikka and naan arrive with a lassi in decadent crystalware, garnished with a mint leaf. I carry my late-night snack out onto the terrace and am hit by a wall of dry heat so forceful it nearly winds me. I take a sip of my drink. The liquid is icy sweet and rushes down my throat, cooling me from the inside out and leaving behind a delicate hint of cumin and lime.

More honking horns and the occasional howl of a stray dog float up from the street below. I look out to the lights of the skyscrapers rising in the distance. Darkness now cloaks the horizon, concealing the unlit. The bronzed temple domes, the skeletons of half-built buildings, the battle-scarred forts, the shadowy, forgotten rivers. Up here in the clouds, the city's beauty feels fleeting and borrowed, which is exactly what makes it so intoxicating.

I let out a long breath. *Finally*. I no longer feel like running away from the world. I want to be a part of it.

I awake to sunlight streaming through the sheer curtains. Between my midnight feasting and jet-lag haze I must have forgotten to pull the drapes. I stretch luxuriously in bed, falling back against the wad of downy pillows.

This is a life I could get used to. Bollywood movies by day, room service by night.

I reach for my phone and text Dad that I've arrived safely. He's out of hospital and at home under the care of nurse Naomi. I'd had a brief freak-out at the airport about leaving him and phoned Naomi. Again. She'd managed to convince me that I was worrying unnecessarily. It was true. I wouldn't be here if he wasn't in such good hands. Naomi will have him on a strict regimen of egg whites and brisk walks in no time.

I also have Dad's words echoing in my head.

'We only get one life, Rosie – and it can be a short one.'

If moving to Mudgee isn't enough to prove that I'm busy living life on my terms, then surely jetting out of the country and across the Pacific on a whim will do it. Dad's opinion matters. But I realised late last night that it's as much about what *I* think as what he does. Probably more so.

We have a day in Mumbai to recover from jet lag before our train to Kerala, where Kindred Spirit is located. I'd questioned the twenty-one-hour train trip over the two-hour flight with SpiceJet, but Markus had informed me that the domestic carrier's oversized baggage fees made flying astronomically expensive. It would have been much easier to broadcast from a studio and not have to cart our microphones, headphones, mixers, audio processors and speakers all the way from Australia, but it was perfectly reasonable for an elephant sanctuary located deep in the Indian jungle not to have such facilities. We also have an elephant's weight–worth of Markus's veterinary supplies.

Once we arrive there, it will be all work and no play for Markus with filming throughout the day and a short break in the middle for our radio show. I know that Cedric has unrealistic expectations about us single-handedly ending the illegal ivory trade live on air.

'If anyone can do it, it's you Rosie.'

I better check in with him too, I think, reaching for my phone and clicking into WhatsApp.

'Hello,' Cedric sounds half asleep.

'Ceddie?'

'Oh my God, it's you, my darling girl! Hang on, let me wake up.'

'What time is it there?' I must have messed up the time difference.

'One.'

'Oh shit, sorry. Let me call you later . . .'

'PM,' Cedric finishes. 'Rough night with Si.'

'I'm sorry, Ceddie. Want to talk about it?' I had hoped it would be smooth sailing to the wedding.

'Are you crazy? No way. Squashy and I want to hear everything about India. Squashy! Mummy's on the phone.

So tell me, tell me – what's it like? Or more importantly, what's *he* like?'

'Cedric!'

'Oh puh-lease, Rosie. Protest all you like, I know that you have a big fat crush on Markus.'

I thought we were done with this nonsense, especially now it's so important for Markus to seem 'eligible' for our audience.

'Stop it, Cedric.' I drop into a whisper. Markus's room is next door, and I don't know how soundproof these walls are. 'You know that I've only just grown to tolerate him.' I don't mention our semi-enjoyable plane ride.

'You sly dog, Rosie! Whatever happens in India stays in India. I hope you have a day of romantic sightseeing planned. Mumbai is known as the city of dreams, you know.'

No, I didn't. But I have a list of precisely seven hundred temples that I'm already stressed about not being able to make a proper dent in. I'm acutely aware of how much time I have to make up for, wasted being terrified of what lay beyond. Like there were vicious monsters lurking outside my small bubble, and not delicious naan bread.

Cedric continues gleefully. 'Speaking of which, I'm expecting quality content from my dream team over there.'

'On it, Cedric. I'm planning to go scope out th–'

I'm interrupted by a loud yawn. 'Listen doll, why don't you buzz me tomorrow once you're all settled in at Kindred?'

'Aren't I the one who is supposed to have jet lag?' I tease, before remembering the Simon situation. 'Go make things right with Si.'

'I will. Namaste, darling.'

'Before you go, Ceddie, I –'

The phone goes silent.

At once, I'm filled with a sense of loneliness. My room, which seemed so grand and full of possibility the night before – and even just five minutes ago – swims around me.

Pull it together, Rosie. You've been here for less than twelve hours.

But I can suddenly feel every one of the thousands of kilometres that separate me from home. Speaking to Cedric has sparked a need for more contact. Reaching out to Dad again will only cause unnecessary worry. Obviously, Penny and Ange are out of the question and although I've become friendly with both Bee and Joanna, I don't have either of their numbers.

I bury into the crisp sheets, but the 1000 thread count provides little comfort. I feel like a stray sock lost deep within the bedding. I pull up the plush gold duvet. It's adorned with delicate embroidered flowers, tiny buds and larger ones, stitched in glistening, metallic thread, forming neat little flower posies.

I'm calling Wes before I even realise. There's no answer, so I follow up with a text message.

Hey Wes, I hope Goulburn is treating you well? Just checking in as promised. I'm over in India, of all places! Here with the show. Really enjoying it so far. I'm not sure if there are any 'big' things here? Google tells me that India has the world's tallest statue, 597 feet! Don't know how tall that is in metres. Will try and locate! Btw it's technically monsoon season here, so I might get lucky with some umbrella politics. I bet they have gloriously colourful brollies!

I press send then start pulling at the threads of the metallic posies. What now? I'm not expecting an immediate reply. I guess it's time for an all-you-can-eat buffet breakfast, then I can get started on my temple itinerary.

I climb out of bed and lift my suitcase off the floor. There's an explosion of colour as I unzip it. Piles of scarves, singlets and sarongs fall out onto my canopy bed. It doesn't matter how neatly I folded and rolled things; turbulence has made its own arrangements. Naomi helped with my packing in Penny's absence, but even I knew better than to bring jeans and my Chuck Taylors in this humidity. I pluck a dusty-pink cotton playsuit from the pile – a Blossoms hand-me-down from Naomi. I wonder if it's suitable temple wear? Once the playsuit is on, I select a plain red scarf and wind it loosely around my neck to disguise my décolletage.

There's a knock, and I quickly stuff the mounds of fabric back into my suitcase before opening the door.

'Morning.' Markus bounds into my room. He hands me a coffee. 'Presumably you take your coffee the same way across the globe?' His smile is wide and white. He appears to avoid jet lag as well as he does plaque.

'Thanks, Markus.'

'What do you say to hitting up a few temples with me today?'

I smile. 'That's exactly what I was planning on doing.'

The thought of not having to navigate a foreign city on my own is especially appealing right now.

'Great. I'll meet you downstairs in ten.'

Once Markus re-emerges in the foyer he's wearing a navy polo, chino pants and has swapped his RM Williams for a pair of well-loved, tan leather loafers. He's not quite TV-ready, but almost.

He lets me take the lead as we spend the day temple-hopping around Mumbai. Each time we step inside the grounds – and leave behind the hustle and bustle of the chaotic streets – we're greeted by fragrant wafts of sandalwood incense and bathed in a peace that's impossible to put into words.

We finish our tour at Shree Siddhivinayak Ganapati Mandir, a temple dedicated to Lord Ganesha, the elephant-headed god. Outside, I shade my eyes from the cloudless sky as I survey the piles upon piles of saffron-coloured marigolds baking in the fierce sun. I'm not sure if it's appropriate for a foreigner to make a purchase, but at each stop the garlands of glowing orange and yellow blooms have grown increasingly magnetic to the point where they're now impossible to bypass. Markus hangs back as I point to one of the overflowing piles. A lady with her head draped in a purple scarf scoops up some flowers and places them into my outstretched hands. They're lightweight and fluffy like pompoms. I hold them carefully as though they're baby ducklings.

With my hands full, I'm unable to reach into my bag for my purse. Markus must see the alarm on my face as he steps forward and hands the woman a thick wad of rupees.

'I'll pay you back,' I mouth gratefully.

He smiles. 'No need.'

Once the flowers are safely tucked in the front pouch of my bag, away from the crush of my weighty water bottle, we ascend the stairs to the temple's entry. The bright white marble glitters gently in the sun, and the climb feels as vigorous as scaling Mt Everest in the 40°C heat. Even Markus has a few hairs out of place when we reach the top.

'Inside?' he pants.

'Definitely.'

The mezzanine is alive with crowds of worshippers making their offerings. We find a free bench and take a seat. Even through my sarong, which was purchased earlier in the day to compensate for the modesty my playsuit lacked, the solid stone feels nice and cool on the backs of my legs.

'Wow. Check that out,' Markus whispers, gaze fixated on the intricate gold dome in front of us.

It is impressive, but I find my eyes on the people. A little boy is trying to balance a fruit basket the size of himself on his head. The basket is overflowing with pineapples, bananas and apples. As he sets it down, I watch him swipe an apple and take a fleshy bite. He glances over his shoulder, presumably to check his mum hasn't spied him munching on his offering. Luckily, her eyes are still closed as she kneels in prayer.

Wes would love it here, I can't help but think. Not just this temple, but India in general. So much colour, and difference, and story. He so badly wanted to travel with me. Not just up and down the east coast of Australia, but further afield. To Japan, to paint the crowds viewing the cherry blossoms. But the prospect of an accidental mother/daughter reunion was just too horrifying. He understood, as he always did, suggesting Bali or Fiji as alternative destinations to test the overseas travel waters. I *knew* he was restless. I *knew* that his brilliant mind and hands were craving something more than I could offer. I can't fault him for his decision to leave me behind all those years ago.

I imagine Wes next to me on the bench. His brush would delight not just in the magnificence of the extravagant gold, but everyone's divine reverence at the sight of it. It's like the crowd belongs wholly to this temple.

We stay for around an hour. I'm not sure if Markus is indulging me, of if he's equally entranced by the buzzing temple activity.

When we eventually leave, neither of us are ready to go back to the hotel, so we take a rickshaw to the Chor Bazaar. Markus chats animatedly to our driver, Jayesh, about the best spot to try the famed 'Bombay sandwich' as we careen wildly over the patchwork of potholes. As Jayesh rounds a tight corner at lightning speed, I'm sent crashing into Markus's solid arm.

Jayesh swivels around to face us, eyes completely off the road. 'Sorry. I drive like a chicken without a head, you know.'

Markus and I exchange grins, our arms still pressed together. I'm surprised that I haven't instinctively shuffled back over to my side.

We drive through some more bumpy roads (my marigolds are definitely crushed by now) until the streets become populated with fewer cows and more street vendors. Then we come to a stop outside the Chor Bazaar.

'Careful,' Jayesh warns as we hop out of the rickshaw. I look down to make sure I'm not about to step in a puddle or a pothole. 'Chor. It is meaning thief.'

Ah, I see. I smile in thanks and grip my bag tightly to my chest as I wait for Markus to pay for our ride. I wonder if he uses Splitwise? Surely *Markus & Pup* isn't funding our recreation too?

We don't make it far into the bazaar before my throat starts to tighten and I feel short of breath. It's a chaotic wonderland – stuff, people, and animals *everywhere*. A hotchpotch of leather trunks, bronze statues, kerosene lamps and Ikat rugs tumble out of the stores lining the narrow streets, while the road itself is a rainbow checkerboard of brightly coloured sarongs littered with shoes, stamps and old typewriters.

A sharp pain shoots through my foot and I let out a faint yelp that's barely audible in the loud sea of haggling. I wipe my clammy hands down the length of my sarong and try to steady my breathing.

In and out.

In and out.

In and out.

'Rosie! What happened?'

Markus has heard me.

'I think a goat just trod on my toe.' I start laughing, but I feel like crying.

The overwhelm really creeps up on you here. One minute you're delighting in the sensory overload, the next it's knocking you to the ground.

'How about we take a timeout and get you a cold drink?'

He doesn't wait for my response before taking my arm and leading me away. One hand is firmly grasped around my wrist while the other arm elbows our way through the crowd. He maintains his grip until we're deposited safely in front of a bustling drinks vendor.

'Coke?' he asks.

'Sure. Thanks.'

We're told not to go off too far: the glass bottles must be returned for his next customers. I try not to think about where the battered bottle has been, and how he has been washing them.

We sit at the flimsy, low aluminium table and chair set outside the drinks wallah, guzzling the brown liquid. I try not to let the glass lip of the bottle touch mine. Wes will never believe I'm doing this! I hope there's a message waiting from him when I'm back in the hotel's wifi.

As I'm emptying the last few drops into my mouth, I notice that Markus's wallet is sitting in the middle of the table – ripe for the picking.

'Markus!' I hiss. 'Your wallet!'

'Don't worry,' he says. 'I read about this bazaar. The name comes from the origins of the items on sale. It's mostly stolen goods that flood the markets.'

'Oh.'

'Not to say there aren't pickpockets everywhere too.' He winks, putting his wallet away.

With my nerves sedated by the sugary soft drink, we return our bottles to the eager stallholder. I can't help but glance back over my shoulder to hopefully catch him submerging the bottles in a tub of boiling water; instead, I see him line them back up on the shelf.

We weave our way to the shadier part of the bazaar and out of the burning sun. At least I've removed my sarong now, but I can still feel the sweat dripping down from my neck. Light pink was probably not the best colour choice for this weather. I trail behind Markus to avoid him catching a glimpse of my sweaty back.

The vibrant, colourful bazaar wares eventually transform into a junkyard of grey twisted metal and rusted, burnt-out cars. Some of the wrecks are the colour of Wes's eyes. *That's a strange thing to think.*

I inspect the piles in front of me: a multitude of spare parts, most of them unidentifiable aside from the obvious motors, gearboxes, and steering wheels.

'Ah, I read about this too,' Markus exclaims. 'There's an entire section of the bazaar dedicated to automotives.'

I didn't take Markus for a car man. But then I've been wrong about him before . . .

'Somewhere here should also be a stall where they sell the stuff from the gloveboxes of the defective cars. How fun is that?'

It takes me half a beat to register what he's said because my eyes land on a dashboard bobblehead, bobbing gleefully in the incense-infused breeze, and the colour drains from my face.

I barely say a word on the way back to the hotel.

'Are you sure you're okay, Rosie?' Markus asks gently once we're finally in the hallway outside our rooms.

'Yes. I'm fine, thanks.' Although I'm positive I look as haunted as I feel.

My hands are shaking so Markus helps me with the key in my door, then follows me inside.

'I think I'll feel better if I just wait for a bit with you. If that's all right?'

'Sure,' I murmur as I make my way out onto the terrace. I look out at the view that held so much promise the night before, but now my eyes can only focus on the eagles picking at food scraps in the vacant lot below.

'Talk to me, Rosie.'

Markus places a soft hand on my shoulder, and I turn around to face him, looking back into my room and at my canopy bed.

I open my mouth to attempt to explain about my mother and her cars and her bobbleheads and her leaving, and how the shock of seeing a reminder of her in the middle of a bazaar in India, where I'm supposed to feel alive and free, was just too much for me to process.

'I'm just tired,' I say instead.

I don't feel ready to share. And I *am* tired. Bone tired. And I'm hot – like I've been sunburnt on the inside.

'Can I get you something to help you relax, maybe?' Markus asks.

I hope he's not going to suggest I have a martini. We've been getting on so well that I don't want to tempt fate by bringing alcohol into the equation. That hasn't worked out very well for us in the past.

'Would you like a Valium?'

'Thanks, but I'll be right. I think it's just early to bed for me tonight.'

'Of course. Let me know if you change your mind though. I find it really helps with my anxiety.'

He clamps a hand over his mouth like he's misspoken. 'I mean, that's not something I've ever talked about publicly – my anxiety, that is.'

Anxiety. Markus has anxiety. How has this never occurred to me? It explains so much – the on-air nerves, his launch-party antics and perhaps even some of his other questionable behaviour. The medication in his bathroom wasn't about him getting high; it was about keeping him calm . . .

'I still had lots of fun today.' Markus changes the subject and gives me a weak smile. He obviously doesn't want to talk about it. That makes two of us avoiding subjects that feel too hard to delve into right now.

'So did I,' I manage as I stifle a yawn. My eyelids are suddenly very heavy.

'Let's go back inside and I'll leave you to rest,' Markus says.

I nod gratefully, but as I start towards the open terrace door my scarf becomes entangled around my leg and I trip and stumble backwards.

'Woah, careful, Rosie!' Markus catches my elbow, stopping me from tumbling over the railing and down into the vacant lot with the hungry birds.

My body seizes up and holds stiff, paralysed by the shock of the near miss.

A moment later it gives out completely, and I fall into Markus's arms.

Chapter Twenty-One

My eyes flutter open. I am no longer in Markus's arms but in my opulent room in the stately Pitoniya carriage on the Maharajas Express, just stirring from a delicious siesta. We'd arrived at Mumbai Central at 10 am this morning ready to board our train to Kerala. I'd assumed it was a standard public sleeper train and had prepped by putting together an 'essentials' kit comprised of toilet paper, hand sanitiser and disinfectant wipes. But when the grand, ruby-red train pulled into the station, I'd swung around to Markus and found him grinning.

'Surprise!' he'd exclaimed, fluttering his fingers like jazz hands in a fashion that strangely did not give me the ick.

Last night, I hadn't expected to feel anything when Markus pulled me in close, especially given the emotional state I was in. But as soon as his arms wrapped around my waist, a sense of calm washed over me. He didn't know the first thing about my family history, so I didn't think it was possible for him to comfort me. But he held me for what felt like hours, until

I started dribbling on his shoulder and he gently led me over to my canopy bed, tucked me in, switched off the light and left.

This morning I readied myself for a barrage of questions about what had prompted my meltdown, but none came. Just a coffee quietly handed to me in the hotel foyer before we left for the station.

As soon as we'd boarded the train, we'd each been given a hot towel with a pair of fancy, silver tongs and a glass of Cristal, before being escorted by our individual butlers to our deluxe cabins where our luggage already sat waiting for us. I was instructed to 'buzz at any time, for anything', and I half thought about testing it out by requesting something annoyingly specific, like some strawberry-flavoured dental floss, before finding myself drawn to the bejewelled king bed, climbing under the thick linen sheets and giant duvet, and promptly passing out.

I'm shocked that *Markus & Pup* has the budget for such lavishness. Maybe it's important that their star arrives in style. It's not like I'm unaware of Markus's expensive taste. The last time I'd drunk Cristal champagne was at Horizons.

I can see out the window from my bed, the luxe gold trim perfectly framing the scenery outside. I'm in a complete trance as the stunning landscape spins past in a lively chocolate wheel of colour. The train trundles by pyramid-like mounds of rainbow spices and paddy fields bursting with wildflowers. We hug the curves of the mountainside, the ominous glow of filtered light splashing striped sunshine across the rich tapestry of my room. Moments later we're squeezing past the backs of houses and people eating their dinner on the tracks spring out of the way.

I don't know how long I watch for, but gradually the scenery becomes more and more shadowy. I hold onto every last morsel of squinting until I can no longer even make out the silhouettes. Eventually, it's completely dark outside. I move to the window, press my nose to the cool glass and look out at the sprinkling of bright stars in the night sky.

How bloody wonderful is this?

I have plans to meet Markus in the dining car at 9 pm, so I manage to tear my eyes away from the window's starry blanket long enough to check my phone. It's 8 pm. Plenty of time to freshen up – and text Wes. After the emotional whirlwind last night, I only noticed his message this morning then had no time to reply.

I open WhatsApp and find myself smiling as I re-read his reply.

Sorry, India!!!! Rosie!!!!! That's amazing. How are you finding it?

My fingers fly across the keys.

I know, right?! I actually used my passport. Can you believe it?

I press send and two minutes later I have a message back.

Sooooo answer me! How is it?!

I could tell him about the glorious temples – the rich colours, the wonderous smells, the alluring people. Instead, I smirk and reply,

I drank from a dirty Coke bottle yesterday

You did not

I did. I reckon approximately 5000 people have sucked from it before me

I need proof

Sorry, this is the only proof I have

I turn the camera to selfie mode and take a quick snap of me in a ruby-coloured robe splayed atop my bejewelled bed. I caption it: **busy lavishing here now**

I'm surprised you're happy with your head that close to the toilet bowl

Wes's message makes me simultaneously laugh and snap back up to a seated position.

What was that 'fact' you used to quote about poo particles? he says.

That they can spread up to a three-metre radius, I type, rolling off the bed to shut the bathroom door that's barely half a metre away. I catch sight of my reflection in the bedroom mirror. My hair rivals one of those pet alfalfa grass heads I made with Dad as a kid. I'll need more time to freshen up than I thought.

I better run, I say. **I'm due in the dining car with Markus shortly**

Oooh the dining car with Markus. How fa-ancy

I'm about to shoot back something about him sounding jealous when my phone pings with another message.

Enjoy!

Relief floods my body. I really don't want to encourage any flirtation. I'm glad I let him know that I'm here, but there's no need to prolong the conversation unnecessarily – or take it in a direction I don't want it to go.

Thanks Wes, I will

In my hand-me-down Blossoms' iridescent blue maxi dress, I unintentionally match the aesthetic of the plush peacock-themed dining car. Markus, who is looking especially handsome in a khaki button-down, also complements the decor. We are seated at one of the intimate tables, separated by a stately light sconce bathing the white linen tablecloth, polished cutlery, fine crockery and glistening wine glasses in a warm glow.

It's like we've walked straight onto the set of *The Darjeeling Limited,* with couples seated two-by-two like a refined Noah's Ark – except we're not a couple.

A carafe of red wine is placed down on the table in front of us.

Markus swivels in his chair to catch the waiter. 'No wine for us, thank you.'

But they've already glided to the next table.

He turns back to me and shrugs. 'Sorry. It must come with the dinner package. We'll get you another drink.'

I wave his words away. 'It's fine. I don't mind.' I nudge my wine glass towards him. It's a rash decision, but for some reason it feels right.

Markus pours, unaware of the true significance of the moment. I watch excitedly as the viscous red liquid glugs into the crystal glass, aromatic fruit flavours and heady tannins stirring my tastebuds.

The wine slides down my throat like ice-cold water after a run, except it's a burst of toe-curling warmth. How have I gone six years without drinking this nectar of the gods? I suddenly feel very silly.

It's a *table d'hôte* menu, which means our only job is to nurse our wines as we're served cloche after cloche of the most magnificent food I think I've ever tasted: signature delicacies like paneer curry, rogan josh and vindaloo (no meat for Markus) accompanied by crispy papadums with mango chutney, mint yoghurt and lime pickles.

'Delicious!' I exclaim as our attentive, white-gloved butler clears our plates. 'I can't believe *Markus & Pup* paid for all of this. They must really value you.'

'Mmmm.' Markus's response is non-committal. I wonder if he's getting nervous about the filming.

'You're going to do great,' I say.

It's too dark to be certain, but it looks like his eyes are glistening – like he's about to cry.

'Thanks, Rosie.' He doesn't look directly at me.

I finish the last of my wine with a final lingering sip and fall into a comfortable silence, the gentle murmur of conversation and tap-tapping of knives and forks on fancy plates from the tables around us our only soundtrack. The carriage sways lightly as we round a corner. It's a shame we're missing out on the spectacular landscape outside.

'Do you think there's anyone hitching a ride on the roof?' I ask Markus, breaking the quiet.

He shrugs. 'Maybe.'

I'm disappointed that he's not more forthcoming. I was eager to make a game out of imagining who might be up there admiring the starry sky.

'Long train trips always remind me of the *Before* movies,' I continue. 'Although I'm sure this amazing train is worlds apart from Eurail. Have you seen those movies?

'No. I don't think I have.'

Oh.

I thought Markus might be up for a fun discussion about one of the most enduring love stories in cinematic history, and whether it's the content of Jesse and Céline's conversations, the charming setting, or the ticking clock that intensifies their connection. No matter. I'll just fill him in . . .

'Well, they're incredibly romantic. Two strangers meet on a train, disembark together, and spend one perfect night exploring Vienna and falling in love. In the next movie, they meet up again – nine years later – and . . .' I trail off as a strange look crosses Markus's face.

Is it confusion? Boredom?

'Ethan Hawke?' I offer just as it dawns on me the look is one of affection.

'It's not ringing any bells,' he says, eyes not leaving mine.

He's staring at me so intensely now that I bump the table and almost knock over my wine glass.

'Listen, Rosie.'

'Yes?' I say shakily.

'I have to come clean about something.'

God, what now? I was truly enjoying myself.

'It wasn't *Markus & Pup* that funded this trip,' he blurts. 'It was me. The studio is taking care of the show's production costs, but it was up to me to get myself here and pay for the accommodation and food and all of this . . .' He gestures to the opulence surrounding us.

'Oh, right, okay.' My mind is racing, trying to process what this means. 'So you paid for me?' I ask carefully.

'Yes.'

'But why?' I don't know if the sudden warmth that springs to my cheeks is from shock or confusion. There's possibly even a part of me that's flattered.

Markus's eyes dart around the carriage, before settling back on me. 'Because I wanted you here with me,' he says.

Chapter Twenty-Two

If the Maharajas Express was the fancy, gastronomic entree, then Kindred Spirit is humble, farm-to-table fare. We arrived here late last night after disembarking at the train station in Kerala and taking a bumpy hour-long van ride to the sanctuary.

We each have a round freestanding hut with a thatched grass roof. Inside is a bed on a bamboo frame with a mosquito net and not much else – definitely no minibar. I love it.

It's mid-morning, but Markus has been filming for hours already. I'd woken to the sound of the tap running in the bathroom next door. I'd lain in bed imagining Markus's large form folded over the tiny clay sink as he brushed his perfect teeth with bottled water.

I bet he cares for his teeth the same way he cares for animals. The same way he seems to care for me.

Once awake, I'd tossed and turned but couldn't get back to sleep. Hardly surprising given the events of the last thirty-six hours. The thing about Markus's admission about financing our entire trip was that it didn't seem like he was boasting or grandstanding. Not like the Markus who had flowers delivered to me at his own house. In a way, his generosity didn't seem like the biggest deal – it felt as natural as handing me a coffee.

Yesterday, after waking at dawn to the first light streaming through my window, I'd wondered if I should pack and get off the train at the next stop. But I'd decided to stay – to test the mood. And we'd had fun. The majority of the day was spent playing board games with Markus in the Rajah Club lounge carriage. We learnt how to play Ludo while drinking more red wine, our hands occasionally brushing while moving our playing tokens across the board.

It's midday when I finally emerge from my hut to find the sun high in the sky. It's different from the dust-blotted sun of Mumbai, with a clear, mellow glow. The sanctuary is a nature-lover's delight. I'm yet to sight an elephant, but I can already understand Markus's passion for Kindred Spirit. Here, you can spend your days interacting with elephants, playing, feeding and bathing them. Ride down the river in a bamboo raft, or simply float away in a tube without a care in the world. Go trekking on endless trails that lead to secret waterfalls and beautiful vistas and, at the end of the day, gather around the fire pit while gazing up at a sky full of stars. A hidden paradise so remote that it is inaccessible by car – we'd been collected from the main road on motorbikes, our luggage and radio equipment travelling behind us in their own private convoy.

But with all of this wonderful seclusion, I am worried about the lack of broadcast facilities. Cedric has been assured that the sanctuary is equipped with a modern education centre with fast wifi, but considering I don't even have power in my hut I'm having difficulty picturing it. It would be remiss of me not to go and check it out ahead of our scheduled interview in a couple of hours.

I walk to the bamboo entrance. It's unattended. We've been advised to only travel chaperoned.

'Hello?' I call out.

There's no response. I hesitate for a moment before deciding to continue on unaccompanied towards the lights flashing in the distance. They blink in time with the swaying palm trees.

I find myself enjoying the quiet stroll, until the trodden grass path comes to an abrupt end, and I'm faced with a wall of reeds two metres high. I swat away a mozzie as I push my way through the wilderness, batting it down with dramatic scissor-chop hand movements. Thank goodness I'm in my activewear and not in any of Naomi's fancy threads. I conquer the last of the grass and emerge into a flatter, savannah-like landscape of rolling grasslands, scattered shrubs and a few isolated palm trees. I've completely lost sight of the lights, but I must be close now.

I step out into the clearing and straight into an elephant. 'Shit.'

My forehead hits its swaying backside with a giant thud. Its butt is thick, leathery and hairy. The coarse hairs prick at my cheek. I freeze. I'm sure I stop breathing for a moment. This creature is huge. I don't know whether to run for my life or remain completely still. My head throbs where I've made contact with its wrinkly butt. Luckily, the elephant isn't the least bit interested in me and continues moving steadily in the opposite direction, completely unfazed.

Phew. That was a close call.

I hurry towards the middle of the clearing.

'Out of the way, girl!' a gruff voice yells.

I've been so focused on my elephant encounter that I haven't even noticed the small group of people standing two-hundred metres away. They're dressed in khaki and huddled around cameras. Markus is standing in front of the cameras.

'Did you hear me? Move!' A man wielding a boom mic is screaming at me. There must be more elephants headed this way. I look around, frantically seeking refuge.

'Where should I go?' I yell back, heart pumping in my chest. Is this how I'm going to die?

'I don't care, lady. Scram!' There's no mistaking his tone. He doesn't give two shits about me or my safety.

'You're in the shot, Rosie.' Markus's voice is panicked and slightly raised, but he's not yelling.

The boom-mic man looks from my desperate expression back to Markus. His face blooms red and he presses his free hand to his temple. 'Is this your little girlfriend, Markus? Explains a few things, doesn't it? Distracted much?' he spits.

'Markus is not –'

'Rosie's just –'

Markus and I respond simultaneously, but boom-mic guy cuts us off.

'Whatever. I really don't give a shit. All I know is that we've been here for hours, and I've gotten fuck all. Just get out of here!' There's fire in his eyes.

'Ah, oh . . . y–yes.' I drop to the ground and crawl to the periphery near where the main group is standing. I stand and brush the dirt off my knees. No one acknowledges my presence.

'*Markus & Elephant*. Take TWENTY-SEVEN.'

'G'day, Dr Markus Abrahams here, coming to you live from – ah – India. We're – ah – down here – ah – at the Kindred Spirit Elephant Conservation Centre and I'm going to take you to – ah – see some of the beautiful animals.' I think he's paused more than he's spoken. And he does a strange pointy finger dancing action while he speaks. He's like a Wiggle in khaki. It's difficult to watch.

Boom-mic guy looks furious. Still, the camera keeps rolling.

'*Markus & Pup* – sorry, I mean, *Markus & Elephant* – are proud supporters of the elephant conservation project.' Again with the weird finger.

'Cut, cut, cut, cut, cut, cut!' boom-mic man yells.

Markus's eyes bulge in terror.

I break away from the group and shuffle over to the lone palm tree, pressing myself against its trunk. I don't want to be responsible for fuelling any further fury.

'I'm sorry, Rick. I really am trying.' Markus's voice rattles. His face is bright red.

Even from my new vantage point under the tree, I can see beads of sweat pooling on his forehead. I have a sudden urge to rush over and give him a hug. Instead, a woman in a khaki skirt hurries forward with a make-up compact and starts dabbing at his face.

'Maybe we could bring in the elephants now? I think that would help put me at ease a little.' Markus says as the woman blots around his mouth.

'I've already told you, Markus. I don't want those damn creatures in shot until you bloody well know what you're doing. At this rate you're not going to get within a foot of them all week. I'll green screen them in if I have to!' Rick's threat seems legit.

Markus looks miserable. 'I understand. I'm sure I can improve. In fact, I know I can. Should we take it from the top?'

'Fourteen shoot days. Fourteen sunrises. That's all we have. Are you getting that through your extremely attractive but extremely thick head? You've successfully wasted one. You better not burn another.' Rick isn't pulling any punches.

'I won't.' Markus hangs his head.

I wish I could call Markus over and remind him of how much his fans love him and all the exposure he's giving the sanctuary. A few days ago, I never would have admitted that to him, but it seems the craziness of India has wiped our slate completely clean.

'Maybe it's the jet lag?'

Shit, shit, shit. I did not mean to say that out loud.

Rick swings around to face me. He looks at me like I'm a piece of loo paper stuck to his shoe.

'Get the girlfriend out of here. Nowwwwwwww!' he bellows.

I half expect two burly men to emerge from the bushes, scoop me up and drag me off set with arms and legs kicking. Instead, a slight man with a moustache and clipboard approaches.

'You heard Rick. You have to leave.'

I'm about to fall into step with my escort when Markus speaks up again.

'Rosie's my radio co-host. She's here to record the show with me. You guys know about that. It's in my contract.'

It's sweet of Markus to defend my honour, but not at all wise considering the precarious position he's currently in. I can tell by the twisting of Rick's face that it's time to make myself scarce.

I mouth 'good luck' to Markus and then head off in what I hope is the direction of the education centre-slash-radio studio, with one eye on the lookout for elephant butts.

Chapter Twenty-Three

How was your romantic dining car experience?

As soon I step foot inside the education centre, my phone pings with a message from Wes. Some texts from Pen also pop up, so I push my mobile back deep into my pocket.

I scan the room looking for confirmation that we'll be fine recording here later, my eyes taking in the adorable elephant pictures covering the walls – elephants bathing in rivers, trunk-tussling and rolling in mud.

Bingo! I breathe out a sigh of relief as my eyes land on our radio equipment, which is laid out neatly in one of the far corners. I'm not sure who or what Ceddie organised to get us all set up; he just promised it would be sorted. Now that I know it is, I can relax a little. I walk over to a poster labelled 'Trunkload of Truths' and proceed to read:

Elephants have the largest brain of any land animal.

The biggest elephant on record weighed 10,886 kilograms.

Elephants eat between 149 and 169 kilograms of vegetation daily.

My stomach grumbles at the last fact, reminding me that I skipped breakfast.

After a quick Zoom with Stacey to ensure I know the right buttons to press, Aisha, the sweet Kindred Spirit attendant who had checked us in yesterday (and told us not to go anywhere unaccompanied – whoops!) sticks her head in and offers to organise a plate of fresh fruit. I don't want to have to traipse back through that film set so I accept eagerly. I highly doubt Rick has let Markus stop for a bite to eat, so at least there will be something for him here.

The food arrives and I feast on wedges of papaya and guava before trying some mangosteen. The white flesh beneath the hard, purple skin has a delicious, delicate flavour that I can't quite put my finger on – it's like peach and lychee in one. Once I'm done, my sticky fingers retrieve my phone from my pocket.

I swipe to delete Penny's messages then click to reply to Wes.

It was very romantic thank you very much

One minute later, I have a reply.

More romantic than our dates?

I grin as I type. **What the $7 movies and Cokes smuggled in from Coles?**

You loved it

He's right, I did. It wasn't often I even made it through the entire movie without slumping on his shoulder and falling asleep. He'd had a special way of making me feel safe like no one other than my dad did.

Remember when we went to see the entire Before trilogy at the Ritz and you faceplanted into your popcorn? I don't know how we ever thought you could sit through 300 minutes of movie . . .

I gasp. **I was just talking about those movies!** I punch the keys enthusiastically.

With Dr Perfect?
With Markus, yes

He definitely sounds jealous. Imagine if I told him that Markus had paid for me to be here. It sounds ridiculous in my head, like I have a sugar daddy or something. Even though, for reasons I can't fully explain, it doesn't feel ridiculous.

I think I appreciate those movies more now, Wes types.
Really? In what way?
I love that nine years later, they meet back up and it's like no time has passed. It's a natural continuation of an inevitable love story

My breath catches in my throat. Even though we've only been broken up for six years, I don't have to be an English lit major to decode his subtext.

But they didn't have the history that we did, I think.

Except Jesse is married to someone else, I type instead. And everything is pretty grim by the last movie
Shhh Rosie. Spoiler!

It's not a spoiler if you've seen the movies. I pause to wipe my sticky fingers on my pants. They're getting stuck to the screen. Anyway, how are you? How's the painting going?

Great actually. Feeling super inspired lately. Creating lots of new stuff. I'm not sleeping much ☺

That's amazing, Wes! I mean the inspired part, not the lack of sleep. Where are you now?

Haha thanks. I got a gig painting a little something at a pub near Ballina – so Big Prawn, here I come!

My stomach flutters as I think of the big, beady eye peering through the window at Putt Putt Planet as Wes and I struck up the beginnings of our new friendship. At the time, I remember thinking it would be impossible for us to achieve – yet here we are.

Btw Bee says hi. Jo gave her the week off, so she decided to jump in the HiLux and come with me

The message catches me slightly off guard. I didn't realise they'd become friendly. Bee hadn't even really known who he was at the Paint & Pinot night. I wonder when that changed? Anyway, not my business. But I still can't help fishing for more information.

I hope she's a better motel buddy than me

Wait. Am I the one who's jealous now?

Let's just say I haven't needed to pull out my cleaning kit

Ouch. Okay, that stung. I was half-hoping he'd say they're staying in some fancy hotel – and somehow also confirm they are in two separate rooms. I love Bee – perhaps that's the problem. I can see how Wes would also enjoy her quirky personality, but I don't like the thought of her in the passenger seat of the HiLux. Completely irrational given that I haven't sat there myself in years.

I'm so caught up with our text convo that I don't notice the time until Aisha re-enters the room with a tray holding two silver brewing pots.

'I brought chai. For you, Miss Rosie, and Mr Markus. I thought you might like it for your show.'

Shit. Is it that time already? I double-check my phone. It's 1.50 pm. This isn't like me at all.

Where's Markus? We're due to interview William Bunker, the principal of Mudgee High, at 2 pm. It was impossible to line up, so Cedric will be livid if we miss it. I suspect Mr Bunker knows we won't be focusing on the sausage sizzle at the school Open Day, but rather on the recent alleged unfair dismissal of pregnant teacher Jenny Lam. Cedric wanted Markus to be part of the discussion – to have a male perspective to balance out my 'passionate' approach. I guess it's obvious I've already made up my mind about the situation.

I glance out the window at the dense green foliage. For all I know, Rick could have Markus in a headlock somewhere deep in the jungle. It's pointless texting and there's no time to send someone to fetch him. I'll have to go it alone. RIP journalistic objectivity.

What's the update on your dad? I hope he's still on the mend?

Another message from Wes flashes up on screen, and with it comes a crazy idea.

Wes . . . What are you doing right now?

By the time I've dialled Wes in (thank God for Stacey's earlier tutelage), we're only ten minutes late to the interview with Mr Bunker. I'm glad Wes is here – and that I'm on the other side of the world. Otherwise, I think I would have had difficulty keeping my hands from Mr Bunker's neck, because William Bunker is in need of a good throttling. It doesn't matter how many times I explain that taking time off work for morning sickness isn't the same as being 'unreliable', he doesn't hear me – or chooses not to. I'm incredibly frustrated by the time Mr Bunker hangs up. I hope that Ms Lam does decide to further her complaint.

Wes does a good job of keeping the conversation from getting too heated in his usual laid-back way. I can't help but wonder if Bee is lurking in the background somewhere.

Markus strides through the door just as we're about to move onto the next segment. He mouths 'sorry' to me as he takes a seat, secures his headphones then jumps straight in with no stuttering. 'Hi, everyone, Dr Markus Abrahams here.'

He must have dosed up on Valium after his morning shoot with Rick.

'Glad you could join us, Markus.' Wes's voice snarks through the speakers in a very unmeasured, un-Wes-like tone. Mr Bunker obviously wound him up more than I realised.

Markus looks confused at the unfamiliar voice.

'Markus, Wes is a friend who joined me for a, shall we say, "colourful" discussion with Mr Bunker. But I think our listeners are ready to put that behind us and hear what we've gotten up to so far here in India,' I explain.

'Thanks, Wes. I'm sure Rosie and I can take it from here,' Markus responds.

'Oh, I'm more than happy to stay on the air, Dr Perfect,' Wes scoffs.

Markus ignores Wes and launches in with a rundown of his day 'filming with elephants'. Everything is given a rose-coloured tint and there's no mention of Rick – although beneath his smooth tones are hints of rattled confidence. At least he hasn't lost his voice.

Before Markus finishes, Wes jumps in with a completely unrelated, yet charming, story about Andy Warhol's love of animals. Apparently, he had a small dog named Archie. They were so close that he accompanied Warhol to interviews, and Warhol would deflect questions to his little sausage dog if he didn't want to answer. I think it's sweet of Wes to try to conjure up some animal-related content. I'm not sure Cedric will feel the same way. At least with the pre-recording, most of this can be left on the cutting-room floor.

Markus interrupts Wes as he's describing how Warhol would hand-feed Archie cucumber sandwiches and starts recounting the story of Squash's close call. Thankfully, he frames it in a way that doesn't make me sound like an irresponsible pet parent. He does mention that it was a painting Squash ingested, but he doesn't go into any detail. I wonder if Wes makes the connection to his gifted peace posie.

Wes punctuates Markus's story with loud commentary. *'And what did you do then, Dr Perfect?'*

It feels like I'm in the middle of some sort of showdown. What beef could they possibly have with each other? They haven't even met. As amusing as I'm finding this battle of egos, I need to regain some order.

'Alrighty, boys, are we all done here? I think we've had enough story time.'

'Agree–,' Wes's voice crackles through my headphones, before his line goes dead.

'Bugger. We seem to have lost Wes,' Markus announces a little too gleefully.

'Mangosteen?' I offer Markus the platter of colourful fruit once we've finished recording. I've pushed us to record some extra time so Cedric and Stacey will have plenty of material to work with. 'There was chai too, but I think it's gone cold.'

'Thanks, Rosie.' He smiles weakly, selects a piece of fruit and then drops down onto a beanbag. 'I'm sorry I was late.' A hand rubs the back of his neck as he sucks on his piece of mangosteen. His pants have ridden up above his tan boots to reveal bare ankles. The top button of his blue linen shirt is undone and there's a hint of dark chest hair. My eyes follow the trail of hair to where it's contained by shirt buttons at the top of his he-vage.

'Don't worry about it. It sounded rough out there. Speaking of, how did the rest of the morning go?' I may as well address the proverbial elephant in the room.

'It was terrible. I don't think Rick got anything decent,' he says with a laugh. It's one of those manic laughs that's no doubt stopping him from curling up into the foetal position.

I drop down next to him, but I don't judge the distance well and have a near miss with his lap.

Markus leans back, resting his broad shoulders against our desk. He sighs deeply as he chews the last of his fruit, the sharp intake of breath deepening his cheekbones. Disillusionment suits him.

'What was I even thinking, Rosie? I thought I could do something truly meaningful here, but it's all about the optics. No one cares about the elephants. I didn't even get to see Eddie.'

'Give it time, Markus. You'll get it.'

'Only thirteen sunrises to go,' Markus mocks Rick's tyrannical bark.

'Try not to get ahead of yourself. Tomorrow is a new day. I can handle everything on the radio show front so you can focus on filming. If *Markus & Elephant* isn't getting the message out there, then *Markus & Rosie* sure as hell will!' Markus has been giving it his all, and I want him to know that he has my support.

'Markus and Rosie. I like the sound of that.' Markus's eyes are on me. 'You really are great, Rosie.'

His gaze hasn't faltered. It's the same intense stare from the dining car, but this time I'm conscious that our bodies are mere centimetres apart.

Heat swiftly rises to my head.

'It's nothing. Really,' I squeak, feeling my cheeks redden.

'I mean it. Thank you,' he says, voice hoarse, eyes smoky. 'I feel more like myself with you than I have in such a long time.'

His head draws closer.

'I–I–I'm glad,' I stammer.

'It's like you give me this calm. When I'm around you, I almost feel like I don't even need my pills anymore . . .' he murmurs.

My body is suddenly buzzing in anticipation.

Markus's mouth travels the remaining distance to mine. Just as he's about to make contact, he whispers, 'Can I kiss you?'

I nod.

The delicate taste of mangosteen still hangs on his lips. I try to switch off my brain as our kiss deepens. This time it's our tongues, not our feet, doing all the exploring.

When we eventually pull apart, Markus is beaming, his pearly whites on full display. It occurs to me that they're the same shade as the marble of Ganesha's temple.

'Well, that was unexpected, wasn't it?' he says.

'Just a little.' I laugh nervously. My brain is still struggling to catch up with my racing heart and tingling lips. I'm going to need some time to process this.

'Gahhhh,' he groans. 'I guess we should get going. I really don't want to, but I should get back to Rick.' He dips his head to give me another peck on my lips. 'To be continued?'

'Sure,' I say.

Markus reluctantly pulls himself to his feet and extends an arm to me. 'Shall we?'

As we make our way hand-in-hand out the door, I catch my reflection in the glass of one of the elephant photos. There's a flush to my cheeks, and my frizzy hair has returned to its Einstein-wild state. My eyes are so bright that I can no longer see the yellow pee spots.

Chapter Twenty-Four

'Yowchie!'

The shallow water that laps up over my ankles is icy cold.

'Watch out, Rosie. There'll be hell to pay if you go drowning their tucker!' Markus calls to me from a few metres downstream.

Hungry trunks wriggle in front of me, and two sets of small eyes focus on the baskets full of bananas and watermelon in my hands. Just a short while ago I was running scared of these giants and now, I'm willingly walking towards them. Willingly walking towards the elephants – and Markus.

I wasn't sure what would happen after our kiss, if we'd ignore it and get on with things, or if we'd fall longingly into each other's arms. We've landed somewhere in between.

It is becoming harder and harder to deny the sweet stretch in Markus's too-tight pants. I no longer think of Markus as that egotistical stranger I met weeks ago, but a generous, caring person. I haven't felt this level of comfort with a man

I'm attracted to in a long while. Perhaps it's because I haven't allowed it, keeping my guard up to prevent heartbreak.

We'd agreed to take things slow, so I've spent the last couple of nights alone, tossing and turning in my bamboo bed. Who knows if it will even eventuate into anything serious? But it feels too good to put a stop to it now.

I'm also fairly certain that I've finally worked Markus out.

Anxiety comes in all forms, and it makes complete sense that Markus's 'charms' had developed as a sort of defence mechanism to handle the limelight – distorting and trans-forming who he really is. I'd been quick to judge him. His smarmy smiles and ridiculous gestures were made all the more palatable now that I understood them. Not that I've witnessed any of that lately. India seems to have a grounding effect on him. Or perhaps – as he's remarked himself – it's me.

But by all accounts, Rick still isn't happy. Markus has been filming and re-filming. Luckily I've managed to whisk him away to enjoy Kindred by night, doing all the cheesy stuff that PG rom-coms are made of, like walking hand-in-hand under the moonlight and taking it in turns to feed each other spoonfuls of dessert. Banana halwa is our favourite.

Tonight, we're feeding Eddie and the rest of his herd. I pick my way carefully over the slippery stones towards Markus. He's standing between Eddie and another elephant, with a long-handled scrubbing brush in hand – and his shirt off.

His pecs are defined, but not in a gross, steroidy way. They're supported by the ripples that make up his abdomen, as defined as the crescent-shaped peaks in the fast-flowing river. Yes, he's basically a clean-cut Tarzan (all that's missing is a tasselled loincloth around his waist), but I'm not about to get swept up in the tide of his hotness. I'm after more than an amazing body.

His manly chest – with its perfectly tame dark mane – has become somewhat of a familiar sight around Kindred. The fierce humidity here makes clothing a sticky plight, so when not in khaki and trembling in front of the camera, it's been shirts off.

I wade deeper into the river; the freezing water sends chills through my entire body but does little to sedate my burning desire. Markus is like a delicious birthday cake I've cut into. I've licked the frosting from the dirty knife, and now I'm waiting patiently for my piece.

Even after such a short amount of time, I feel a certain claim over that bare chest. I don't know how I'll go back home, with all of the Dr Markus Abrahams groupies and trending hashtags. That's if we even last that long. Who knows what Markus is thinking?

I continue wading towards him, admiring his muscled arm as he works the brush and scratches at Eddie's expansive leathery back. I'm knee-deep in the murky water when the burning finally subsides. I've also acclimatised to the temperature, and the water now feels refreshing after a day spent in the muggy heat.

I tuck my dress up into my swimmers so it doesn't get too muddy. I hope Markus notices the extra bronze to my leg. The jungle surroundings have meant an improvised beauty regimen. Luckily, I thought to pack some tinted sun cream, which I've applied liberally to freshly shaven legs.

I step up onto a mossy stone beside Markus, steadying myself with a hand on one of his broad shoulders.

Just as I find my balance, Eddie's trunk juts out at me, whacking the basket of fruit with force and almost sending it – and me – flying. Markus's arm instantly goes around me.

'Careful!' Markus berates Eddie. 'Rosie is precious cargo.'

A renewed warmth trickles through my body, but this time it's closer to my heart.

He sets me back on my rock, as effortlessly as moving a chess piece, and waits for my reassuring smile before returning to his scrubbing.

Eddie and his mate's appetites are endless, but unfortunately my baskets of fruit are not. They're emptied in about two minutes flat, with the last piece of watermelon cradled and scooped into Eddie's mouth before Markus has a chance to instruct me on what to do next. I'm not exactly in my element.

The empty baskets don't deter them, and they sniff for more. I back away slowly. One 'harmless' nudge and I'm likely to end up face first in the Periyar River.

'Sorry, boys, I'm all out. Are they even both males? I don't know why I assumed that.'

Markus has moved to scrub the mud off the other side of Eddie, so I can no longer see his face, only his muscular legs.

'Spot on, Rosie. They're brothers.'

'Awww. That's sweet.'

'They're a formidable pair – had a tough start to life.' Markus ducks back under Eddie's large body and moves next to the other elephant. 'Eric here has had it particularly rough. I'm not sure if you can tell, but one of his back legs is a bit wonky.'

Now that he's pointed it out, I can see that the back leg closest to me is a little shorter than the others. As if sensing that we're talking about him, Eric tilts his head to look at me. A watery, blackened eye meets mine. I see sadness. He's staring so intensely, like he's reading my mind or trying to send me a subliminal message. His eye becomes glassier as we stare but, just when I think the wetness is about to spill over into a fat tear and roll down his leathery cheek, a wrinkled lid closes over and our trance is broken. I'm left staring at an enviable set of thick lashes.

'Both Eddie and Eric were separated from their mother as infants, crammed into crates, gouged with bullhooks and beaten mercilessly. They were lucky to survive, but they're not without their scars. We found Eddie first – Eric was only rescued a few months ago. That's why he's a bit more tentative.'

'How horrible!'

Markus continues to scrub as he talks. 'Unfortunately, being taken from their mother at such a young age means they missed out on invaluable survival skills. During their early years, calves follow their mother everywhere to feed and learn everything they need. These poor guys never really got that chance, which means a life of captivity – they'd never survive out in the wild. Sadly, they would have spent longer in their mother's belly than with her in the outside world . . .'

Perhaps this is what I'd felt between Eric and I – the silent pain of missed time with our mothers. Although, I'm sure Eddie and Eric were very much wanted. I shudder as I imagine their mother being tranquillised, roped and dragged away from her calves. Mine willingly walked. It's hard to know which scenario is sadder.

I plunge my hand into the water. Like a slap to the face, the chill pulls me out of my dark thoughts and back to the river. It's still too soon to open up to Markus about Mum. I'm not ready to go there.

I wade towards the bucket of soapy water balanced on the rocky ledge next to me. 'Can I help you wash them?'

I can't do anything to change what happened to them, but I feel like I need to do *something* to help now – even if it's just giving a good back scrub.

'Look at you go, Rosie.'

Markus grins at me like a proud sensei. It's funny how differently I feel about that smile now compared to that first time at Lesters.

'Normally that would be totally fine, but we're trying to minimise any forced human interactions with Eric until he's all settled in. Professional handlers only, unfortunately. Eddie is also extremely protective of his brother, so I'm not sure how he'd react.'

'That makes sense,' I say.

Duh. Just because I'm finally familiar with Squash's preferred Delightful Tuna Gourmet flavour doesn't make me instantly qualified to handle an elephant. Actually, Squash has two favourite flavours. I hope Ceddie is alternating them each morning.

'It's amazing that they were reunited,' I say.

'Yes, we got really lucky. It was Eddie who helped us make the connection.'

'What do you mean?'

'When Eric first arrived, Eddie wouldn't leave him alone. He'd frequently be by his side, always nudging him and poking him gently with his tusks. We started to have our suspicions, so we had them tested and it was a match!'

If only Markus could bring this enthusiasm on set, he'd have no issues with Rick.

'That's lovely. Are you covering their story in the documentary?'

'No, unfortunately not. Rick thinks it's best to stick to the science.'

'Ah, that's a shame.'

'Yeah.' Markus hangs his head and I sense the mood beginning to shift.

'Do you have any siblings?' I ask, an attempt to redirect the conversation.

The long handle of the scrubbing brush slips though Markus's fingers and falls into the river, making a big splash. Markus snaps into action and dives into the water before it can sink to the bottom or be swept away by the current.

'Got it!' He stands back up triumphantly, his chest glistening with droplets caught in his body hair. He's transformed from Tarzan into a hot water deity. 'Sorry, Rosie, were you asking me something?'

My question now feels redundant, but I'm keen to move beyond those washboard abs and learn as much about the real Dr Markus Abrahams as possible – especially since he's already proven to be somewhat of an enigma. I may know where he lives and how he takes his coffee, but not much more.

'I was wondering if you have any siblings? It's just learning that these two are brothers – it makes you think about how powerful that bond must have been for them to find each other again. I'm an only child, and I always wondered what it would be like to have a sibling.'

I think of Penny, who comes from a large family of eight and often referred to me as 'her sister of choice'. I'm sure she won't notice writing one less Christmas card this year.

'Um, yeah, same,' Markus says.

'Oh, really?'

I respond perhaps a little too eagerly, but I'm delighted to discover that our common ground stretches beyond physical attraction.

'Yup, it's only me.' He's speaking so softly that I can only just make out his words over the rushing water.

I've obviously hit on a sensitive topic.

It's silly to assume we grow out of our sensitivities as we get older, when we so often grow into them. I'd been too focused on being down a mother to have any hang-ups about being an only child. Sure, at times it would have been nice to have the camaraderie of a sister or brother, but mostly Dad and my self-made support system of Wes and the girls had been enough.

'Ah, I've heard it's not all that it's cracked up to be anyway – just lots of bullying and constant competition,' I continue.

Shut your mouth and change the subject, Rosie.

But I don't want to derail our conversation completely – not when we are teetering on the edge of something meaningful. Then again, I don't want to risk Markus asking about my mother.

A hiccup escapes from Eddie. It's not an adorable, delicate sound but more of a roaring, unsettled belch. I'm grateful that I'm a decent distance away, as I can tell from Markus's twisted face that there's an accompanying smell.

We both laugh, and Eric peels his eyes open then shuffles forward and curls a protective trunk around his brother's own trunk, forming a misshapen figure of eight pattern.

'Sorry Eric,' I address him. 'We're laughing with your brother – not at him. Actually, scrap that, we're laughing at him.'

I beam at Markus, and he responds with another howl. 'I wonder how good that fruit was? Elephants have been known to get a little tipsy from over-ripe fruit,' he says, attempting to pull himself together before succumbing to more peals of laughter. 'Have you ever seen a drunk elephant, Rosie?'

'Only Dumbo.'

Markus is now the one hiccupping.

Is that another thing he likes about me? That I make him laugh? Somehow, I've managed to put off analysing things too much, but at some point my brain is going to unwillingly dive into the inner workings of this coupling to try to decipher how it makes sense. The hot TV star vet with, well . . . me.

'You're the best, Rosie.'

'Um . . . thank you?'

'Seriously though, I know I've said it before but you're the one keeping me sane through this whole nightmare.'

His giggles are gone. Eddie and Eric are quiet, and we are left with the lull of the flowing river and chirps of cicadas high up in the trees. Being in the middle of a remote jungle makes it feel like we're the only two people on earth.

'Marrrrrrkuuussss!'

Rick's voice bounces off the rocky outcrops crowding the riverbank.

'Where in God's name are you? I need you for an evening shoot. Nowwww!'

'Shit!' There's panic in Markus's voice and he starts gathering up the washing things. He upends the scrubbing brush and gives both elephants a gentle tap from behind to get them moving back towards their night-time enclosure.

'Raincheck, Rosie?'

Chapter Twenty-Five

The soap suds drain away, and I groan inwardly as I catch myself pretending the milky bubbles have formed a heart shape. Who even am I? And what's happened to the unlucky-in-love Rosie? Not in my wildest dreams could I have imagined that I would be in India with my own radio show and a celebrity TV vet (and maybe soon-to-be boyfriend). Yet here I am.

They say that love finds you when you least expect it, and while it's definitely not love, maybe it could be one day. It's the most hopeful I've felt in years.

I've gone from despising Markus to wanting nothing more than for him to make *Markus & Elephant* a massive hit – for both his career and those poor elephants.

But at this point, that's going to take some kind of miracle. His performance still hasn't improved, and night shoots are continuing to make up for lost time. When Markus suggested that it may be best for me to leave for a few days to try to appease Rick, I was more than happy to oblige. Even though he keeps telling me what a calming influence I have on him, I know he doesn't need me as an extra distraction right now.

Which is why I've taken myself off to a local retreat for the weekend. I don't want to add to his – or Rick's – increasing stress. There'll be plenty of time to develop whatever is growing between us.

'Karma of Kerala' wasn't my first pick of retreats. It's smaller and not as conveniently located as its competitors – with a swampish rather than beachside vista – but it had last-minute availability. I wasn't about to spend the weekend holed up in the education centre reading ele-facts.

As I lather my body with the complimentary bar of Sandalwood soap, I picture Markus soapy and wet in the shower with me. I can all but see him standing in the steam of hot water as the soap lather gathers in the crevices of his muscular body. A sudden whoosh of water from the luxe shower head jolts me from my *Fifty Shades* moment as it spurts out at lightning speed onto the concrete shower floor. It already feels strange being away from my cold hut shower – and Markus.

Will we pick up where we left off once I'm back at Kindred? How about when we're back home in Mudgee? Does Markus even want something serious? It certainly feels that way, since he's the one who pursued me.

It's almost anti-climactic that there's no one to tell about him. I'm still deciding on the best approach with Cedric, and it's too early to say something to Dad – I don't want either of them getting carried away before I know what the future holds. I'd love nothing more than to dissect Markus's every look, touch and elephant fact with Penny, but that's obviously out of the question.

A sadness descends on me. There had never been any doubt in my mind that she'd be right there by my side when – *if* – love finally happened for me again, but things change. I'd come to terms with Mum not being there to watch me walk down the aisle long ago, but not my best friend.

Aisle? Don't be ridiculous, Rosie!

I've never been one to Pinterest my favourite boho wedding looks and DIY lolly buffets. I don't even enjoy watching *Say Yes to the Dress*. So why am I suddenly leap-frogging over our entire courtship and marrying us off? We haven't even gotten to second base. The scalding heat of the shower must be messing with my head.

My hands are completely shrivelled by the time I turn off the taps and step out of the warmth.

It's late afternoon once I've dried off, and I pull on a gym top and leggings and make my way downstairs to the Palm Room for a 5 pm Bikram yoga session. The room is as hot and sticky as downtown Mumbai. There are women contorted in every position – some in basic child poses, others in complex binds and headstands. There is an immense gulf between the limber young women in Lululemon yoga gear, rolling out rubber mats on the hardwood floors, and the ash-smeared older women wrapped in cheesecloth fabrics. I don't know where I fit in. I'm no pro yogi, but thanks to Ceddie I know just enough Vinyasa to not look like a complete idiot.

After an hour of profuse sweating, I return to my room feeling more grounded. I shower again, rearrange the toiletries so they're in neat rows on the counter and begin pacing the room in my bathrobe. Now what? It's another hour before dinner. I glare at my laptop, which is taunting me from the bed. Maybe I've watched *Eat, Pray, Love* too many times, but I was really expecting to have all of my devices confiscated at check-in for a mandated digital detox . . .

I check my inbox and answer a few work emails. There's nothing from Markus. No WhatsApp messages either. I try not to feel too disappointed. I've only been gone a few hours, and the whole point was to give him space. Hopefully, he's killing it and has returned to his confident *Markus & Pup* TV self. I don't want to be known as the girl responsible for the demise of Australia's favourite TV vet.

I spend another twenty minutes scrolling through Instagram before becoming aware of irresistible aromas drifting into my room – smoky onion, garlic and fragrant spices.

Finally, it's dinnertime.

The 'Jaipur' dining room is awash with pastel pink and completely fabulous. I'd read that Maharaja Ram Singh of Jaipur painted his whole city pink in colour to welcome guests, and this colour palette and hospitable sentiments have been embraced wholeheartedly at Karma of Kerala.

The food smells amazing. On offer is a row of bain-maries filled with vibrantly hued vegetables, curries and naan. A mustard-coloured dal bubbles away at the far station. The server piles my plate high with a medley of colour, until it's swimming in deliciousness.

Weighty plate in hand, I survey the room. There are a handful of lone women, some I recognise from yoga, dotted at each of the tables. I'm happy when I spot a free table in the corner of the room. We're not at one of those strict silent retreats so we're allowed to chat, but it feels good not to. One of my neighbours is loudly cracking pappadums in half and stuffing them into her mouth. The sound effects are as bad as a nail filer on public transport, but I do my best to block out the noise and focus on the delicious meal in front of me. *Less judgement, more namaste*, I think, as I shove a forkful of curry into my mouth. The sauce is thick and buttery.

I'm going in for another bite when a woman in a full-length red sari with gold beaded detail sidles up to my table.

'Chai?'

She sets a tray of teas on the table in front of me. Her hands are covered in intricate henna, and she has sets of coloured metal bangles up both arms.

Head bowed, she lines up four ramekins and starts pouring tea from the various silver pots. There's a scarf bundled around her head. As the liquid swishes into the cups, she looks up at me. 'Nut mylk?'

My fork crashes down onto my plate as our matching green eyes meet. Bright orange curry splatters up onto my T-shirt.

'Mum?!'

There's a flicker of recognition in her eyes before they glaze back over.

'Rosalie! What brings you to India?' She addresses me calmly, as though we chat regularly about the best way to launder our whites.

'Um, work . . .' I manage. My head is thumping. I glance over at the pappadum girl, willing her with everything in my aching post-Bikram body to glance in my direction and rescue me. I'm not prepared for this.

'Sounds like you're very successful then, dear.' She sets the teapot down alongside the ramekins and starts arranging some nutmeg and cinnamon sticks into an Instagrammable shot.

I take in the rounded nose and rosebud mouth of her focused face. Even after all of these years, it's like looking in the mirror. I can't see her frizzy hair under her faux turban. I push my own wild mane out of my eyes and wish I'd straightened it.

'What are *you* doing here?' I ask.

Is it possible that she's heard me on the radio and come looking for me? Markus isn't up to speed on all things estranged mother, so maybe she stopped by Kindred and he pointed her this way?

Her green eyes light up like the 'go' signal. 'I moved to India a few months ago to start Chai Me. Did you know chai is a superfood? It enhances the immune system, fights inflammation and has antioxidant properties. By the way, my name is Suni now, darling. A guru gave me my rightful name last year. It's supposed to bestow love, money and success.'

I'm sure my face is painted with disdain. I should inform her that I go by Rosie, and not Rosalie. Have done my entire life.

But her attention is no longer on me. She's digging around for something in her embroidered shoulder bag, perhaps trying to locate her newly issued birth certificate with 'Suni' typed in thick black lettering in the place of 'Marie'.

Mum stops fussing in her bag and moves in closer to my table. Oh God. Is she going to hug me?

'I'll quickly snap this for our socials. You know how it is, it's all content, content, content,' she trills as she leans over me and swipes on the iPhone that has materialised in her henna-ed hand.

Of course she's not trying to embrace me.

'So, what do you think?' she asks, still snapping away.

What could I possibly think? I haven't laid eyes on her for twenty years and now she wants my opinion on her new name? I couldn't care less.

'What blend is your favourite?'

Ah, she's still talking about the tea.

'We've sourced the loose leaves directly from local artisan farmers. The range includes masala, chocolate, Thai – every blend your heart could possibly desire. Best of all, it promotes weight loss. Drink our teas for a month and you're guaranteed to lose up to five kilograms. No more sweating it out at yoga. Shaun thinks Chai Me is going to be the next big thing. It was his idea to start promoting in retreats. I think it's genius. *He's* a genius; you must meet him.'

Shaun the schmuck must be her new bank account.

'What happened to Japan and the cars?' I croak.

'Keep up, Rosalie! I haven't done that in years. Entrepreneurship is fast-paced. You have to know when to pivot!'

She's schooling me as though I'm eight years old, and she never took an eternal leave of absence from motherhood.

Instead of exerting more energy controlling my reply, I take a sip of one of the teas. The liquid is too hot and burns my throat on its way down. I quickly shot the rest of the teas, spluttering as I force them down like a batch of warm oysters. I'll deal with my scalded tongue later; I just want this moment to be over. I can't believe I avoided the cherry blossoms all this time because I didn't want to risk seeing my mum, even by accident, yet I ran into her in India!

'So, what do you think?' she asks, eyes greedy and eager.

'They're fine.'

'Come on, Rosalie. Admit it, they're magic! You always were very picky.'

Please don't pretend to know a thing about me.

'So, what work do you do?' Mum starts neatly stacking the empty ramekins, her bangles tinkling like torturous wind chimes. She was clearly too concerned with firing off 'business opportunity' messages to ever bother reading my LinkedIn profile.

'I host a radio show.'

'Impressive! The apple really doesn't fall far from the tree, does it? I always hoped you'd be a mover and shaker like me. Keeps things interesting, doesn't it?' She winks.

I am nothing like you.

'I was just thinking about some radio advertising for

Chai Me. Isn't it funny how the universe works, delivering what you need exactly when you need it?' Mum exclaims.

I'm exactly what she needs? The irony of her words would be too much even for Shakespeare.

The dining room is now nearly empty. The pappadum girl must have left to join the after-dinner natural soap making workshop. I want to go and make soap.

'Rosalie?' Mum is staring at me expectantly.

'Yes?'

'I was just saying sorry for leaving.'

Wait, what? I must have misheard her.

'Sorry?' I ask, cautious.

'I'm apologising, Rosie.'

I clench my fists to stop myself from instinctively jamming my fingers in my ears to drown out her response. I need to hear this.

'I know there's lots of making up to be done . . .' she continues.

For years I've been adamant that I didn't want her anywhere near my life, but now that she's standing in front of me it's only right that I should at least hear her out. Perhaps Markus has softened me.

'Here you go.' Mum presses a Chai Me branded silver tin into my hands. 'It's Cinnamon Berry, blended with subtle notes of coriander and cumin, so the sweetness isn't too overwhelming.'

'You're giving me tea to say sorry?'

She has to be joking.

'Yes, I know it doesn't make up for everything, but I can arrange for some more boxes to be sent to you. It's from our premium range. And great for digestion,' she adds proudly.

'Thanks,' I say, quickly tucking the tin into my bag, expression and tone flat.

'It would be great if you could do a little plug for Chai Me on your show, too. That would be fantastic. Shaun and I . . .'

NO. I won't stand for a second more of this rubbish.

I push back my chair and stand. 'Namaste, Marie.'

'Wait, you're leaving, Rosalie? I thought we could chat about my radio marketing strategy.' Incredibly, she appears to be frustrated with me.

'We're done, Mum.' I look straight into her green eyes, then stride out of the dining room.

Chapter Twenty-Six

I don't want to go back to the emptiness of my room and my meticulously arranged toiletries.

I approach the lone groundsman who's crouched smoking behind the greenhouse and pay him five-hundred rupees for the rest of his pack.

Then, I climb the stairs to the hotel rooftop. I count them as I go: *one, two, three, four, five.* The intense concentration helps calm me.

But by the time I reach the top, I'm still shaking, and although it's late, the sun is still shining. *Ugh.* How dare it shine! I want a monsoon, or dark rain clouds violently rolling in, to match my mood. The sun demands participation in life – a picnic in the park, a beach walk. That is all well and good for the sun; it has Mother Nature guiding it through eclipses and global warming. I'm sick of the sun shining. I'm sick of trying to dance in the rain. I'm sick of pretending I have it all together.

I reach into my pocket and pull out the packet of Marlboros. I take a cigarette and light it. I inhale deeply. The taste is wretched, but I persist. With each puff I feel myself swelling with powerful defiance.

FUCK YOU.

SERIOUSLY, FUCK YOU.

I light up another and then another. Each curl of smoke proffers up yet another question that wisps away unanswered.

WHY DID YOU LEAVE?

DID YOU NOT LOVE ME?

It's the salty breeze whipping across the rooftop, not the nicotine, that eventually calms me. I take a few more puffs before stubbing out my final cigarette and sending it off the side of the building.

I'm left with incredible sadness. The paddy field below is quiet. Not a soul or cow as far as the eye can see.

I thought I didn't care. I was sure that I didn't. But in one interaction, the great wall I've spent two decades construct-ing has come crumbling down. Suddenly, that untouchable place I've bricked myself into isn't so untouchable. The dull pang in my abdomen that has been a constant companion is now a searing pain. I'd learnt how to protect it, how to disguise and ignore it, how to swallow it down so deeply that it didn't eat me up inside. But there's no running from it now. Resentment is the foundation of hatred, and I don't want that living anywhere inside me, even at scary deep-diving depths, skulking in the darkness where it can still be recovered. In the past, every time I felt it bubbling to the surface, I'd try stamping it out like a sick game of whack-a-mole.

My mum left.

I can wallow and wonder all I want, but I know I'll never understand. Even if I was literally able to crack open her brain and pick apart its contents with tweezers, it wouldn't give me the answers that I need. Maybe she's unwell. But that doesn't mean I have to be okay with her leaving. Because I'm not.

I'm not sure that I've ever admitted that before – even in my head.

This is too much to deal with on my own. I plunge my hand into my handbag. It brushes against something hard and unfamiliar. The tea. My hand springs back like it's touched a ticking bomb, then perseveres past the tin to my phone.

It's 7.30 pm. Markus is probably still filming. I'm sure he wouldn't mind a quick call, but Rick certainly would. And I don't know that it would end up being quick. After all, there's my whole messed-up relationship with Mum to fill him in on. I definitely don't want to worry Dad, so I message the only logical person.

Are you still awake? I just ran into Mum

I consider lighting another cigarette while I wait for Wes to reply. I'm reaching back into my pocket when my phone beeps.

What?! Please explain! Wait, hold up. Are you okay?

I'm fine. Well not really, but I will be

You always are, Rosie. But it's also okay not to be

I'm not sure how much truth there is in that. I was in pieces after our break-up. If it wasn't for Pen and Ange pulling me out of my spiral and dragging me to brunch, I probably would never have gotten over Wes.

I ran into her at this retreat in India

Wow. What did she say? Is she still living in Japan? Sorry, you're probably working through this all yourself

She's selling chai tea. Her new thing

I'm typing furiously, replies tumbling out of my fingers before they've even formed in my head.

This is huge, Rosie. How are you feeling? Bloody Marie. The things I want to say to that woman!

I can picture him on the other end of the phone, re-arranging his face into that special look seven-year-old Wes reserved for behind Mum's back – a face with crossed eyes and a sticky-outy tongue, the kind that meant if the wind changed, he'd be in real trouble.

I guess I'm in shock

It sounds fucked, Rosie

I exhale deeply then send another message.

It wasn't easy. I didn't say half of what I wanted to. None of it really

I'm sure you did just fine. You know how to hold your own

I let slip a sliver of a smile.

You mean like at the reunion?

Haha yeah. But seriously, please don't be hard on yourself. That's exactly what she wants

Thanks Wes. I know you get it . . . your dad was almost as bad

I'm probably overstepping by bringing up his dad. But I'm on a rooftop in the middle of India talking to my ex-boyfriend about my estranged mother, so I don't know that anything is off limits.

Actually, my old man passed away last year

Oh wow.

Gosh. I'm sorry. I had no idea

We always said our lives would be much easier if they were dead. Or if they never existed in the first place and we were simply dropped by storks or left at some ritzy orphanage where chores were optional – and I could bring Dad. But the reality is much different.

Thanks. Cancer got him in the end. And it's okay. I'm okay. It took him being on his deathbed to kinda accept me. That's why I came back home – to spend his final months with him, and to be there for Mum. He even apologised and told me that he wanted me to do what made me happy. He had a buyer lined up for Preston Imports and everything. You would never have believed it, Rosie

That's great, Wes

I can only imagine what that meant to him. It must be one of the reasons he's painting again. His dad never missed an opportunity to remind him of the starving-artist life. I hated seeing him give up on his dreams because of his closed-minded father.

Yeah. I didn't think that would ever happen. I still catch myself trying to impress him up there you know

I'm sure he's proud, Wes

Thanks, Rosie. Anyway, enough about me. Have you told Markus?

Why would he ask about Markus? Does he know that there's something going on between us? But he didn't refer to him as Dr Perfect . . . does that mean he no longer cares? The thought sends a disappointing thud hurtling to the pit of my stomach.

Not yet

I'm sure he'd say the same as me. Marie is a fool

I wonder how Wes would respond if I revealed that I haven't told Markus anything about my mum.

Suni

Sorry?

It's Suni now, not Marie. She changed her name

Oh God

Tell me about it. And you're right. I should tell Markus

I have the man of my dreams waiting for me back at Kindred. I'm not about to let my freak run-in with Mum/Marie/Suni ruin that.

Thanks, Wes

Any time Posie x

Chapter Twenty-Seven

It's good to be home – or as close to home as a straw hut in a remote part of India can get.

I left the retreat right away, but it's pitch black by the time I arrive back at Kindred.

Markus isn't expecting me back tonight, but hopefully he's still awake so we can drink a couple of mango lassis and talk through the shock I've just had. No more trying to handle things on my own.

The huts are arranged in a long row and mine is somewhere in the middle, I'm just not sure where. My plan is to get as close as possible and then hope that I eventually stumble on the right one.

I navigate the dark dirt path, giving a wide berth to the chorusing frogs in wayside puddles, and stop outside a hut that looks familiar. Who am I kidding? They all look like my hut.

'Hello,' I call out, straw rustling as I brush through the doorway.

For a few moments the world stands completely still. I close my eyes in case maybe, just maybe, this is a bad dream, and when I open them again the scene in front of me will have disappeared. After a few seconds, I manage to pry my eyes open and nausea hits in full force. The butter chicken curry – or maybe it's the chai – is churning in my guts. I think I'm going to be sick.

There, in all of his naked glory, bathed in the warm glow of the lone kerosene lamp, is Markus. With Eryka on top of him. Both appear to be chiselled from the same perfect rock, with their stellar physiques and not a spot of cellulite between them.

They freeze, horrified expressions plastered on both their faces, as I take a step into the room. Eryka instantly covers her hands over her perky breasts, while Markus tries to sit up, the exertion further deepening his six-pack.

The room is silent as they untangle themselves. Eryka wraps herself in the thin bedsheet then hands Markus a pillow. My throat itches, like there's an army building forces in there, readying itself to burst out on the attack.

'What the fuck is this?' I screech.

Markus climbs down from the bed, careful not to move his carefully positioned pillow, and puffs up his chest.

'It's not what you think. Actually, I'm not who you think,' he says evenly.

'What is *she* doing here?' I demand.

Have Eryka and Markus been hooking up this entire time? Could I really have been this stupid? I know we've only just started out but I really thought we were building something, and that despite his erratic behaviour, Markus was one of the good ones . . .

Eryka moves forward, sympathy etched on her face, and tries to embrace me. I dart sideways before she can touch me, ramming my hip into the bamboo bed frame.

Fuuuccckkk.

I breathe deeply, holding my stomach tightly as nausea gives it another violent whack. I try to temper the sickening waves with a steely expression.

'I'm sorry, Rosie. We never meant to hurt you.'

She seems genuinely distressed, which is evident from the one line that has formed on her normally crinkle-free forehead, above her flawlessly arched brows.

Who wouldn't want that sort of perfection? I mean, it's completely irresistible. But then why would Markus pretend with me? That's exactly why I was so suspicious in the first place. It didn't feel right that he'd pursue little old me over his model fiancée. I should have listened to my instincts. Why oh why had I changed my tune and allowed myself to start falling for him, when I could see plain as day that it didn't make any sense?

'Just give it to me straight, please.' I'm done with the game-playing.

Markus exchanges a glance with Eryka. Why isn't he in a rush to explain it all? It's Eryka who speaks again. 'It's really not what you think.'

Markus puts a reassuring arm around her waist. His hand cinches in the sheet, emphasising her enviable hourglass shape. She wears a bedsheet better than I wear a designer gown.

'We're together,' Eryka says simply.

And there it is. I stare at the dirt floor. If I had a shovel, I'd start digging. I'm horrified and slightly heartbroken all at once.

Eryka continues. 'What I'm trying to say is that *Chad* and I are together. This is Chad, Markus's twin brother.'

Whaaaat?

'Twin brother?' I squeak.

I'm having difficulty processing what she's saying.

Markus steps towards me and sticks out a hand, while the other one holds his pillow in place. 'Chad Abrahams, nice to formally meet you, gorgeous. I'm Markus's identical twin. Well, almost identical. Unlike Markus, I work out.'

I don't hurry to accept his outstretched hand, so he retracts it and flexes his bicep. His skin is baby smooth, not an arm or chest hair in sight.

'Chad!' Eryka chastises him in the same way she did at the fashion event. Except this time, with a 'new' name.

'You'll have to excuse him. We just flew in last night and the jet lag is obviously making him misbehave more than normal.'

My mind is racing.

'I don't know why my brother thought his stage fright would be suddenly cured. I should have come and done this gig from the start. Saving the day – and the network's money – yet again.'

For the first time since I entered the hut 'Markus' looks directly at me, and winks, transporting me straight back to the same narcissistic arsehole from my date at Lesters and the Scuttlebutt event.

'So, you're the real Dr Markus Abrahams? And your name is Chad?' I say slowly.

'Bingo.' Chad winks again.

'I'm so sorry, Rosie,' Eryka sounds exasperated. 'Don't listen to him, he's all bark. I know this is a lot to take in, but Chad is actually an actor. He's big in Poland – where we met. And he's not the real Dr Markus Abrahams. The one you've been doing your radio show with and – well – dating, is the real Dr Markus Abrahams. Chad put his career on hold to fly to Australia and take over when Markus started having his panic attacks, about a year or so ago.'

'Yes, so I'm currently carrying *Markus & Pup*. Which makes me the star,' Chad interjects, voice like honey. 'It was a mistake to step aside, even briefly. We've gone straight back to square one. I thought that finally having love in his life would get him back on track, so we could return to Poland sooner – but it was completely premature. Markus is in such a bad way that we were on a plane back to India a mere forty-eight hours after touching down in Warsaw!'

My head is spinning. I don't know what to think.

'W–w–what do you mean?' I stammer.

Eryka nudges him. 'Chad! You're scaring the poor girl! You may as well tell her everything now.'

Everything . . . what is *everything*?

Chad clears his throat. 'It was a complete fluke that you were the one I picked out at Lesters. You are exactly his type – er, natural. Relatable, if you will. I just had no idea you were going to be Markus's co-host on that little country radio show. That was supposed to be Markus's test to see how he fared back in the spotlight – well, more like the lukewarm-light. Before that, he'd just been holed up at Horizons for months, seeing the occasional patient, but nothing more. Thank God I demanded we had somewhere decent to live while we were in Mudgee – somewhere big enough for all of us to live our lives. Who knew we were going to be there for this long! I pulled out all the stops that night you came for dinner – the flowers, the love-song dedication – but Markus sabotaged it all with his stupid takeaway Thai.'

Eryka jumps in. 'Chad! You know how over the top you can be. It's not everyone's style . . . just because it happens to mine.' I watch her transform from chastising him to drooling over him.

It's completely unhinged.

I edge closer to the door.

Eryka turns back to me. 'It's been hard to lie to everyone. I knew it would be easier to stay in Poland, but I couldn't bear to be away from Chaddy-boy for so long. And, of course, I couldn't keep pretending to date Markus when you came along – especially when it became obvious that he liked you. What a scandal that would have caused – more so than our "breakup"! We just want to see Markus back to his regular, healthy self.'

'Yeahhhh, except this whole thing has been a bit of a waste in the end, hasn't it?' Chad chimes in again. 'After that viral lamb TikTok thing happened, his confidence skyrocketed, and he insisted that he was well enough to do this elephant show. I was so eager to get back to our life in Poland that I was stupid enough not to question it. I suggested he take you along with him and use it as an opportunity to win you over. I even lent him the funds to do it in style. And then the SOS call came so –'

I've heard enough.

I hear Eryka call after me as I rush through the open door.

'Rosie, honey! Come back! Please. We're on your side.'

But I'm already sprinting out into the darkness.

Somehow, I locate my hut and have my belongings packed in two minutes flat. I wheel my suitcase up the rocky path, with only my phone lighting the way.

I've almost made it to the bamboo entry when I see Markus striding towards me.

Fuckity fuck.

He's looking down at a stack of papers and appears very much like the 'real' Markus. Not that I know who that even is anymore.

I quickly dim my phone's brightness and try to glide past quietly, with thoughts of a kind-faced air hostess offering up hot cups of tea and fuzzy bed socks spurring me along.

Unfortunately, my suitcase has other ideas. One of the wheels catches on a large rock lining the path and my case becomes airborne. It flies through the air before crashing at Markus's feet.

'Rosie?' Markus looks up, confused. 'What are you doing back already?'

'You should probably ask Chad,' I say, ice-cold. I bend down to collect my suitcase.

I feel Markus's horror thick in the air before an urgent hand grabs my arm.

'Rosie, please. Stop. I can explain.'

I can't see him properly in the dark, but I picture the colour draining from his face and his khaki shirt drenched in sweat and slicked to his body. Not because he gives a damn about me, but because he's been caught out in his little web of lies.

I shrug his hand away. 'There's no need. I've heard everything that I need to.'

I already feel like the world's biggest fool. Just let me go.

'Please! Rosie! I wanted to tell you, but Chad didn't think it was a good idea until we were sure that we could trust you.'

'Trust,' I spit. 'Now that's an interesting construct. I believe we have wildly different definitions of that word.'

I continue wheeling my suitcase, Markus trailing behind like a stray dog desperate for scraps. Aisha is at the small bamboo desk.

'I need a ride to the taxi stand. Now, please.'

'No! You're staying here,' Markus cries. 'We can figure this out, Rosie.'

His words ricochet off me as I help Aisha lift, then strap,

my aluminium case onto the back of her motorbike. She straddles the bike, and I clamber on behind her.

'Let's get you out of here, ma'am,' Aisha whispers as she kickstarts the engine and we roar off into the distance.

'Where to, lady?' the driver asks as I slide into the back of his taxi half an hour later.

'Kochi airport.'

We whizz through the streets that are just as – if not more – alive at night under the moonlight and bright streetlamps. So much beauty and life, yet so much hypocrisy. Shanties alongside five-star hotels, and shoeless people peddling basic wares outside fine jewellery stores that require appointments to enter their gated doors. Things are never as they seem. Nothing in this world is as it seems.

We're not long into the trip when my tears start. Not many at first, but enough for the driver to check on me in his rear-view mirror. Through my tears, I focus on the string of wooden beads hanging from the mirror, swinging side to side, hypnotically. There's a glistening gold charm dangling from the end of the beads. An elephant. Another damn elephant.

'He Ganesha. He protector,' the cab driver says, his compassionate brown eyes locking with mine in the mirror.

Protector? Really? Well, Ganesha's doing a pretty shit job with me. Was he protecting me when Mum walked out? How about back when Wes annihilated my heart? Or when my best friends decided to follow suit? And now, shouldn't Ganesha be at his most powerful while I'm in his homeland? So, why the blindside with Mum, and now this Markus shit? Can't he let me be happy for even half a second? Seriously. What. The. Fuck.

I'm crying like a baby now.

'New beginnings,' the driver continues in a meditative hum.

I sniff and wipe my face with my arm. I may be having a meltdown, but that's no excuse to be rude. I'm sure the driver has his own problems. He's probably working overtime just to keep a roof over his family's heads. The last thing he needs is a whiny Westerner to deal with. I give him an appreciative look and reach into my handbag for a tissue.

But when we finally pull up to the airport, I'm still a sobbing mess.

'That's two-thousand rupees. I give you special deal.'

I accept the kind driver's price and his offer to carry my bag into the terminal. I wonder if I can ask him to stay with me until I've sorted my flights, but he's got other fares to take and money to make.

Instead, I hand over the tin of Chai Me.

'A gift for you.'

'*Nandi.*' The driver thanks me as he sets the tin on the dashboard underneath swinging Ganesha then moves to help me with my luggage.

The departure hall is jam-packed. I search the crowd for some friendly faces to carry me through the next few hours – perhaps a woman my age who is also travelling alone. But I'm greeted by a sea of nondescript people. I join the back of the long line at the check-in counter and wait. No one speaks to me.

An hour passes before I reach the front, enough time for me to count the number of smiling families and couples: fifty-seven. My eyes are still watering as I approach the stern woman at the counter. A delicate red bindi is pressed between her eyebrows, a diamond stud glints in her nose and she's wearing a gold sari with the airline's peacock logo mono-grammed on the pleated fabric draped over her shoulder.

'I'm sorry, ma'am. There are no seats until tomorrow.'

'Please. I'll pay double. Is there any way I can get on the flight tonight?' Desperation drips from my voice. I don't enjoy begging, but I'm out of options. How do I convince her that this is a true emergency?

The negotiation continues for another few minutes until the woman has repeated five times in no uncertain terms that she *cannot* help me.

'Are you sure?'

'Yes.'

She's done with pleasantries. I open my mouth to finally spill every last messed-up detail of the last few hours/my entire life, but nothing comes out. Not even a squeak of a voice. I clear my throat and try again. Still nothing. I must look like one of those silly carnival clown games, wide-mouthed and waiting to be fed balls – except there's nothing fun about this situation. If I say it all out loud and give it oxygen, it will become big, scary and *real*. Too real.

I can only nod my head and accept my fate silently as the counter lady's long nails tap away at her computer. There's one final dramatic click of the mouse. 'Aaand that booking is done.' Her wide phoney smile is more jarring than joyful. 'You don't have to be back here until 9 am tomorrow.'

And just like that, I'm dismissed.

I back away slowly from the counter and am nearly knocked over by a pair of hormone-fuelled, grabby teenagers dressed in colourful beachwear and obviously still immune to the cruelty of this world. It won't be long before life starts to bump and grind away at them, and they become as disillusioned as the rest of us.

What now? The blackout curtains and soundproof windows of an airport hotel will do too good a job of blocking out the world, and I don't need to be alone with my thoughts right now – especially with a fourteen-hour flight ahead of me.

I search the terminal until I find the perfect darkened bar. I down a neat whiskey and order two more before leaning back in my chair and losing myself in the background chatter of excited travellers.

If I try hard enough, I can pretend I'm one of them.

Chapter Twenty-Eight

I'm seven mini-bottles of chardonnay in before Millie, the air hostess, cuts me off. And fair enough. I've been downing them faster than she can serve me. Eventually I stop using the tiny plastic glasses and chug straight from the bottle. Clearly, I'm trying to make up for all of that lost wine time.

We'd had an unspoken arrangement – call it girl code. Millie had taken one look at me and added an extra bottle to my dinner tray, and it had escalated from there. But now she was doubling down on the peanuts and smuggling Oreos into my seat pocket to soak up the alcohol. The welfare of fellow passengers was at stake – primarily the lady sitting next to me.

I'd taken an instant dislike to my seat mate. Typically, I'd welcome the opportunity to have a chat and hear the life story of a stranger. Right now, it would have served as an excellent distraction. But from the moment she'd squeezed past me into the window seat and dragged her long, wild hair over my body, it was war.

I'd tolerated overhearing her requests for a vegan meal and coconut milk in her coffee, despite not having pre-ordered either. *'I'm newly Hindu. I'm on the way home from a life-changing month's stay in an ashram.'* But when the thin gold bangles running all the way up her arm started clanging loudly with every slight movement, I'd gritted my teeth and amped up the drinking.

I know my feelings have zero to do with what this woman is or isn't doing and everything to do with the fact she reminds me of Mum. I close my eyes and lean back into my chair. Hopefully a nap will help me sober up.

Jingle jangle, jingle jangle, jingle jangle.

Arrrrgggggh. It's tinkling torture.

Somehow, I manage to doze off, and the next time I open my eyes the jingle-jangle woman is digging into a breakfast sausage that doesn't look very vegan-friendly.

I look past her big hair and inauthentic breakfast and out the window. There's a slice of light on the horizon. I focus on that sliver as we start our descent into Sydney. By the time we're hovering over Wollongong, the sky is streaked in fierce reds and bursts of orange. The shapely coast of the Sutherland Shire is spectacular from this high up; deep blue water cuts into stretches of yellowed sand and, behind that, lush greenery. Botany Bay glistens in the early morning sun, jewelled with sailboats bobbing up and down. As we dive further down, I see specks of tiny people working the brightly coloured sails. I bet they don't have a care in the world, except whether they should order a glass of crisp chardonnay with tonight's salt and pepper squid.

Emotion washes over me as the plane finally touches down on the tarmac. Is it relief? I'm not sure. Some of the weight that has been laying heavy on my heart since the dining room at Karma of Kerala has lifted, but I'm hit with a fresh wave of what-the-fuck-is-next?

Millie waves 'Suni the Second' past and gives me a quick squeeze goodbye. She hands me another mini-pack of Oreos and smiles. 'One for the road.'

By the time I'm ushered through customs and waiting at the baggage carousel, I've well and truly sobered up. My suitcase pops up onto the conveyor belt. Boy, has that suitcase witnessed a lot. I swing the twenty-three kilo weight down onto the ground beside me. I'm completely exhausted.

As I walk out through the arrivals gate and towards my connecting flight to Mudgee, no one rushes to greet me. How could they? I haven't told anyone I'm coming back. I don't want Dad to worry unnecessarily, and I'm not sure what to say to Cedric.

I'm back in town before I know it. There are the same old, wide streets, the tall steeple of St Mary's – and Lesters. I wonder if Bee is back from her trip with Wes, and where in the country – or the world, even – he is now. It was amazing to have him at the other end of the phone while I was in India, but it doesn't feel right to go running to him about Markus.

My taxi pulls up outside my old terrace apartment block. How is it that my whole world has been turned upside down, yet the building looks exactly the same? The paint is still peeling off the balustrades, and the lawn still needs to be mowed. This isn't home. But I'm not sure what is anymore. I climb the stairs and unlock my front door. More of the same. I let out a big sigh. It's extra white. Extra sterile. Not even Squash to greet me.

I glance at my mobile, which I've dumped on the entry table with my keys and Oreos. It's been switched off since I arrived at Kochi airport.

Has Markus even bothered messaging? And how about Cedric? Luckily the cab driver was busy listening to *The Best of Celine Dion* and not Gold 86.7 FM. We should be on air right now. We'd pre-taped the show, so at least there wouldn't have been a last-minute scramble. Cedric doesn't deserve that kind of egg on his face.

Turning my phone back on is the final step in my re-immersion into reality. Once that screen lights up, I'll have to face everything and figure out how I'm going to deal with this big mess.

It's now or never.

I press the 'on' button. The screen lights up for a moment before the empty battery light flashes and the screen goes back to black.

Of course, my phone is dead. Being unlucky in love is an awful enough cross to bear, but I now know it's something far greater. The universe hates me. I've had a black mark on my head from the moment I was born. Mum could see that I wasn't worth the bother, clear as day. That's why she'd packed her things and split. It's the same reason Wes didn't stick around, why Markus chose me as the butt of his joke, why Penny couldn't be bothered being honest with me and why Ange just plain couldn't be bothered. It's who I am. There's nothing fortunate or lucky about me. My career at Slice only took off because I worked so damn hard at it – and I sacrificed everything just to have something worthwhile, only to have it turn around and reject me too. If this is my lot in life, then why try at all? I've been a fool for attempting to fight fate.

I flop onto the couch. I leave my Converse on. Fuck the all-white leather.

I thought that a fresh start in Mudgee might actually be the answer. Provided I kept my Tinder active, my floors sparkling clean and my fridge free of expired milk and limp greens, I'd catch a break with my love life too. How wrong I was.

I want to disappear like loose change between the couch cushions, into an oblivion where the universe and its cruelties can't reach me, where I don't have to feel lied to or betrayed ever again. I'll build a wall so tall and so wide that Jon Snow would be proud. I'll make myself untouchable with gladiator-style armour or a *Harry Potter* invisibility cloak. Or maybe I'll simply disappear to a remote island in the Pacific.

Who else have Markus and Chad been fooling? It can't have been just me. It's likely also Cedric, the lovely folk at Kindred Spirit and every last Dr Markus Abrahams fan. They all deserve to know they've been duped.

I retrieve my laptop from my suitcase and login to Facebook. My hands hover over the keyboard as I consider my approach. I squeeze my eyes shut, trying to conjure up the blind fury I felt when I first laid eyes on Eryka straddling Markus. I mean, Chad. I clench my teeth. *Think angry thoughts, think angry thoughts, think angry thoughts.*

SCANDAL ALERT! WILL THE REAL DR MARKUS ABRAHAMS PLEASE STAND UP!

But just as soon as it arrives, the rage that had thundered in my ears earlier is gone. My pulse is no longer racing. Is it because I know deep down that I've only got myself to blame? That after the myriad warning signs, I was still stupid enough to fall for his act? How could I have let myself go there? Especially given all of the bullets I've dodged in the past. I should have been smarter. I normally am. This is my reward for lowering my guard, even for a moment. There's nothing to achieve – only further humiliation – by announcing it all to the world.

I abandon my Markus post. But instead of closing the lid of my laptop, my fingers lead the trackpad mouse straight for the search box. It's rare for daughters to stalk their own mothers online, but it's a place I have found myself many times before.

I type the letters 'S-U-N-I R-O-Y-C-E' into the grey box. No doubt Facebook was first to know about her new identity. *Bingo.*

A photo of my mother loads. It looks like she's created a brand-new profile. I double-check that her usual account is still there. Yup, here it is – complete with the photo of her striding across Shibuya Crossing in all-business black. This new profile features a different, close-up shot. In it, she's wearing a giant flower crown. Pink blooms fall across her forehead and her dark, curly hair is gathered to one side and cascades loosely over her shoulder – the way I'm sure my hair would fall if I encouraged the curl. She's smiling widely. You could be easily fooled into thinking she's a free-spirited, maternal goddess, the type of spirit who fell in love with her baby girl the moment she laid eyes on her.

Occupation: Owner at Chai Me.

I click on her latest album and study a few photos. It's the launch of Chai Me at a hideously cliché Bollywood set with Oriental rugs aplenty. In most of the shots, Mum is sporting a bright yellow kaftan with henna art running up and down her arms. There's also an album of a beachside seafood dinner with an unfamiliar silver fox: most likely Shaun, her new 'investor'-turned-suitor. Dad was once that hopeful suitor, spellbound by Mum's natural beauty and her passion for business. I can see how he and Mum would have initially connected, talking all things company structures. But I'm still not sure how or why it worked for so long.

I don't know what I've come to her profile looking for, but there's nothing new here. Different guy and setting, same old money-making, manipulating story. Did I really think I'd find a long, heartfelt public apology to me laid out neatly on her page for myself and all of her six thousand friends to see?

Six thousand 'friends'. My scoff sends me into a

body-shaking coughing fit. I cough violently for the next few minutes before I'm able to calm the tickle in my chest. I'm still breathing rapidly, and my nose feels stuffy. Don't tell me Suni the Second generously passed on some vegan-friendly strain of influenza – that's the last thing I need right now.

Time for some preventative ginger tea . . . Ugh, tea. Will I ever be able to enjoy a hot drink without thinking about Mum's stupid sorry tea?

I'm done stalking. I'm about to click out of her profile when something catches my eye.

1 Mutual Friend.

I double-click into her friends' list.

When Wes Preston's lopsided smile loads, I'm certain that my brain short circuits. I slowly rise to my feet. As soon as I'm upright, the blood rushes from my head and I stumble forward, vision blurred. I'm suddenly seeing double. Two laptops, two coffee tables, two litter boxes, two aluminium suitcases.

I lie flat on my back on the cold floor. The room is spinning ferociously. This is either the beginnings of an awful flu – or I'm having a panic attack.

The air seems thinner. Paper thin, in fact. I start breathing rapid small, shallow gasps, coughing between the tiny pockets of air. Then, the walls close in on me.

Chapter Twenty-Nine

'Rosie, wake up!'
A loud voice startles me alive.

Squash's little furry face is centimetres from mine. A hand goes to my throbbing head. It hurts. My throat is dry. I have no idea what time or day it is, or where I am. Eyes blurry, my hand shoots out in blind search of my phone. I feel the long-haired threads of my rug. Right. I'm on the floor of my apartment.

'Are you okay?' It's the voice again.

So, apparently Squash talks now. Just how hard did I hit my head?

'Oh, praise be, sweet baby Jesus. You've returned from the dead!' Cedric's wide, worried face appears next to Squash's tiny one.

'Ceddie?'

How long have I been out for? I squirm uncomfortably on the floor, push Squash's warm body from me and sit up. My eyes dart around the room, searching for a clue to explain

Cedric's visit. My eyes land on my suitcase. Fuck. It all comes flooding back. My mum, Markus, Chad, Eryka . . .

So, it wasn't a nightmare.

But how does Cedric know that I'm home? As far as he knows, I'm still in India recording a hit radio show and ending the ivory trade. This is not how I'd planned on breaking the news that his big celebrity radio star is a massive fraud.

'Are you okay, Rosie?' For all of his concern, Cedric doesn't appear terribly surprised to see me lying on the floor of my apartment in Mudgee.

'I'm fine. I think . . .'

Aren't I fine? My hand goes to the top of my head to feel for an egg. Should I get it over with and tell him now? He obviously already knows that something is up.

'What a relief! I thought you'd be a right mess about Markus.'

Oh, nooo . . . so he already knows. I eye my laptop, discarded on the rug next to me. I don't remember posting anything. I'm still in a sleepy fog but last I recall, I'd been so distracted stalking Mum that I'd abandoned my Markus exposé altogether. And then – oh God – there was the Wes and Mum connection. I can't even begin to comprehend what that's about yet . . .

It appears from Cedric's expression that I've posted *something* about Markus . . . I'm just not sure what.

'I'm so sorry, Ceddie. I should have come straight to you so that we could figure this out together before I went ahead and broadcast it to the world!'

'Oh, babe! You're not to blame. It wasn't you.'

What does he mean?

He passes me his phone, which is open on the homepage of the *Daily Mail.* I read the first headline:

Celebrity TV vet confesses to secret on-air twin

Under the headline are two, large-scale coloured photos: one of Chad smiling widely, with his Lego hair and dinner-plate-white smile, and one of Markus in his scuffed boots, crouching down next to Eddie. Seeing them side by side like this makes me feel like an even bigger fool. It's so obvious that these are two completely different men. How did I not see this?

'*This* is how you found out?' I ask Cedric tentatively.

'Nope. Markus called me as soon as you left. You made quite the run for it, I hear.' A proud smile tugs at the corners of his mouth.

'I wasn't sure what else to do. Under the circumstances, I mean . . .'

'Of course you didn't, doll! What a right shock that would have been.'

Tell me about it – and that's only a tiny slice of the nasty surprises India served up to me.

'How did Markus sound? Was he okay?' The question is out of my mouth before I can stop it.

Cedric's already crouched on the floor but drops to his knees and stretches out next to me. His arms go under his head like he's on a weekend camping trip gazing up at the stars, not discussing my great escape from India while looking at my peeling ceiling.

'He's been trying to call you.'

'My phone's dead,' I respond quickly.

'He cares, Rosie.' Cedric flops his head on my shoulder. 'I know I was having some fun teasing you guys before, but I'm staying out of it from now on. Especially with what's gone on. Apparently, the team at *Markus & Pup* knew all about it, and I guess there was no real need for me to know – but he should have told you.'

'I feel like a fool, Ceddie. We kissed, you know.'

'I know. Markus told me.'

'He did?'

'Yeah. He pretty much confessed everything to me. I do feel bad for the guy. Sounds like he's really been going through it. And I think the weight of this secret was just making everything so much worse for him. I'm the one who encouraged him to speak out about it publicly.'

Squash climbs up onto me and I reach down to stroke his head. He purrs.

'Thanks for coming over to check on me, Ceddie,' I say.

'Don't be silly, doll. You went MIA! Like, I wasn't going to wait until you turned up dead in a ditch.'

I laugh weakly. My head is still throbbing. I'm not sure if it's the effect of the mid-air bottles of chardonnay or if I fell.

'What time is it anyway?' I ask as I creep up cautiously onto all fours. Just in case I'm emerging from a days-long coma.

Cedric helps me up off the floor. 'It's 10 am.'

'And the date?'

'Monday, 5 June 2023,' he says, unable to disguise his amused expression.

I arrived home forty-five minutes ago.

Phew. No MRI necessary then.

'So, what do you want to do about the show?' Cedric asks once we're seated on my lounge.

I sigh. 'I don't know. I'm just not sure that I can keep working with him when I can't even think about facing him right now.'

I don't want to be difficult, but I can't imagine feeling much differently any time soon.

'I thought you might say that. Which is why you need only give me the word and I'll give Markus his marching orders. No further questions asked.'

I can't help but smile, aware that his jokey tone masks genuine sacrifice. It sounds as though the Abrahams twins are splashed across the news right now, and the marketer in me knows that will do wonders for the show's profile. The idea that Cedric would be prepared to throw that away for me means the world.

But I can't let him do that. Not when I'm not confident that I even want to stay here.

'I'm so sorry, Ceddie. I don't want to let you down.' I swallow to try to hold back my tears. I'm unsuccessful. 'I don't know where I belong right now, but I don't think it's in Mudgee,' I sob.

'Don't cry, doll. I understand. This is about so much more than a radio show.'

'I don't want to leave you in the lurch though. I don't even know if I want to leave permanently. I was just starting to get properly settled here . . . but I need to go back to Sydney and get my head sorted.'

I think about crisp early morning strolls under the wintery trees at Galdwell Park and home-cooked dinners with Dad and Naomi and my heart instantly feels lighter. There's also important, hard, yet soul-healing chats about Mum to be had.

'You're not leaving me in the lurch,' Ceddie says. 'Because you're fired. You can't just jump on a plane and go MIA and not expect there to be consequences!'

Tears are still streaming down my face. Giant, grateful ones.

'Fired with a glowing reference, of course. Because I'm sure as hell not letting you give up on radio!'

We both stand and Cedric envelops me in one of his rib-cracking hugs. When he eventually loosens his grip, I step back to look at him. His purple frames are skewiff on his face. I'm going to miss that face.

'Now, do you need Uncle Ceddie to mind Squash?'

'Nope,' I say, beaming as I scoop my cat up off the floor and snuggle him to my chest. 'He's coming with me.'

Chapter Thirty

Are you back in Sydney? I fire off the text to Wes as I'm boxing up the last of my belongings.

I am. Why? Are you?

Soon to be. Can we meet?

I'd love that. When will you be here?

Saturday?

Let's do it

Wes suggests meeting at Galdwell Park. I try not to think of the sentimentality behind it, just the convenience of it being equidistant from my childhood home and his.

What with everything I need to organise with my rushed move, the rest of the week flies by. As I walk through the park's gates on Saturday morning, I'm both excited and terrified. Excited, because Wes has somehow made his way back into my inner circle and I'm looking forward to seeing him, but terrified that any explanation of his Facebook connection with my mother might blow us back up.

Wes is sprawled on the grass at our meeting spot near the largest duck pond. He's wearing a cap, so his face is in shadow, but he's in his distinctive orange check shirt that only Wes would wear. There's a sketchpad in his hands.

I watch him from afar as he sizes up the pond visitors. It's a scene I've witnessed many times before, although normally not from this angle. I used to be sprawled right next to him, conjuring up exciting stories to match his drawings.

It's too cold for rowboats, but there are plenty of young families and couples on the fringes of the park enjoying their Saturday morning picnics. Wes is mesmerised by one couple in particular – a boy and girl no older than eighteen, laughing and flirtatiously feeding each other croissants. They're a few moments away from a full-blown food fight. As I approach, I can see they've both come up well in the drawing. He has big, bouffant hair and she has a smile as wide as the Harbour Bridge, which I know Wes's artistic hand must delight in.

My stomach tightens.

'Hi, Wes.'

'Rosie!' Wes jumps up and plants a kiss on my cheek. 'Welcome home.'

His thick beard tickles my cheek and my skin tingles. Not just my face, but down my spine too.

'Thanks. And to you, too.'

'But I wasn't exactly off travelling the world!'

We stand awkwardly in front of each other. Wes edges closer like he wants to embrace me, but then doesn't.

'I'm really sorry, Rosie,' he says eventually. 'I take it that you weren't aware Markus was a twin?'

I've tried not to read too many of the articles – there's a lot out there – but I know I've been mentioned in a bunch of them as Markus's 'romantic interest'.

'I was not. Things certainly took quite a turn after you and I messaged.' I smile to show Wes that I'm not about to crumble in front of him.

'He's a right fool. I knew there was something I didn't like about that guy. How are you holding up?'

We sink down onto the grass.

'I'm okay. I've moved back in with Dad and Naomi – just for a bit. I couldn't stay in Mudgee.'

'That's understandable. How did you even find out?' He reaches over and squeezes my hand. I'm surprised by how natural it feels.

'It's a bit of a story . . .'

'A Rosie Royce story? You know they're my favourite.' He grins at me, his entire face lit from within.

I take a deep breath, comforted by his strong grip on my hand, and launch in. I brush over the details of Markus's and my love story (if you can even call it that) but give him a blow-by-blow of the traumatic twin reveal, starring Eryka and her pert breasts. Once I'm finished, I see him trying to suppress a smile.

'Okay. It's not *that* funny.' Maybe I liked him better when he was at least trying to act sensitive.

'You're right, it's not. Although you have to admit that it sounds more like *The Bold and the Beautiful* than real life.' He puts a hand over his mouth, but there's no disguising the twitch of his lips. Next thing I know, Wes's whole face contorts with laughter.

I'm horrified for a second, but then I start giggling too.

'Remember when we sprung your dad watching that?' Wes laughs.

'Yes. He was in his Ridge Forrester era. I can't believe I was actually relieved when he ditched the suits and re-discovered Led Zeppelin,' I say.

'I can imagine your boyfriend, Hans, and Ridge Forrester being great mates,' Wes teases.

I poke out my tongue at him and suddenly we're rolling around on the grass, clutching our stomachs. It's a good few minutes of utter delirium, until the muscles in our cheeks and tummies begin to ache and we lie down, looking up at the clear blue sky. There's not a cloud in sight.

'So, did you like India?' he asks after a while.

I have to pause for moment to consider his question. Even though I got the shock of a lifetime – two shocks, actually – I don't think beautiful, majestic, enigmatic India should be penalised. In a way it gifted me a sort of rebirth.

'I fucking adored it,' I say at last.

'I'm so glad, Rosie.'

It's easy to get carried away in Wes's company. We've always had this magic energy whenever we're together. He makes me feel light and carefree in a way no one else does. But I can't forget the reason I wanted to meet up with him in the first place.

'Wes, I need to ask you something . . .' I say towards the sky.

He props himself up on his elbows and looks down at me. His face looks extra rugged from this angle, his rust eyes shining bright. I remember him looking down at me in this exact way, in almost this exact spot, when we were half the age we are now.

'I knew it! You were so blown away with my radio skills that you want to offer me a permanent guest spot on your show.'

'Ah, not exactly . . .'

'Joking, Rosie!'

His expression changes in a flash, from silly to serious. He knows this is no time for games. He can still read me so well. In his hands, I flutter like the pages of an open book.

'So how *are* you feeling about seeing your mum?' he asks, eyes tinged with concern. 'Is that why you wanted to meet up?'

'Okay, I guess. It's strange because, as you know, I was never under any illusion that one day we'd work it all out and play happy families. I thought I'd made peace with that. But somewhere deep inside, I guess I still cared.'

In my head it had always been simple. The better I did at life, the more it proved that her leaving didn't matter. If that meant pushing myself through the tough times, then so be it. Now, I was feeling less okay and less like it even mattered. Having the whitest whites or being the best at my job didn't prove anything. And it certainly would never make my mother love me in the way I needed her to.

'Of course you cared, Rosie.' His voice drips with compassion. It's so familiar and warm.

I need to ask him before I chicken out.

'But Wes?' I sit up and swivel to look at him properly.

'Yes?'

'It's just that . . .' I find the words getting stuck in my throat.

'Yes?'

'Well, I wondered . . .'

'Yes?'

'When I . . .'

'It's okay, Rosie. Say whatever you need to.' He reaches for my hand again.

I take a deep breath. 'Firstly, I can't thank you enough for being at the other end of the phone when I was in India. That really did stop me from completely self-combusting. I honestly mean that.'

'You don't need to thank me, Rosie.'

'What I'm confused about, though, is why you're friends with my mum on Facebook?'

There. I've come out with it.

'Ah, right, that . . . Yes, I can see how that might seem strange.' He looks down at the ground and starts picking at some blades of grass. I wait for a moment, but he doesn't continue.

'So . . .?' I prompt. I've been over it so many times in my head and I still can't come up with even one reason that makes sense to me.

'Well, I had a few things to say, and it's the only way I could get her to listen . . .'

'What kinds of things? What do you mean?'

'Here,' he says, pulling his phone from his pocket. 'It's probably easiest if I just show you.' He taps his screen a few times then passes the phone to me. 'I thought the best chance of her seeing the message was to add her as a friend.'

But I'm no longer listening to him, my eyes glued to the screen.

Marie, Suni, whatever your name is now . . .

It wasn't okay when you missed her birthdays, or when you weren't there to see her riding a two-wheeler for the first time. It wasn't okay when you weren't around to console her when she flew over the handlebars and chipped her two front teeth or witness her taking her debating team to glory with her crushing closing (she was amazing!!!). It wasn't okay when you were completely absent for her high-school graduation and didn't get to witness her being the only student to wear Converse under her formal dress, like an absolute rockstar.

You're the one who missed out. You're the one who missed seeing her shine in the way only Rosie does.

If you're not planning on being back in her life for real, can I kindly suggest that you ship the fuck out. I won't let anyone steal her sparkle ever again.

Sincerely,
Wes
'That entrepreneurial boy who sold paintings' from down the street.

I feel like I need to re-read it to process what's written here. What *he's* written.

'Please don't get mad, Rosie. I just got so angry hearing how upset she'd made you in India. I thought it was high time someone held her accountable for her actions. Rich coming from me, I know. I just couldn't have her hurting you all over again.'

'She hasn't replied?' I say shakily, seeing that there's no message under his.

'No.'

The word lands with a violent thud.

I hand the phone back, heat creeping all the way up my neck to my ears. I'm unsure if it's second-hand embarrassment I'm feeling, or shame. I wish he hadn't opened that can of worms again, reminding me that my emotions are still very much entwined with my mother's actions, or in this case – as so often is the case – lack thereof.

'Look, as I said, Wes, I really appreciated your support while I was in India. But that doesn't give you the right to start meddling in my life now. I really don't need you messaging my mum on my behalf. If I wanted to message her, I would.'

Pain streaks across his face and I instantly regret my words.

'You're right. It's none of my business,' he says.

My chest pinches. But I don't want him to stop caring either. I *want* him to be in my business.

'That might be my cue to get going. I have lots to prep for tonight.' Wes goes to stand up.

'Tonight?'

'I have my art show opening.'

Wow. He really is doing this thing. My heart soars and I take a deep breath, trying to gather myself and stuff my feelings back down – overwhelming pride but also some sadness that I haven't been around to witness any of it.

'That's great, Wes,' I choke out.

His eyes lock with mine, gaze fierce. 'Thanks Rosie.'

A chill blasts through my body that's so intense I have to turn away. I focus my attention on the playground to the right of the pond where two boys are playing on the jungle gym. An elderly man watches them from the park bench. His eyes follow them intently, darting as the boys bounce around. You can practically see his chest swelling with grandparent pride.

I turn back to Wes. 'That's Grandpa Ben. He picks up Charlie and Ryan every Saturday at 8 am so that their parents can have a sleep-in. It's the highlight of his week. Especially since losing Dot last year. Charlie has Dot's eyes.'

Wes settles back down to sit, and we watch as the boys clamber up to the highest rung of the climbing frame, hook their legs over the beam at the very top and dangle upside down, their faces growing redder by the second. They call out to Grandpa Ben. 'Look at us! We're flying!' Grandpa stands, clearly nervous that he may soon have broken limbs on his hands.

'Who wants an ice cream?' he calls back.

Clever Grandpa Ben. The boys unfurl themselves and sprint towards the park bench.

'A little early for Mr Whippy, isn't it?' I laugh, turning back to Wes.

His eyes are already on me, studying my face with an expression that I can't read.

'You do remember how many of those cones we used to smash right, Rosie?'

I can't help but grin. 'You're talking about ice cream cones, right?'

'Of course.'

Poor Dad gave me far too much credit in those early years, thinking I could be trusted to fix myself a nutritious lunch when he had to go open the office on the weekends. Ironically, I'm the one now wrestling the dessert spoon from his hands.

'Mum really fucked up, didn't she?' I say suddenly.

It feels good to finally say that out loud. Not just in my head, alone on a random rooftop in India, but standing right here, in Galdwell Park, metres from my house, with Wes as my witness. I see the two boys and the old man walk away from the playground, all holding hands.

'Yes, Rosie. She really fucked up.'

Wes's hand goes out and gently strokes my cheek and I instinctively reach for him. When I feel his arms go around me, I start to cry.

'Don't you ever want to delete everything that's ever happened and start again?' I sob against his shoulder.

'Sometimes,' he murmurs into the top of my head. 'But that also means saying goodbye to a lot of good stuff, too.'

I wipe my eyes and pull back to look at him.

'You might not be able to rewrite your past, Posie. But goddamn am I excited for what's to come.'

Chapter Thirty-One

'Lunch?' Dad calls the second I step foot back inside the house. I'm a bit wobbly on my feet from my emotional catch-up with Wes and was hoping to slip back in quietly.

'Dad! You should be resting.' I follow his voice into the kitchen. He's standing at the bench in striped flannel pyjamas lifting a chocolate mud cake onto Naomi's best Royal Albert cake stand. He looks like an adorable criminal caught red-handed.

He'd been delighted to see me when I'd walked in the door from Mudgee. He'd been less delighted to hear about 'Suni'. But instead of handling it his usual way, by not saying much at all, we'd spoken about everything. How Mum being so absent in my life had made me feel – how it had made him feel. It felt good to talk things through with Dad and be reminded that, despite everything, I'm loved unconditionally.

Dad reads the paper each morning with his tea, so he knew about Markus (unfortunately the story was yet to be tomorrow's fish 'n' chip wrapping), but he was wise enough not to dig any further on that front. All he knew was that things hadn't ended well in India, I was no longer on the radio and I didn't want to talk about it.

I was relishing our time together, which included a disproportionate amount of fussing from me.

'Daaaaad, you just had a heart attack! Honestly, you can't be trusted. Where's Naomi? Also, it's about thirty degrees in here. Those pyjamas are much too warm. You'll make yourself sick. Turn down the heat or go and put your Led Z tee on.'

Dad receives my orders exactly as he's done for the past twenty-eight years – calmly.

'Naomi has gone to the movies – I thought she deserved a day off from waiting on me. The cake is not for me. And Led Zeppelin is in the wash, so it will have to be Beastie Boys.'

He finishes arranging the cake, then takes out three patterned saucers, a handful of teaspoons and a knife. If Naomi is out, then what is this all about?

Dad kisses me on the top of the head as he scooches past. 'I'll leave you to it while I go change. Carry all this into the dining room, won't you, love?'

He rushes off towards his bedroom before I can question him further.

I grasp the cake stand in one hand and the pile of plates, spoons and a knife in the other. My ears are assaulted by heavy rock music as my precarious balancing act makes its way up the hallway. I have no idea how Naomi puts up with Dad's permanent midlife crisis. Rock music and random cake making!

Once I've rounded the corner into the dining room, I make a beeline straight for the old-school stereo, rest the cake plates on the TV unit and turn the volume down.

'Ahem.' A woman clears her throat.

I look up to see Penny sitting stiffly at the dining table, hands arranged carefully in the lap of her powder-blue pants suit. Ange is sitting quietly next to her.

What the hell, Dad!

I am too emotional for this. And how is it that they're here together? Penny has obviously not said a word to Ange about her 'affair'.

'Hi, Rosie,' Penny's voice wavers slightly. Penny's voice never wavers.

Ange wipes her palms on her greyed sweatpants.

'Hi, guys.' The softness in my voice surprises me. I'm still angry, but there's no denying that I've missed them.

I move to the table and set the cake and plates down.

I bet it was Penny who requested the cake from Dad, as sweet as sweet can be. She could charm the pants off anyone. Literally. Which, ironically, is how we got into this mess.

I start cutting into the cake.

Penny sits up straighter. 'How have you been, Rosie?'

I don't respond, just push a plate towards each of them and take a seat at the head of the table. It's unfortunate that the Markus stuff is such public knowledge. I wonder if Dad has also said anything about me running into Mum? I plunge my spoon through my slice, breaking apart the chocolate sponge and mousse layers.

'We're your best friends. Let us be here for you,' Penny tries again.

'Best friends don't lie to one another,' I say, looking pointedly at Ange, who has pushed away her plate.

I'm not about to spill the beans. I've well and truly learnt my lesson with the Dave drama. I take a bite of cake and chew so aggressively that I barely hear Ange's whisper.

'I know, Rosie.'

My head snaps up. I must not have heard her correctly.

'Sorry?'

'I know,' Ange repeats, louder this time. 'Penny told me.'

My hardened exterior instantly gives way to a softness as spongey as the cake layers. *Gosh. Poor Ange!*

'Are you okay?'

'I can't say that I've slept all that well, but I'm glad I know.'

Wait a second . . . If she knows, how could she possibly be sitting next to Penny in her powder-blue suit like nothing has transpired?

Penny reaches over and clasps Ange's hand. She turns to face me. 'I was disgusted with myself for keeping it a secret for so long. I went over to Ange's house the moment you left mine, Rosie.'

I swing around to face Ange. 'And you're going to just forgive her?' I ask incredulously.

'Well, I'm not sure it's that simple,' Ange says. 'But I want to work at it.' They exchange a glance thickly laden with words that have clearly already been spoken one hundred times over.

'Unbelievable,' I mutter under my breath. Where was my grace for much, much less?

'I'm here to apologise to you, Rosie. You didn't deserve the silent treatment, or my anger. I know you were just looking out for me. I'm so sorry.'

'So, *now* you're sorry?' My voice doesn't even sound like me. 'Because you want to forgive Penny, you can't possibly stay angry at me?'

'No. It's because I know now that I was wrong.'

Ange pushes back her chair and comes over to my side of the table. She places her hands on my shoulders. They're warm and heavy, like a weighted blanket all snug and secure.

'Your dad told us what went down with your mum in India. I can't believe it! Her behaviour was – it *is* – inexcusable,

Rosie. Especially after having my own kids, I don't think I'll ever be able to fathom it – except that she's obviously missing the empathy gene. Completely fucked up. But if you can't change what happened, then you have to work out a way to not let it affect your life. Easier said than done, I realise. After what I've just been through, I know that to be especially true!'

'This isn't about my mum. It's about Penny.'

'You deserve happiness, Rosie,' Ange continues. 'But you won't get it if you push away the people who care about you the moment they make a mistake.'

'So you both think this is all my fault?' I swing around to look at Penny. 'That I haven't given the losers in my life enough second chances?'

Ange starts to answer, 'That's not what I meant at all, I –'

'Enough, Rosie. Seriously, enough!' Penny interjects. 'You don't get to just lump us all in with your mum, and stupid Markus and every bad date you ever had. Yes, I fucked up. Fucking royally, actually.' She pauses and exchanges another meaningful glance with Ange before continuing. 'But does that mean that's it? We simply cease choosing each other over everyone else? Years and years of friendship erased like it never even existed? Is that how things seriously work for you, Rosie? I witnessed you doing this with Wes and I supported you. And I've watched you pick apart and shut down every potential partner without giving them a real chance. Yes, there are some shitheads out there – but that's life, Rosie! I guess I just never thought that you'd do the same thing to me.'

I tilt my head to look up at Ange who is still standing above me, face ashen.

'Do you agree with her?' I ask quietly.

'Yes, Rosie. I do.' She pulls the chair out next to me and sits down. 'He's stayed in touch you know.'

'Who has?'

'Wes. He's been checking in with me pretty regularly over the years. Just a text or email here and there.'

'What? What do you mean?'

'He got the message loud and clear that you wanted to be left alone once you blocked him, but he also wanted to make sure you were okay.'

'So you've been feeding him information about me?' I ask hesitantly.

'Only that you're happy and doing well. Don't worry, I never gave him any real details. I thought his interest would die off with time, but it never did. When I saw him at the reunion, I just had to give him your number. I was so hopeful that you guys were finally going to sort things out and be together – just as it's always been written in the stars.'

I'm quiet.

'Are you mad?'

'No.' It would be easy to get worked up about this – yet another secret kept from me. But I'm not angry. Not even a little bit. I'm only sad that I didn't know sooner.

Over cake (yes, we go back for seconds) I fill them in on the Markus/Chad fiasco. Their chocolate crumb dusted mouths hang open while I describe the Kindred Spirit hut scene in pixel-level detail. Next, we chat about Mum. At first, it's difficult to pinpoint exactly how I feel – shocked, angry, disappointed, sad – but with the girls' support, I manage it. Then Penny brings up the Chai Me website on her phone and we all laugh evilly at the icky green packaging and horrible Comic Sans font.

In this moment, nothing feels as right as sitting in my old childhood living room with my old childhood friends, pouring out my heart. I know unconditional love – Dad has ensured that's the case – but I was naive in thinking that it was always going to be perfect. I know now that the love of friendship demands more. It isn't always perfect; it endures the good, the bad and the ugly. But those unpredictable twists and turns of our lives are made that much sweeter once we squelch on through the hard shit and out the other side together.

Hours pass. We gasp; we laugh; we cry. Dad slips into the room and the stereo is switched back on, belting out classic rock tunes. So then we dance.

Chapter Thirty-Two

It doesn't take much to convince both Penny and Ange to accompany me to Wes's art show.

Penny is able to find out pretty easily that it's at Verge Gallery, a small place in Surry Hills. Apparently, she used to sleep with the owner. (She watered his plants when he went to Bali a month after they broke up, so they're still on good terms). And Ange . . . well, as long-standing president of the Wes Preston fan club, she's changed out of her sweatpants and into my jacquard cocktail dress before I've even run a brush through my hair.

Verge Gallery is not a massive space, so there's nowhere to hide – something that would have been an impossibility with Penny in tow anyway.

'We'll have some of your good stuff,' she barks at the lanky man standing behind the gallery's makeshift bar, which is really a picnic table topped with a few bottles of Jacob's Creek chardonnay. His face scrunches. 'Don't pretend you don't know exactly what I'm talking about. I'm on intimate terms with the owner, Jasper Connell, and this one . . .' Penny pulls me alongside her, '. . . used to fuck the artist, Wes Preston. Don't mind the sneakers. Cute casual is her thing.'

'Shhhh, Penny!'

I glance over to where Wes is standing by the far wall. A small crowd is gathered around him. Thankfully, he doesn't appear to have heard Penny's eloquent proclamation. I didn't even get to say a quick hello before being marched straight to the bar – not that I'm complaining. A drink will help take the edge off.

Penny swivels to face me. 'What? Aren't you proud of me for finally deciding to embrace your lack of style?' she says, before lowering her voice. *Now* she decides to whisper! 'Stick with me, girls. I know how these things work. They always have good bottles stashed away for the VIPs.'

Ange and I exchange an amused glance. It feels good to be back with the girls.

'Look, you can pretend all you want to be satisfied with this cat's piss and Jatz crackers, but I won't.' Penny stares daggers at the bartender until he bends down under the table and emerges with a bottle with a gold-foiled top.

'Now, there's a good boy!' Penny exclaims, turning to me triumphantly. 'You couldn't have drunk that other stuff anyway.'

'I'm back on the wine actually,' I say smoothly.

'Well, well, well, now isn't that an interesting development,' Pen teases, poking me in the ribs. Ange doesn't look even vaguely surprised, just delighted.

Armed with our glasses of Moët, we make our way over to Wes. Ange grabs my hand and gives it a squeeze but drops it as soon as we're in Wes's eyeline. Ange's subtle support is the yin to Penny's extroverted yang.

It's only now that we're in arm's reach of Wes that I take note of the canvases hung behind him. The artworks are a mixture of sizes, but all are textured with blobs of violent colour – splashes of dark purples, reds and greens. They're very bold, but they also seem, well, very angry. The opposite of the lopsided grin that's currently spread across Wes's face.

'Rosie! What a lovely surprise. Hi, Penny, hi, Ange.' He leans in and gives each of us a peck on the cheek, hesitating a moment longer at my cheek. It's like there's a magnetic force stopping him from pulling away. Or maybe I'm just imagining it?

He's changed from a cap into a sleek black beanie. It's slouched at the back, transforming his usual 'throw on and go' look to off-duty street style. *Sexy* off-duty style.

'Preston, just so we're clear, I'm here to support Jasper's gallery, not you. Also, could you not have popped on a suit for your big night?' Penny gives him a disapproving once-over.

I don't think things would be right in the world if Penny and Wes weren't at each other's throats.

'I'm pretty sure Wes is allergic to suit wool, isn't that correct?'

His mouth twitches. 'Yes, that's correct. Deathly allergic, just as Rosie is to wine.'

My eyes go straight to his and we hold each other's gaze.

'Earth to Preston, Rosie! Are you still with us?' Penny waves a manicured hand in front of our faces. 'It's like there was just a glitch in the Matrix.'

I laugh so breathlessly that I feel woozy and need to glance down at the sturdy ground.

When I look back up, Wes is watching me.

I swallow thickly and avert my gaze.

'Well, aren't these impressive,' I say extra brightly, gesturing to the artworks behind us. Even if these particular artworks aren't exactly to my taste.

'Yes, Oscar's done a really great job of capturing the emotion of World War II.'

'Oscar?' I ask.

'Yes. He's the artist I'm exhibiting with. Jasper thought that his moody works would provide an excellent contrast with my BIG Things exhibit.'

My hopeful heart twinges at the word 'big'.

'Where are your pieces then, Wes?' I ask.

'This way.' He turns and leads us over to the far corner of the room. 'Real estate was at a bit of a premium,' he says as he comes to a halt in front of the back wall. 'Here we are.'

I can tell by the way he tugs at his beanie that he's nervous.

Before I get a chance to take in the artworks, Penny jumps in. 'I don't get it. Where are the big things?'

I wish she and Ange had hung back to critique Oscar's dark smoke plumes between gulps of champagne, and given Wes and I some space.

As my eyes take in the colourful artworks, my heart catches in my throat. Just as Penny has observed, there are no big things. There's no Big Golden Guitar, no Big Merino, no Big Prawn. There's not even a Big Banana. Of course not. The focus isn't on the novelty architecture, it's on the people – the gawking adults, all happy and child-like, the disgruntled teenagers who have been dragged on family trips against their will, the toddlers all snotty nosed and red-cheeked, and the couples – giddy on each other's love.

All at once, a rush of emotions floods my body. It hits me like a waterfall gushing on a rainy day. There's admiration and adoration for Wes's obvious talent, but a sadness, too. And, perhaps, a kind of hope. We were one of those couples. Maybe we could *still* be one of those couples . . .

'What do you think?' Wes asks with a tentative smile.

'I still don't get it,' Penny exclaims. 'You couldn't have thrown in at least *one* big thing. Make it make sense, Preston.'

'It makes sense to me,' I say quietly.

Ange takes one look at my face, grabs Penny's hand and drags her away to look at the neighbouring exhibit.

'It was so strange being back at the Big Banana with Bee the other week. Our road trip feels like a lifetime ago, doesn't it?' Wes says, once they've disappeared around the corner.

'It does,' I murmur, fighting the urge to say more. To tell him how much I've missed him and let him know that I might be willing to give us another go. I can't believe it's taken until this very moment to realise that's what I want.

Maybe I *should* say something to him? Isn't that what I've learnt from my time in Mudgee and my disastrous trip with Markus? Not to hold back. To be honest about how I'm feeling.

Wes's shiny rust eyes examine my face as I drift closer to him. I open my mouth, but my breath catches in my throat.

Rosie, this is your chance. Take it.

'Wes, I –'

'Wes!'

The cheerful voice is heart-achingly familiar. I watch the delight explode across Wes's face. If he was happy before, he's now positively ecstatic.

I turn around to greet a smiling Bee. She's looking extra cute in ripped denim overalls and a messy biro bun.

'Rosie! You just disappeared on us! How the hell have you been?' She embraces me warmly before attaching herself to Wes's side.

'Yeah, good thanks,' I croak, barely able to focus.

When he slips an arm around her waist, I have to avert my eyes.

'Wowie,' she gushes, her twinkly eyes fixated on the BIG paintings. The paintings I stupidly thought were for me. 'These turned out *so* well, Wes! Well done!'

She leans in to inspect the red-cheeked toddler. 'Oh my God, remember this little guy? He was so petrified of that fugly cane toad.'

I feel a sharp stabbing in my chest, right near my heart. She's probably well-versed in umbrella politics too. I'm such an idiot. I've spent so much time refusing to acknowledge my feelings for Wes, and now it's too late.

I've only got myself to blame.

Chapter Thirty-Three

We're out of Maltesers before we even hit the M4.

'Daaaaaaddd, can we stop soon? I'm hungryyy!'

I'm not sure what it is about being in the backseat of a hot, stuffy car that reverts you right back to being a teenager. I can practically smell the Golden Arches, and I need to pee.

Dad isn't even at the wheel; Naomi and I wouldn't allow it. But he's commandeered the radio while Naomi is driving – at least until we hit the Blue Mountains, then I've offered to take over. I was more than happy to drive myself to Mudgee for Ceddie's wedding – it's not like it's an unfamiliar trip – but Dad and Naomi have insisted on coming along to check out a nearby wedding venue of their own. I'm one hundred per cent supportive of anything that's going to get them closer to walking down that aisle.

'I'm sure there's a bag of party mix in the seat pocket in front of you,' Dad takes a moment out from DJ-ing to advise. I'm happy to go along with his daggy selection of rock until we near the 'danger' broadcast zone. Although, I shouldn't have to remind him to skip over Gold 86.7 FM.

I may be sleeping in my childhood bedroom, but I know that returning to Sydney was the right move. Two weeks on and I'm feeling much more settled, and I've even started thinking about sussing out a radio job in Sydney. This clusterfuck of a situation had revealed plenty of nasty surprises – but one delightful one. I love my new career in radio. So much so, I miss it. I miss speaking my mind and telling stories – bringing a show to life, painting pictures with a thousand words. I miss the rush of being on-air and off-script, never knowing what newness and brilliance will emerge from rolling with the punches. Crazily, I even miss pulling myself out of bed at the crack of dawn each morning.

It feels different from Slice. When I was in the throes of agency life, my job was everything. It served the purpose of giving me purpose. With no one special by my side, what would my life even amount to without my job? I don't feel that way now. How could I? Here I am, bundled in the backseat of our family car with Squash next to me, my gorgeous almost-stepmum in the driver's seat and gem-of-a-human father in the front belting 'Whole Lotta Love' at the top of his lungs. The same dad who would do and continues to do anything for me – including escorting me back to my demons in Mudgee under the ruse of wedding-venue hunting. I have new friends who adore me as much as I do them, and old friends who refuse to leave my side. I am surrounded by love.

I know that I'm not just going to be able to walk straight into a radio-hosting job. Mudgee was a fortunate break. Penny reckons the whole Markus schmozzle will help me get a foot in the door, but I'd prefer not to mention it.

'You have to milk it for every last pasteurised drop, babe.'

I'd agreed to let her suss out some of her connections for any going opportunities. I'd be happy to start with a production assistant's role and work my way up from there.

I'm relieved that our fractured little trio is on its way to repair. I had dinner with Pen and Ange last week at We Rice Above. It was a cracker of a night. Penny had come armed with a Blossoms garment bag and thrust it into my hands as we were leaving. Once we were on the street, away from potential Adobo sauce splatters, I'd unzipped it to find the Sebastian Worthington along with a beautiful handwritten note attached to the hanger.

Gotta have you looking fire at the wedding. Reunion take deux! P.S. told you we'd make our $ back on this bad boy. Big mwah!

I glance at the red dress hanging over the empty passenger seat on the other side of the car. So much has changed since that tight silk last hampered my breathing. I'm so done with the showbiz frills. For any other event I'd be tempted to go comfort-first, but not for Ceddie's wedding. He deserves me at my most glamourous.

Plus, I'd be seeing Wes too. I told Penny that he had likely been invited as Bee's plus one, but it's like she failed to hear me. After our gallery visit, she was firmly in camp Preston too. *'I saw the way he was looking at you, Rosie. The man's in love with you!'*

But she hadn't seen the way he'd looked at Bee.

I'm also nervous about seeing Markus. Cedric had warned me that he'd been invited. I'd handled it maturely and simply thanked him for the forward notice. I assumed that meant Markus was still on the radio; Cedric had assured me that our timeslot was sorted. I imagine Markus had tried contacting me – to save face with Cedric, if nothing else – but I'd blocked his number. Funnily enough, though, my initial fury hadn't returned. Markus could walk into Cedric's wedding flanked by an entourage of hot women and I really wouldn't give a damn. I don't care that he – or rather, Chad – has already seen me in the Sebastian Worthington, at the Scuttlebutt event. I don't need a revenge outfit.

'Can you pass me one of those lolly bananas, love? Maybe a tiny milk bottle and race car, too,' Dad requests from the front as his duet with Led Z comes to an end and Pink Floyd starts up. Poor Squash is in his cat carrier meowing up a storm. I don't think he's enjoying the music selection.

'Just one, Dad. You'll have to choose.' I roll my eyes as I go digging in the seat pocket, listening for the sound of rustling plastic. There's a wad of newspapers in the way, so I pull them out onto my lap.

The article on the front page of the paper catches my attention.

A tale of brotherly love

It's different from the other articles, which have been virtually impossible to avoid. Instead of loud headlines and half-page pap photos with minimal words, there's a lengthy article.

I abandon my hunt for Allen's lollies and start reading.

'There's no such thing as a perfect twin. Chad just wanted to help me out.'

They're the most famous faces in the country right now, but do we really know the full story about the Abrahams twins' double act? We sit down with Dr Markus Abrahams, celebrity vet of the hit show Markus & Pup, *to hear how his struggle with mental health prompted one of TV's biggest scandals.*

When Markus's twin, Chad Abrahams, was a little boy, he dreamt of being an actor. As he grew, the dream grew with him. Markus, on the other hand, wanted to be a vet. He graduated top of his class from the School of Veterinary Science at the University of Tasmania and opened his own veterinary practice in Hobart not long after. Chad remained steadfast in his goal to become an actor, but unfortunately things didn't go as he'd hoped.

'He went to audition after audition, but he couldn't catch a break,' *Markus reveals.*

'It was a tough time for him – and me. He'd go to Sydney or Melbourne for work opportunities and come back so defeated. It was hard to enjoy my own veterinary success when my brother was struggling.'

The turning point came when Chad went backpacking around Europe and found himself auditioning for a local soap opera in Poland, M jak miłość, *(L for Love), before promptly landing the part.*

Around the same time, Broad Star Entertainment, the production company behind Channel 19's Markus & Pup, *held nation-wide auditions for an on-air vet. Championed by his brother – who was quickly becoming one of Poland's rising stars – Markus attended the Hobart auditions.*

'I thought it would be a tiny production and give me the opportunity to broaden my veterinary skills – and it did at first. Then the show became bigger and bigger, and they purchased the land just outside of Mudgee to purpose-build the TV studio. I think that's when it first dawned on me just how massive it had become.'

Markus went onto share that, as the viewership contin-ued to skyrocket, so did his nerves. Things reached rock bottom around a year ago, when the show was moved to a prime-time slot.

'I was always in the studio under the bright lights and barely spent any time doing the thing I loved – caring for the animals. I started having these panic attacks, to the point where I could no longer film. That's when the production company and my agent suggested we bring Chad in, to give me a chance to rest – I had contracts to fulfil and there were lots of advertising dollars on the line.'

By this stage Chad had been living in Poland for close to a decade with his model girlfriend, Eryka Polanksi. (Ed note: now fiancée)

'No one really knew I was a twin; it just had never seemed relevant to bring up. And luckily, Chad was keen to try his hand at some method acting. The soap opera was on a break, and he thought it would be a fun challenge to move back to Australia with Eryka for a bit.'

For a while it appeared to be working, and with Markus out of the spotlight and on the road to recovery, he was able to resume some private veterinary practice and eventually pick some of his own projects, including charity work with Kindred Spirit Elephant Conservation Centre in India and a co-host spot on a Mudgee radio show.

'Unfortunately, that's also when it all started to come undone,' Markus shares, his demeanour downtrodden.

I glance up from the paper. Dad and Naomi are deep in conversation. Dad has seemingly – and very suspiciously – forgotten all about his milk bottles and race cars. Did he leave this here for me to find? I still haven't said much to him about what happened with Markus, but somehow Liam-bloody-Neeson always knows what's what. I go back to the article.

Sadness overcomes Markus as he describes how the Chad switch-up affected a budding romance in his life.

'Unfortunately, my dishonesty backfired big time. Rosie was someone special.' (Ed note: believed to be Markus's radio co-host, Rosie Royce.)

I stop reading. The combination of seeing my name in that sentence and the bag of Maltesers I've just inhaled is making me feel sick. I crack open my window a fraction to let in some fresh air. Instead, I'm hit with a whack of M4 car fumes. As the strong, leady taste sticks to my tongue, the words from the article roll around in my head.

Did he really care about me? Is it possible that despite everything that's happened, Markus *is* actually genuine?

What's next for Dr Markus Abrahams? You can still catch him on the airwaves of Gold 86.7 FM with new co-host and show producer Cedric Cool, who has temporarily stepped into Royce's vacant seat. However, Markus & Pup won't be back on our screens anytime soon, if ever, with the network announcing a permanent hiatus and Chad believed to have returned to Poland.

When asked if love was still on the cards, Markus considers the question carefully, 'I don't think I'm quite in the place for that yet. But certainly one day.'

Ed note: Let's hope that one day rolls around soon because this handsome vet is a certified catch!

I silently fold the paper, tuck it back into the front seat pocket and reach for my phone. I have a text to send.

Chapter Thirty-Four

I already want to turn around and hightail it out of here. Dad and Naomi dropped me at the entrance to the 'secret location' not even five minutes ago. I'd been finally ready to face Markus, but instead, I've spotted Wes at the end of the long driveway. And he's with Bee. I'd prepared myself to see them together, so I should be fine. But I'm not.

Dust kicks up around me and I breathe in the earthy aroma as I force myself to walk down the dirt drive. I'm thankful that I followed the invitation's dress code and borrowed a pair of Blossoms boots to team with my dress – neither heels nor my white Converse would fare well on the red dirt. A lambswool shawl, draped over my shoulders, completes my look.

Luckily, no one greets me as I approach the neatly trimmed lawns and rows of twisted vines, now just woody twigs dotted with shrivelled grapes. It's a spectacular saturated Tuscan palette of greens, burgundies, beiges and browns.

I consider turning and sprinting back down the drive as my eyes find Wes and Bee again. This is not how I'd pictured my 'homecoming'. Seeing them huddled over one of the rustic wine barrels swapping intimate sweet nothings is almost too much to bear.

Oh fuck, they've seen me.

Bee waves and blows me a kiss, then ducks off towards a timber-cladded building, presumably the cellar door. Wes begins weaving around the wine barrel tables and through the crowd towards me. *Shit.* I don't know what I'm going to say to him. Can I really just pretend that everything is normal and ignore that, in fact, everything has changed for me? I'm the one who insisted that we remain friends, and that's all I'd wanted. He stops in front of me.

'Rosie, hey!' He's excited to see me.

'Hi!' I keep my voice light but I can feel my heart beating in the back of my throat.

'Do Cedric and Simon know all of these people? Or is it some sort of rent-a-crowd? Here I was feeling lucky to have scored an invite.'

I should say something about Bee. To prove that I'm fine with it.

'Ha! Probably a rent-a-crowd. Wes – ah – I meant to say the other night at the gallery, that I'm really happy for you and Bee,' I blurt.

'Yoo-hoo!' We're interrupted by Joanna's cheery greeting as she stands at the edge of the vineyard. She's underneath an ornate candelabra chandelier that's hoisted up high on a steel pole and dangling from a chain over the vines, like an alfresco fairytale. 'Welcome, everyone!' Her eyes stop on me, and she gives me a big smile. Her warmth puts me at ease, and I beam back.

Cam joins her at her side. His polka-dot bow tie matches her swing dress. 'Good afternoon, ladies and gentlemen, friends and loved ones, welcome to the wedding of Cedric

Cool and Simon Farrell. For those of you who don't know me, my name is Cam and this is my lovely wife, Jo. In addition to hosting you tonight, we have been asked by our lovely grooms to be your emcees for the evening. I hope you were surprised that the secret wedding venue is right here at the Lesters Estate! The ceremony will be starting soon, so I'd like to ask everyone to make their way to the other side of the vineyard, take a seat and await the arrival of the handsome couple!'

As the crowd traverses the vines, I lose sight of Wes. I high-five Stacey, air kiss Kathy from Mudgee Dance Academy and give Jack a big squeeze. 'My segment's been extended to an hour, young pup,' he whispers in my ear.

I'm swept along with the surge of excited wedding guests until a firm hand catches hold of my arm.

'Rosie. Do you have a second?'

Markus.

I turn to face him. He's as attractive as ever in a navy suit and his signature scuffed boots, but my heart continues beating steadily.

'Of course I do.'

'Thanks for your text.'

'You're welcome.'

'To be honest, I was surprised to receive it, especially after you hadn't responded to any of my messages. Obviously, I wanted to see you to apologise . . . for everything.' His voice drips with remorse and he hangs his head. His hair is tousled, not Lego-slick.

'It's okay, Markus. It really is.'

'It is?' He looks at me, eyes wide with hope, and I feel a sudden pang of guilt for letting him believe even for a moment that we can repair things. The thing is, I've realised we never really had anything *to* repair. He told me he didn't have a brother and I had no idea until that *Herald* article that he grew up in Tasmania. I really didn't know the first thing about him.

'Like I said in my message, Markus, I totally get how you got caught up in that mess, and I'm really glad you're prioritising yourself now.' I choose my words carefully so as not to lead him on.

Because it wasn't only him withholding. There must have been a reason why I never mentioned a thing about Mum. I don't want to take away from the fun adventures we shared in India. There were times when his strong arms were my only source of comfort, and I'll always appreciate that. It was just a case of being in each other's lives for a season.

If anything, I'm proud that I lowered my defences with Markus. If I hadn't, I probably would never have gone to India, things would never have developed between us the way they did, and I might never have faced the hard truth about how Mum leaving really impacted me – and finally taken steps to lay that ghost to rest.

I certainly don't regret anything.

'So, there's really no hope for us?' he asks. His piercing blue eyes cling to mine.

'I think you already know the answer, Markus.' I smile sadly.

He is a good guy. Just not *my* good guy.

'You can't blame a man for trying.' He gives me a perfectly white, wistful smile.

'I don't think you'll have any trouble with the ladies whenever you're ready to get back out there.' I laugh lightly and subtly gesture to where Kathy is hovering nearby, waiting to pounce. 'Just promise me that you'll keep Chad as far away from your love life as possible!'

'Deal.'

As we break apart from our goodbye embrace, Kathy intercepts Markus and I hurry through the vines, foliage brushing up against me like encouraging hands coaxing me onwards.

I stifle a gasp as I emerge on the other side. The scene before me is breathtaking. A festoon of fairy lights is strung above the stretch of lawn, an extra layer of twinkling stars in the dusky evening sky. There's hanging plants, terracotta flowerpots and lanterns aplenty. Jo and Cam have created the quintessential lover's wonderland.

I'm so taken with the aesthetics that I almost fail to notice the brick wall that stands tall behind the altar, spotlit by a track of LED lights.

It's a painted mural. The convincing detail vibrates with colour and energy. It radiates off the wall, as if the bricks have difficulty containing the painting and it's spilling out into real life, into three-dimensional form. It's an expansive scene of the Lesters' bar, with people everywhere. There's Joanna and Cam in the foreground, so vivid it looks like they're standing right there in front of me. Bee's there, too, behind the bar, hair pulled up in a messy ponytail, elbows leaning on the teak countertop. Wes has captured her cheeky expression perfectly. Then I see me. Sitting up at the bar with a radio mic in front of me, a bottle of hand sanitiser in one hand and a banana in the other. My heart grows warm.

The music starts up, so I duck into the back row of chairs and move to the end. Simon stands in front of the wall, looking nervous and excited. Everyone stands as the first bars of 'Purple Haze' sound through Cam's jukebox, which has made its way here from Lesters and is positioned to the right of an arbour made of branches, vines and flowers.

Cedric appears at the end of the aisle. He's wearing a spangly purple jacket. He pauses and pulls a ball of fluff from underneath his jacket and triumphantly thrusts it in the air like Simba the lion cub. It's Madge! I look around frantically for Squash, whom Dad should have deposited in Ceddie's care, at the couple's request. Just as I'm about to start panicking, Ceddie reaches into the other side of his jacket and retrieves another fluff ball.

There he is! I stifle a giggle when I see that Squash has a ring box strapped to his back. I hope Cedric's not expecting them to walk down the aisle like obedient golden retrievers. But he stows Squash under one arm and Madge under the other and starts toe-tapping down the aisle.

As Cedric stops under the archway, the song transitions into 'White Wedding'. His eyes are brimming with tears as Simon moves towards him, positively sparkling in a dark green suit that perfectly complements his ginger hair. I can tell he's applied powder to his face but there's a cluster of freckles on his nose that's too dark to cover up. His nose is running and his eyes glassy as he nears Cedric. How could Cedric have ever believed – even for a second – that this man was ever not completely in love with him? Cedric and Simon exchange vows, rings and finally a kiss, and the crowd erupts into cheers. Once the paperwork is complete, Cam rescues Squash and Madge and hands Cedric a microphone and a glass of champagne.

'You would think this bit would be less nerve-racking, given my day job. But I'm shitting myself.'

Cedric pauses to down the contents of his glass.

'It's not every day that you marry the love of your life.' Cedric stops again to peck Simon on the lips. We all cheer. 'And there will be plenty of time later tonight to get sentimental about all the reasons I adore this man, but first I have a few announcements.'

He opens up his spangly jacket and pulls a square of folded paper from the inside pocket.

'First up, I want to thank Joanna and Cam Lester for bringing not just one, but *two* fabulous venues to Mudgee. I know that I can speak for the entire town in saying thank you.'

There's a thunder of applause as he gestures to the wonderland surrounding us. It might be my imagination, but is there a faint rumble of real thunder in the distance, underneath the clapping . . .?

'Of course, it would be completely remiss of me not to acknowledge the talented artist responsible for the unbelievable wall art, so lifelike that earlier today I tried to ask painting-Jo when the first round of hors d'oeuvres was due out – which is a delicious stuffed zucchini flower, for anyone who's interested.' The crowd laughs. 'Why don't you come on up and say a few words, Wes?'

Wes emerges from the back row of seats. I'd been too overwhelmed earlier to notice how handsome he looks in a rust-coloured blazer and chinos. I wonder if he even owns a suit anymore, or if they've really all become kindling. He waves an acknowledgment to the crowd and then tries to slink back into the shadows, but Ceddie thrusts the mic into his hands.

'Thanks, Cedric. I'm stoked you like it. A lot of heart went into it. But I really couldn't have pulled off the final touches without my assistant, Bee. She helped me with the finer facial details. You may have noticed her studying you a little too closely when she last served you – we wanted to make sure we got every detail bang-on. And to think I *almost* didn't discover her talents! Of course, once I did, I just had to whisk her off onto the road for a bit to help me with the collection for my latest exhibit.'

A burning flush creeps across my face. I think Bee is great – amazing, in fact – and that's the problem. I'm not sure I can sit here while Wes goes on and on about how wonderful she is. But I'd be making a huge scene if I left now. I have to sit it out.

'So, a big thanks to Jo for giving Bee the time off to see some of this lovely sunburnt country with me. I take no responsibility for any hunky backpackers she may have met along the way ... If she doesn't stick around, it's not my fault!'

Joanna boos good-naturedly. Wait – what have I missed? I scan the crowd for Bee and locate her standing on the other side of the aisle, hand in hand with a guy with dreadlocks.

My flush is quickly chased by cooling relief. Wes and Bee aren't an item?

Wes hands the mic back to Cam who has returned empty-handed after, presumably, depositing Squash and Madge safely in Dad and Naomi's pre-arranged care.

'With the thank yous out of the way, it's time to clear the chairs for a pre-dinner boogie under the stars. Cue the music!'

This is *not* the standard run of events. I love it.

As the zucchini flowers circulate, the vineyard heaves with music and the town of Mudgee moves and shakes to 'Stayin' Alive'. Ceddie and Simon are having the time of their lives rocking out to the music with their matching rapid-fire hip movements. It's not long before Bee and her dreadlocked fella, then Markus and Kathy, join them on the dance floor. Markus gives me a wave as he whirls past.

I'm sticking to the edges, nibbling on a mini quiche and keeping one eye out for Wes, when Jo approaches with a bottle of red in hand and a tray of wine glasses held above her head.

'Rosie, my love! Would you like a sneaky taste of our new pinot? We don't have enough for distribution yet – pinot noir grapes are so fiddly to grow, but we found a few bottles from last year's crop to give us a head start.'

'Sure,' I say after a beat. 'Fill me up.'

As Jo pours, my eyes follow a decadent drop of red as it runs down the bottle's label before settling into a heart-shaped smudge.

'Enjoy!' Jo says as she spins off into the crowd, balancing glasses like a practiced acrobat.

Led Zeppelin's 'Stairway to Heaven' comes on and I sip my pinot as I wander over to the jukebox. I wonder if it's too early for the Nutbush? I'm searching for a rogue coin in my purse when the first splatters of rain land on my head. I fold a hand over my glass to shield my wine.

Oh no! I wonder if there's a wet weather plan? I guess we can all crowd into the cellar door.

But just as quickly as it starts raining, it stops.

'Is this height to your satisfaction, miss?'

I don't think I'll ever not recognise that lazy drawl. I look up to see Wes holding an umbrella over my head.

Meanwhile, he's getting soaked, the white shirt under his jacket slick against his body.

'Quick, come under!' I laugh. 'Shit, I hope they have the jukebox insured.'

The heavens have really opened now. Wes raises the umbrella to his height, and I shuffle back underneath, pressing myself into his tall frame, careful not to spill my wine and stain his shirt.

My skin prickles as Wes towers over me. We haven't been this close since, well, 2017.

'Wait. Is that wine?' he asks, his breath preternaturally warm on the top of my head, like his words are a snug beanie.

'It is,' I say, taking a careful sip.

'And you're enjoying it?' he asks cautiously.

'I am,' I reply. 'I've recently developed a new taste for it.'

I wish it wasn't so awkward to tilt my face to look up at him so I could sneak a look at his expression.

'Well, isn't that good to know.' He sounds like he's smiling.

'Hurry! Throw the bouquet, Cedric, so we can all go inside!' Simon's frantic cries pierce the air. A frenzy of men and women form on the grass in front of the happy couple.

Cedric blows a kiss to the drenched crowd before turning his back and throwing the bouquet, a dreamy teardrop of velvety pink petals, over his head towards the chaotic, and increasingly muddy, pit of singletons.

I watch as it sails through the air. Two women jump simultaneously, but neither are able to catch it mid-flight. Instead, the bouquet hits our umbrella before bouncing off and neatly depositing itself in a puddle at my feet. I bend to retrieve the flowers.

When I stand back up, the umbrella has been cast aside and Wes has moved in front of me, his eyes fixed on mine and his inky hands holding out a postage stamp-sized watercolour painting.

'Rosie Royce.' My heart thunders in my chest. 'Will you *finally* accept my sorry flowers?'

A fat rain droplet lands like a single tear in the middle of the tiny peace posies, causing the colours to bleed into each other. I'm starting to cry too, but I beam through the rain and tears.

'Yes, Wes. I will.' I pause. 'On one condition though.'

'Yes?' he asks, voice shaky.

I set my wine down on the grass, then stand back up.

'That you accept mine too.' I don't wait for a response before pressing the bridal bouquet into his arms. The delicate, dripping wet flowers look perfectly at home in Wes's large, inky hands.

The peace posie painting flutters down to the ground, landing in a bath of pinot.

Wes leans in and kisses me.

There's a tingling in my toes that makes its way up my legs to the pit of my stomach, where it lingers before planting itself and transforming into a glorious, familiar warmth. It radiates throughout my entire body.

If this is never ever, then I want it forever.

Epilogue

Six months later

'Rosie! Would you please stop moving?'

I poke my tongue out at Wes and continue wriggling my toes.

'Careful, or I'll paint you that way,' he warns.

'You are not Leonardo DiCaprio, and I am *not* one of your French girls. I'm getting a cramp,' I say, shifting again on the grass in a futile attempt to get more comfortable. 'Is there any catering on this set?'

I crane my neck to look across Galdwell Park, praying that Mr Whippy will magically appear across the lake.

'Is that the faint chimes of "Greensleeves" I can hear in the distance?' I exclaim, trying to will an ice-cream truck into existence. 'I swear whoever decided that creepy music was the perfect soundtrack for seven-year-olds to purchase their double-scoops with sprinkles needs to be shot. It may be perfect for a possessed clown, but not . . . Oh! I think I can see a van!'

'Rosie!'

'Okay, okay.' I swivel back to face a dismayed Wes and his easel. He's wearing his teeny tiny football painting shorts, and I've been very much enjoying the glorious full thigh-to-calf view. I make a mental note not to complain the next time Wes disappears to the gym for 'leg' day. Although, now that the BIG gallery is officially open, gym visits have become few and far between anyway. Thanks to Penny 'launching the shit' out of the gallery with a Scuttlebutt collab and her A-list network (there's no bad blood, but we thought it best to leave Markus off the guest list), Wes has been run off his feet with a constant rotation of local exhibitors appearing alongside his own art. So those delicious-looking calves are more likely shaped by climbing up and down ladders than pumping iron.

Of course, Penny is delighted she has a 'vibey' new place to swan around with dates – or with Ange and I on a Friday or Saturday evening (the only nights of the week I can stay up past 8 pm).

What with my new radio job and the gallery, we've both been burning the candles at both ends, which is why I'm so excited for our holiday to Japan next month. Yes, we are finally booked to see those cherry blossoms. Dad and Naomi are joining us as the last stop on their epic three-month, around-the-world honeymoon, and I've roped them into helping me execute a surprise proposal.

I've read that the beauty of seeing the *sakura*, or cherry blossoms, bloom is in experiencing a moment that is temporary: *mono no aware*, a phrase that tries to encapsulate the impermanence of nature. But I am determined to capture the moment forever. I've organised a Japanese illustrator to sketch the scene as I drop on one knee in Tokyo's Ueno Park.

I can hardly wait, and I also can't wait until I don't have to keep my secret any longer – I've almost ruined it a bunch of times!

I readjust myself yet again, pulling a stick out from underneath my butt. That's better.

'Honestly, how do you sit behind that mic for hours on end?'

'I don't. Unlike Ceddie, Tess lets me plan out the show to the last millisecond. So I can schedule a run of songs, then duck to the kitchen and wolf down brekkie. I sometimes even take a walk.'

I miss Ceddie desperately, but my job as the solo host of a growing independent morning drivetime show is going well, and I am happy. I'm also lucky I can do digital marketing work on the side to help pay the bills and our insane Sydney rent. Wes and I have already been back to Mudgee a handful of times, each time with Squash in tow. He is terrible in the car but has thankfully taken a shine to Wes's beanie, curling up on my lap, the soft wool tucked under his tiny paw like a baby blanket. The pompom doubles as entertainment whenever he stirs.

'Pffft.' Wes's eyes don't leave his artwork. 'You don't take a mid-show stroll.'

'You don't know that.'

He stops painting and looks up at me. 'Yes, Rosie. I very much do.'

It's true. At the most, I'll dash to the bathroom at the end of the hallway. But only if I'm so desperate to pee I think I'll wet my pants. The show is doing so well, I don't want to do anything to risk messing it up.

'Just give me five more minutes of your time, then I'll take you for pizza,' Wes says.

'Not a family-friendly place I hope?'

He peers over his canvas, a puzzled expression on his face.

'Those shorts are R-rated,' I tease.

'An R-rated pizza joint then,' Wes shoots right back.

'Ohhh, imagine the people watching there! Strippers, poles and pizzas.'

I have a theory that regular bantering with Wes helps keep my radio skills razor-sharp. Lucky we're so fluent.

Wes's shoulders bounce up and down. 'Don't make me laugh, Rosie. I'll ruin the painting.'

'What's this even for again?'

'I told you. I'm working on this technique that I'm rubbish at. It's –'

'FUCKKKK!' My screech pierces through the air, and I jump to my feet. 'GET AWAY, GET AWAY!' I yelp as I slap my burning backside. 'I've been sitting on an ant nest!' I rush over to Wes. 'Check me, check me please! I think I can feel one crawling into my crack.'

Wes drops his paintbrush and bends down to inspect my behind. I'm wearing a dress, so his hand shoots up underneath and he starts swiping haphazardly. The stinging subsides just as quickly as it arrived, replaced by a delicious warmth.

'Better?' he asks.

'Much,' I say, manoeuvring my body slightly until his hand brushes up against an entirely *different* area. He looks up at me and smirks.

It doesn't occur to either of us that this is completely inappropriate behaviour for a public park until a couple walking past with their dog does a double take before dragging their poor dachshund away.

Wes retracts his hand, and his smirk transforms into a wide grin.

'Imagine if it were you and me observing us? How do you think you'd describe our story?' he asks, still kneeling on the ground.

I can see from his eager expression he's itching to share his assessment. 'Hmmm. You go first.'

'Boy and girl return to the childhood park where they fell in love, to fall back in love, and can't help but get a bit frisky.'

'Awww, that's lovely.'

'I agree. Getting frisky is lovely,' Wes remarks.

'You know I mean the falling back in love part . . . Hey! This is really good,' I exclaim, Wes's painting suddenly catching my eye.

It makes sense now why Wes refused to let me sit on a picnic blanket. The green grass perfectly complements my eyes.

'You even got the shade of the piss bits right,' I say, leaning in more closely to inspect the painting.

'Of course I did. I've put in a lot of hours staring into those eyes. I was going for mildly dehydrated wee, like should-drink-a-glass-of-water-but-will-probably-survive-if-you-don't.'

'Do you think you'll ever get sick of matching my eyes to the health department's urine colour chart?'

'Never ever.'

His words send a contented ripple throughout my body.

My wee eyes explore the rest of the painting. Wes has me sitting cross-legged on the grass in my dress and Converse. My face is a mixture of bemused and bored.

My gaze shifts to my arms, which rest at my side. One of the hardest things about being an amateur model is not knowing what to do with your hands. I wonder if Kate Winslet had the same issue in *Titanic*. She appeared to solve the problem by arranging them delicately around her face. Also, by being naked. Not hugely park appropriate – as just confirmed by the couple with the dachshund.

Wes has drawn a ring on one of my hands. It's not to scale like the rest of the details, but more the size of one of those jumbo ring pops. I never wear jewellery . . . and

I'm not wearing any now. Wait. That's the left hand, fourth finger . . .

I turn around, confused, and look down at Wes. He's rearranged himself onto one knee and is holding a ring box.

'No. Get up! Get up!' I hear myself exclaim before I'm able to form a coherent thought. My heart is pounding so loudly it feels as though it's about to leap from my chest.

His face drains of colour.

Shit.

'No, no, no. It's not that. I *want* to marry you.' I fold down on the ground next to him.

Wes clutches the ring box tightly to his chest. 'Fuck, Rosie. Are you *trying* to kill me?'

'It's just that I sort of had something organised myself . . .'

I trail off as I see his pulsating temple.

'But a proposal right now would work just fine, too. In fact, I'd really love one,' I say.

Wes blinks, like he's trying to puzzle together my words, before a goofy, lopsided grin unfurls from the corner of his mouth. 'Well, I'm glad. Because your dad, Naomi, Pen, Ange, Ceddie, Bee – the whole gang – are waiting for us back at our apartment. Cam has the champagne on ice. And, yes, before you ask, there's catering. And wine.'

My mind instantly goes to whether he's ordered enough food, then switches to wondering whether we've emptied Squash's litter box . . .

But the moment Wes flips open the ring box, and I see a vintage posy ring – a cluster of tiny sparkling diamonds set on a dainty band and nestled on the soft velvet pillow – everything else fades away.

It's happening now. Not among the cherry blossoms in Ueno Park, but right here, underneath the gum trees at Galdwell Park.

'Rosie Royce?' Wes's rust eyes bore into me.

'Yes?' Even though I know what's coming next, my knees feel weak. I'm going to buckle from raw emotion.

'Will you marry me?'

I don't hesitate.

'Yes, Wes. The biggest, BIGGEST yes.'

Acknowledgements

Rosie Royce has been with me in some form for close to a decade, so I'm delighted (not as delighted as Rosie – she's always had A LOT to say) that her story has finally made it out into the world.

To my dearest little duck, JoJo – Rosie is and will forever be your homegirl. Danica, thank you for your early college-dorm cheerleading. Dedicating this book to you was an easy decision. And to Penny, the final member of my holy-beta-trinity. 'How did we get here?' I'm still not entirely sure, but I'm so honoured to have your talents and calm by my side. Your character namesake remains, even though I know that you know that it's not you.

As always, my deepest thanks go to the amazing team at Pan Macmillan, especially my publisher Geordie Williamson for taking a chance on me (and romance!), Belinda Huang for your invaluable editorial input and patience, and publicity queen and friend, Candice Wyman. Thank you also to Rufus Cuthbert for your marketing prowess, Samantha

Sainsbury for dotting my i's and crossing my t's, and Debra Billson for the cutest cover that makes me smile each time I look at it. Thank you to the sales reps who work tirelessly to get my books into bookstores, and all the behind-the-scenes contributors. And to the booksellers. I see you and thank you for being the biggest champions of Australian-authored stories (I'm looking at you, Josh Hortinela and Anna Loder).

Clare and Biggie-C, thank you for letting me borrow Squash (I'm sorry about Squish!). Kylie, thank you for your meticulous proofing and friendship – keep up the good work and Daisy might make a cameo one day. Danielle, let's dine at Harry's until we're old and grey(er). Nathalie, thank you for helping me come up with the perfect title.

To the people of Mudgee/*Moothi*. I hope you'll forgive me for fictionalising parts of your magical town. Every time I went to give it a new name, I just couldn't. I hope it's read as the tribute I intended.

To my family, I love you. Thank you for sharing in my successes with me. A special shout-out to Nora for my BFF necklace. (Hot tip to my other nieces and nephews: bribes enthusiastically accepted.)

To the Australian writing community – you are such a wonderful bunch! I love the conversations I have with you at bookish events and online. I still can't believe that authors I have fangirled for so long are not only 'my contemporaries' but have been so incredibly supportive. It's my mission to pay it forward. Special mentions go to my talented work wife Clare Fletcher, as well as Victoria Brookman, Genevieve Novak, Amy Lovat, Vanessa McCausland, Ali Lowe and Natalie Murray for helping me stay tethered this year.

And finally, to the readers who have loved and reviewed/ sent me the most glorious messages about *Duck à l'Orange for Breakfast*. I'm not sure what I did before I found my

Bookstagram peeps. I'm so tempted to name a few special people, but I'm terrified that I'll forget someone, and I suspect you already know who you are! So, I'll just say 'Duck, Duck, Goose' to you!

Never ever in my wildest dreams could I have pictured all of this. Thank you.

This book was written on Guringai and Gadigal Country and partially set on the traditional lands of the Wiradjuri people. I acknowledge the Traditional Owners of these lands – the original storytellers – and acknowledge their deep, personal and significant connection to the land, water and community. I pay my respects to Elders past and present. To learn more about the Wiradjuri people and language, please see the Mudgee Aboriginal Land Council (www.mudgeelalc.com) and the Wiradjuri Language and Cultural Heritage Recovery Project.

Duck à l'Orange for Breakfast

Maxine 'Max' Mayberry, an ad executive with writing ambitions, is holed up in a friend's apartment after discovering her long-term boyfriend in bed with another woman. If that wasn't bad enough, Max has recently been diagnosed with a brain tumour.

Enter Johnny: a cheeky yet charming Tinder pen pal and the perfect distraction. Together, Max and Johnny flirt and cook their way through *The Laurent Family Cookbook* (a recipe book from Max's ex-boyfriend's pretentious French family) without ever meeting in person.

The 'Fork Him' project starts as a joke, but soon transforms into something more meaningful as Max undergoes brain surgery, travels to Paris for a fresh start, and decides whether she believes in herself enough to chase the life – and the man – she really wants.